———————— ★ ————————

"Do you think that the girl, Milly Watsername, was murdered then?"

"Nothing will be sure until the coroner gives his report," said Donaghue. "But I'm almost sure what the report will be. When her husband's body has been removed perhaps you could suggest sleeping in her cell with her. Would you mind doing that?"

"You think it's as grave as that?"

"I do," said Donaghue. "I think it may be even graver. At no time must she be left alone."

———————— ★ ————————

"There's an undeniably charming tone to it all..."
—*Publishers Weekly*

"Mr. Donaghue unravels a puzzle worthy of the most baffling cases of Agatha Christie."
—*Mystery News*

ANNA SHONE

MR DONAGHUE INVESTIGATES

WORLDWIDE.

TORONTO • NEW YORK • LONDON
AMSTERDAM • PARIS • SYDNEY • HAMBURG
STOCKHOLM • ATHENS • TOKYO • MILAN
MADRID • WARSAW • BUDAPEST • AUCKLAND

To the memory of my father,
Eugene Whiston, an Irishman and storyteller
who loved the language of the Bard

MR. DONAGHUE INVESTIGATES

A Worldwide Mystery/May 1997

First published by St. Martin's Press, Incorporated.

ISBN 0-373-26238-8

Printed in U.S.A.

Contents

PART ONE

ONE

An appointment

A TALL, SMARTLY DRESSED woman in her early fifties strode resolutely along the quiet Hampstead mews. Her excellent posture lent her an aristocratic bearing which was enhanced by her simple but expensively cut suit and professionally styled bob of dark hair. The woman glanced cursorily at the numbers on the buildings as she passed them, then stopped abruptly at a door marked 17.

She pressed the bell below a brass plate inscribed with the name U. F. Donaghue, glancing at her watch as she did so. The intercom crackled and a disembodied female voice asked for her name.

'Mrs Trescott,' the woman replied, leaning forward on her high stiletto heels to speak into the intercom. 'I have an appointment with Mr Donaghue at 4.30.'

The voice answered her in a tone of practised politeness. 'Mr Donaghue is on the third floor. There's a lift to your right as you enter the hall. Please take a seat in the waiting-room and Mr Donaghue will call you as soon as he's ready.'

'You'd think it was the bloody doctor's,' Mrs Trescott muttered to herself as the crackling voice switched itself off and a rather aggressive buzz indicated that the polished oak door was now unlocked.

The woman tutted impatiently and entered the simply decorated and highly polished hallway. Following the voice's instructions she took the lift to the third floor and found herself on a spacious, softly carpeted landing whose single doorway bore the inscription 'U. F. DONAGHUE—PRIVATE INVESTIGATOR'.

She pulled the door open to find herself in an exquisite waiting-room, furnished with cane chairs plumped out with brightly coloured cushions, a jungle of exotic plants in one corner, glossy magazines piled neatly on a bamboo and glass table. Her stiletto heels sank into the pile of a salmon pink wool carpet that blended perfectly with the oriental décor.

Mrs Trescott sighed and lowered herself on to one of the cushioned cane chairs close to the jungle of plants and resisted the temptation to take off her shoes and place her now aching feet on to the table.

Instead she leaned forward and massaged her rather coarsely bulging calves with her fingers. Then she threw back her dark, elegantly coiffured head, stretching the muscles of her finely boned face, the exercise dispelling the fraught expression that had crossed her features for several days now.

She leaned forward to select a magazine from the table. As she did so the door in the wall opposite opened and a tousled head with what appeared to be the face of an ageing monkey imprinted on it, appeared in the doorway and beamed enquiringly at her.

'Mrs Trescott?' the face enquired.

Mrs Trescott nodded and rose to her feet.

'Do come this way,' the monkey face begged as its bearer, a small man dressed in an expensive but crumpled linen suit, stepped to one side of the door lintel to allow her to pass. He smiled up at her admiringly as she entered the spacious office. Mrs Trescott was a head taller than the little man and a good deal more handsome.

'Take a seat, Mrs Trescott,' said the man, indicating the comfortable leather chair before his desk. His pleasant voice bore the soft burr of the educated Dubliner. The little man quickly shuffled his way round to his side of the desk and installed himself comfortably in his own swivel chair, leaning backwards and loosening his tie as he did so.

'It's getting warmer…the weather,' he said. 'Perhaps we're in for an Indian summer. Who knows,' he added smiling, 'England might get a glimpse of the sun this September.'

Mrs Trescott found that the little man's soft brogue had a curiously tranquillizing effect on her. She stared at him in puzzlement. She was almost certain that he had his feet resting up against the side of his expensive oak table. In the attitude in which he was sitting his short legs could not possibly be touching the floor. She glanced at the name plaque resting on the desk which read 'ULYSSES F. DONAGHUE'.

'I take it you are Mr Donaghue,' she asked uncertainly.

'Ulysses F. Donaghue, the very same,' he answered, smiling brightly at her and revealing as he did so a row of tobacco-stained teeth.

Mrs Trescott returned a reluctant smile that instantly took ten years from her fine, rather fraught features.

'Well, Mrs Trescott,' said Ulysses Donaghue, 'what can I do for you?'

He leaned back in his chair and regarded the woman quizzically, his small bright blue eyes scrutinizing her—a smartly dressed woman, although he had noticed as she walked into his office that there was a run in one of her stockings, but very handsome, preserved by the natural strength of her bone structure and musculature.

The handsome face frowned. The woman looked at him hesitantly. It was evident that she was in some kind of dilemma.

Ulysses Donaghue leaned forward. He picked up a gold-plated fountain pen and twiddled it between short well-manicured fingers.

'Perhaps I can offer you a cup of something? Coffee, tea?' he enquired gently.

Mrs Trescott relaxed visibly.

'I'd just *love* a cup of tea,' she said in apparently great relief. She pronounced the word love 'luv', with a marked Lancashire accent.

Donaghue tapped the old-fashioned bronze bell on his desk and the office door opened to admit a strikingly beautiful young woman who advanced gracefully into the room.

'A pot of tea for my client, Bridget, and a milky coffee for me. Thank you, Bridget,' he added and the young woman nodded approvingly before smiling politely at Mrs Trescott and turning on her elegant ankles to leave the room.

Mrs Trescott regarded the girl's retreating figure appraisingly. A mass of red ringlets, bound decorously at the nape of the neck by a green velvet ribbon, cascaded down the elegant back that tapered to a tiny waist above the longest, finest legs that Mrs Trescott had ever seen on a female.

'A beautiful girl,' she commented admiringly. 'Your secretary?'

Donaghue sighed. 'Yes, my very competent secretary, Bridget. I don't know what I shall do the day she decides to marry her very handsome fiancé and improve the human stock with tall beautiful children.' Donaghue sighed again as he gazed at the now closed office door. He appeared to be engaged in some personal private reflection.

Mrs Trescott's face constricted into a grimace of consternation.

'Mr Donaghue...' she said. She hesitated.

Ulysses Donaghue looked at her enquiringly.

'Mr Donaghue,' she repeated, 'would you mind very much if I took off my shoes?'

Donaghue's rather disorderly eyebrows rose a millimetre.

'My feet are killing me in these high heels.'

'By all means, Mrs Trescott,' exclaimed Donaghue. 'Take them off—liberate your toes. There is nothing in the world worse than painfully constricted feet.' He glanced down at his own feet which were resting comfortably, encased in tan brogues, against the lower drawers of his desk.

Mrs Trescott slipped off her smart high heels with a sigh of relief then sat back comfortably in her seat, flexing her cramped toes.

'Ah,' she said. 'It can be a painful business keeping up appearances.'

'Now, Mrs Trescott,' said Donaghue coaxingly, 'perhaps you would like to tell me why you have come to see me.'

'Well,' said Mrs Trescott. 'I... It's going to be difficult to explain... You see, I've got nothing really to go on...just a feeling.' She hesitated, trying to find her words. 'It's about my daughter...my only daughter. I have a feeling that something... something bad is going to happen to her. I have a feeling, ridiculous as it may sound, that she is in danger.'

'In danger?' queried Donaghue.

'Let me explain,' said Mrs Trescott. 'My daughter is Salome.' She regarded Donaghue fixedly.

He regarded her in turn in mystification.

'Salome?' he repeated.

'Yes, Salome. You know—the pop singer. Well, she's more an actress now.'

'Salome?' repeated Donaghue, utterly perplexed. Donaghue, although he considered his taste in music eclectic, rarely watched television and had never bought a tabloid newspaper in his life. He had never before heard of a singer called Salome.

'Bridget,' he said as his elegant secretary entered the room with a tray, 'have you heard of a pop singer called Salome?'

'Of course I have,' said Bridget indignantly. 'Who hasn't?'

Donaghue refrained from answering Bridget's question. Instead he invited her with a motion of his hand to place the tray on the desk before him and Mrs Trescott.

'What about Salome?' Bridget asked.

'This lady is...er...Salome's mother.' Donaghue had difficulty enunciating the girl's name. How on earth could any self-respecting mother call her daughter Salome!

'Salome's mother!' Bridget's almond shaped green eyes widened and she gazed at Mrs Trescott in admiration. 'I think Salome's terrific,' she gushed.

Mrs Trescott beamed.

'Of course,' said Bridget, bending a little from her exceptional height to peer at Mrs Trescott's face, 'I can see the resemblance now.'

Mrs Trescott beamed even more brightly.

'I wear Salome shorts,' said Bridget proudly. 'When I go to discos, of course—not to work.'

'You've certainly got the legs for them,' commented Mrs Trescott as she smiled up at Mr Donaghue's beautiful secretary.

Donaghue coughed and motioned to Bridget to leave him with his client.

'Salome shorts?' he enquired, his voice lowered, when the office door had closed behind Bridget.

'Salome's stage outfit became all the rage among young girls,' Mrs Trescott explained. 'Haven't you noticed, Mr Donaghue, that all the young girls at the moment are wearing shorts instead of skirts?'

Donaghue had, in fact, noticed the current ubiquity of young girls' legs. He could not fail to but he had no notion of who or what initiated fashions among the young.

'It's all down to my Sandra,' said Mrs Trescott proudly.

'Sandra?'

'Salome is my daughter's stage name,' explained Mrs Trescott.

'You don't think I'd call my only daughter Salome, do you?'
She flashed a sudden brilliant smile at Donaghue which made
him start.

'Absolutely not, Mrs Trescott,' he said.

Mrs Trescott sipped her tea. 'She's a lovely girl, Sandra. She's
got a lovely nature—you can't judge her by her behaviour on
stage.'

'I've never had the pleasure of seeing her on stage,' said Donaghue.

'Here,' said Mrs Trescott and she fumbled in her bag and
withdrew two photographs which she thrust at Donaghue across
the table.

One portrayed a pretty girl in her early twenties, glossy brown
hair spilling over delicate shoulders—the eyes green and clear,
the skin English peaches and cream, the mouth smiling and girlish. The second picture portrayed a dazzling young woman
dressed in scanty satin shorts, glossy tights, high-heeled shoes
and a tight, revealing top—the whole glitzy affair topped by a
leonine spiky blonde wig. The face, heavily made up, in no way
resembled that of the girl in the first picture.

'Her stage act is just an act,' Mrs Trescott went on. 'In real
life she's not at all the sex maniac she appears on stage. She is,
in fact, an excellent actress—she's planning now to drop singing
and go seriously into acting.'

'Is that so?' Donaghue muttered. He was studying the two
pictures intently, his head bent.

'And what,' he asked finally, lifting his rather unkempt head,
'is the origin of your feeling of apprehension?'

'I really can't say,' said Mrs Trescott, her features clouding.
'Only a mother's intuition, I suppose. I just feel that she's in
danger. I can feel it in my bones. If you have any children you
must know what I'm talking about.' Mrs Trescott appeared to be
on the verge of tears.

Donaghue coughed. 'Ahem...' he said. 'God, in his great plan
of evolution, did not select my good self as a procreator of the
race. He must, I imagine, have had his reasons.' Donaghue spoke
almost regretfully. 'But that does not mean,' he added, 'that I do
not believe in the power of intuition—on the contrary, I place
great faith in it and in particular in the much greater intuition of
women.'

Mrs Trescott dabbed at her eyes with a paper handkerchief. Donaghue spoke to her in a gentle, sympathetic tone.

'You will have to tell me, my dear lady, a little about your daughter's lifestyle—where she lives, with whom, et cetera.'

The soft lilt of the little man's brogue again exerted a tranquillizing effect on Mrs Trescott. She delved once more into her handbag and brought out a folded newspaper cutting which she passed over to Donaghue. The photograph depicted Sandra without her stage outfit but wearing an expensive fur coat, arm in arm with a small man considerably older than herself. The picture had been taken in some public place—possibly an airport terminal.

'I take it she is a tall girl,' Donaghue commented, 'or else her companion is extremely short.'

'That's her husband and you're right,' said Mrs Trescott. 'He is short.' Her tone was not without a note of disdain. 'He has a weakness for tall women—short men often do.' Her face reddened slightly as she finished speaking. She evidently remembered that she was talking to a short man.

Donaghue smiled. 'It's true,' he said. 'I am a small man and I have a weakness for tall women.'

'I suppose you recognize him,' said Mrs Trescott, nodding to the newspaper.

Donaghue looked apprehensively at the photograph. He couldn't for the life of him put a name to the small, balding man in the picture although he did have a notion that he had seen him before. The investigator's bright blue eyes squinted. The name would, of course, come to him in time. His formidable memory never failed him—it was only a question of time for what he called the peripheral data relegated to the unconscious to come to the surface of his conscious brain.

'Thelonius Kapp,' Mrs Trescott stated curtly.

Thelonius Kapp. Donaghue had, of course, heard of Thelonius Kapp. As his secretary, Bridget, would have said—who hadn't?

Thelonius Kapp was one of the most successful film directors in Hollywood and therefore in the world; but film directors, though they usually bore renowned names, were rarely blessed with remarkable faces—which was why they were film directors, Donaghue supposed, and not the stars they directed.

'I take it from your tone that you don't approve of your daughter's choice of husband,' Donaghue commented.

Mrs Trescott frowned.

'It's not exactly that I don't approve—it's just that I don't think he's...well, suitable. I mean, the difference in age—he's sixty-six or sixty-seven, she's twenty-five. He's more than forty years older than her—he's old enough to be her grandfather. It's not natural. He's old enough to be *my* father, for God's sake!'

Donaghue winced inwardly at Mrs Trescott's taking of the Lord's name in vain and wondered if there might be a slight touch of jealousy in her attitude; but the genuinely fraught expression on the woman's face convinced him otherwise.

'Do you think she's in danger from him?' he asked.

'I'm not really sure,' she said worriedly. 'I don't know him very well—I've only met him twice. He appeared very polite and considerate on the surface. But these film people... I've heard stories about him—when he was younger, sleeping with every young actress that came his way. But then they say that they all do that—and you don't know what to believe in the papers.'

Donaghue nodded in fervent agreement.

'I...I don't know whether she's in danger from him. He seems to dote on her—in fact, they seem to genuinely love each other—for the moment. I don't expect it to last though. Surely a young girl would get bored with an old man after a while. The old get stuck in their ways, even if they're a bit Bohemian like this Kapp, and Sandra's not a stupid girl. She's bright—she was studying law when she got caught up in the pop world.'

'Law?' queried Donaghue. He couldn't quite associate the image of a sober lawyer with the picture before him of a half-naked girl under the stage lights.

'Yes,' said Mrs. Trescott. 'She was planning to become a barrister but she got involved with some music students who asked her to sing in their group. She has a lovely singing voice.'

'A talented girl all round,' commented Donaghue.

'Oh yes,' Mrs Trescott agreed proudly.

'And what exactly would you require of me—in the way of services, I mean?' Donaghue asked.

'Sandra and her husband—she calls him Theo—will be in London in two weeks' time. They'll be staying in their flat in Chelsea. She'll come up for a few days to visit me in Rochdale but most of their stay in England will be in London. He's making a film or something—they'll be here for about a month. I'd like you to keep an eye on her—a watchful eye—to see that she comes to no harm. I can afford to employ you full time. Money is no object—Sandra keeps me well provided for.'

'You haven't thought of asking the police?' enquired Donaghue.

'The police!' snorted Mrs Trescott derisively. 'In my experience the police do not exactly rush into dangerous situations—they prefer to arrive after the danger is over. It's only human nature I suppose—look after your own skin. The Starsky and Hutches only exist on television.'

'They are, unfortunately, mere mortals like you and me, Mrs Trescott,' said Donaghue. 'What makes you think I might be any more heroic?'

'I don't expect you to be heroic,' said Mrs Trescott drily, 'but I'm sure you will be more *discreet*. I've yet to meet a discreet policeman. And I've been told, Mr Donaghue, that the reason for your success is your great discretion.'

Donaghue's rather pallid complexion deepened very slightly with pleasure at Mrs Trescott's words of praise.

'As the great man himself said, "Discretion is the greater part of valour." He was, as in everything he said, perfectly correct.'

Donaghue's eyes misted as he spoke and Mrs Trescott regarded the little investigator suspiciously.

'You know, Mrs Trescott,' he said, his small piercing blue eyes peering at her intently, 'I have the profoundest respect for the English—not being of the race, that is—and do you know why?'

Mrs Trescott shook her head.

'Any nation that could produce a Shakespeare cannot be all bad,' he said. Donaghue's moist eyes were lifted to a spot on the ceiling. He appeared to have drifted into another private reverie.

'Can I rely on you then, when my daughter arrives?' queried Mrs Trescott.

'Of course,' said Donaghue, dropping his eyes instantly to her face. 'With pleasure, my dear lady. I'm off tomorrow on a much-needed ten-day holiday. I suggest that you come back to see me a couple of days before your daughter arrives in London. Then you can give me details of her schedule, addresses, et cetera.. Shall we say 10th September at the same time—teatime?'

Mrs Trescott smiled in agreement.

'And don't worry, my dear lady,' said Donaghue as he rose from his seat. 'All's well that will end well.' He raised his eyes to heaven in a gesture of supplication. 'If the great Bard forgives my misquoting him.'

Mrs Trescott slipped on her shoes, shook Donaghue's hand with a firm grip and, feeling a great deal better than when she arrived, left the office.

Donaghue sat back in his swivel chair, a frown creasing his leathery, simian features.

The words that he had just quoted to his client he had uttered glibly—they had not, in fact, been the words that he had wanted to utter at all. What had sprung into his mind had been indeed from the same work but lines of a different hue altogether. What he had really wanted to say to Mrs Trescott had been: *'The hind that would be mated by the lion must die for love.'* The investigator wondered why. He reached out for his packet of slim cigars, lit one and inhaled, leaning back reflectively in his chair.

Ulysses Finnegan Donaghue believed profoundly in three things—in God, in the phenomenal astuteness of Shakespeare's observation of human nature, and in the power of intuition. He nursed a fourth belief, less certain than the other three—that the human brain was cleverer than most of its bearers believed it to be. He, Donaghue, believed that the human brain, when not hampered by alcohol, drugs or irrational fears, might possibly be almost as clever as God's own.

He frowned. He had no idea why but he felt, along with Mrs Trescott, irrational though the feeling was, that her fears for her daughter might not be without foundation.

TWO

Donaghue on holiday

THE MORNING FOLLOWING Mrs Trescott's visit dawned bright and sunny—a glorious golden, late summer Saturday. Donaghue's prediction had been correct—England had been blessed with an Indian summer. Not that it would have mattered to Ulysses Donaghue had this particular Saturday turned out to be the normal grey drizzly morning that could be expected at the end of August. He was leaving that morning for his favourite holiday retreat—the village of St Pierre la Croix in the South of France, which lay well off the beaten track and was unsullied, as yet, by the tourists that swarmed like ants only a few kilometres away on the Riviera coast.

Donaghue leapt out of bed as nimbly as his slightly bulky weight would allow, released the blind on his bedroom window so that it flew up with a clatter, and regarded contentedly the verdant view of Hampstead Heath that lay before his eyes.

His office was situated on the other side of the Heath directly opposite his bachelor flat: a perspicacious choice of lodging and workplace as it forced upon him the pleasant duty of walking or cycling (as the fancy took him) the two miles or so across the Heath each morning to work—his sole form of daily exercise and one which, if he performed it briskly, would counteract the adverse effect on his arteries of the dairy butter that he partook of each morning at breakfast on his toast.

Mrs Percival, Donaghue's cook and housekeeper of long standing, disapproved vehemently of her employer's altogether too Irish liking for butter which he spread far too liberally on his morning toast and melted in great quantities on the potatoes that she carefully prepared for him daily in polyunsaturated oil.

Mrs Percival's great concern in life was the hearts of the men in her culinary care, those of her husband, Mr Percival, her sons,

Eric and Kenneth Percival and her employer, Ulysses F. Donaghue.

'One day,' she warned him regularly, 'you'll drop dead, just like that—with no warning at all—just like that.' She would qualify the rapidity of her employer's demise with a foreboding snap of her thick fingers.

'My Percival has margarine,' she informed him. 'Not so much as a dab of butter—my Eric and my Kenneth neither. They're not going to peg out on me like Mr Jenkins in the corner shop did on Mrs Jenkins. It was all that butter he got for nothing that done it. Men haven't got the staying power,' she would add wisely. 'They've got no chance if they eat too much animal fat.'

Donaghue was sure that Mrs Percival watched too much television and read too many women's weekly magazines. He would respond to her warnings of doom and gloom with a tacit nod of his shaggy head. He had learnt over the years that it was not worth arguing with those of purely Anglo-Saxon stock—and Mrs Percival, along with all the male Percivals, was of such stock.

It was evident to Donaghue that at no point in their evolution had any Percival set foot beyond the watery boundaries of their sceptred isle and equally evident that no Percival had ever had occasion to mingle their genetic heritage with that of the last conquering invaders of England—to wit the Normans, who, on the whole, had mingled only with the indigenous nobility and royalty. Such genetic segregation was testified to, not only by Mr and Mrs Percival's ruddy Saxon solidity, but also by Mrs Percival's vehement hatred of the upper classes to whom she referred scathingly as the 'Toffs'.

I'd rather work any day for an Irishman than a Toff,' Mrs Percival had declared when Donaghue had interviewed her for the post sixteen years earlier. Donaghue had waived aside his suspicion of a veiled insult in Mrs Percival's declaration in the face of the ardent enthusiasm with which she had set to cleaning and tidying his somewhat dusty and disorderly bachelor flat.

'Cleanliness is next to godliness,' she had declared. 'The only reason the Toffs think they're cleaner than the poor is because the poor do all their cleaning for them and don't have time to do it for themselves.'

Donaghue found himself reduced to silent admiration of Mrs

Percival's simple Protestant ethic of the life-prolonging benefits of hard work and sanitary poverty.

Donaghue, then only thirty-five, had not yet managed to come to terms with the great dilemma in his life—namely that of marrying the opposing effects of his Jesuit teachers and his Epicurean parents who, though not in the least religious, had sent him to be educated by the Dublin Jesuits in the hope that their son, whom they had named after the two great works of their hero, Joyce, would follow in the master's footsteps and become a new Irish literary giant. Donaghue had failed them miserably, manifesting no talent whatsoever for creative writing, but developing instead a formidable memory which, in order to please his adored parents, he devoted to the assimilation of the great works of English and Irish literature—quantities of which flowed from his lips in much the same way, he imagined, that the ink had flowed from their authors' pens.

Donaghue tempered the guilt he felt at having disappointed his parents by convincing himself that, unlike Mrs Percival, he was not one hundred per cent genetically pure. Somewhere in the Donaghue evolution a Spanish *conquistador* had dallied with a Donaghue maiden or matron—hence the very unCeltic sallow hue to Donaghue's leathery skin.

For sixteen years a very cordial *entente* had established itself between these representatives of two warring nations and religions. Mrs Percival 'did' for Donaghue and Donaghue accepted her admonitions in respectful silence and paid her handsomely for her services.

He could hear her now moving about in the kitchen preparing his breakfast.

'Mr Donaghue,' she called, 'I'm making you poached eggs—you'll need a good start to the day if you're off to that French place. You know you won't be eating properly once you set foot on that plane.'

Donaghue slipped into his light summer kimono and declined to inform Mrs Percival that the food on French planes was exceptionally good and usually accompanied by a half-bottle of Perrier Jouet champagne. Such information would, he knew, not impress Mrs Percival at all. Instead he made his way to the bathroom calling out as he went, 'A hot English breakfast will do the world of good, Mrs Percival. Weak food best fits weak stomachs, and my stomach is, as you know, the strongest part of me—as you have seen fit to make it.'

'Eh?' called Mrs Percival, popping her head around the kitchen door.

'I'll be having a quick shower, Mrs Percival,' Donaghue called out, 'and I'll be ready in two flicks of a cat's tail.'

'More gab than sense, that one,' Mrs Percival muttered to herself as she turned the eggs on to a plate and placed a square of best dairy butter with great disdain into the butter dish.

Five minutes later Donaghue entered the sunny kitchen dressed in a pair of light Italian-style cotton trousers and a silk shirt, his normally unbridled hair reduced to a damp cap that imparted to him the aspect of a well-dressed medieval serf.

'I don't know why you want to go gallivanting off to those foreign places when there are perfectly good holiday resorts here in England,' Mrs Percival complained as she placed his plate of eggs before him. 'It's not good for the health, foreign food.'

'I've no doubt, Mrs Percival,' said Donaghue as he picked up the morning's newspaper, 'that I will live to a healthy old age thanks to your solicitous care. I am, as your own good Henry the Eighth was, a man of an unbridled stomach.'

Mrs Percival cast a disdainful eye at the burgeoning rotundity of Donaghue's midriff.

'Your stomach will be the death of you,' she commented sourly.

'No, Mrs Percival,' Donaghue protested, peering at her over the top of his newspaper. 'In that you are wrong. We will all die of one thing and one thing only—every last one of us of the same thing and it isn't the stomach nor the heart.'

'And what might that be?' queried Mrs Percival suspiciously.

'LOB,' said Donaghue.

'LOB?' repeated Mrs Percival.

'Yes, LOB—Lack of Oxygen to the Brain,' declared Donaghue triumphantly. 'Some die of PLOB, Progressive Lack of Oxygen to the Brain, and many of us, sadly, die of CLOB, Chronic Lack of Oxygen to the Brain, but we all die of the same thing in the end—even your cholesterol-free Percivals,' he added under his breath.

Mrs Percival tutted in tacit disagreement as she poured boiling water into the teapot. Donaghue, profiting from a moment's respite, returned his attention to his newspaper.

His gaze was arrested on the second page by a fuzzy picture and a headline above it which read: HOLLYWOOD DIRECTOR THELONIUS KAPP ARRIVES IN PARIS WITH WIFE SALOME.

Donaghue studied the picture closely. Kapp he recognized from the cutting that Mrs Trescott had shown him the day before—the same compressed expression of the lips, the same hard, sharp glint in the small dark eyes, the same black leather coat—but Salome, or Sandra, as Donaghue preferred to designate her, was unrecognizable to him. The girl, it seemed, was a chameleon. With a change of hair-style and a new outfit she became an entirely different woman. He would keep the picture—a woman who changed her image as often and as easily as this Sandra Kapp might be difficult to keep a watchful eye on.

'Come along now, Mr Donaghue.' Mrs Percival's cockney twang shook him from his contemplation. 'Eat up—you've got a plane to catch in two hours.'

AN HOUR LATER at Heathrow airport Donaghue was waiting patiently in line to have his single suitcase weighed and checked in. Donaghue's was the plane for Marseilles; the queue next to his was destined for Paris. Donaghue's attention, as he glanced round at his fellow travellers, was arrested by a tall, striking young girl standing in the Paris queue. The girl had also been noticed by the elderly blue-haired woman standing directly in front of Donaghue who was staring openly at her, as indeed were almost all the passengers within sight of her.

It wasn't so much the girl herself as her attire that attracted their attention. She was dressed in glossy shorts so scanty as to be indecent and a tight-fitting vest that revealed the rounded contours of her breasts. Her long slender legs tapered into bright red stiletto-heeled shoes and her small pale face was rendered utterly anonymous by the thick black lines painted around the eyes and the wild mass of straw-blonde hair that covered much of her face and splayed out from her head. Huge ear-rings in the shape of crucifixes hung from her tiny ear lobes.

'Salome shorts,' Donaghue found himself repeating silently—one of those Salome look-alikes that Mrs Trescott had spoken so proudly of. Indeed this girl could have been Salome herself for all Donaghue knew. How odd, he mused to himself, that these young girls, in their effort to make themselves noticeable, lost all trace of their individuality.

The elderly lady in front of Donaghue, whose ruddiness of complexion exceeded even that of Mrs Percival, noticed Donaghue looking at the girl and whispered conspiratorially at him, 'They might as well walk around stark naked—really!'

'Fortunately the weather is warm,' Donaghue commented, then noted to his surprise that the Salome look-alike was accompanied, not by the ear-ringed punk who stood indifferently to one side of her, but by the tall, smartly dressed, clean-cut young man who stood at the desk checking in two suitcases. The pleasant-faced young man, who was wearing fashionable photosensitive tinted spectacles, had turned to whisper something in the girl's ear. The girl shook her blonde head and started to cough—a rasping, wheezing cough that made her narrow shoulders tremble.

'It's not surprising she's got a cough,' the elderly woman hissed in Donaghue's ear. 'Dressed like that!'

Donaghue declined to express his opinion that the girl's cough was not the result of a viral infection but rather that of an asthma sufferer. He had learnt in his long experience never to argue with elderly Anglo-Saxon women of a ruddy complexion.

ONCE ENSCONCED in his habitual window seat at the rear of the plane, Donaghue banished all thought of Salome and her infamous shorts from his mind. He was on holiday—albeit a short one. He was on his way to Marseilles where the temperature would be at least ten degrees higher than in England—he loosened his tie in anticipation—and where he would have no need of his thermal underwear.

From Marseilles he would take the train to Toulon: for Donaghue, a refreshingly delightful prospect. French trains arrived and left on time, a miracle, to his mind, of temporal and spatial engineering and, in addition to being smooth, silent and comfortable, were equipped with well-stocked bars and restaurants. Ah, French food, he mused. He sighed in anticipation of the meal of salmon mousse and steak Tartare with gratin de pommes de terre, followed by a selection of excellent cheeses and all accompanied by a '78 Bordeaux, which would be served to him in approximately fifteen minutes' time.

At Toulon he would be met by his old friend, Clothilde Blanche, who would drive him at terrifying speed to her delightful villa in the equally delightful village of St Pierre la Croix that lay nestled in the hills behind Hyères. His spirits sank momentarily at the one black cloud on his sunny blue horizon—the utterly appalling journey in the passenger seat of Clothilde's car. He dreaded to think what car she might have this year. Toulon to St Pierre—forty kilometres of petrifying fear and horror.

Donaghue's greatest fear was not simply, as is common to most mortals, the fear of death—it was rather the fear of death in an appallingly horrible accident and in particular in an accident on one of those interminably winding French country roads where French drivers like his friend, Clothilde, took his life into their hands in a ghastly French drivers' version of Russian roulette. Donaghue, who was an inveterate non-gambler, knew that in that game the odds were stacked heavily against him. A simple resolution to treat himself to a half-bottle of an '83 Bandol while on his way to Toulon alleviated his anxiety a little and lifted the cloud that had descended on to the blue skies of his prospective holiday.

A passenger installed himself noiselessly into the seat next to Donaghue's, rousing the investigator from his reverie. He glanced sidelong at the passenger's profile and was greatly pleased to note that his neighbour was staid, middle-aged and male, the immaculate grey suit bespeaking a sales manager of a long-established biscuit manufacturer—the kind of passenger who would study his market research reports assiduously throughout the journey and leave his fellow passengers alone. The elderly blue-rinsed lady with the ruddy complexion, Donaghue was relieved to notice, had installed herself noisily six rows in front of him.

The man, as he took his seat, nodded silently and glumly at Donaghue, attached his seat belt and settled down to study the huge wad of market research reports that he had placed upon his knee.

'REALLY, CLOTHILDE,' said Donaghue in utter despair as he bent himself almost double to enter the impossibly low, sleek, two-seater vehicle that Clothilde had double-parked in the car-park at Toulon's railway station. 'Each time I come down you've bought an even lower, even faster car.' The tone of Donaghue's voice was plaintive, so much so that Clothilde looked at him reprimandingly.

'Ulysses Donaghue, you are the most exasperating man alive—and I've met a few in my time. You claim to detest every minute you spend on the road, so I endeavour to halve that time, and you still complain—that, I suppose, is male logic!'

'Logic is a multi-faceted affair, as you well know, Clothilde,' replied Donaghue peevishly. 'If, in the halving of the time I spend on the road, I reduce my life expectancy by more than fifty per cent then, from a purely mathematical point of view, it would be infinitely more logical to spend what time I necessarily must on the road in a slower, generally safer vehicle. Personally, Clothilde, I would prefer to walk.'

'Walk, pah!' snorted Clothilde. 'What do you take yourself for? I suppose you think you're still a youth hosteller and could hitch-hike a lift from a farm tractor to take you from Toulon to St Pierre. Really, Ulysses!' Clothilde snorted once again in utter derision.

Donaghue, who had met Clothilde thirty years earlier in a youth hostel in Stockholm, fastened his safety belt and looked over at his friend's coarse features in apprehension. The '83 Bandol that he had bought on the train had dulled the sharp edge of his consciousness but not sufficiently to quell his fear of being blown to smithereens in a high-speed collision with another high-speed car.

'You know, Clothilde,' he said, 'in the long years I have spent on this earth, I have never been able to come to a satisfactory conclusion as to why civilized man, with all his highly technical intelligence and refinement of culture, should choose to hurl himself through time and space in a fragile and highly combustible box-like container when he could, with his highly developed intelligence, devise a means of transporting himself about that is infinitely less life-imperilling.'

'It's only a question of economics, you know that, Ulysses,' snapped Clothilde. 'The combustion engine has not yet killed enough human beings to make it a threat to mankind.'

'143,362 people were severely injured by vehicles with combustion engines in this country last year, 18,199 in this region alone.' Donaghue's tone was melancholic. 'I call that a threat—perhaps not to the whole race but certainly to this member of it.'

'It's a question of ratio,' said Clothilde as the sports car leapt forward and Donaghue's eyes snapped shut. 'As long as the co-efficient of obsolescence in the car is inferior to that of the human being, the number of cars produced will increase. The day a car is mass produced that lasts a human lifetime or longer things will change—but that day, of course, will never come.'

Clothilde glanced over at Donaghue.

'For goodness' sake, Ulysses,' she snapped, 'open your eyes. Do you think that by keeping them closed whatever you fear will go away? Such a tactic is the refuge of an over-sensitive small boy.'

As far as Donaghue was concerned the tactic of an over-sensitive small boy worked wonderfully well in distressing situations such as the one he was in now.

Then his eyes flew open unwittingly as Clothilde's finger poked him sharply in the ribs. He kept them open reluctantly wondering what on earth was the point as the beautiful Provençal scenery, that he knew lay to each side of him, was rendered utterly invisible by the car's speed, appearing to him, as they flashed through it, as nothing more than a series of surrealist streaks of light and colour on a moving canvas.

He glanced down at his watch—12.15. He calculated that, at the speed of sound at which Clothilde was driving, they would travel the forty kilometres to St Pierre la Croix in approximately five minutes.

'Well,' said Clothilde cheerfully as she reached out and patted Donaghue on the knee. 'Despite your deplorable and offensive lack of trust in my driving ability, I am very, very pleased to see you. We've some splendid exhibitions to see and I've prepared a special weekend treat for you. I won't say any more about it now. I'll explain when we arrive over an iced rosé and marinaded olives.'

Donaghue turned to smile weakly at his old friend. His eyes

were drawn irretrievably to the speedometer. They were moving at two hundred kilometres per hour. His face paled to the colour of Clothilde's favourite goat's cheese.

THREE

A flat in Paris

IN HIS PENTHOUSE FLAT overlooking the Seine, the renowned American film director, Thelonius Kapp, sat reclining in a long leather easy chair surveying the magnificent view of the French capital afforded him by his panoramic double-glazed window. The air-conditioning, which hummed discreetly somewhere in the depths of his vast apartment, was the only sound to disturb the utter silence of the penthouse despite its central position in a noisy and bustling capital city.

To one side of his chair a small period table bore the remains of a bottle of pure malt whisky, a heavy-bottomed glass, a silver cigarette case, a pipe and what appeared to be an antique snuff box.

Kapp reclined reflectively, his eyes half open, looking down at the view below. His gaze came to rest on the top of the newly constructed Louvre Pyramid which glittered like a monumental diamond in the midday sun. A scintillating monument to what? Kapp thought. To a politician's temporary glory? He smiled to himself. How foolishly short-sighted politicians were. A monument should be built not to one's temporal deeds but to one's eternal soul. He, Kapp, was building a monument to his soul—a monument albeit in stone and plaster, but much more than this trinket below, this edifice in steel and glass. His, Kapp's, monument would be constructed of human souls. He reflected happily on the medieval abbey that he had bought two years before in Provence, an ancient twelfth-century monastery which had been completely restored to its former beauty and magnificence. The monastery he had transformed into a convent inhabited now by a silent order of Carmelite nuns. The abbey would become once again a centre of spirituality and an eternal monument to his,

Kapp's, eternal soul. Kapp looked down at the Pyramid with disdain.

He reached out to refill his glass. Damn—the bottle was empty. He could have sworn it had been half full when he'd poured it last. He rose and made his way unsteadily to the bar in the corner of the room and selected another bottle. He returned to his seat by the window, opened the snuff box and took from it a small pill which he popped into his mouth. His beady black eyes glazed for a second.

Where was Sandra? He looked behind him into the empty room. Was she in the shower? He called her name. The vast room answered with silence. He called again more loudly this time, his voice cracking as he raised it.

Had she said she was going to take a shower? What had she said? What time was it? He peered at his watch. 12.45. Was she fixing lunch? Sandra fixing lunch? No, Sandra never cooked— Milly cooked. He leaned forward in his chair and turned his head again.

'Milly! Milly!' he yelled imperiously. Milly failed to answer his call. Kapp slumped back into his chair, lit his pipe, which contained a mixture of tobacco and cannabis resin, and smoked thoughtfully.

Why had he come to Paris? Ah, yes, to meet that new young French actor—what was his name? Carrer, yes, that was it—who was going to play the male lead in his new film. What was the film called? A glint of something that approached apprehension entered the glazed black eyes. What was the goddamned film called? He couldn't for the life of him remember. He turned his shaved head again and peered into the depths of the sunny air-conditioned room.

'Sandra!' he called. 'Sandra!'

SANDRA KAPP EMERGED from the ladies' toilet on the ground floor of Charles de Gaulle airport and walked purposefully towards the central staircase. Her face, without its stage make-up, was pretty and bland. Her light brown, almost mousy hair hung straight to her shoulders. She carried a hessian shoulder bag and was dressed simply in a pair of light blue jeans and a plain white T-shirt. In her dark glasses she appeared as just another of the hundreds of young French students who thronged the airport on their way back to colleges and universities at the end of the summer holidays.

She wended her way through the throng in total anonymity— no one would have recognized the tall, mousy-haired girl as the blonde and extravagant pop singer and actress, Salome.

She climbed quickly up the wide steel central staircase to the second floor of the terminal where the passengers from London had already passed through customs control and were waiting around aimlessly for the luggage to appear on the moving luggage belt.

'Carl,' she called out and a tall, fair-haired, clean-cut young man, who was standing with his back to her some distance away, turned and smiled in recognition. She approached him and lifted her face to offer him the customary French brush of cheek on cheek. The pleasant-faced young man removed his tinted spectacles as he bent to kiss her, his intelligent grey eyes luminous in the halogen light of the airport building. Then, replacing his glasses, he looked rapidly over each shoulder as if looking for someone else.

'Did you come specially to meet me?' he said in a soft American drawl. 'You didn't come with Mr Kapp, did you?'

'Mr Kapp is indisposed at the moment,' Sandra said. 'And in any case he would never have come to the airport to meet you.' She smiled. 'I came because I was bored and, to tell you the truth...' A frown replaced the smile. '...it gets me down sometimes, being around Theo.'

'That's understandable,' said the American.

She reached out and took his hand, holding it tightly in hers so that the knuckles stood out white against the skin.

'I have to get away from him sometimes,' she whispered. 'You can understand, can't you, Carl?' Her voice was low as she spoke. 'I need the company of a younger man sometimes...someone my own age, who's not half crazed with drugs. I need to be with someone whose thoughts are clear and whose body is healthy.'

Tears misted her eyes and her companion smiled with great tenderness at her, stroking her hair gently with his hand. Then she smiled once again.

'Anyway,' she said with feigned cheerfulness, 'I really came because I thought that it would save you the trouble of having to find your way to the Louvre or hail a taxi. I know it's your first time in Paris.'

Sandra Kapp's voice, as she spoke, exhibited a curious combination of American and Lancashire intonations.

'I *am* a big boy now,' the young man said humorously as he selected his suitcase from the luggage belt. 'I can find my way about in the world even in places I have never been to before.' He smiled brightly, revealing an array of perfect white American teeth. 'But I think you came for a different reason,' he said to her quietly as they moved away towards the central staircase.

Sandra stopped walking, gripped her husband's secretary by his elbow and said urgently, 'Look, Carl—I have to talk to you.'

Carl Petersen frowned at her.

'You haven't changed your mind?' he said.

'It's not that I've changed my mind,' she said. 'It's just that…'

'You're not sure,' he said anxiously. The grey eyes behind the spectacles flickered for a second to reveal a momentary expression of sympathy.

'It's just that…' she said hesitantly. 'Well, sometimes, some days, I think he knows.'

'Knows what?' asked Petersen solicitously.

'Well, just knows what's going on.'

Petersen looked at Sandra, his eyes betraying a measure of anxiety.

'I think we'd better find a quiet corner in a bar somewhere,' he said quietly, 'and talk about this, don't you?'

'Yes,' said Sandra worriedly. 'Yes, I suppose we had.'

The two descended the stairs and left the terminal—to all appearances a very ordinary and unremarkable young couple.

FOUR

Preparing for a journey

MARK KINGSFORD WOKE with a start to the sultry tones of Salome's latest top ten hit. He had timed his disc player to wake him at 8.30 and had chosen Salome, his favourite female vocalist, for the purpose.

He managed, just in time, to stop his head from hitting the ceiling as he sat up in his high mezzanine bed. He had moved into the much sought-after converted loft in Camden only a week before and was not yet accustomed to the limited space between the duvet and the rafters. He climbed nimbly over the edge of the wooden structure and dropped naked to the floor below, ignoring the ladder constructed to one side for the purpose of ascent and descent.

Grabbing T-shirt and jeans from the wardrobe below, he ambled, whistling cheerfully, into the kitchen, flicking the switch on the coffee percolator as he passed, then, throwing his clothes over his shoulder, reached up and grasped the lintel of the bathroom door and swung himself, Tarzan fashion, into the shower.

A quick, cool shower and he emerged damp and refreshed. He towelled his dark hair into an unruly mop, slipped into his clothes and then, casting an appraising glance at his handsome, amiable reflection in the bathroom mirror, returned, humming along to Salome's song, to the kitchen which was now filled with the pleasing aroma of percolating coffee.

Cup in hand and his bare feet up on the coffee table, Mark picked up his notebook and quickly jotted down his itinerary for the day.

10 o'clock: pop into office, pick up Diner's Express card (left on desk), see editor, avoid Fiona at all costs.
11.15: catch plane to Marseilles, lunch on plane.

12.30 (French time): pick up hired Golf in Marseilles and drive to Hyères. Call in at Corinne's flat—stop for coffee (if she's there)—then on to St Pierre la Croix.

Sometime this evening: Salome, meet Mark Kingsford! Mark Kingsford, meet Salome! HOT DOODIES!!!

Mark listened in rapture to Salome's dulcet tones for a minute or so while he sipped his coffee.

'Salome!' he said aloud when the track had finished. 'I'm going to meet Salome—can you just beat that!'

Interviewing Salome and her husband, Thelonius Kapp, would be Mark's first foreign assignment as film correspondent of the reputable national newspaper, the *Daily Courier*. Not only was young Mark an ardent fan of the beautiful Salome but this would, in addition, be his first trip to the fashionable South of France. The abbey, owned by Kapp, where he and his wife had deigned to be interviewed, was of course some way from the beaches with all those beautiful topless French girls, but the interview would only take an hour or so—and then he would be off to the sun and the sea and the girls. He'd been spending an hour every evening for the last two weeks in the local gym and he felt in remarkably fine form.

He picked up the notes he had made the previous evening in preparation for his interview with the famous couple.

Kapp—not known as a sympathetic character—said to be dictatorial with his actors and actresses—rarely allows himself to be interviewed by the press—reputed as a great *'tombeur de femmes'*—said to have been, when younger, an inveterate 'couch caster'—numerous actresses over the years have filed paternity petitions against him—none succeeded in court. Extensive amorous activities apparently ceased since meeting and marrying the singer, Salome.

Bought the abbey at St Pierre la Croix two years previously—had it rapidly restored to its former glory and is inaugurating it this weekend as a centre of retreat.

Kapp had made a statement to the *Courier* explaining the spiritual purpose of the abbey. He had made it clear that he wanted no pre-publicity of the inauguration which was to be a quiet affair, the director and his wife arriving incognito. The first retreat, like all those that followed, would be open to those members of the public who sought genuine spiritual solace. He did not want the abbey, on its inauguration, to be filled with loud-mouthed journalists, television cameras and autograph-hunting adolescents. The abbey of St Pierre la Croix was to remain, as it had always been, a place of tranquillity.

Its silent order of nuns would welcome novices from every nation. They would live in comfort and security, offering to anyone, young or old, from every corner of the globe, a temporary escape from the stresses of the material world through a monthly retreat, which would provide three days of spiritual contemplation in the calm and delightful cloisters and grounds of the ancient abbey. In the abbey chapel, famed for its perfect acoustics, the guests could pray or meditate in silence or experience the tranquillizing effect on body and soul of the voice of the young Franciscan monk, Brother Martin de Porres, whose rendering of Gregorian Latin chant was said to be almost angelic.

Kapp, in his statement, had said that he hoped his abbey would provide an alternative, for the young, to drugs—that once they had experienced the 'high' of spiritual retreat, they would never bother to seek such a high artificially through drugs again. The statement had been signed by Kapp's wife, Salome, who, of course, had great influence among the young.

Mark smiled to himself. Kapp, it was well known, had indulged in every drug produced, natural or synthetic. It was rumoured in media circles that he was, in fact, a heroin addict. Up to the present Salome, in her short dizzying career, had managed to avoid any scandalous reports of sex and drug abuse.

Still, thought Mark, he would reserve judgement for the moment he was face to face with the celebrities. Having worked in the media for two years now he was well aware of the sometimes scandalous extent to which facts were distorted or even invented by the sensation-seeking press.

Mark popped his notes into his attaché case, checked that his camera was equipped with batteries and film and wondered whether he should leave a note for Fiona.

On reflection he decided no. Fiona was not exactly his girl-friend—not any longer. She was, at present, a mere colleague.

She was bound to call round at some time during the weekend and discover that he'd gone and she was bound sooner or later to learn that he had replaced Larry Turner for the Kapp interview. She'd be furious, of course—would have insisted that she accompany him to do the photos—but he was not going to have Fiona ruining what remote chance he might have of charming the talented and beautiful Salome.

He picked up the disc cover with its picture of Salome in her famous shorts and blonde wig and danced round the small sitting-room, blowing kisses to the image and holding it at arm's length as if it were a dancing partner.

'Salome,' he said amorously, 'this is your lucky day.'

Then, noticing the time, he grabbed his case, camera and blouson jacket, ran tanned fingers through his hair so that it fell into its habitual tousled disorder, threw himself a last approving glance in the hall mirror and left for France.

FIVE

A villa in Cannes

MIREILLE PARMENTIER, in the bedroom of her villa on the out-skirts of Cannes, zipped up her lightweight suitcase and then positioned herself in front of her triple mirror to put the finishing touches to her make-up. Her face, that of a B-movie starlet, was ravaged, not by her forty-two years, but by the deep frown lines between her brows and the clefts that ran from her nostrils to the corners of her mouth, established, it would seem, from the grim set of her lips.

At first sight of Mireille Parmentier's face the observer was struck, first of all, by the expression of anger and deep-seated anxiety and only later by the still-present beauty and symmetry of the features. The neat platinum blonde hair was cut into an expensive and exquisite bob; the skin was evenly tanned, in dark contrast to the hair, and beautifully preserved by the meticulous care of her husband, Loic, a chemist, who provided Mireille with the latest discoveries in skin protection long before they came on to the market.

Loic, lounging in the cane basket chair beside the bedroom window, which gave out on to a magnificent view of the Med-iterranean, watched his wife reflectively as she carefully applied her lipstick.

'Mireille,' he said in his quiet, dispassionate voice, 'I really do think we ought to cancel this weekend.'

Mireille turned her blonde head and frowned at her husband angrily.

'*I'm* going,' she said. '*You* can stay if you like.'

Although the set of her mouth remained relentless the dark eyes softened—took on an expression of entreaty. 'But I'd rather you came,' she said tenderly.

As always Loic was disarmed by the almost childlike tone of

plaintiveness his wife used when she wished to persuade him to
her way of thinking. As always he relented.

'I just don't think it will do you any good,' he said.

'You're wrong,' she said. 'I've waited all these years for a
chance like this. I'm not going to let it pass me by.'

'I just think that—psychologically—it won't do you any
good,' Loic said.

'It *will* do me good,' she maintained. 'It's the only thing that
will do me good.'

'The retreat will be beneficial—the atmosphere will probably
do you good—but you know what you need. You need to do a
therapy. That's the only sensible way to purge the unconscious
of its problems.'

Mireille turned on her husband furiously.

'Unconscious? *Unconscious?*' she said, her voice raised almost hysterically. 'My problem isn't a problem of the unconscious—it's a problem of the conscious.' She tapped her temple
angrily with a scarlet fingernail. 'I've suffered consciously for
years and years—it's that I want to purge, it's that I want to get
rid of. Talking to some calm collected psychologist who's never
had a real problem in his life isn't going to purge me of what I
suffer. Only one thing will purge me of that: vengeance.'

She pronounced the word with a quiet controlled emphasis.
Loic regarded her in mild consternation.

'Really, Mireille,' he said. 'You don't have to be melodramatic
with me.'

'I'm not being melodramatic, Loic,' she said. 'I'm being sen-
sibly realistic.'

'And how do you propose to wreak this vengeance?'

Mireille turned back to the mirror and applied her mascara.

'I don't know,' she said. 'I really don't know. I'll decide when
I see him, when I'm standing before him face to face.'

She looked at Loic's reflection in the mirror. He gazed steadily
back at hers. Her face suddenly crumpled into an ugly mask of
anguish. She laid her head on her hands and sobbed quietly. 'I'll
deal with him when I see him,' she repeated, mumbling through
her tears.

Loic rose and approached his wife. He placed his hands gently
on her shoulders and studied his narrow tanned face in the mirror.

He was the same age as his wife but looked ten years younger. His gaze dropped to the nape of her neck.

Mireille had been unusually fraught lately. He believed that she should see a doctor, preferably a psychotherapist. But persuading Mireille to do anything she didn't want to do was nigh on impossible—as impossible as trying to persuade a cat to release the mouse gripped in its teeth.

Loic stroked his wife's hair, the expression on his face one of consternation. His wife was an intelligent woman, albeit a profoundly unhappy one. He had never, until now, had reason to fear that her unhappiness might affect her behaviour.

SIX

On a motorway near Aix-en-Provence

'HAVE YOU CHECKED the tyres?'

The tall, elderly woman rapped out the question at the young garage mechanic in the service area just north of Aix-en-Provence.

'Yes, madame,' the mechanic answered nonchalantly.

'It's "mademoiselle" not "madame",' the woman corrected the young man who, she considered, was badly in need of a shave. 'Have you filled the windscreen wiper container?'

'Yes, madame.'

'Mam'zelle!'

Really, young people nowadays had no memory for anything—probably smoked cannabis every morning before coming to work.

'Have you checked the oil?'

'Yes, mad...mam'zelle.'

The young mechanic gazed up at Mademoiselle Thérèse Mendes France in embarrassment. Somehow, to his mind, the title 'mam'zelle' and this hawk-faced, grey-haired, quite terrifying old woman simply didn't go together.

'Right,' said Miss Mendes France. 'I can get off in confidence then?'

'How far are you going?'

'To St Pierre la Croix, north of Hyères.'

'Hyères?' said the young man. He looked at her wryly. 'Mad...mam'zelle,' he said, 'if this thing gets you to Hyères it'll be running on the grace of God.'

At the mechanic's words Miss Mendes France did a surprising thing. She placed a muscular arm around the young man's shoulder and hugged him. She smiled a grisly smile that revealed neglected yellowing teeth.

'You know, young man,' she said, 'you've probably never said a truer word in your life.'

She leaned close to him and whispered in his ear, 'Let me tell you something—grace is exactly what that car does run on. And do you know something else? It's what I run on too!'

Then she released him and, slipping a hundred francs into his hand, she folded her long body into the driving seat of her twenty-year-old 2CV and drove off.

'Mam'zelle!' called the mechanic after her. 'Your change!'

Miss Mendes France waved a large arm out of the window. 'Keep it,' she called. 'Use it for petrol when you run out of grace.'

The young mechanic shook his head as he followed her progress out of the garage.

As she circumvented the petrol pumps, Thérèse Mendes France calculated that it would take her a little over two and a half hours to get to Hyères. If she didn't want to pull into another service station she had better answer the call of nature now rather than later.

Having availed herself of the rather dingy WC behind the garage, she was about to pull off on to the slip road when her attention was drawn to what appeared to be a scuffle going on some yards in front of her. Two rather brawny men were in the process, it seemed, of harassing a young woman. Miss Mendes France jerked the 2CV to a halt, clambered out and bounded on her long legs towards the group, noting as she ran that the girl, who appeared to be pinned up against the garage wall, was slight, dark and obviously terrified. She was crying out in a foreign language that Miss Mendes France recognized as English, 'Please let me go! Please let me go!'

One of the men appeared to be fumbling with the girl's clothing. Miss Mendes France tapped him on the shoulder. The man turned his head in surprise then laughed suddenly and derisively at the ugly old woman who was glaring at him reprimandingly. His companion had also, for an instant, turned his surprised attention from the girl to the old woman.

'Clear off, you ugly old bat,' sneered the first man, whose shoulder Miss Mendes France was now gripping firmly in thick steely fingers.

'It's you, I think, who are going to clear off,' said Miss Mendes France matter-of-factly.

The second man snorted with merriment at her words and the first man opened his mouth to speak, but before the words could form themselves he found himself being hoisted up into the air and over the elderly lady's shoulder. He attempted to grab the lapel of her jacket for something to hold on to but her movements had been too swift. Before he knew what was happening his head had hit the tarmac of the slip road with a sickening thud and before losing consciousness he experienced a violent spasm of nausea in the pit of his stomach. The second man, who had watched the unexpected flight of his companion through the air, was too slow in his reaction to prevent Miss Mendes France from grabbing him by the collar of his shirt and precipitating him on to the same airborne trajectory.

Miss Mendes France then grasped the trembling girl and propelled her into her car. She drove quickly back to the other side of the garage and pulled up in the car-park before the service area shop.

'They attacked me as I came out of the toilet,' the girl said in accented French. Her voice trembled nervously. 'I thought they were going to rape me.'

'Of course they weren't going to rape you,' said Miss Mendes France. 'Not in broad daylight. They were just playing with you—not that I'm saying that's any worse, mind you.'

She handed the girl a paper handkerchief. 'Wipe your eyes,' she said. 'You'll feel better in a minute.' She leaned over her seat, delved into a holdall on the back seat and pulled out a thermos flask. She poured a cup of steaming coffee into the plastic cup and handed it to the girl.

'Here, drink this,' she said. 'It'll bring the colour back into your cheeks.'

The girl sipped the black liquid gratefully.

'You're English, I take it from your accent,' said Miss Mendes France.

The girl shook her head. 'Scottish,' she said.

Miss Mendes France appraised the girl's pale, rather pretty, narrow face with its large blue eyes and glossy black hair. Very definitely Celtic, this one.

'Ah yes,' she said. 'One forgets that the British Isles are made up of four separate nations, each impossibly proud of its language and culture.' She smiled. 'Let me introduce myself. I am, I believe, as French as my name—Thérèse Mendes France, *Mademoiselle* Mendes France. I am not and never have been married. I am *not* a madame.'

'Fiona,' said the girl. 'Fiona MacKinley—Ms.'

'Ms?' queried Miss Mendes France. 'What on earth is Ms?'

'Ms is for women who don't want to reveal whether they're married or single—it's in between.'

'In between!' snorted Miss Mendes France. 'Why should any woman be ashamed of revealing her marital status? I am a single woman and proud of the fact. Such a notion would never be accepted in France. Frenchwomen have established a relationship of absolute equality with men without sacrificing their femininity at all and without entering into futile battles of words with the male of the species as you Anglo-Saxon women tend to do.'

Fiona looked at her companion in silent admiration. The fact that this particular Frenchwoman declined to enter into battles of words with men had been testified to a few minutes earlier. She had, evidently, other means of tackling them.

'Well, my dear,' said Miss Mendes France. 'How are you travelling? You're not hitch-hiking, I hope?'

'No,' said the girl. 'My car's over there.' She indicated a rather battered-looking Morris Minor. 'It's broken down,' she said dejectedly. 'I was told that those cars last for ever but they obviously don't. I was wondering what exactly I should do when the two men...'

'Where are you heading for?' Miss Mendes France asked.

'I'm going to the Haut Var. The abbey of St Pierre la Croix. It's in the hills above Hyères.'

'Well, that's an extraordinary thing!' exclaimed Miss Mendes France. 'That's exactly where I'm going. I take it you're going to do the three-day retreat. Are you a Catholic then, my dear?'

'Well, no,' said Fiona. She hesitated. 'You don't have to be a Catholic to go on a retreat, do you? Not at this abbey, anyway.'

'Well, nevertheless,' said Miss Mendes France in delight, 'I think it's an extraordinary coincidence. Well, not coincidence— I don't actually believe in coincidence. I am pretty sure that someone had it in mind that I thought to answer nature's call at the particular moment I chose to, don't you agree, my dear?'

The girl nodded mutely, evidently rather unsure as to how she should react to the formidable old lady sitting next to her.

'Well, Fiona,' Miss Mendes France went on, 'perhaps the best thing to do would be to leave your car here in the capable hands of the garage mechanic and you accompany me down to the abbey. You can pick up your car on the way back. It would be a dreadful shame for you to miss Brother Martin de Porres.'

'Brother Martin de Porres?'

Miss Mendes France looked at Fiona curiously. 'Didn't you know that the celebrated Brother Martin de Porres is singing during this the first retreat of the abbey?'

Fiona reddened and shook her head.

'In that case,' said Miss Mendes France, 'you're in for a treat. Now,' she said in a businesslike manner, 'perhaps we'd better transfer your baggage from your car to mine, then arrange to leave it with the mechanic.'

Fiona nodded. Miss Mendes France drove off and parked the 2CV alongside the Morris. Fiona pulled out her luggage which consisted of a nylon holdall and a huge camera bag which she placed on the back seat of the Frenchwoman's car.

Then, having left the Morris in the safe care of the young mechanic, they joined the motorway and set off in the slow lane for Toulon.

'Thérèse,' said Fiona. 'May I call you Thérèse?'

'Certainly, my dear,' assented Miss Mendes France.

'Thérèse, can you please explain how you managed to hurl those two men about the way you did?'

'It's quite simple, my dear,' said Miss Mendes France. 'Even a snippet of a girl your size could lift men like that if you'd been the French judo champion for eight years running.'

Fiona's large blue eyes widened as she gazed at Miss Mendes France in admiration.

'But let me give you some advice,' said Miss Mendes France rather gruffly. 'Until you get a black belt in judo don't wear those kind of clothes while travelling alone.'

Fiona looked down at her summer travelling outfit which consisted of a sleeveless T-shirt and short tattered jean shorts.

'Are you saying,' she said indignantly, 'that I can't wear what I please—that those men have got the right to attack me because

I wear shorts? They can wear shorts and nothing else and I wouldn't dream of attacking them!'

'No, of course I'm not saying that,' said Miss Mendes France. 'Of course they haven't got the right to attack you. Dear me! You modern feminists, you really are so naive! You refuse to see what's in front of your eyes. Men are the way they are. Dressing like that is like waving a red flag to a bull. If you do it, don't be surprised if the bull charges—just be prepared.'

Fiona smiled. 'Do you think men are like bulls, then?' she asked. 'Do you think they have no control over their behaviour?'

'I most certainly do,' said Miss Mendes France. 'Which is why I never married one.'

Fiona looked across at her companion, a bemused smile on her small pretty face.

Miss Mendes France went on, 'It's not that I don't understand that some women feel the need to attract a man in order to satisfy their maternal urges. I understand that perfectly. What I fail to understand is why they feel the need to *live* with one. As far as I'm concerned,' she said firmly, 'men, like charging bulls, are best avoided.'

SEVEN

Mr and Mrs Bloch

MAXIMILIAN BLOCH smiled wistfully at his wife, Adèle, who stared glumly out of the window of the first-class carriage of the Paris-Nice TGV. He leaned across and patted her comfortingly on the knee.

'You wait, Adèle,' he said reassuringly. 'You'll return from this retreat saying that it was the most marvellous experience of your life. The trouble is that your feet are too firmly planted on terra firma—you don't allow your spirit to soar.' He lifted his tanned arm in a theatrical gesture of flight. He had wanted to add, 'which isn't surprising with your weight,' but his wife would not have taken his words in the humorous spirit in which they were meant. Adèle Bloch took her weight far too seriously for that.

Adèle glanced at her husband sulkily.

'It's all right for you,' she said. 'You don't have problems of self-esteem.'

What Adèle had said was, in fact, absolutely true. Maximilian Bloch had never suffered from problems of self-esteem. A remarkably handsome man of mixed ancestry—a German father, a French mother, Turkish and Russian grandparents—his physical beauty was only now, in his forty-second year, becoming marred by the burgeoning of the Epicurean's mid-life midriff. His remarkable success as a post-modernist painter had established him firmly in the upper echelons of the Parisian art world, so that nowhere in the domains of his personal and professional life was there room for the slightest self-misgiving. On top of that, his artist's concern for the spiritual over and above the temporal rendered him immune to the more mundane anxieties that plagued people like his wife.

Adèle's problem was a simple if banal one—once a very beautiful woman, she had, in early middle age, run excessively to fat, so that all trace of her formerly finely chiselled beauty had disappeared. But what Adèle failed to understand—or rather failed to believe when her husband tried to convince her of it—was that, although to the outside world she appeared just another large, middle-aged lady, to him, Maximilian Bloch the artist, she now possessed an equally powerful, if different, kind of beauty. What Adèle Bloch refused to believe was that Maximilian actually *liked* her fat, that, as he declared to her often, he actually loved her rolling hills of flesh.

'The female shape is only a matter of fashion,' he explained to her. It was also, as it had always been, a matter of personal taste. As the English so astutely said, beauty lay in the eye of the beholder.

But none of Maximilian's proclamations of love could repair the damage done to her ego by the media's insistence that the perfect woman was slender and shaped like the curved branch of a willow.

'It's because of Kapp, isn't it?' Maximilian said kindly. 'You'd be happier about going if he wasn't there—isn't that so?'

'I suppose I would,' she said grudgingly.

'It's because of him that I *want* to go,' declared Maximilian.

'I know,' said Adèle disconsolately.

'What an amazingly far-sighted thing this man has done,' exclaimed Maximilian. 'A truly artistic act on a monumental scale. To actually create a spiritual domain—to create on a new artistic dimension.'

'I wouldn't go so far as to say that,' muttered his wife sceptically. Maximilian had a tendency at times to soar to rather farfetched flights of fancy.

'He's using people, human beings—their bodies and souls—to create a wholly new form of kinetic art, a kind of spiritual dance that will carry on as long as people feel the need to participate in it—which, of course, they always will. Man cannot live by consumption alone. Kapp knows that; therein lies his genius. It's in that knowledge that he shows himself a true artist.'

'He's a male chauvinist,' grumbled Adèle.

'They said the same about Picasso,' contested Maximilian. 'But that doesn't make him less of an artist.'

'It's well known what Thelonius Kapp thinks about women,'

said Adèle grumpily. 'The beautiful ones are only good for sleeping with, the ugly ones for cleaning up after him, and the older ones—well, as far as he's concerned, the older ones should be put mercifully away at menopause. He actually said that in an interview for some girlie magazine.'

'An appalling attitude,' agreed Maximilian. 'Absolutely unpardonable and stupidly narrow-minded, to my mind. He doesn't know what he's missing—a vintage Bourgogne is infinitely more delectable than a Beaujolais nouveau.' His dark eyes smiled at Adèle as he spoke. 'But there must be some reason for his attitude. He was probably brought up by some old hag of an aunt who beat him and turned him off ugly women for life. I believe he had an appalling childhood. His mother was raped and murdered before his eyes at the age of nine—or so he says. The trouble is, you never know how much to believe of what these film celebrities say. People who live their lives in a world of fiction must, in the end, have difficulty distinguishing between what is real and what is not.'

'Well,' said Adèle swiftly, 'whatever the reasons, you can't expect me to look forward to meeting a man who would have me quietly put away for my own good just because I'm... I'm...overweight.'

'Adèle, my darling,' said Maximilian, 'my lovely, plump, Titian beauty—you've got to stop worrying about what others think of you.' He leaned towards her enthusiastically. 'Get that paranoia out of your system—make that the *raison d'être* of this retreat. Use the tranquillity and silence of the next three days to reflect on your inner turmoil—and you'll see, the spirit will triumph over the flesh. It always does.' Maximilian's handsome face broke into a dazzling smile. *'Fly upon the wings of angels,'* he sang gaily, *'And your flesh, your plump, succulent flesh, will sing with joy.'*

Adèle smiled self-consciously at her husband. She reached out and placed her plump hand on his.

'What would I do without you, Maximilian?' she said, tears pricking the corners of her eyes.

EIGHT

Dr Renoir and his wife Felicity

TWO CARRIAGES DOWN in the same TGV, Dr André Renoir sat close to his wife, Felicity, protectively holding her hand in his. Dr Renoir, an obstetrician, had, three weeks earlier, diagnosed his wife's first pregnancy. Having brought into the world literally hundreds of infants during his ten year career as a gynaecologist, Dr Renoir now found himself obsessed to the point of paranoia with the progress of his first child's gestation. It was for that reason that he had insisted that they participate in the weekend retreat in Provence. The experience, one of utter tranquillity and serenity, would leave an indelible mark on mother and foetus, which was in its tenth week of development and in the process of forming its organs of perception.

Felicity was suffering from severe bouts of nausea and fatigue and needed to spend as much time as possible in an environment that was as calm and restful as possible. It was for reasons of safety that Dr Renoir had insisted that they travel by train and not by car. Trains were, statistically, much safer than the road— as well as that, the TGV, an incredibly smooth train, would cause less trauma to the delicate stomach of a pregnant woman.

Felicity had concurred, accepting André's superior wisdom in matters of the female reproductive system.

'The baby's outer ear is in the process of being formed,' Dr Renoir explained to his wife. 'By Sunday the tympanum will be fully developed and on Sunday Brother Martin de Porres will sing in the chapel of the Abbey of St Pierre. Imagine, Felicity,' he said rapturously, 'that the first sound to be heard by our child will be the angelic tones of such a voice. What a marvellous start to life this little chap will have.'

Felicity declined to protest that at ten weeks it was not possible, even with the help of modern scanners, to discover the sex of an embryo. Instead she asked, 'Can the foetus hear what's going on outside the uterus?'

'Of course it can,' said Dr Renoir. 'Once the ear is formed it can hear—that's what it's made for.' He smiled sweetly at his wife. 'Of course the extraneous sounds might be muffled by the amniotic fluid but clear sharp sounds such as the notes of a song or loud sudden noises must register on the ear-drum. It's for that reason that you, the mother, and I, the father, must ensure that the early sounds the infant hears are ones conducive to a tranquil development of his personality, not a traumatic one. You must treat your baby, even in its undeveloped state, as if it were already born. You wouldn't subject him, when he's born, to sudden shock, would you?'

'No, of course not,' Felicity agreed. She didn't like to ask André, but she wondered how he knew exactly what the ten-week foetus perceived with its undeveloped sensory organs. As a nurse in a maternity unit in the hospital where she had met her husband, she had noticed that new-born babies were remarkably impervious to extraneous sounds, even sudden loud noises such as the switching on of a vacuum cleaner next to their cots. Still André was a gynaecologist and he must know more than she did.

'Perhaps you'd like a little salad,' he urged. 'A light cheese soufflé, something like that—you need your vitamins, you know. I can order it from the restaurant car.'

Felicity's plain but intelligent face suddenly turned green, constricted into a grimace and she leaned over her husband and vomited on to the beige carpet of the compartment. Unfortunately some of the projected matter landed on her husband's stay-press linen trousers and some clung to the ends of her shoulder-length ginger hair.

'Oh dear! Oh dear!' exclaimed Dr Renoir, leaping up from his seat. 'How unfortunate.' He looked around distractedly for something to wipe up the mess with, then reached up and grabbed the travelling bag which he had placed in the rack above their heads. He struggled with the zip repeating, 'Oh dear, oh dear!' in distress.

Dr Renoir had monitored the progress of innumerable pregnancies but no pregnant woman had ever vomited on him before. He struggled impotently with the bag's zip which appeared to have stuck.

Meanwhile his wife was busy wiping the carpet and her hair with a paper handkerchief that she'd retrieved from her handbag. Then she instructed her husband to sit down so that she could clean off his trousers.

'Oh dear, how unfortunate,' said Dr Renoir, gazing at the rather distasteful stain that now marked his formerly immaculate trousers.

'Sorry about that,' Felicity giggled. Then, having thrown the soiled handkerchiefs into the rubbish container, she sat back into her seat, her face no longer green but now healthily flushed from her exertions.

'Do you know, André,' she said, 'I'd give absolutely anything right now for a hamburger.'

NINE

St Pierre la Croix

LADY OLIVIA Carter Bonnington rose from her very comfortable old-fashioned bed in the Auberge des Tuileries in the village of St Pierre la Croix. The short nap had left her feeling refreshed after the tiring journey from Paris where she had been staying with her closest friend, Hermione, wife of a member of the diplomatic staff at the British Embassy.

Hermione, after a discreet scrutiny of her friend's face, had made the suggestion that Lady Olivia take part in a church retreat and had mentioned the Abbey of St Pierre la Croix, having read about its restoration in a Church journal.

Lady Olivia, as directress of a large cosmetics company, spent a great deal of her time travelling and was showing, as her friend pointed out, signs of fatigue.

'You have no idea, Olivia,' Hermione had said, 'how *resuscitating* a retreat can be. I do two a year...it takes years off you.'

The promise of rejuvenation had impressed Lady Olivia. An elegant and youthful appearance was essential to her social and professional position.

'Perhaps I could fit three days into my schedule,' she'd said to Hermione. 'It's a long time since I've visited the beautiful *arrière pays* of Provence. It'll make a refreshing change from London and Paris.'

She now removed the cucumber slices that she had placed on her eyes while she slept, then checked in the mirror that they had done their job. Good, no puffiness. Lady Bonnington had had the bags removed from below her eyes twelve months earlier and the fatty pouches of her upper lids removed six months before that. The skin of her face had been lifted and the first traces of a double chin erased shortly after the bags had been removed. She had just turned fifty-one at the time. Now, at nearly fifty-three, with her breasts restructured, the excess fat of her stomach removed by liposuction and any cellulite that threatened to attack her rear kept at bay by strenuous exercise, Lady Carter Bonnington looked, in her expensive underwear, scarcely thirty-five.

She shook out her dark cap of glossy hair, threw off her dressing-gown and glanced appraisingly at her splendid figure in the wardrobe mirror. Then she sat down to apply her makeup.

The operation finished, she appeared another five years younger. She slipped into a simple Chanel-style summer costume, placed a gossamer silk scarf around her neck which she secured with a simple gold clip, checked that her nail varnish was without cracks then, locking her door behind her, descended the ancient stone stairway of the inn for dinner.

The restaurant was crowded as it always was. The auberge catered, not just for its guests, but for tourists and the local population among whom the auberge chef was considered one of the best in Provence. People travelled great distances to sample his famed lunchtime daubes and terrines and his celebrated evening *cuisine traditionelle.*

The young waiter, who had fallen in love with the tall, elegant Lady Bonnington as soon as he had seen her on her arrival earlier in the day, ushered her obsequiously to her table for one at the auberge window.

She thanked him with her English-accented but impeccable French and the young man almost fainted with delight.

She sat down, carefully arranging her skirt so that it didn't ride too high and afford the little man at the next table a view of the tops of her thighs. She glanced at the man and his companion, grimacing inwardly. Goodness gracious, she thought— she'd never seen such an ugly couple.

HAVING SPENT a quiet afternoon drinking rosé and sampling Clothilde's olives, Donaghue had accepted his friend's suggestion that they take a brisk walk up to the Abbey of St Pierre which, she informed him, had been fully restored since his last visit to the village. They might, she had added, dine later at the village inn, to which suggestion Donaghue had readily agreed as he was well aware of the deplorable level of Clothilde's culinary skills.

On the way up to the abbey, which was situated three or four kilometres east of the village, Clothilde informed Donaghue of the surprise that she had in store for him—namely a three-day retreat in the abbey itself, which was to start the following day, Sunday.

'A retreat!' Donaghue said in surprise. He had not been on a retreat since his last year at his Jesuit college in Dublin. Not that he was averse to retreats. He had always found, even as an adolescent, that the few days of prayer and meditation, even when forced upon him, had exerted a surprisingly calming effect on body and soul.

'Some American film director has bought the abbey—paid an absolute fortune to have it restored,' said Clothilde. 'He's established an order of Carmelite nuns in it and is inaugurating it this weekend as an international centre of retreat.'

'Evidently a good practising Catholic, this director,' Donaghue mumbled guiltily. Ulysses Donaghue had, all his adult life, tried unsuccessfully to shake off the inhibitory moral shackles, as he saw them, of his Irish Catholic education. But he had come to the conclusion, now, in his fifty-second year, that one's early formative education was like chewing gum on the hair—it stuck to the core of one's personality and could never be removed.

'A recent convert, as far as I know,' said Clothilde.

She was striding along the narrow country lane that led from the village to the abbey. Her thick-soled walking shoes took her along at a brisk pace. Donaghue, on his short legs, had difficulty keeping up with her.

'...dissolute when young,' Clothilde went on, '...getting on now so probably turning to religion in his old age after a life of debauchery. Rather too easy that, if you ask me—thinks he can buy his way into heaven, I suppose.'

'And who is this American camel trying to get through the eye of a needle?' asked Donaghue.

'None other than the famous Thelonius Kapp, no less,' said Clothilde. 'No one's supposed to know he's here but you can't keep anything from old Madame Beaulieu in the boulangerie. He's going to put St Pierre la Croix on the map with his international centre of retreat—probably turn the village into another St Tropez. I'll be moving out if that happens.' Clothilde tapped her elm walking-stick crossly on the ground as she walked.

'Thelonius Kapp,' said Donaghue. 'How very strange.'

'Strange, yes—it will be strange, Hollywood coming to St Pierre la Croix,' grumbled Clothilde.

'I say strange because only yesterday his mother-in-law, a fine-looking woman fifteen years his junior, came to see me. She wants me to keep an eye on her daughter, Kapp's rather beautiful young wife, when they come to England in ten days' time.'

'They'll be doing the retreat here first,' said Clothilde. 'He will, anyway—I don't know about his wife. Yes, that is a curious coincidence.' Then she lifted her stick and pointed it in front of her. 'There it is,' she said, as they came in sight of the abbey gates.

The two stood at the arched gateway and gazed down the long driveway lined with plane trees to the distant walls of the abbey.

'I've kept an eye on the restoration,' said Clothilde. 'It seems to have been done properly. I haven't been inside yet but we shall see when we go tomorrow morning.'

'I suppose Kapp is there now,' mused Donaghue.

'I would think so—it is his property, after all.' She glanced at her watch. 'Shall we get back to the auberge? I booked a table for 7.30.'

AT THEIR ALCOVE TABLE in the inn Donaghue appraised the attractive woman who had seated herself at the table next to theirs. He leaned towards Clothilde and said in a hushed whisper, 'An extraordinarily beautiful woman that—vain, I would imagine, to an extraordinary degree. Not a young woman either, but if you look at her face you will see none of the expression that comes with age. She has *no character whatsoever in her face.* Isn't that extraordinary?'

'Surgery,' said Clothilde. 'It leaves only an expression of mild surprise. I suppose if you had your face remodelled you would react with surprise each time you looked in the mirror: Goodness me, who's that? Ah, it's only me!'

Clothilde spoke caustically and the flabby landscape of her face concertinaed into one of her rare sardonic smiles.

'She must have been extremely beautiful as a young girl,' said Donaghue, glancing over at the woman who returned his glance with an expression of mild irritation and an aversion of her aristocratic head.

'Hard to say what she might have looked like,' said Clothilde drily. 'I wouldn't imagine that there's much of the original individual left. The face has been lifted, the nose remodelled, the eyes are debagged. The chest is silicone and the stomach unnaturally flat. The legs, I think, are her own. I wonder who the surgeon is. He or she is remarkably good.' She smiled her craggy smile. 'As good as me, I'd say.'

Clothilde had exercised the profession of plastic surgeon at the Burns Unit of Toulon Naval Hospital for thirty years.

'How old is she?' Donaghue asked. 'She looks thirty-five.'

'Fifty, I'd say—maybe fifty-five,' said Clothilde.

'Extraordinary,' said Donaghue. 'How can you tell?'

'The hands, of course,' said Clothilde. 'There is no surgery yet that will hide the age of the hands, even those that have never even dipped themselves into a bowl of washing up. No one has yet perfected the technique of hand transplant.'

'Age cannot wither her,' said Donaghue absently, *'nor custom stale her infinite variety; other women cloy the appetites they feed, but she makes hungry where most she satisfies...'*

'Are you talking about *that* woman?' said Clothilde disgustedly. 'Really, Ulysses, don't tell me you've fallen in love with her. You might as well fall in love with one of those blow-up rubber dolls.'

'That was the Bard's description of Cleopatra,' Donaghue explained, 'who, I've heard it said, was quite plain. He was describing, not her physical beauty but her sensuality—which has nothing, of course, to do with beauty. This woman—she is making sure that age does not wither her, but somehow,' he said reflectively, 'I don't have the impression she would satisfy any man she made hungry. I have the feeling that she is the kind of woman who profoundly dislikes men.'

'Unlike me,' said Clothilde, patting her friend Donaghue on the hand, 'who adores them.'

PART TWO

TEN

Sunday morning

AT 8 A.M. on Sunday morning sixteen people sat in groups of four at the solid oak tables of the large guest refectory in the Abbey of St Pierre la Croix. Two white-robed novices, one plump and bespectacled, the other tall and graceful, served them a Continental breakfast of freshly percolated coffee, croissants baked in the abbey's bakery and delicious apricot and fig jams made by the nuns themselves from the abbey's extensive orchard of fruit trees. The novices served the guests with mute decorum and the guests themselves, seemingly cowed by the awesome splendour of the vaulted refectory, ate in an equally reverent silence.

Donaghue and Clothilde found themselves sharing a table with a rather formidable-looking elderly woman whose face Donaghue found vaguely familiar and her companion, a pretty young woman with, Donaghue considered, rather shrewd large blue eyes. The elderly woman had introduced herself as Thérèse Mendes France, the name instantly reminding Donaghue and Clothilde of a younger Thérèse, famous thirty years earlier as the French Olympic judo gold medallist. Miss Mendes France had then presented her companion, Miss Fiona MacKinley, photographer by profession, whom she had met on the journey down to the abbey.

Donaghue had noticed that the rather amiable-looking young man at the adjacent table was throwing a surreptitious glance over his shoulder from time to time at the pretty young Fiona, who, Donaghue decided, was known to the young man, although, it seemed, she preferred to pretend otherwise as she made no response to his repeated glances in her direction.

Seated next to the pleasant-faced young man was the surgically reconstructed woman whom Donaghue and Clothilde had seen in the village auberge. Donaghue wondered what a woman like that could possibly be doing on a spiritual retreat. The woman was gazing into the middle distance in much the same expressionless way in which she had gazed out of the auberge windows. Seated opposite her were a couple, he a balding, rather agitated man in his early thirties, she calm, of plain but intelligent features—a nurse, Donaghue decided, which conjecture was promptly confirmed by Clothilde who whispered hoarsely in his ear, 'That's Renoir, a gynaecologist. I've met him once or twice. From Lyons. Married a nurse. I'd say she was pregnant from the way she's picking at her food.'

'He doesn't appear to be a satisfied man,' commented Donaghue. '*Mal dans sa peau*, as the French so germanely describe the condition.'

'You're right—he isn't a satisfied man,' said Clothilde dourly. 'Never will be, if you ask me—wants to be the greatest gynaecologist in France—forever submitting dull articles on the formation of the foetus to monthly periodicals—expresses some peculiar notions on genetics, along the lines of outdated eugenics, racial superiority and all that. Fortunately nobody takes him very seriously.'

Donaghue's glance passed over to the table beyond the Renoirs. Two couples sat facing each other: a dark exceptionally handsome man with his overweight wife beside him and, on the other side, a well-dressed, distinguished-looking man whose long suntanned features bespoke a successful businessman or scholar. He sat with one arm curved around the back of his wife's chair.

Donaghue studied the woman's face with interest. A woman, somewhat older than her husband, on whose beautiful but fraught features was written some profound emotional disturbance. An unhappy woman, Donaghue thought, although her husband appeared utterly solicitous. What, he wondered, could have brought such suffering to a woman's face? The exceedingly handsome man sitting opposite was saying something to her and smiling charmingly at her. His plump wife sat fidgeting uneasily beside him. Another one who's 'unhappy in her skin', thought Donaghue. Curious that at one table there should be two such couples, the husband apparently happy with his lot, the woman not at all. The overweight woman was glancing nervously every now and again at the fourth table that was adjacent to theirs and directly in front of Donaghue. Her glance rested alternately on Thelonius Kapp and his pretty young wife who shared the table with a bespectacled man in his early thirties and a young woman of twenty-something.

Donaghue's eyes came irresistibly to rest on the face of the famous film director. Was he looking, the detective asked himself, at the face of an unhappy man or that of a sick man? Donaghue wasn't sure. The black eyes, which darted here and there, appeared to focus nowhere. The young man sitting opposite Kapp, whom Donaghue recognized with surprise as the man he had seen with the Salome look-alike in the Paris queue at Heathrow airport, leaned across the table and tapped the film director on the arm, evidently trying to gain his attention. It was obvious that the clean-cut young man was an employee of the renowned Kapp—his PR man or personal secretary perhaps. His blond hair and lightly tinted spectacles glinted in the early morning sunshine that streamed in through the arched windows above their table.

Donaghue's gaze rested curiously for a second on the girl sitting next to him and opposite Sandra Kapp. Could this thin-cheeked, painted young woman possibly be the girl he'd seen in the young man's company at the airport? No, he was sure it couldn't have been—despite the anonymity of the girl's Salome-style outfit, it would not have concealed the really rather brainless expression on this girl's thin, heavily made-up face. A mouse, Donaghue decided—this one was very definitely a mouse. The girl in the airport had been no mouse. She had been softly pretty, her prettiness rendered anonymous by her outfit, rather like Salome herself—or Sandra, as she really was.

He looked across the thin girl's streaked blonde head at Kapp's young wife. Yes, he said to himself—there is something anonymous in such perfect prettiness. He recognized her easily from the photograph Mrs Trescott had given him—the brown hair hanging neatly to her shoulders, the face free of make-up or jewellery, the skin healthily tanned, the green eyes roaming curiously around the room but returning inexorably to her husband whose hand she had covered with her own and on whose distracted face she gazed with open love and solicitude. There was, Donaghue noticed, an expression of anxiety in the girl's intelligent green eyes.

'There are very few in this room,' Donaghue confided to Clothilde, 'who are not troubled in spirit.'

Thérèse Mendes France, who had heard Donaghue's remark, interjected, turning her grey head sharply in his direction. 'It's only natural, Mr Donaghue, that those whose spirits are troubled should seek the tranquillizing therapy of a retreat. One could compare it to the seeking of water by a man dying of thirst.'

'And you, Miss Mendes France,' asked Clothilde somewhat caustically—Donaghue had after all been speaking to her—'are you here because you are troubled in spirit?'

'Of course,' retorted Miss Mendes France. 'We all suffer from a spiritual malaise. It is the nature of our state. I, in common with every other member of our wretched species, am not without sin. The day we live in God's good grace is the day our spirits will be well. But that day, sadly, has not yet come.'

'For some perhaps it has,' said Clothilde curtly.

'Show me one,' retorted Miss Mendes France. 'In this room show me one person whose spirit is not troubled.'

'I think there might be one,' said Donaghue quietly.

'You mean yourself, I suppose,' said Miss Mendes France accusingly, glowering at Donaghue as she spoke.

'Oh no, not me, not me,' Donaghue assured her. 'My spirit has long been troubled and will remain so, I daresay, until my dying day. No, I'm talking about him...' And he indicated with a nod of his unkempt head the dark handsome man at the third table. Miss Mendes France turned her grey-capped head to look.

'That is a happy man,' said Donaghue wistfully. 'I've never seen such a happy man.'

'Happiness,' said Miss Mendes France rather haughtily, 'is not, to my mind, the criterion of peace of soul.'

'In that, my dear lady,' said Donaghue deferentially, 'I have to disagree with you.'

'As is your right,' said Miss Mendes France curtly. '*Call no man happy until he dies—he is at best but fortunate!* I am in complete agreement with Herodotus.'

'Ah,' said Donaghue. '*But earthlier happy is the rose distilled, than that which, withering on the virgin thorn, grows, lives and dies in single blessedness.* I tend to agree with the great Bard.'

Miss Mendes France glared darkly at Donaghue.

'Are you implying...?' she began.

'What I am saying,' said Donaghue, 'is that man is a rose distilled.'

Miss Mendes France's intended response was nipped in the bud by the sudden clang of a gong from the far end of the room. The guests, who had by now finished eating, turned their attention to the diminutive figure of the Mother Superior who had welcomed them on their arrival and ushered them immediately into breakfast. She was standing now before the assembled gathering, a portable blackboard beside her to which she had pinned a large plan of the abbey and its grounds. The plan depicted the two principal cloisters around which the abbey and its buildings were constructed. The first, larger cloister was bordered by an arched colonnade that surrounded the central garden and gave off on to the guests' cells—four double cells to the east side and eight single cells to the west. At the southern end of the cloister stood the beautiful Chapel of St Pierre la Croix, famed for its perfect acoustics. At the northern end was the smaller Lady Chapel of La Sainte Vierge standing between the Mother Superior's office and the library. Directly opposite were the guests' refectory and the showers. A narrow arched walkway linked the large cloister to a second smaller cloister which housed the cells and refectory of the small community of nuns who inhabited and maintained the abbey. Beyond the smaller cloister lay the abbey's outbuildings—the ancient wine press to the north-east and the cellars, olive press and kitchen to the east. The grounds comprised kitchen gardens, orchards and a large expanse of vineyards which extended north and east for eight to ten hectares.

The community of nuns, the Mother Superior explained, grew their own vegetables, baked their own bread, raised chickens and rabbits, tended vines and fruit trees and processed their own olives. They were, to all intents and purposes, self-sufficient. The food served to their guests was almost one hundred per cent organic—only the milk products and red meats were brought in from outside.

'As Mr Kapp, our benefactor, has declared,' the Mother Superior turned as she spoke to smile at Thelonius Kapp, 'no expense must be spared to make a retreat here in the abbey as comfortable as possible. The guest cells are air-conditioned in summer, heated in winter. Each cell is equipped with a comfortable bed, cupboard, desk, toiletries and wash-stand. The nov-

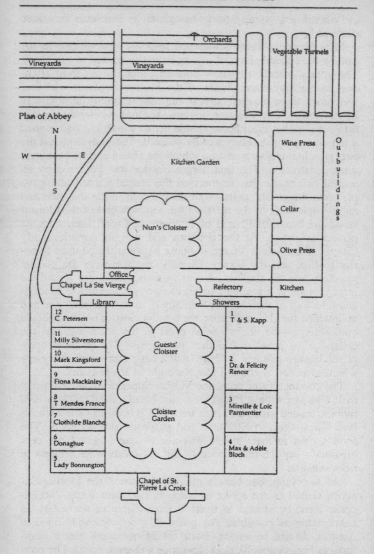

Plan of Abbey

Orchards

Vineyards

Vineyards

Vegetable Tunnels

N
W — E
S

Kitchen Garden

Wine Press

Outbuildings

Nun's Cloister

Cellar

Olive Press

Office

Chapel La Ste Vierge

Refectory

Kitchen

Library

Showers

12 C Petersen		1 T & S. Kapp
11 Milly Silverstone	Guests' Cloister	
10 Mark Kingsford		2 Dr. & Felicity Renoir
9 Fiona Mackinley		
8 T Mendes France		3 Mireille & Loic Parmentier
7 Clothilde Blanche	Cloister Garden	
6 Donaghue		
5 Lady Bonnington		4 Max & Adèle Bloch

Chapel of St.
Pierre La Croix

ices are at the service of the guests and there are buzzers in each cell for the purpose of summoning a novice. Naturally the cells were originally built to house nuns and do not therefore have sufficient room for private bathrooms to be installed, but showers can be taken in the fully fitted shower and washroom adjacent to the refectory.

'It is the wish of Mr Kapp, and ours too,' the Mother Superior added, smiling graciously at the assembled guests, 'that, in order for the spirits to benefit from what the retreat has to offer, your physical needs should be satisfied to as great a degree as possible. This we have attempted to do by providing you with a reasonable degree of comfort. I hasten to add that the members of our small order do not enjoy such luxuries. I must also inform those guests who might not be aware of it, that ours is a silent order. I, of course, as Mother Superior, am permitted to speak as I am now doing. You may at any time address me or the attendant novices but I do beg of you—on no account converse with the other nuns nor expect a spoken response from the novices that attend you.'

The Mother Superior turned to the plan of the abbey and tapped it with the pointed baton she held in her hand.

'The grounds of the abbey are entirely at your disposal for contemplative walks and the chapels are open at all times for silent prayer. You must consult the schedule for times of Mass, prayer readings and Gregorian chant. The schedule is, of course, simply a guideline for your retreat—you are not in any way obliged to follow it. In a retreat at the Abbey of St Pierre la Croix you are absolutely free to do as you wish. A copy of the schedule is displayed in each cell but it is, in any case, very simple.

'8-9: Breakfast in the refectory.
9: Mass in the Chapel of La Sainte Vierge given by Brother Martin de Porres.
10-12: Bible/Gospel readings in the Chapel of St Pierre la Croix.
12: Lunch.
1-2: Free time (siesta).
3-4: Gregorian chant in Chapel of St Pierre la Croix sung by the celebrated Brother Martin de Porres.

4-6: Free time (afternoon tea served in refectory).
6: Vespers in Chapel of La Sainte Vierge, followed by Mass.
8: Dinner in refectory.

'This evening at 9.30 a video film showing the history of the abbey and its restoration will be shown in the library and on Monday evening (tomorrow) Brother Martin de Porres will give a short lecture on church music again at 9.30 in the library. On Tuesday evening, the last evening of the retreat, we would ask the guests to assemble for a fraternal meeting—we will not call it a prayer meeting as not all our guests are of the same religious persuasion—but simply an informal gathering of the guests for a discussion of the benefits and/or shortcomings of the retreat. None of the evening activities, of course, are in any way obligatory. A retreat, we believe, is for the liberation of the soul and of the body—a retreat from the banal and stressful worries of everyday life. We have no wish whatsoever to impose any restraints upon our guests. The library, of course, will be available at all times for contemplative reading, and I myself will be at your disposal should you wish to come to see me. You will find me in my office next to the Chapel of la Sainte Vierge.

'Now, I will just call out your names—a kind of roll call—so that you can at least know each other by name. First of all our very esteemed proprietor and benefactor, Mr Thelonius Kapp, and his wife Sandra.'

All heads turned to the first table where Sandra Kapp smiled demurely and nudged her husband who frowned distractedly at the group of guests.

'At the same table Mr Kapp's secretary, Mr Carl Petersen, and Mrs Kapp's beautician, Miss Milly Silverstone.'

Carl Petersen smiled around at the assembled guests, inclining his fair head; Milly Silverstone, a wide smile on her red-lipsticked mouth, rose to her feet and waved a hand jangling with bracelets in an arc above her head. 'Hi, everybody!' she called out in a strong New York accent. 'Pleased ta meetcha!'

'At the second table,' the Mother Superior indicated the table adjacent to the Kapps, 'Monsieur and Madame Parmentier, Mireille and Loic, and Monsieur and Madame Bloch, Maximilian and Adèle.'

The four people turned their heads in acknowledgement, the two men smiling, Mireille frowning and Adèle reddening in apparent embarrassment.

'At table number three, Lady Olivia Carter Bonnington and Mr Mark Kingsford. Mr Kingsford is a journalist here to interview Mr Kapp and his wife on this the memorable first retreat of the restored abbey. With them are Dr and Madame Renoir, André and Felicity.

'At table number four, Mademoiselle Thérèse Mendes France whom many of you will recognize, I am sure, as a former French judo champion, accompanied by Miss Fiona MacKinley, from London, and last but not at all least, Mr Ulysses Donaghue and his companion, Dr Clothilde Blanche.'

Donaghue and Clothilde smiled benignly at the group and the Mother Superior clasped her hands together in a heartfelt gesture of welcome.

'I will now leave you to enjoy your retreat,' she said, 'but before I do, may I wish you one and all a peaceful and spiritually uplifting stay.'

A low wave of murmured thanks rose from the assembly and the Mother Superior departed with a swish of her black robes. The guests, after a few moments of uncertain silence, started to shift their chairs and rise to their feet. Only the four at Thelonius Kapp's table remained seated.

The guests drifted out of the refectory into the morning sunshine, Donaghue and Clothilde in the wake of Miss Mendes France and the young Fiona MacKinley.

'Well,' said Miss Mendes France, glancing at her watch, 'I'm off to Mass. What about you, Fiona?'

'Er...no,' stammered Fiona whose eyes were following the progress of the dark-haired young reporter, Mark Kingsford, who was making his way rapidly along the west side of the cloister colonnade. 'No, I won't go to Mass—I wasn't brought up a Catholic.'

'As you wish,' said Miss Mendes France. 'What about you, Mr Donaghue?'

'I shall attend evening Mass,' said Donaghue. 'I intend to avail myself of the less strident morning temperature to explore the grounds. It will be far too hot in the afternoon.'

'Well, we shall see each other again no doubt,' said Miss Mendes France, creasing her face with deliberation into one of its unaccustomed smiles. And she took off, striding on her long powerful legs across the narrow arched walkway that led from the refectory to the Chapel of La Sainte Vierge.

'And you, Fiona,' asked Clothilde, 'what do you intend to do this morning?'

'I think I've met one of the guests before,' the girl replied. 'I'm just going to check,' And she took her leave, turning quickly into the covered colonnade through which the journalist had passed.

'I'm sure she knows that young man quite well,' Donaghue commented as he followed her progress along the shady colonnade. 'And I think he knows her too.'

At that moment Thelonius Kapp emerged from the refectory, his wife's arm linked in his. The couple were followed by the secretary, Carl Petersen, and the pale-faced Milly Silverstone. Kapp appeared to be walking with difficulty, his wife, Sandra, supporting him.

Donaghue, stepping to one side to allow the small group to pass, was shocked by the film director's appearance. His stooped posture was that of an old man, his face, grey and pallid, that of an old sick man. The eyes gazed ahead of him blankly, black discs devoid of all expression of emotion or even, it appeared to Donaghue, of intelligence.

The group passed along the walkway towards the cloister, Sandra leading her husband to their cell which was the first on the east colonnade. Carl Petersen and Milly Silverstone continued on to the west colonnade, Petersen entering the first cell and Milly Silverstone the second.

'Well,' said Clothilde to Donaghue, 'shall we explore the grounds then, Ulysses—as you said, while the temperatures aren't too high?'

'Certainly,' said Donaghue as he consulted the plan of the abbey's grounds that had been left along with the retreat schedule in each cell. 'Shall we take a walk out to the eastern vineyards? I'd very much like to see the old wine press which has, I believe, been fully restored.'

'OK,' said Clothilde, 'but first I'll pop back to my cell to fetch a bottle of mineral water. You know what I'm like, Ulysses—can't go very far without drying up.'

Donaghue smiled wanly at Clothilde's departing back as he leaned against the central stone pillar that supported the ancient walkway. From this vantage point he was offered the splendid view of the large cloister garden, surrounded as it was by its arcaded colonnade. The cloister garden, with its simple wooden seats shaded by knotty plane trees and its banks of shrubs and flowers, would offer, in the heat of the afternoon, a pleasant spot for the quiet reading of *A Midsummer Night's Dream,* a paperback copy of which Donaghue had nestled in the back pocket of his trousers.

He sighed blissfully, his hands comfortably ensconced in the pockets of his loose linen summer pants, his stomach replete with the excellent arabica coffee and freshly baked croissants that they had been served for breakfast. As he waited contentedly for Clothilde to return, the door to Kapp's cell opened quietly and Kapp's wife, Sandra, stepped out. She made her way quickly along the walkway to the opposite colonnade, passing Donaghue on her way. She smiled briefly and politely at him before entering the west colonnade and stopping before the first cell door which was opened to her knock by Carl Petersen.

'I have to speak to you,' Donaghue heard her say.

The secretary, his expression grave, invited Mrs Kapp into the cell. She entered the solid oak door and closed it behind her.

A girl possibly in danger, Donaghue reflected, but had no time to develop his thought as Clothilde had returned and taken him by the arm and was leading him off in the opposite direction into the smaller cloister from which they would have access to the abbey vineyards.

ELEVEN

In the abbey gardens

MARK KINGSFORD made his way rapidly around the curved buttressed wall of the nave of the large Chapel of St Pierre la Croix and strode quickly up along the east wall towards the vineyards that lay to the north of the abbey. He had taken the long way round in order to avoid bumping into Fiona MacKinley who, to his intense annoyance, had turned up at the retreat. She must have packed her bag as soon as she'd discovered his deception and left London immediately. Couldn't the damned girl let him do anything on his own? All right, he had—once—professed that he loved her and they had even talked about marriage, but just because you slept with someone now and again didn't mean that you have to have them attached to you with a pair of handcuffs, did it? Good God, thought Mark, she would be even more limpet-like if they were ever married. Mark really didn't understand Fiona. For all her possessiveness she professed to be a feminist— but didn't feminists believe in liberty and equality, each free to do their own thing, all that sort of thing? Fiona said one thing but did the opposite. It was highly confusing. And on top of that she knew how much he liked Salome. He was sure that she'd come down to the abbey expressly to stop him from speaking to the singer alone. Fiona could be infuriatingly jealous at times. He was beginning to have serious doubts about his relationship with her.

He had reached the first row of vines. Away in the distance, at the far end of the field, he could see a group of nuns, maybe a dozen or so, working laboriously, their black-robed backs bent, picking the grapes ready for the year's wine-making.

He stopped, digging his hands into his jeans pockets, to admire the almost impressionist scene. Lost in his contemplation he failed to hear the soft pad of a footfall behind him, then turned his head with a start when Fiona tapped him on the shoulder and said caustically, 'Must have been very short notice this job, Mark—you didn't even have time to leave me a note on my office desk, telling me where you were going.'

'Now look here, Fiona,' said Mark crossly, 'if you've got any plans to jeopardize this job, I'll...I'll...'

'You'll what, Mark Kingsford?' demanded Fiona tersely. 'Break off the engagement we've never made or find yourself another girl to sleep with? Someone like the tarty Salome, I suppose.'

'Salome?' said Mark. 'What are you talking about? Do you imagine Salome would be interested in me?'

'Isn't that what you were hoping,' said Fiona, 'when you rushed grovelling into McCade's office to get the assignment?'

'I didn't grovel and I didn't hope anything,' said Mark peevishly. 'Anyone would want an assignment like this one.'

'Yes, like me for instance,' retorted Fiona. 'But not for the same reasons. *I'm* not interested in looking down the cleavage of some tarted-up sex maniac who's probably got Aids from the drugs and orgies she indulges in.'

'As a matter of fact Salome isn't like that at all,' said Mark. 'You saw for yourself in the refectory just now. The sexy image is only part of her stage act. She's actually quite reserved in her private life—a great deal more reserved, I might add, than you, Fiona. And again,' he added, keeping his eyes on the distant fields and well away from those of Fiona which were darkening in anger as she glared at him, 'there's nothing wrong with a woman dressing up sexily—men like it.'

'Like it!' shouted Fiona, her face now red with fury. 'Of course they like it.'

Tears began to glitter in the corners of her large blue eyes. 'You're just like all the rest of them—you want everything. You want your women to be saints during the day, like these nuns,' she waved a furious finger at the distant bent black figures in the field, 'working for you and waiting on you all day—in silence preferably—and you want them to turn into whores like that stupid Salome at night! Well, I'm not either—I'm just myself. I can't put on any acts, so if you want a woman like that you'll have to marry an actress. Marry Salome! Maybe she'll consider leaving her famous husband for you—that's if drugs and sexually transmitted diseases don't kill her first.'

Fiona turned furiously to leave, tears pricking her eyes, and almost collided with Donaghue who, accompanied by Clothilde, was strolling along the path in the direction of the abbey outbuilding that housed the wine press and cellars.

Donaghue, who had overheard the final few phrases of Fiona's lament, was sufficiently conscious of her distress to excuse her embarrassed turning of her head and her failure to acknowledge his presence. Instead she hurried away, half walking, half running, back in the direction of the abbey.

Mark nodded sheepishly at Donaghue and Clothilde and bade them a half-hearted good morning.

'Rather a splendid scene, isn't it?' commented Donaghue, indicating with a wave of his arm the spread of vineyards dotted with the black figures of the nuns, verdant hills rolling away into the distance behind them, the sky the brilliant clear azure of the South of France—and all bathed in the warm golden light peculiar to Provence. 'How reminiscent of Cézanne and Van Gogh,' he said.

'It's wonderful,' agreed Mark. Then he added dourly, 'Life would be great if people weren't so bloody prejudiced.'

'You're referring to the young lady's evident dislike of our host's wife, Salome?' Donaghue asked.

'It's pure prejudice,' said Mark vehemently. 'She doesn't know the girl at all—never even spoken to her. You shouldn't judge people until you know them, should you?'

Mark gazed after Fiona forlornly. 'Well,' he said, 'perhaps I'd better go and try to make amends. See you around.'

And off he set after his girlfriend, the neat musculature of his trim body visible through his tight-fitting jeans and T-shirt.

'There goes a young idealist who expects love to be an affair of the mind. He expects her to treat their relationship rationally, as he does.'

Donaghue winced as he received a sharp dig in the ribs from Clothilde.

'Are you implying that women aren't rational and men are?' she demanded accusingly.

'Not at all,' retorted Donaghue with indignation. 'You, my dear Clothilde, are eminently reasonable. But in my experience as an observer of human behaviour, young women in search of a partner and women who are mothers of children rarely act primarily from reason.'

'I, of course, come into neither category,' said Clothilde, 'having never sought a partner and consequently having had no children. You may, as you usually are, be absolutely right. That young lady for example, from what I heard of the tone of her voice, was speaking from a highly charged emotional viewpoint and not at all a rational one.'

'She is jealous of Sandra Kapp—or rather she is jealous of Salome, the singer.'

'She's English,' said Clothilde somewhat derisively. 'She has absolutely no notion of how to seduce a man. The singer Salome, or Sandra or whatever she calls herself, at least makes a rather crass Anglo-Saxon attempt to be seductive to men. The Englishwoman really has no understanding of the difference between eroticism and pornography. From what I've seen of her I wouldn't call Salome's half-naked prancing around on stage erotic. That rather silly Fiona has nothing really to be jealous of—all she needs to do is something about the way she dresses. No man is going to be charmed into bed by a woman dressed in well-worn ex-army duty shorts and heavy walking boots. For some reason that I fail to understand, Englishwomen have never learnt the simple lesson in the game of reproduction that men like women to be sexy. It astounds me that the race manages to reproduce itself at all!'

'If I remember rightly, Clothilde,' said Donaghue, 'when I first met you, when you were twenty-five and I a mere stripling of nineteen, you were wearing baggy shorts to the knee and men's socks beneath hiking boots.'

'Ulysses,' said Clothilde reprimandingly, 'really, you can be infuriatingly illogical at times. I wasn't, at that age any more than I am now, looking for a man. My manner of dress is in keeping with my motivation. The same cannot be said of that young woman—she appears to exist in a state of permanent emotional dichotomy.'

'I do agree,' said Donaghue as he gazed thoughtfully after the retreating figure of the young journalist. He took Clothilde's arm.

'Shall we take a detour before going to the wine press? That must be the vegetable garden over there.' He pointed in the direction of a row of polythene-covered tunnels that stood a short distance from the abbey outbuildings. 'I'd like to see what we might expect in the way of organic fruit and vegetables.'

Clothilde nodded in agreement. The path they were on led directly to the wine press building. Three tubs of grapes stood before the open door. A black-robed figure emerged from the dark interior and pulled one of the tubs inside. The first grapes, Clothilde reflected: they would be pressing them the following day.

They took the fork in the path that led to the vegetable garden, skirting, on their way, the eastern field whose vines had been depleted of their grapes. They found themselves at the entrance of a walled garden containing several long polythene-covered tunnels, which served, Donaghue conjectured, as the fruit and vegetable greenhouses.

As they stepped through the small wooden gate that marked the entrance to the garden Donaghue said, 'It seems that there are no cats in the abbey.'

'No cats?' said Clothilde mystified. 'Really, Ulysses, you can be obscure at times—and how can you possibly make a statement like that when we haven't yet seen the whole of the abbey? How on earth do you know there aren't any cats?'

'Because I've just seen a rat. There wouldn't be a rat in one of these tunnels if there were a cat. I suppose if there were cats the nuns might be tempted to speak to them. It's difficult not to talk to a cat, don't you think?'

'Ulysses,' said Clothilde a little worriedly, 'sometimes I think you might be going a bit soft in the head in your old age.'

Donaghue, ignoring Clothilde's remark, popped his head into the first tunnel, which housed carrots and garlic. The novice working within lifted her head in surprise then, quickly averting her eyes, resumed her work. Donaghue stopped himself in time from saying, 'Don't mind us, we're just nosing.' They were not of course to address the nuns or novices.

The second tunnel housed the melons. They wandered through, Donaghue bending and touching the odd melon for its ripeness, then exited at the other end, their nostrils filled with the sweet and delicious odour of the ripening fruit. As they were about to enter the third tunnel, the one housing peppers and courgettes, Donaghue stopped Clothilde in her tracks by grasping her arm at the elbow.

'Ssh!' he hissed. They listened. They could hear the sound of hushed voices whispering in the tunnel.

'Two of the novices are having an illicit chat,' Donaghue whispered to Clothilde. 'Let's not cause them any unnecessary guilt.' He coughed loudly before entering the tunnel and wasn't in the least surprised to catch a fleeting glance of white as the truant talker fled the tunnel at the other end. The young novice working on the plants kept her head bowed assiduously as Donaghue and Clothilde made their way through the rows of plants towards her. She couldn't, of course, resist looking up at them as they passed and Donaghue caught a glimpse of an exceptionally pretty wide-eyed face whose cheeks were tinged with dots of guilty pink. Seeing the girl bent over her work he had, at first, thought she was the novice who had served them at breakfast. She was as tall and slender, but where the novice in the refectory had been serenely beautiful this one possessed the innocent prettiness of a schoolgirl.

'Extraordinary that such a pretty young thing should want to become a nun,' said Donaghue as they left the tunnel, 'particularly in this day and age, when female beauty is highly rewarded and revered and not hidden away as it used to be.'

'Happily, there are still some young people who are not led like sheep by the media or fashion moguls,' said Clothilde.

'She must be a recent newcomer,' said Donaghue, casting a surreptitious glance back at the tall young novice as she bent to her task of picking the ripe peppers. 'Hasn't lost the habit or desire to talk yet.'

After a brief visit to the aubergines and tomatoes Donaghue and Clothilde set off back along the path towards the gate, glancing as they did so into each of the tunnels that they had visited. As they passed the pepper tunnel again the pretty young novice looked up at them guiltily.

'I wonder who the other one was,' Donaghue said. There had been a very plain-looking novice in the carrot tunnel and two diminutive Asian novices working with the aubergines and tomatoes. 'I bet she was not quite so young or quite so new. I wonder what it was they had to say to each other that was worth breaking the prime rule of the order.'

'Probably asking for a tampon,' said Clothilde dourly. 'Goodness, Ulysses, can't you ever stop trying to find things out? You
are on holiday, you know. Good God, what are you doing now?'

Donaghue had bent down into a squatting position. He had
picked something up from the gravel of the path and was dusting
it on his sleeve. He stood up.

'What is it?' asked Clothilde. 'Roman remains or something?'

'Not at all,' said Donaghue. 'It's a brooch of some kind—
looks rather like a large ear-ring.' He held out the heart-shaped
object for Clothilde to inspect it. 'Is it yours?' he asked.

'Good God, no,' said Clothilde wrinkling her fleshy face in
disgust. 'I wouldn't wear such a gaudy thing.'

'I wouldn't exactly call it gaudy,' said Donaghue, studying the
brooch which had a spring clip on the back and was golden in
colour, the metal embossed with a pattern of oak leaves. 'It's
heavy—I think it's gold.'

He turned it over in his hand. There was indeed a hallmark
and above it the initials C.M.

'It's expensive,' he said.

'Expensive but garish to my taste,' said Clothilde. 'I find such
trinkets utterly unnecessary and silly, like cuff links. Thank God,
Ulysses, I've never seen you wearing cuff links.'

'It would never occur to me to buy them,' said Donaghue and
added somewhat sorrowfully, 'and no one has ever bought me
any.'

'Well, you won't get any from me,' retorted Clothilde. 'I
wouldn't be seen dead with a man wearing such foolish trinkets.'

'I suppose this must belong to one of the guests,' Donaghue
mused. 'It's only recently been dropped—though I can't remember any with the initials C.M. But it's not likely to be the property
of one of these novices.'

'You can hand it to the Mother Superior when we get back,'
said Clothilde. 'Shall we get on?' She glanced at her watch.
'9.45. I'd like to spend an hour in the chapel before lunch.'

Donaghue pocketed the gold clip brooch and the two set off
through the garden gate and along the vineyard path that led to
the wine press, Clothilde using her elm walking stick to get off
to a good brisk stride. She grumbled at Donaghue as she walked.

'I suppose you're going to spend the whole of the retreat trying
to solve the mystery of the garrulous novice and the unknown

brooch. Don't you think, Ulysses, that you ought perhaps to see a psychologist? You appear to have an almost pathological need to discover what you don't know. You really should be able to switch off from your work and become a normal ignorant human being like everybody else. Do you catch me trying to reconstruct people's noses or worrying about unsightly bags under people's eyes while I'm on holiday? Of course you don't. You know what they say— all work and no play...'

'You're right, Clothilde, absolutely right,' Donaghue agreed. 'Unfortunately it isn't as easy for me as it is for you. You work with your hands, so you can quite easily stop and do nothing with them for a week or so. I work with my brain and as you know seventy-five per cent of the work done by the brain is done unconsciously. For instance, having seen the girl, Sandra Kapp, I can't help thinking about her mother's anxiety about her—why her mother feels she's in danger.'

'As far as I can see,' said Clothilde, 'she's in no danger whatsoever. And, in any case, her mother isn't paying you to watch over her here—she'll be paying you to work in England in eight days' time. You're not working now, Ulysses, you're on holiday. You've just got to be more disciplined with yourself.'

'It's not a question of discipline,' said Donaghue. 'The brain is not like the hand. I can put the conscious part of my brain to other things but I have no control whatsoever over the unconscious part. The brain controls the hand and can instruct it to stop functioning but what controls the brain—now there's something I'd dearly love to find out.'

Clothilde laughed a hoarse laugh and linked her arm in Donaghue's.

'You know, Ulysses,' she said, 'that's what I really like about you—your utterly ordered confusion. In fact, what I like about you generally are your very coherent contradictions—your humble arrogance, the meticulously chaotic way in which you think things out, even your dress which is always shabbily elegant. I like you, Ulysses,' she proclaimed as she strode rapidly along, 'because you remind me of *life*.'

Donaghue smiled sheepishly at his friend. He was only half listening to her eulogy. His thoughts were elsewhere.

TWELVE

Conversations in the cloister

IN THE FOURTH and last cell on the east colonnade of the guests' cloister Adèle Bloch sat listlessly on the sturdy wooden double bed. The air-conditioned cell was comfortable, the original stone walls given a contemporary, rustic aspect by the natural pine ceiling and newly tiled floor. Adèle sat, her hands in her large lap, her eyes gazing dully at the pretty pastel rug that decorated the floor beside the bed.

'Come with me, Adèle,' Maximilian Bloch begged his wife. He was busy packing pencils and a portable easel into a knapsack. 'I must sketch those nuns working in the fields before the grape-picking is finished. It will do you good to get out into the sunshine—get a nice tan...'

Adèle sighed. 'A tan?' she repeated distractedly. 'I'm not really bothered about a tan.'

'You're still worried about Thelonius Kapp and what he'll think of you when he sees you—that's it, isn't it?'

'I know what he thinks. I saw the way he looked at me at breakfast.'

'You're wrong, Adèle,' said Maximilian fervently. He squatted on the rug before his wife and took her hands in his. 'Adèle, you are deluded by your false misgivings. That man didn't see anything. He didn't see me or you or anybody else in the room.'

'What do you mean, he didn't see anybody? He looked at me. I saw him. I saw the expression on his face.'

'He looked in your direction, perhaps, but the expression you saw on his face was what you wanted to see. The man is ill or on drugs. His eyes were blank—he saw nothing. Didn't you notice? Even his wife had difficulty getting his attention.'

'She is so pretty,' said Adèle wistfully, 'and so slim. She's perfect.'

'There's no perfect beauty,' said Maximilian. 'And if there
were, it would be doll-like and infinitely boring. What makes
beautiful women beautiful are their defects. Tell me,' he said,
gripping his wife's hands tightly, 'who do you consider the most
beautiful woman here on this retreat?'

'That Englishwoman, Lady Olivia something or other,' said
Adèle. 'She's the most perfectly beautiful.'

'She is the least attractive woman here,' said Maximilian cat-
egorically. 'And the prettiest? Who do you consider the retti-
est?'

'Kapp's wife, that Salome—she's the prettiest,' said Adèle
morosely.

'She is indeed the prettiest,' agreed Maximilian, 'but an utterly
bland prettiness. As a result she is in fact rather ordinary she
is not in any way, in her natural state, the kind of girl you would
notice on the street. She has to embellish her prettiness to an
extraordinary degree to make herself remarkable—as she does
on stage. I find such bland beauty utterly uninteresting.'

'The English girl, the photographer, she's pretty,' said Adèle.

'Yes,' said Maximilian. 'She is prettier than Kapp's wife. She
is a girl with a passionate spirit that animates her features.'

'And the American girl who works for her?' Adèle asked looking sidelong at her husband. 'What do you think of her?'

'Too thin for my taste and far too heavily made up—nothing
healthy and natural about her. She has the city pallor badly concealed by layers of make-up. She has, I think, a cheerful nature
but lacks intelligence—not, on the whole, my type.'

Adèle dropped her eyes to her hands which she pulled from
her husband's grasp. She twirled her fingers through her hair
nervously.

'Who do you think is the most beautiful woman here, Max?
Tell me truthfully,' she said.

'For me undoubtedly the doctor wife,' said Maximilian. 'I can
see in her eyes a profound understanding of the human psyche.'

'She's the plainest,' said Adèle, her voice low.

Max looked at her in alarm. She appeared to be on the verge
of tears.

'You're an artist,' she said in the same soft tone, 'you don't
see the world the way normal people see it. What most people
consider ugly you consider beautiful. You think I'm beautiful

but most people out there…' She waved a plump hand to indicate the world beyond the cell door. '…most people out there think I'm grotesque.'

'Oh dear,' said Maximilian, a pained expression creasing his handsome face into a frown. 'There doesn't seem to be anything I can say to convince you. Look, Adèle,' he said, 'just come with me—sit with me while I sketch. You'll see, you'll feel better once you're out there breathing the pure air of the fields.'

'I'm sorry, Max,' she said taking his hand once again in hers. 'I feel too fragile right now to go out. I want to stay here for a while. I'll do a bit of yoga. I'll feel better after that.'

Maximilian rose, looked down at his wife and shook his head sorrowfully.

'Oh, Adèle,' he sighed as he slipped his knapsack over his shoulder. 'Oh, my dear Adèle.'

AT TEN O'CLOCK in cell number one, the first of the double cells, Sandra Kapp sat on the small simple wooden chair that accompanied the oak desk and watched her husband sleeping. The expression on her face was one of extreme sorrow. He lay on his back snoring fitfully, his mouth hanging open, a much older man in his sleep than awake.

Suddenly he sat up, bolt upright, his eyes wide open and staring directly in front of him.

'Sandra,' he called hoarsely, lifting one hand and holding it out like a blind man in front of him.

Sandra rose and approached him. She took his hand in hers. He continued staring blindly ahead as if he didn't see her.

'Sandra.' His voice was raucous and desperate. 'Get a doctor. I'm dying.'

'You're not dying, Theo,' Sandra said gently. 'You've smoked too much dope, that's all. You're all right.'

She attempted to push him back to a lying position but with surprising strength he resisted. Then he yelled so loudly that everybody in the abbey must have heard. *'Get me a doctor, Sandra!'*

She jumped up quickly and ran out of the cell and along the colonnade to Dr Renoir in the next cell.

DONAGHUE, accompanying Clothilde back along the gravel path that led from the vineyard to the wine press, could not resist plucking one of the small purple grapes from its stem and popping it into his mouth.

Clothilde tutted in disapproval. 'Those are not table grapes,' she scolded. 'They're full of pips and the skins are tough.'

'But they taste marvellous,' said Donaghue as he chewed with great pleasure on the succulent fruit. 'Grenache, I'd say...monks always produced the better wines.'

He squatted down to inspect one of the gnarled trunks.

'*Vitis vinifera,*' he said. 'The ancestor of all fine European wines, saved from extinction by an American hybrid which now forms its root.'

'Do you mean to say that our vines are American?' exclaimed Clothilde in incredulity.

'Only the root,' Donaghue reassured her. 'The French vine is grafted on just above soil level...a very cordial *entente* to my mind. It happened in 1860 when——'

Donaghue's speech was roughly interrupted by Clothilde hauling him to his feet.

'You can tell me the history of French viticulture later,' she said. 'I want to have time to look at the press...and I've no doubt you know all there is to know about wine presses and their evolution. You can tell me that later too.'

She ushered Donaghue along the path towards the heavy oak door of the press building, stooping to avoid the lintel as she pulled the door open and entered the dimly lit room within.

Donaghue, one or two centimetres shorter than Clothilde, had no need to duck his head.

'Medieval man was, on average, nine inches shorter than us,' he said. 'Had I lived then I would have been considered tall.' He added this somewhat wistfully as he looked around at the low-ceilinged room which felt surprisingly cool after the heat outside.

'I can't understand why they didn't restore the building to the height of modern man,' said Clothilde. 'After all, it is modern man—or should I say modern woman—who's going to work in it. Some of those novices are taller than most men!'

Donaghue nodded in regretful agreement as they approached the large slatted tub of the single press that stood in the centre of the stone-flagged room. Three containers filled with grapes stood against a far wall.

They peered over the rim of the ancient oak tub of the press, gazing at the huge circular wooden weight that lay at the bottom. Through the centre of the weight rose a thick screw-shaft on which the wooden weight would rest while the tub was filled with the grapes to be crushed.

Clothilde looked querulously at the tall wooden shaft.

'It looks a highly dangerous contraption to me,' she said. 'I wouldn't trust a centuries-old pole like that to hold that huge weight. It could come crashing down on one of those novices' heads while they're putting the grapes in the tub. Why on earth didn't Kapp install modern equipment with modern safety standards? I am quite appalled that those young girls should have to work in such conditions.'

'He obviously wanted to restore the abbey exactly as it was and the nuns to function as they used to.'

'Like workhorses, you mean,' snorted Clothilde. 'It's a wonder he doesn't have them treading the grapes with their feet! I suppose he considers this highly dangerous wooden weight as a labour-saving device!'

'Grapes have not, traditionally, been trod in this region,' Donaghue informed Clothilde. 'Treading was done in Spain and Portugal where it's still done to this day in some villages.'

'I suppose crushing with a wooden weight must be marginally more hygienic,' said Clothilde. 'Safer for the drinker if not for the presser.'

'There is no danger,' said Donaghue. 'These presses were built by craftsmen. They knew what they were doing. The thread on the shaft holds the weight. It can't possibly fall.' He gazed up at the ancient shaft, inspecting the twisting thread. 'It's been well restored,' he said. 'I imagine it must have become worn over the years.'

'Despite your considerable knowledge of the subject, Ulysses, you are not an expert,' said Clothilde. 'I wouldn't trust it.'

She leaned into the tub as she spoke, running a finger around the curved slats inside.

'Well, at least it's clean,' she declared. 'Though one wonders if they've treated it for woodworm. Given the choice, I think I'd prefer a drowned worm in my wine to insecticide!'

Donaghue smiled. 'Remember what the Mother Superior said—everything produced in this abbey is organic. I imagine that applies equally well to the wine!'

AT A LITTLE AFTER TEN o'clock Mireille Parmentier left the library after a pleasant half-hour's browse. Her husband, Loic, was resting in their cell having worked late the previous evening. She had finally selected a book on the history of the abbey and decided to read it in the shade of the cloister garden.

She felt curiously light-hearted. The abbey was astonishingly beautiful and tranquil as if its ancient walls had absorbed the centuries of devotion and prayer that they had been witness to. She felt as though her whole being had been lifted, lightened— a very pleasing sensation.

As she stepped lightly into the colonnade, Dr Renoir came out of the Kapps' cell and almost collided with her.

'I...I...do beg your pardon, Madame...Madame...' he stammered.

'Madame Parmentier,' she said, holding out a slender hand in greeting. 'You're Dr Renoir, if I remember the name rightly?'

'Renoir...yes, Renoir,' said the doctor distractedly as he limply shook the proffered hand.

'Is Mr Kapp ill?' asked Mireille, indicating the door of the first cell with a nod of her blonde head.

'His wife called me out to him but when I arrived he was sleeping. She said he'd had some kind of fit. I must admit the man has a sickly pallor...but he was sleeping soundly so I didn't wake him up.'

'A strange man, Thelonius Kapp,' said Mireille as she and Dr Renoir moved away from the Kapps' cell. 'I had no idea the abbey was owned by a film director.'

'He obviously didn't want it publicized,' said Dr Renoir. 'One would expect the place to be crawling with TV cameras and journalists but I suppose film directors need a refuge of some sort where they can escape the media.'

'You know, Dr Renoir,' whispered Mireille leaning conspiratorially towards him, 'I think he takes drugs.'

Dr Renoir recoiled involuntarily from Madame Parmentier's proximity. There was a sensuous quality to the woman's features that disturbed him. Dr Renoir had always felt ill at ease in the company of this type of glamorous woman.

'You're right, Madame Parmentier,' he said. He shifted nervously from one foot to the other. Mireille reached out and gently touched his arm, making him start.

'I'm going to sit in the shade of the cloister garden,' she said. 'Perhaps you'd like to join me, Dr Renoir?'

'Eh?' queried Renoir in astonishment. 'S...sit in the garden?'

'Why not?' said Mireille. 'It's such a lovely morning.'

She smiled a slow, languorous smile which made Dr Renoir blink at her in confusion.

The doctor, who had never in his life been seduced by a woman, was saved from the appalling dilemma he found himself in by a choked gurgle that came from the second cell along the colonnade.

'That's my wife, Felicity,' he stuttered as he turned and ran in the direction of the cell door.

Mireille regarded him humorously then, shrugging her small shoulders, turned into the cloister garden where she selected the shadiest seat and settled down to read her book.

DONAGHUE AND CLOTHILDE, on their return from the wine press, went directly to their respective cells to change from their walking boots into footwear more suitable for church. They had decided to spend the last hour before lunch in the small annexe Chapel of La Sainte Vierge in tranquil meditation.

'Give that ever-snooping mind of yours a rest,' Clothilde had advised him and Donaghue had agreed.

At 10.55 they met in the colonnade outside the cells, their two pairs of feet comfortably encased in soft leather sandals, Donaghue's short stubby toes wriggling contentedly in their unaccustomed sock-free state. They followed the colonnade up towards its northern exit, nodding in greeting to the blonde Frenchwoman, Mireille Parmentier, who sat, a book lying open on her lap, on one of the wooden seats under the plane trees in the centre of the cloister garden. As they made their way up the shaded colonnade, which was pleasantly cool in contrast to the now blistering heat of the late morning sun, they spotted Maximilian Bloch who had just emerged from his cell and was striding purposefully along the west gallery. The painter beamed a bright good morning to Donaghue and Clothilde and smiled over at the seated Madame Parmentier, who nodded her blonde head and smiled politely in reply.

Donaghue and Clothilde, having stopped to bid good morning to Maximilian Bloch, resumed their trajectory only to have it interrupted once again, this time by the sight of Dr Renoir whose cell door had suddenly flown open and precipitated the doctor into the cloister. He gazed around at them, his hands flapping in a highly agitated manner.

'Oh dear, oh dear,' he muttered. 'My wife's being violently ill,' then added by way of an explanation, 'She's pregnant. I must find a mop to clear up the mess.' Then he took off up the colonnade in the direction of the refectory.

'You only have to call a novice,' Clothilde called after him. 'There's a buzzer in the cells for the purpose.'

'My wife did so,' the doctor called over his shoulder as he ran, 'but there didn't seem to be any about.'

'You go on to the chapel,' said Clothilde pushing Donaghue forward. 'I'd better go across and help the poor girl. Her husband doesn't appear to be in a fit state to look after her. I'll join you in a minute.'

Clothilde hurried away to the other side of the cloister and Donaghue wandered off up the colonnade towards the chapel. As he reached the last cell, that of Carl Petersen, Thelonius Kapp's secretary, his attention was caught by voices coming from inside the cell, whose door was very slightly ajar. He could hear the nasal tone of the American's voice quite clearly.

'You can't change your mind now,' Petersen was saying, his voice calm and solicitous.

A quiet female voice answered, 'I can't go through with it— I can't do it to him.'

'You do love me, don't you?'

'You know I do.'

'Then you know there's no other way.'

'Yes, I suppose there's no other way.' The answering voice was barely audible.

Suddenly the cell door closed. Donaghue remained where he was for a moment or so wondering curiously who Kapp's secretary was speaking to. He reprimanded himself mentally. Some-

times, he had reluctantly to admit to himself, his insatiable curiosity bordered on nosiness. It was really no business of his who
Carl Petersen was in love with. Nevertheless he stood where he
was waiting to hear the voices from the cell once again. But the
conversation was muffled now by the heavy oak door.

Then, unexpectedly, as he was about to move away, the sound
of another voice assailed his ears but not, this time, hushed and
low like the voices he had heard from Carl Petersen's cell. This
voice was strident and raucous like the cry of an animal in distress. The voice came from Thelonius Kapp's cell directly opposite that of Carl Petersen. It was a man's voice that howled
out hoarsely and distressfully, *'Sandra! Sandra!'*

The two words echoed mournfully around the cloister then
there was silence. Donaghue gazed around at the empty colonnade and garden. The Frenchwoman, Mireille Parmentier, had
disappeared from her seat. It was a curious disquieting silence
after the strange howling voice of Thelonius Kapp. Then the
silence was broken by the sounds of Felicity Renoir retching
once again in her cell.

The lines from *All's Well That Ends Well* came sharply into
Donaghue's mind again as they had done in his office two days
before when Mrs Trescott had visited him: *The hind that would
be mated by the lion must die for love.*

At that moment Dr Renoir, mop and bucket in hand, rushed
past Donaghue and sped down along the colonnade. Donaghue
turned towards the Chapel of La Sainte Vierge and entered its
carved oak door, his head bent in reflection.

THIRTEEN

Lunch in the refectory

AT TWELVE O'CLOCK the guests assembled in the refectory for their first lunch of the retreat. They took their seats as they had at breakfast with one small change. Fiona MacKinley asked Lady Carter Bonnington if she could have her place next to Mark Kingsford with the result that the Lady, who had agreed somewhat reluctantly, found herself in the company of Thérèse Mendes France, Donaghue and Clothilde.

Dr and Madame Renoir sat opposite Mark and Fiona, Maximilian and Adèle Bloch sat opposite Mireille and Loïc Parmentier and at the first table Thelonius Kapp sat with his wife, his secretary and his wife's beautician as he had at breakfast.

Two young novices served the guests. They brought out hors d'oeuvres of fresh melon, salad and crudités, raw vegetables grown in the abbey gardens, with homemade mayonnaise. This was followed by a menu of Gratin Dauphinois, pork cutlets or mussels served with the abbey's rosé of the previous year. The main course was followed by a selection of cheeses and after that a dessert of fresh fruit salad and a spiced apple tart baked that morning in the abbey's kitchen.

For most of the meal a rather tense silence reigned at Donaghue's table. It was obvious to anyone who cared to look that Thérèse Mendes France was considerably put out by having to sit next to the exquisitely dressed Lady Carter Bonnington. They were indeed an ill-matched pair—Miss Mendes France with her iron grey cap of hair and shapeless sweatshirt over a long white cotton skirt, Lady Carter Bonnington in a silk sheath dress, her sleek black hair brushed back into a chignon from the smooth sheen of her line-free forehead, her sculpted profile outlined in elegant contrast to the hawklike protuberance of Miss Mendes France's nose and the grim set of her mouth.

Donaghue, having presented Clothilde and Miss Mendes France to the new table guest, asked politely of Lady Olivia if she happened to be related to the Carter Bonningtons of Exhampton. 'I had a case down that way some years ago,' he said. 'A small question of missing heirlooms.'

Lady Olivia looked at Donaghue curiously. She recognized him as the ugly little man who had sat at the table next to hers in the auberge restaurant.

'Not at all,' she said, inclining her head politely. 'I am called Carter Bonnington simply because I linked my name, Carter, to that of my husband at marriage.'

'Would your husband be Cecil Bonnington, the plastic surgeon?' asked Clothilde.

'As a matter of fact he is,' said Lady Carter Bonnington in surprise.

'Ah,' said Clothilde, 'I've seen him once or twice at medical conferences. I don't think I ever saw you with him.'

'No, you wouldn't have,' said the Lady. 'I have no interest in the theoretical aspect of his work.'

Clothilde declined to continue the conversation. The Lady's polite but succinct replies left her with the impression that, as an aristocrat, she considered her partners at table of too low a social class to converse with. At the same time Clothilde was fascinated to see the workmanship of Sir Cecil Bonnington at such close quarters. She stole a surreptitious glance at the Lady every now and again as she ate.

Lady Bonnington, catching Clothilde's eyes, smiled graciously at her, thinking that the woman was extremely rude to stare in that overt manner. She sighed inwardly. It was only natural, she supposed, that a woman as ugly as this Dr Blanche would be unable to keep her eyes off a face as beautiful as hers. She ate her lunch with slow deliberation. Her friend Hermione had told her (and Cecil had confirmed it) that the more thoroughly you masticated your food the more satisfied you felt and the less you ate. The food at this abbey was excellent. If she wasn't careful she would leave several kilos heavier than when she arrived!

Miss Mendes France, sitting next to the elegant Lady, ate her mussels with grim determination. Clothilde devoted all her attention to her pork and Donaghue picked at his gratin, his eyes wandering reflectively around the room. The two novices were standing sentinel at the far end of the room waiting for the diners to finish the main course. He noticed that one of them was the pretty young thing he'd seen in the pepper tunnel, the illicit talker. The other, in sharp contrast to the almost angelic pretti- ness of her companion, was the exceedingly plain girl whom he'd seen working in the carrot tunnel and whose close-set eyes were rendered even smaller and closer-set by the largeness of her nose. Bright pink pimples dotted her chin and narrow forehead.

Then his gaze fell inexorably on Thelonius Kapp's table. The film director appeared, as he had at breakfast, distracted. His beady black eyes gazed blankly before him or roamed aimlessly about. His wife, Sandra, was speaking to him solicitously, evi- dently trying to persuade him to eat. He appeared to be picking at his food in a desultory fashion. Donaghue watched the girl, a feeling of unease creeping over him as he did so. She didn't look at all well. Her face was pale with that pallid green tinge of the sick. Her eyes were pink-rimmed as if she had been crying. She had looked fine at breakfast. What had happened in the three hours since to make her look like this? Had they been taking drugs together in their cell? Smoking cannabis made the eyes pink-rimmed but as far as Donaghue knew did not impart a sickly pallor to the skin. Cannabis also depleted the blood sugar level so that the taker craved sweet food. Sandra was trying to per- suade her husband to eat the apple tart that was served with the coffee but she herself neither ate nor drank. At one moment she took a piece of tart as if to taste it then, with a slight grimace, handed it to her husband. He refused, grimacing in the same manner as if imitating her expression in much the same way, Donaghue thought, as a small child being fed by its mother.

After watching the rather curious eating habits of the Kapps, Donaghue came to the conclusion that Sandra was ill and Kapp high on some drug or other, something much stronger than can- nabis. He thought of Kapp's long mournful cry from his cell an hour earlier—the cry of a man not in his right mind. But why did Sandra Kapp look so ill? Despite Clothilde's repeated re- minders that he was on holiday, Donaghue couldn't help thinking about the girl and the danger, albeit imagined by her mother, that she might be in.

When the meal was finished the guests left the refectory and the novices set to clearing the tables.

The guests congregated aimlessly outside in the shade of the arched walkway, the women looking curiously at Kapp and his entourage as they emerged last from the refectory door. Sandra, still pale, her face clouded by an expression of anxiety, steered her husband quickly into the shade of the cloister towards their cell. Milly Silverstone followed her mistress and Carl Petersen, bidding the others goodbye, made his way towards his own cell on the opposite gallery. Mark Kingsford, who was standing with Fiona MacKinley watching the progress of the Kapps, suddenly leapt forward and sprinted after the couple. He intercepted them just as they were about to enter their cell.

'Mrs Kapp,' he said, tentatively touching Sandra's arm.

'Yes?' queried Sandra Kapp, her pale face frowning.

'Mark Kingsford, London *Daily Courier*—about the interview. Do you think…'

'The interview?' said Sandra tiredly. 'Oh, the interview. I'm sorry, but right at the moment it's not convenient. My husband isn't well. You'll have to arrange it with his secretary. Cell number one—his name's Carl Petersen.'

Mark, disappointed, thanked her and ambled back to Fiona's side.

'Damn,' he said. 'I've got a feeling that this job's not going to come off. Kapp's ill. He couldn't talk to himself let alone anyone else in the state he's in—and she doesn't look that good either. God, they're an odd pair.'

'Drugged up to the eyeballs,' said Fiona. 'He's probably dying of Aids.'

'I suppose I'll just have to wait until he's better,' said Mark glumly. 'I was hoping to get the interview over and done with on the first day then bugger off and hit the beaches.'

'Where were you thinking of going?' Fiona asked.

'Oh, I don't know—St Tropez, Cannes. Just follow the coast —stop off where I fancy.'

'Sounds good to me,' said Fiona. She looked at him sidelong and smiled coyly at him. 'Mind if I come along?'

Mark placed a tanned arm around her shoulders and hugged her.

'As long as you don't make me wear blinkers on the beach,' he said, smiling cheerfully. 'Anyway, we'd better make the most of our stay here—it looks as though we'll be here for the whole

bloody retreat. So what shall we do this afternoon? We don't
have to stay here in the abbey, of course—we could sneak off
to the beach at Hyères if you fancy.'

'Actually,' said Fiona, 'I'm going to stay to hear Brother Martin sing at three o'clock.' She looked absently at the lintel of the
refectory door. 'I believe he's incredibly good-looking.'

'Oh really,' said Mark frowning. 'As a matter of fact I forgot
that he was coming. I did intend to listen to him sing. I'll join
you.'

He looked at his watch. 1.15. 'How about a couple of hours'
grape-picking before the monk sings?'

'Fine,' said Fiona brightly. She linked an arm in Mark's and
they set off, following the south wall of the refectory in the
direction of the vineyards.

CLOTHILDE RETURNED to her cell and Donaghue to his, she with
the intention of sleeping and he of availing himself of the comfort of the air-conditioning and some time alone to reflect on
what possible danger the young Sandra Kapp could be in. Her
husband was undoubtedly in a very bad state, mentally and physically. He was either ill or heavily drugged. Was he in such a
state that he could do harm to his young wife? If his mind was
unhinged by drugs, yes—but what could a man in such an appallingly weak condition do to her? She was physically stronger,
it seemed, than he was.

Donaghue sat back comfortably against the head-rest of his
bed and lit one of the small cigars that Clothilde forbade him to
smoke in her presence. Two small questions were niggling at
him. He wondered whether they could possibly have anything to
do with Sandra Kapp. One concerned a face that he was sure he
had recognized and the other a voice that he was equally sure
he had never heard before. He closed his eyes, relishing the illicit
pleasure of his cigar, and reflected on the problem.

DR AND FELICITY RENOIR returned to their cell for a siesta and
Mireille and Loic Parmentier set off on a tour of the abbey buildings. Maximilian Bloch returned after lunch to the vineyard to
continue his sketching and Adèle, his wife, returned to their cell.
She spent some time pacing indecisively up and down the small

room. She was feeling better than she had at breakfast, due in no small way, she knew, to the spectacle of the Kapps at lunchtime. They had looked terrible, both of them. Perhaps Max was right. Kapp might not have actually noticed her. He did appear to be an ill man—and Max was right about another thing. Beauty was ephemeral, short-lived, not anything to be valued too highly. She smiled. She had made up her mind. She would do something positive. She would go to the fields and pick grapes with the nuns. It would surprise Max to see her there. She changed quickly into a loose cotton skirt. How pleased he will be, she thought happily as she closed the cell door behind her.

CARL PETERSEN, in his cell, searched his pockets for his lighter. He couldn't find it. Briskly he left the cell and made his way back to the refectory. He peered around the half-open door and noticed that the novice on duty busy cleaning the tables was the tall, pretty one. He turned, smiling, hurried back to his cell and pressed the buzzer to summon the novice.

AT 1.45, after a short nap, Miss Mendes France strode energetically towards the vineyards. She wanted to see the restored wine press which, she had read, dated from the fifteenth century. Passing the gate of the fruit and vegetable garden she smiled in admiration at the general order and tidiness of the long polythene tunnels. Order in the garden to her right and industry in the fields to her left. The nuns were busy working away in the vineyards. She spotted the young English couple working among them. She smiled once again—a sensible girl, that Fiona MacKinley. Naive, of course, and emotionally immature—she had a lot to learn—but basically sound. She wasn't sure about him, but then Thérèse Mendes France wasn't sure about any male. As far as she could see he appeared to be one of those shallow contemporary young men who cultivated their muscles then squeezed them into tight-fitting clothing and whose only concerns in life were girls and fast cars—not a thought in their heads of anything other than the pleasures of the flesh.

Her eyes, roaming over the fields, detected Maximilian Bloch, the painter, half hidden among the olive trees at the southern end of the field. She noticed that he'd been careful to conceal himself from the working nuns. She supposed that he wanted the scene to be as natural and unposed as possible. Altogether, she reflected, a very satisfactory start to the retreat. She glanced at her watch. 1.55. She had plenty of time to get to the wine press and back for the Gregorian chant in the main chapel at three o'clock.

LADY CARTER BONNINGTON, in her cell at the bottom of the west gallery, kicked off her high-heeled shoes and lay down on her bed. She picked up her handbag, fumbled around inside, frowned, then drew out a packet of cigarettes. She smoked contentedly, lying back against the bedhead, enjoying the relaxing effect of the nicotine. She didn't like to smoke in public—not now that Cecil and most of the medical profession had given up. Her firm silicone-lined bosom rose and fell as she inhaled and expelled the smoke. She reflected on the unpleasant hour she had spent in the refectory. It was really rather inconvenient to be placed at the same table as that gruesome old judo champion Mendes France and the garrulous Dr Blanche. She had been much happier in the company of the handsome young journalist and the agitated doctor and his pregnant wife. At least they'd had the manners not to stare at her—but then, she reminded herself, she was an extraordinary-looking woman, more striking now, in many ways, than when she was younger. People were bound to look at her. In fact, to be truthful, she had to admit she liked it but it was just that sometimes it was...well...inconvenient.

She glanced at her watch. 2.15. She must remember at 2.30 to phone Cecil. She had phoned him the day before from Hermione's, but he liked her to phone every day. Dear Cecil—a gentle, tolerant man, but he could be jealous as a panther in love. He had no need to be, of course. She had never been unfaithful to him. But she understood the psychology of jealousy. He was unfaithful to her and so believed that she would deceive him in turn. Suspicion haunted the guilty mind. She smiled. Well, even if he had reason to mistrust her he'd have nothing to worry about here. There was no one remotely interesting to a woman like her at this abbey.

She smiled again—the young journalist perhaps, if she'd been twenty-five years younger, and the painter was good-looking but he was an artist and artists were notoriously untrustworthy. The doctor was too highly strung, an apology for a man. Monsieur Parmentier...now he was the kind of man a woman could be attracted to, but he was obviously devoted to his wife. As for the little Irishman, he was a joke—a face like a monkey and short fat legs. Standing up, his head had barely reached her shoulder! She imagined him taking her arm, leading her into Cecil's draw-ing-room at their annual hunt ball. The thought made her giggle aloud. She clamped her hand to her mouth. He had the cell next door to hers. What would he think if he heard her giggling to herself? He'd said something about a case in Exhampton. He was obviously a policeman although he didn't look like one—probably just a constable or a sergeant. She pictured the scene again—she in her newest designer gown, the Chanel in cream silk, he in his crumpled suit. The major-domo announces them: Lady and Constable Donaghue. She giggled again, keeping her hand to her mouth to stifle the sound. How she would enjoy telling Hermione about the people at this abbey.

She checked her watch—2.25. She must go now and phone Cecil.

AT 2.30 THELONIUS KAPP woke with a start from the deep sleep he had fallen into on return from the refectory. He looked around, startled.

'Sandra!' he called sharply.

His wife, who was lying beside him, sat up and stared with surprise at her husband. He was looking at her strangely—sus-piciously and aggressively, the small black eyes sharp and clear.

'Thelonius,' she said, smiling at him. 'You look better, almost your old self.'

'Sandra,' he repeated, shaking his bald head as if to dispel the fog that had been clouding it. 'I've been dreaming vividly—a terrifying dream. I dreamt you were trying to kill me.'

Sandra smiled. 'Thelonius,' she said, 'your dreams express your fears. You've been ill. When a person is ill they have fears of dying—it's normal.'

'Pass me a joint,' Kapp said sharply.

Sandra reached out to the enamelled box on the bedside table.

She handed him a thick hand-rolled cigarette that contained a mixture of cannabis and opium.

'I don't remember feeling ill,' Kapp said. 'I feel fine.'

'It's that kind of illness,' said Sandra. 'It affects the mind. The drugs you take don't help.'

'You know I can't manage without them,' Kapp muttered gruffly. 'I'm hooked, you know that.'

'They'll kill you in the end.'

'You think it's better to live a long, dull, joyless existence than a short ecstatic one. I don't. I'll go when it's time to go but I'll go happy. Goddamn it, Sandra, I only want to be happy— isn't that what anybody wants?' He looked at her sorrowfully. 'You know me by now. You know that without the drugs I'm black, pessimistic, miserable. I can't help but think endlessly of the almost infinite capacity for evil of the human psyche. How would you like to spend your whole damned existence in that state?'

'I understand, Theo,' said Sandra, caressing his hand. He gripped the proffered hand and leaned towards her.

'You only live once, Sandra. You have to live to the limit.' He spoke passionately, his beady eyes glittering like two black diamonds. 'Enjoy every pleasure, see every beautiful thing there is to see in this beautiful creation, create what you cannot find, take what you cannot buy.'

He brought Sandra's slender hands to his lips and kissed them. 'You are the most beautiful thing in creation that I have seen. I have taken you and I have helped to create you. But...' He lifted his finely formed fingers and cupped them around his wife's face. '...I do not want to own you. You're not my possession—you're not my prisoner. I want you to remain beautiful—and a human being is only beautiful when he is free. I want you to be truly free. You know that, don't you? I want you to give me the ultimate love and the ultimate love is only ever given freely.'

'I know,' Sandra whispered, tears filling her eyes. 'I know what you want.'

'Sandra,' he said, 'I'm hungry.'

Sandra smiled brightly through her tears. 'You are getting better,' she said. 'I'll call a novice and order your lunch.'

She pressed the buzzer and a few seconds later the young novice shyly opened the cell door.

'Mr Kapp will have his lunch now,' said Sandra. 'Salad, chops, cheese and dessert—and a pot of weak tea for me.'

The novice nodded and returned fifteen minutes later with a loaded tray. Kapp ate with relish, cleared every plate. Sandra regarded him with satisfaction and sipped her tea—then she grimaced and put the cup down.

'What is it, honey?' Kapp asked. 'Aren't you well? You don't look too well—perhaps you caught the same goddamn virus that I got.'

Sandra, frowning, shook her head. 'I don't know. I just feel a bit off colour. My head's a bit fuzzy.'

'Here,' said Kapp. He picked up a small leather snuff box from the table beside the bed and tipped some of the contents on to his palm.

'Have a little coke. It'll clear your head.'

Sandra hesitated.

Kapp, smiling broadly, proceeded to arrange the white powder into two thin lines, one of which he sniffed up into his left nostril by means of a tightly rolled piece of writing paper. He invited Sandra to do the same.

'Go on, honeybunch,' he said.

Sandra took the roll of paper and sniffed up the powder. Then she rose, took Kapp's tray and, grasping his hands, pulled him to his feet.

'Come along, Theo,' she said. 'It's almost three. Brother Martin will be singing in the chapel. Quick—we don't want to miss it.'

Kapp, on his feet, placed a muscled arm around his wife's waist. He pulled her towards him and kissed her passionately on the lips.

'Baby,' he said in a hoarse whisper, 'Baby, in thirty minutes when the monk has finished singing, you're gonna take my hand and lead me back here. You're gonna pop some Ecstasy—yes, you are, just for once, to please me. Then you're gonna dance for me like the first Salome did for Herod. Then you're gonna make love to me. Waddya reckon? Am I right about that—or am I wrong?'

'You could be right,' Sandra whispered, tears filling her eyes.

'An' then I'm gonna make love to you like nobody's ever

made love to you before. Waddya reckon to that? Do you reckon that I'm right about that too?'

'I reckon...I reckon...' Sandra stammered. Then she laid her head on her husband's shoulder and wept.

FOURTEEN

Death in the abbey

AT THREE O'CLOCK Thelonius Kapp and his wife entered the Chapel of St Pierre la Croix. The other guests were already there, seated in silence as seemed fitting within the ancient walls of the twelfth-century church.

A monk, dressed in a long white habit, stood before the high altar facing the congregation, a solitary, ethereal figure, his close-cropped head bent, apparently in prayer.

The Kapps walked slowly along the central aisle towards the empty first pew. The eyes of the guests moved from the figure of the monk to those of the celebrated couple.

Thelonius Kapp genuflected before entering the pew, then, as he rose from his knees, he staggered so that his wife had to help him to his seat. As soon as they were both seated the chapel regained its reverent silence. The monk lifted his head and the guests gazed in fascination at the young man's face—a face of such pure youthful beauty that it almost took their breath away. For an instant they felt, all of them, that they were looking at the face of an angel. The monk's eyes closed and he started to sing. The pure notes filled the chapel, echoing from the ancient walls until the air was resonant with their cadence. One by one the eyes of the congregated guests closed as the music of the monk's voice washed over them, transporting them, so that they felt that their spirits were being lifted from their bodies and carried upwards. For what seemed an aeon they remained motionless, transfixed by the almost hypnotic effect of the young man's voice—then suddenly a different sound, a harsh ugly sound, penetrated the purity of the monk's chant. The eyes of the congregation flew open and they saw to their astonishment the bizarre spectacle of Thelonius Kapp, standing in the first pew, his arms raised as if in supplication and issuing from his mouth a long terrible cry that was amplified to a truly terrifying degree by the perfect acoustics of the chapel.

The monk, his eyes still closed, oblivious even to the awful sound of Kapp's cry, continued to sing, but the guests were no longer listening to him. They were watching Kapp who, his arms still aloft, had thrown his head back in a gesture of great suffering. When his howling cry came to an end he turned his head, his eyes wild and furious.

'*Come away!*' he cried, his voice raucous and resonant. '*Come away death! Fly away, fly away breath! No, no, it's...*'

He opened his mouth to speak again but no word issued. Instead his face contorted into an ugly grimace of pain and he fell suddenly. His wife, Sandra, who had been clinging on to his arm, let out a piercing cry as he crumpled heavily on to the floor.

Milly Silverstone in the pew behind screamed a high-pitched hysterical shriek and Carl Petersen, standing at her side, pushed heavily past her to gain the aisle. The other guests remained for a second or two in shocked silence as the clear notes of the singer rang out. Then Dr Renoir sprang from his pew into the aisle followed quickly by Clothilde Blanche. The Mother Superior who had been standing at the back of the chapel hurried up the aisle, Mark Kingsford and Fiona MacKinley behind her, and the remaining guests hesitantly left their seats to approach Kapp's pew.

Dr Renoir bent over the motionless figure of Kapp which lay crumpled on the floor beneath the pew. Sandra Kapp, her face ashen, knelt beside her husband. The doctor, after a brief examination, lifted his head and said solemnly, 'The man is dead.'

Carl Petersen, standing over Sandra Kapp, looked down at his employer, his face pale and fraught.

'He appears to have suffered heart failure,' said Dr Renoir. 'A coroner will have to ascertain the exact cause of death. I'll need some help to carry him back to his cell.'

Carl Petersen helped the doctor to lift the crumpled body of Kapp and they carried him out of the chapel and up along the colonnade to his cell. The Mother Superior hurried after the doctor; Sandra, accompanied by Clothilde and Milly Silverstone, followed them with Donaghue and the two journalists lagging behind at a discreet distance.

The other guests returned soberly to their respective cells.

IN KAPP'S CELL Dr Renoir, with Carl Petersen's help, laid the
film director on his bed. He closed the eyes, which were staring
glassily at the ceiling, and drew together the lips, which were
blue in colour and pulled back from the white porcelain teeth in
a snarl.

Sandra Kapp, her face drained of all colour, approached the
bed and gazed down at her husband.

'I'd like to be alone with him,' she said quietly.

'Of course,' said the doctor and he ushered Petersen, Clothilde,
Donaghue and the journalists out of the cell. Milly Silverstone,
who stayed to comfort her mistress, was the last to leave.

In the colonnade outside the cell Carl Petersen, evidently
greatly troubled, said in impeccable French to Dr Renoir, 'So
you think it's a heart attack?'

'It looks like it,' said Dr Renoir hesitantly. 'But I can't be
sure. I'm a gynaecologist—pregnant women rarely suffer from
heart attacks so it's not something I come across very often.
There will have to be a coroner's report to ascertain the exact
cause of death.' The doctor frowned. 'He doesn't look the type
to have heart problems to me—too lean, no excess fat—but then
I'm not an expert and I don't know his history. Was he, as far
as you know, a drug taker?'

Petersen coughed drily. 'I believe he did indulge,' he said
cautiously.

The sound of Sandra Kapp sobbing came from behind the
closed door of the cell, followed by the sound of violent retching.

'I think perhaps somebody ought to stay with Mrs Kapp,' Donaghue murmured. 'Perhaps you, Clothilde.'

Clothilde nodded in assent.

'I'll stay with her,' declared Milly Silverstone. 'Jeez,' she said,
shaking her small streaked blonde head as she followed Clothilde
into the cell. 'Who'd a thought that he'd peg out on us like that—
in front of everyone, right there in front of everybody! Jeez!'

A few minutes later Clothilde emerged from the cell with a
distraught Sandra on her arm.

'I've persuaded Mrs Kapp to come and sit with me in my cell,
Milly,' she said, addressing the little beautician, 'you go and ask
a novice to come and clean the sink where Mrs Kapp was sick
and to bring a pot of tea for Mrs Kapp in cell number seven.'

Milly dutifully went off, passing on her way the Mother Su-

perior who bustled up to Dr Renoir and said, 'I've called the
police. They'll be here in fifteen minutes with a police surgeon—
the death has to be reported to the authorities.'

'In that case,' said Carl Petersen soberly, 'I'd better go and
get Mr Kapp's papers, identity documents et cetera.'

'Yes, of course, all that has to be done,' the Mother Superior
agreed worriedly.

Carl Petersen hurried off to his cell and the Mother Superior,
somewhat flustered, returned to her office to await the police.
Mark Kingsford and Fiona MacKinley took off after Carl Petersen, leaving Donaghue alone in the colonnade. He stood aimlessly for a moment or so then opened the door to Kapp's cell
and entered it. He closed the door quietly behind him.

He approached the bed and gazed down at the dead man's
face. An illustrious face—a face that had appeared in many
newspapers and on numerous screens. Yet who really knew who
this man had been? His wife perhaps—or his secretary. He was
not, Donaghue could see from the set of his features, which were
determined even in death, a man who had revealed his inner self
to many people. This old man had once been a young man, the
bald head once covered with hair. Black hair, Donaghue imagined. What manner of young man had he been? Debauched and
immoral by all accounts—but the media of course exaggerated
or even invented. From all that Donaghue had learned, Thelonius
Kapp had been a hard, ruthless man, ready to mow down anybody who stood in the path of his own ends. And yet his young
wife appeared to have loved him.

Donaghue gazed at the dead man's face thoughtfully. Frown
lines—or were they anxiety lines?—were etched between the
black eyebrows. The features were narrow and delicately
sculpted—the face, Donaghue thought, of a man who had suffered, perhaps all his life. Since he had arrived at the abbey
Donaghue had not had occasion to see Kapp's face at such a
close range. Even in death, Donaghue could see that Kapp had
borne his age well—the skin was good, weathered but finely
textured for a man of sixty-six years. The hands, blunt and hairy,
were the hands of an aesthete.

The eyes of the little investigator roamed around the room,
coming to rest on the table beside the bed which bore an array
of small ornate boxes, some enamelled, some lacquered, one or

two in embossed leather. Donaghue lifted each lid in turn. The
largest contained several long hand-rolled cigarettes—joints of
some kind. One of the small leather boxes contained a dusting
of white powder, undoubtedly cocaine. A rolled-up tube of writing paper, lying beside it, testified to the fact that the dead man
had recently partaken of the box's contents. No doubt the cocaine
had played its part in his death. An inspection of a second leather
box revealed small white pills that resembled aspirin. Donaghue
had no idea what they might be—amphetamines, perhaps, or
LSD. Two other boxes contained tablets and pills of various
shapes and colours whose identities Donaghue could only guess
at—new concoctions of drugs appeared every week on the drug
markets. One of these, he guessed, would almost certainly be the
new pleasure drug, Ecstasy, but he had no idea which. The coroner's report would provide the answer. Donaghue was careful
not to move or handle the contents of the boxes. A vellum notebook lay to one side of the table. Donaghue lifted its glossy
cover. The notebook was empty. A gold fountain pen lay open
beside it. Donaghue absently picked up the pen's top and replaced it. Solid gold pen nibs should not be left to dry of their
ink. Then he picked up the notebook and slipped it into his
pocket.

As he left the cell he almost collided with Thérèse Mendes
France who appeared to have been on the point of knocking on
the door. A worried expression clouded her features.

'I've come to see if there's anything I can do to help. The
poor girl must be in a terrible state.'

'My companion, Dr Blanche, is looking after her along with
her assistant, Milly Silverstone. They're in Dr Blanche's cell,
number seven, if you'd like to offer your services,' Donaghue
informed her.

'I shall first say a prayer for the dead man,' said Miss Mendes
France and she entered the cell, closing the door behind her. A
few minutes later she emerged just as the duty novice arrived to
clean the cell.

FIFTEEN

A diagnosis and another death

DONAGHUE, in his cell, sat at the simple oak table and retrieved from his pocket the vellum notebook that he had picked up in Kapp's cell. With it he drew out the gold clip brooch that he had found that morning in the vegetable garden. He placed the brooch on the table beside the notebook. Then he leaned over, scrabbled around in his travelling bag and brought forth an HB pencil. He opened the notebook at the first page and proceeded to rub gently across the top half of the page. As he did so a message appeared, white against the grey of the pencil, the letters having been imprinted into the paper from what had been written on the previous page, which had, evidently, been removed. The message, written in a firm elegant script, read: *We died as we lived—high in the saddle of life!*

'Extraordinary,' said Donaghue aloud to himself. 'Now where can the original possibly be?'

He gazed reflectively at the message. Life, as far as Ulysses Donaghue saw it, was formed from a complex construction of multi-dimensional jigsaw puzzles. This abbey, this retreat, represented one such puzzle—a small one of perhaps fifty or so medium-sized pieces—but some of the pieces were missing and some, though present, didn't quite fit into the puzzle as a whole. This message, for example, and the clip brooch he had found, and Thelonius Kapp's face—and something else, some small piece that shouldn't be there, a small thing that niggled at the back of his mind and hadn't yet come to the forefront of his consciousness, some little thing that he had noticed unconsciously and had relegated to that area of his brain that he called his IDR or Irrelevant Data Reserve. He would remember it, he knew, when its relevance became important.

But the jigsaw and its missing pieces all came back, he was

sure of it, to Mrs Trescott's visit to his office to express her
concern for her daughter's safety. She had thought that her
daughter was in danger from Thelonius Kapp but that was not
now the case—or was it? Donaghue stared in puzzlement at the
message on the paper. *We died as we lived*—a suicide note, it
would seem. Had Kapp committed suicide? He had certainly had
the wherewithal with his arsenal of drugs, but why 'we' and why
had the original note disappeared? Had they planned a suicide
pact, he and his wife, and had Sandra then chickened out? A
logical conclusion but not, to Donaghue's mind, a probable one.
Sandra Kapp, from what he had seen of her, was, like her mother,
not a person to chicken out of anything.

The hind that would be mated by the lion—the words came
back. But, he reflected, it was the lion who had died—or was it
the case, as he suspected in the peculiar relationship between
Thelonius Kapp and Sandra Trescott, that she had been the lion
and he the hind? He rather thought that that might have been the
case.

His reverie was interrupted by a knock on his cell door. Clothilde entered.

'I've left Mrs Kapp with her assistant, Milly,' she said. 'The
police have arrived and would like to speak to me and Dr Renoir.
Perhaps you'd like to join us, Ulysses. You know how you hate
to miss out on anything that's going on.'

'It's true,' agreed Donaghue, smiling. 'It's my nature—it
doesn't allow me to be indifferent.'

He slipped the notebook and the brooch into his pocket and
accompanied Clothilde to the Mother Superior's office where
they recognized the moustachioed features of Sergeant Bonifay,
known to both from the village gendarmerie, who introduced the
lean bespectacled man accompanying him as Dr Giles Mons, the
police surgeon. The sergeant presented Clothilde and Donaghue.
The others in the room had evidently already been presented to
the doctor.

Carl Petersen, seated beside the Mother Superior, nodded at
Donaghue and Clothilde, his regular features crossed by an expression of profound anxiety. On the other side of the Mother
Superior's table sat Dr Renoir and beside him Mark Kingsford
and Fiona MacKinley.

Dr Mons got down to business immediately.

'I have examined the dead man and have come to one or two conclusions, but first may I ask what you think, Dr Renoir and Dr Blanche?'

Clothilde spoke first: 'We are of course specialists in our own fields, not in any way cardiologists, but we both came to the same conclusion that the man suffered a massive cardiac arrest.'

'Although we both agreed,' added Dr Renoir, 'that he didn't appear the susceptible type.'

'I agree absolutely,' said Dr Mons. 'My opinion is that the arrest was due to a massive dose of poison.'

'Poison!' exclaimed Clothilde. 'Do you mean he was deliberately poisoned? Do you think he was murdered?'

'As to the origin of the poison, that, of course, I cannot say at this stage. Poison can be taken deliberately, accidentally or unwittingly. In other words the man could have committed suicide, been murdered or accidentally taken whatever it was that brought on the arrest of his heart. There were, I noticed, an army of drugs beside his bed. It's quite feasible that he overdosed, either deliberately or accidentally. An autopsy will reveal the exact cause of death.'

'An autopsy isn't obligatory, is it?' asked Carl Petersen. 'I'm not sure that his wife would...'

'It is obligatory,' said Dr Mons, 'if the police suspect foul play—if the death doesn't appear to be a natural death.'

'And you don't think this appears a natural death?' said Petersen.

'No, I'm not sure that it is,' said the doctor. He gazed keenly at Petersen. 'Mr Petersen, as you were Mr Kapp's secretary I am obliged to ask you one or two possibly indiscreet questions. You are not, of course, obliged to answer them but if you would do so it will help enormously in our task of establishing the cause of your employer's death.'

Petersen nodded gravely.

'Were you aware, Mr Petersen, of the extent of your employer's drug addiction?'

Petersen's face reddened slightly.

'I was aware that he indulged in drugs of various kinds, but I never investigated it—if you understand my meaning. I ignored it. It was none of my business, what he did in his private life.'

'Of course, of course,' said Dr Mons. 'But as far as you know, he regularly partook of such drugs as cocaine, opium, cannabis, Ecstasy—perhaps even heroin?'

'As far as I know, yes,' said Petersen.

'And did your employer, as far as you know, have any personal problems—health problems, perhaps, which might have led him to take his life?'

'He did make several visits to his doctor recently. He never spoke to me about the nature of the visits but I am aware that several were made. I put them down to the normal ailments of the...er...not so young.' The secretary coughed, raising a manicured hand to his mouth. 'As a matter of fact I believe that Mr Kapp committed suicide.'

'And what makes you think that?' the doctor asked.

'Because I found this on the bedside table when we took the body back to the cell.'

Petersen produced a piece of vellum writing paper which he passed to the doctor who read aloud the message written on it.

We died as we lived—high in the saddle of life.'

'A suicide note, as far as I can see,' said Carl Petersen, 'much in Mr Kapp's style, I feel.'

'But why "we"?' asked Clothilde. 'Why did he not put "I"?'

'He was quoting from one of his films, *The Life and Death of the James Brothers.* He always held a secret admiration for the outlaw.'

Mark Kingsford opened his mouth as if to speak then closed it again, saying nothing.

'If there is a possibility of suicide there will have to be an inquest,' said the police surgeon. 'Mrs Kapp will, of course, have to be consulted.'

'I'm not so sure that this is the right moment,' said Carl Petersen.

'She's resting right now,' said Clothilde. 'She's rather distraught.'

'The decision will have to be made fairly quickly,' said the doctor. 'She will have to be consulted.'

'I'll fetch her then,' said Clothilde. She rose from her seat but at that moment the door of the office was flung open and an ashen-face Sandra entered the room. She gazed, stricken, around at the gathering.

'It's Milly,' she whispered, her voice barely audible. 'I think she's dead.'

Carl Petersen had risen to his feet, his face drained of colour. 'Milly!' he exclaimed in a strangled voice and ran from the room. The others followed quickly save Clothilde who took Sandra Kapp's arm and sat her in a chair. The girl started to sob hysterically and Clothilde placed a comforting arm around her shoulders.

In Clothilde's cell, number seven, a curious cameo met the eyes of Carl Petersen who was the first to arrive at the scene. Thérèse Mendes France and the white-robed monk, Brother Martin, were bent over the still form of Milly Silverstone which was slumped on the rug in the middle of the cell. Dr Mons and Dr Renoir gazed down at the dead girl. She had obviously died in pain—her face was contracted into a grimace of agony and her body doubled up. She had evidently been violently ill before death, the bile on the floor beside her bearing witness to the fact.

Dr Mons knelt down to examine her, his expression grim.

'Poison,' he declared. 'Arsenic, I'd say.' He looked up at Sergeant Bonifay. 'Call Inspector Joly in Hyères. There's something seriously wrong here.'

The Mother Superior, rubbing her hands together in great agitation, accompanied the sergeant back to her office.

Carl Petersen, his control having deserted him, appeared on the verge of tears. He gazed down at the dead girl.

'Milly,' he said. 'Milly...?'

The doctor stood up and looked questioningly at Thérèse Mendes France and the young monk. Miss Mendes France held out a muscled arm and shook the doctor's hand firmly.

'Thérèse Mendes France,' she said. 'I was in the next cell when I heard Mrs Kapp scream. I came in immediately. The girl had just vomited and died—just like that. Absolutely frightful. There was nothing I could do.'

'And you, Brother?' asked the doctor.

'I was passing along the colonnade,' Brother Martin explained. His voice was soft, almost girlish. 'I heard a scream from the cell. This lady, Miss Mendes France, had heard it too. She'd come out of her cell into the colonnade. We came in here together.'

Mark Kingsford, squeezed into a corner of the cell with Fiona

MacKinley, gazed avidly at the body on the floor as if noting every detail.

Within a few minutes a small gathering of guests had congregated at the open door. Felicity Renoir pushed her way through to her husband's side, looked at the scene then rushed out of the cell holding her hand over her mouth. Maximilian and Adèle Bloch, accompanied by Mireille and Loic Parmentier, hovered inquisitively in the colonnade outside the door.

Donaghue stepped out of the cell and stood beside Maximilian Bloch. The painter's handsome face bore an unaccustomed expression of gravity.

'Such a young thing to die so horribly,' he said sadly. 'And so soon after her employer—one wonders whether the two deaths might be linked.'

'Perhaps she was his lover,' suggested Adèle.

'I really don't think so,' said Maximilian. 'She wouldn't be his type.'

'Perhaps it's an epidemic of some kind,' said Adèle worriedly. 'The doctor said poisoning—perhaps it's food poisoning.' Her plump hand went to her stomach.

'If it was food poisoning more people would be ill,' said Loic Parmentier who was standing beside Adèle. 'We all ate more or less the same thing at lunchtime.'

'Don't worry, Mrs Bloch,' said Donaghue. 'An inquest will determine the cause of death.'

'That's all very well,' said Mireille Parmentier, 'but if it is indeed poison the inquest won't be able to say where it's come from.'

'That's very true, Madame Parmentier,' concurred Donaghue, turning his head as the small entourage within the cell emerged. The last to leave was Dr Mons, who closed the door and instructed the assembled guests not to enter the cell under any circumstances. He advised them to return to their former activities and assured them that there was nothing to worry about, nothing contagious, and that a police inspector would arrive soon to take care of the sad and sorry business.

The guests slowly dispersed and Donaghue, accompanied by Mark Kingsford and Fiona, followed the doctor and Carl Petersen back to the Mother Superior's office. Dr Renoir made his excuses and returned to his cell to attend to his wife, almost bumping into Lady Carter Bonnington who was striding along the colonnade towards her cell.

'Goodness me, the cloister's crowded,' she commented. 'What's going on?'

'They found that American girl, Mrs Kapp's hairdresser or whatever she was, dead in her cell—just ten minutes ago,' Dr Renoir explained somewhat breathlessly.

Lady Carter Bonnington's elegant hand flew to her mouth.

'They think they've both been poisoned. I don't like the look of it at all,' Dr Renoir said. 'I'm going to keep a careful eye on my wife. There could be a homicidal maniac around.'

'Good God,' said Lady Bonnington. 'If that's the case I'm packing up and leaving immediately.' And she flew off round to her cell on the west colonnade, her long white silk skirt billowing out behind her as she hurried along.

In the Mother Superior's office Dr Mons instructed Sergeant Bonifay to go to the kitchens and find out what Thelonius Kapp and Miss Silverstone had eaten for lunch and whether they had ordered anything to eat or drink between lunch and the time of their deaths. Mr Kapp had died at about 3.05 and the girl approximately thirty-five minutes later at 3.40. It was now 3.55.

Sergeant Bonifay, before departing, informed the doctor that Inspector Joly from Hyères would be arriving within the quarter-hour.

The doctor sat down beside Sandra Kapp and said apologetically, 'I know this must be distressing for you but I have to ask you one or two questions.'

Sandra nodded tearfully.

'Can you tell me exactly what your husband ate for lunch?'

'He ate lunch in the cell—he didn't have any appetite at lunch-time. He had salad, chops, cheese and a dessert of apple tart.'

'And did you eat the same?'

'No, I had no appetite. I've had no appetite lately.'

The doctor looked at her curiously.

'Are you unwell?' he asked.

'I've been feeling rather strange since this morning.'

'In what way?' asked the doctor. 'Indigestion? Stomach pains?'

'No, not exactly. I've just had no appetite and I've felt tired.

I was sick. I vomited when they brought Thelonius back to the cell. I suppose it was shock.'

'I think perhaps you should be examined by a doctor. Perhaps Dr Renoir or Dr Blanche here could see to that.'

Dr Blanche nodded in assent and the doctor continued his questioning.

'While you were in Dr Blanche's cell with Miss Silverstone, did you or she eat or drink anything? I believe Miss Silverstone ordered you a pot of tea?'

'Yes, but I didn't drink it. I found I didn't really fancy tea after all.'

'And Miss Silverstone, did she drink any of the tea?'

'I don't know,' said Sandra tiredly. 'I fell asleep. She might have done.'

'There was no sign of the pot or cup in the cell. I suppose a nun must have come to take them away?'

'I suppose so,' said Sandra. 'I really can't say. I was asleep. I woke up when I heard Milly retching.'

She sobbed, placing her head in her hands.

Sergeant Bonifay appeared at the door.

'Back to the kitchen, Sergeant,' said the doctor. 'See if you can track down the pot of tea and cup that were taken to Dr Blanche's cell, number seven I believe, for Mrs Kapp, twenty minutes or so ago. They might not have been washed up yet. If you find them bring them back here.'

Sergeant Bonifay disappeared and the doctor turned back to Carl Petersen and Sandra Kapp.

'Mr Petersen and Mrs Kapp, do either of you know of any drug or drugs that Miss Silverstone might have indulged in?'

Sandra shook her head vehemently. 'Milly didn't like drugs. She didn't even smoke.' She sobbed. 'She was full of life—full of life.'

Carl Petersen, his face still ashen, spoke hesitantly. 'I didn't know her very well,' he said, 'but she didn't appear the type.'

'Ah well,' said the doctor, terminating his interrogation. 'The inspector will be here shortly. It'll be for him to decide whether an inquest is necessary or not.'

Sergeant Bonifay entered the office once again and reported that the pot and cup had been washed up. It was impossible to say which had been used from the dozens of identical cups and pots in the cupboards. He described the lunch served to Thelonius Kapp, which corresponded to Sandra Kapp's description. Those plates and cutlery had been washed and put away also.

The doctor nodded. He asked no further questions and a tense silence descended on the room. Donaghue motioned to Clothilde to speak to him outside and quickly left the office. Mark Kingsford and Fiona MacKinley were standing in the walkway close to the office door.

'It's unbelievable,' Mark was saying to Fiona. 'Kapp kicks the bucket and then his wife's hairdresser does the same thing—makes you wonder.'

'Do you think they were having an affair—a double suicide?' suggested Fiona.

'Can't see it myself. If you were married to a woman like Salome would you be interested in a feather-brained thing like that hairdresser? Poor kid,' he added graciously as an afterthought.

Fiona looked at Mark stonily. 'Love has no criteria,' she said caustically.

'But what a scoop,' said Mark excitedly. 'What if it works out that their deaths are not natural? Suicide or murder, it'll make a good story and we're here on the spot.'

'We'll have to talk to Mrs Kapp,' said Fiona. 'When she's in a fit state to talk.'

'*I'll* have to talk to her,' said Mark. 'You seem to have forgotten, Fiona, that this is my assignment.'

'OK,' said Fiona reluctantly. 'You do the talking, I'll do the pictures.'

Donaghue, unable to avoid overhearing the conversation, turned to the young journalist.

'Mr Kingsford,' he said deferentially, 'I take it you will have done a bit of research on Thelonius Kapp before coming down to interview him. You'll have, perhaps, some documents of his early career—newspaper cuttings, photos, that kind of thing?'

'Of course,' said Mark. He looked at Donaghue suspiciously. 'You're not a journalist, are you?'

'Oh no, not at all,' Donaghue assured him. 'As a matter of fact I'm a private investigator. Ulysses F. Donaghue—you might have heard of me.'

'Ulysses Donaghue!' exclaimed Mark. 'Are you Ulysses Donaghue? Goodness me. I imagined someone...'

'Taller?' suggested Donaghue. 'It's curious how people always expect private investigators to be tall, Hollywood types in trenchcoats. You can see now that Hollywood does not in any way reflect reality.'

'Every journalist on Fleet Street has heard of you,' gushed Mark. 'You're considered a quite extraordinary fount of knowledge.'

'I have a capacity for retaining seemingly trivial details,' said Donaghue modestly, 'and am happy to share what data I have accumulated in my memory bank with others. Would you happen to have some of the aforementioned documentation with you? I am in the employment of Mrs Kapp's mother and the documents you have might help me in my investigation.'

'Really?' said Mark, his eyes lighting up at the possibility of a second story. 'Perhaps we could work together, Mr Donaghue. If they discover that the deaths are suicide or murder, that is. There'll be a story behind them if they are.'

'Undoubtedly,' agreed Donaghue.

'Of course, even if they're natural deaths it'll still make great copy. Thelonius Kapp dying at the inaugural retreat of his abbey. What he himself calls his spiritual monument becoming his tomb—it's a great story.'

'But an even greater one if he's committed suicide or been murdered, eh?' said Donaghue.

'Would your investigation for Mrs Kapp's mother have anything to do with Kapp himself?' asked Mark.

'I really don't know,' said Donaghue. 'I haven't actually started the investigation yet. As a matter of fact I'm on holiday —but it may have, it may well have. If I come across anything that may be of interest to the press I'll pass it over to you—you can be assured of that.'

'Thank you, Mr. Donaghue,' said Mark enthusiastically. He held out a tanned hand. 'I'll go and dig out those cuttings for you. They'll be ready when you want to look at them.'

Mark and Fiona disappeared into the guests' cloister and Donaghue turned to Clothilde who had emerged from the office and was waiting to speak to him.

'Clothilde,' he said. 'Can I ask of you a service?'

'Of course, Ulysses,' said Clothilde.

'Can you keep a particularly careful eye on that young woman?' He indicated the office door with a nod of his shaggy head. 'Mrs Kapp, I mean, of course. She is, I believe, in great danger.'

'Really?' said Clothilde. 'Are you sure about that, Ulysses?'

'I'm fairly sure,' said Donaghue gravely.

'Do you think that the girl, Milly Whatsername, was murdered then?'

'Nothing will be sure until the coroner gives his report,' said Donaghue. 'But I'm almost sure what that report will be. When her husband's body has been removed perhaps you could suggest sleeping in her cell with her. Would you mind doing that?'

'You think it's as grave as that?'

'I do,' said Donaghue. 'I think it may be even graver. At no time must she be left alone.'

At that moment the shadow of a large bulk fell over them and Clothilde turned to find standing behind her her old friend, Chief Inspector Henri Joly of Hyères Commissariat. The two embraced, kissing each other on the cheek as the French do. Donaghue held out a stubby hand to the inspector.

The inspector's large, bovine face broke into a smile at the sight of the little detective. He had know Donaghue for many years, having dined with him on several occasions at Clothilde's home in the village. Donaghue had, from time to time, helped with one of his local enquiries.

'I am very happy to see you,' he exclaimed, clapping Donaghue on the back and shaking his hand vigorously. 'With you here we'll get this business over in half the time.'

Inspector Joly's joy was genuine. At the moment that he had received the call from the abbey he had been in the process of packing his suitcases for a long-awaited trip to his sister's farm in Brittany. With the English detective's help he might only have to delay his holiday by a couple of days.

He finished shaking Donaghue's hand and his broad face resumed its habitually bland expression.

'Can you take me to Dr Mons,' he said. 'I believe we have two suspicious deaths on our hands.' He looked around at the ancient walls of the abbey cloister and sighed. 'And in such a beautiful place, on such a beautiful day.'

PART THREE

SIXTEEN

An investigation begins

TWO HOURS AFTER the bodies had been removed to the police mortuary, Inspector Joly, sitting in the Mother Superior's office, received the pathologist's report: in both cases cardiac arrest due to arsenic poisoning. In Kapp's case the arsenic had been supplemented by a cocktail of powerful drugs which could possibly have killed him without the aid of the arsenic but almost certainly the arsenic had been the mortal element. The inspector made notes as he listened.

The only other person in the office with the inspector was Donaghue. The Mother Superior had given them the use of her office as it contained the only telephone in the abbey. She herself had returned to her cell in the nuns' cloister to pray for the souls of the two dead people.

Clothilde had accompanied Sandra Kapp back to her cell. The girl had appeared reluctant to return to the place where her husband had lain dead but as there were no empty cells she had no choice. She accepted with great relief Clothilde's suggestion that she sleep with her in the cell.

The inspector finished writing and put the receiver down.

'Cocaine, LSD, Ecstasy, opium, cannabis, amphetamines and a nice little box filled with arsenic.'

'Powder?' queried Donaghue.

'Mixed with cocaine. Not a mixture I would have chosen—a painful way to go, arsenic. I suppose his liver was hardened to the others and he added the arsenic to make sure that the deadly cocktail worked.'

'So you assume it was suicide?' Donaghue asked.

'There's nothing to suggest otherwise. It's hardly likely that a murderer would leave the arsenic there for everyone to see.'

'There was some white powder,' Donaghue reflected. 'I assumed it was cocaine. There wasn't much.'

'Enough, so the forensics say, to kill everybody in the abbey. Come to think of it, I remember seeing one of those boxes filled with white powder. I, like you, assumed it was cocaine.'

'You say it was filled,' said Donaghue. 'I could have sworn it was almost empty.'

'There were dozens of small boxes on the table. You probably looked at another one.'

'There were twelve.' said Donaghue. 'Only one contained white powder.'

'Well, full or not,' said the inspector, 'it was arsenic not cocaine and it killed him—and the girl too, though how she got it into her system is a mystery. They must have done it together—a pact of some kind.'

'I'm not so sure of that,' said Donaghue. He recounted briefly Mrs Trescott's visit to his office in London and her fears for her daughter's safety.

'So you think,' said the inspector, perplexed, 'that Sandra Kapp was meant to die in place of the girl—but if she'd wanted to commit suicide with him she would have done so.' Then the light of understanding dawned on the inspector's broad face. 'Ah, of course, that's it. They planned a double suicide—hence the note. She must have put the arsenic in her tea, fallen asleep and the girl drank her tea instead.'

'Does one have forty winks before committing suicide? I hardly think so,' said Donaghue. 'There are things that somehow just don't fit in all this. I think the possibility of foul play should be investigated.'

'You seriously think that this could be a case of murder?' said the inspector with disappointment. He looked regretfully at Donaghue. 'I suppose I should consider what you have to say. You do have quite remarkable prowess in your field, after all.'

Donaghue inclined his untidy head modestly. 'I have had a number of successes to my credit,' he said.

'Well,' said the inspector glumly, 'I'll bow to your successful English—or should I say Irish?—intuition. We'll investigate the possibility of murder. If it is murder there would, of course, have to be a motive. Have you any ideas on that score?'

'The general motives for murder are money, passion and psychosis. In my opinion people murder most commonly for money, less commonly from passion and only very rarely from mental derangement. In Kapp's case the motive could be all three. He was a wealthy man who, in his lifetime, had had many passionate love affairs and, from what I know of him, caused a great deal of emotional trauma in both his private and his professional life. As for the girl, I would strongly suspect that her death was in some way connected with his—how, I'm not sure. But first of all I think we should speak to the novice who was on duty during and after lunch. Whoever it was, she will have served dinner to Kapp in his cell and served the pot of tea to Milly Silverstone.'

The inspector pushed the button on the desk that would summon the service novice from the kitchen. The girl appeared within a few seconds. She was the plump and bespectacled novice who had served the guests at breakfast.

'Please be so good as to bring us the duty roster,' the inspector asked.

The novice indicated a sheet pinned to the wall behind his head. He turned to look at it.

'Sunday 11 a.m. to 1 p.m.: Novice Sister Veronique and Novice Sister Marie Pierre. 1 p.m. to 4 p.m.: Novice Sister Veronique and Novice Sister Dominique,' he read aloud.

'Would you be so good as to send Novice Sister Veronique to this office,' he said addressing the duty novice. Then he added, 'On the authority of your Mother Superior I am to inform you that, for the purposes of this enquiry, you may answer any questions I or Mr Donaghue here might put to you.'

The girl looked nervously from one to the other and quickly left the office. Five minutes later came a knock at the office door and another novice tentatively entered. Donaghue recognized her as the pretty young thing he'd seen in the vegetable tunnel that morning and who had served lunch at midday.

'Novice Sister Veronique?' enquired Inspector Joly.

The pretty novice shook her head.

'You may tell us your name,' said the inspector coaxingly. 'You may speak.'

'I'm Novice Sister Marie Pierre,' the girl said. Her French, Donaghue noticed, was, like his own, English-accented.

'Are you English?' he asked.

She nodded.

'Which part of England are you from?'

'London.'

The inspector addressed the girl. 'It's marked on the roster Novice Sister Veronique and Novice Sister Dominique for the after-lunch session. Sister Veronique is, I take it, the novice who served lunch with you from twelve till one? The novice with a rather spotty complexion?'

'Yes.'

'And Sister Dominique, who is she?'

'One of the novices who served at breakfast.'

'The tall one or the shorter one?'

'The tall one.'

'Sister Veronique's name is marked on the roster for the session from one to four. Why have you come in her place?'

'She asked me to do her duty for her, so I did.'

The girl coughed nervously placing a slender hand in front of her mouth, the gesture drawing the attention of the two men to her perfectly symmetrical face which, though devoid of all make-up and artifice, was quite remarkably beautiful, the skin pearly, the full lips deep red. The green eyes looked anxiously back at the admiring men.

And how, Donaghue wondered to himself, had this Sister Veronique communicated her wish? Was she, perhaps, the second illicit talker in the greenhouse tunnel? This girl, he reflected, was obviously worried that her breach of the rule of silence might be found out.

Donaghue smiled, hoping to put her at ease.

'So you were on duty in the kitchen from eleven o'clock to four?' the inspector asked, speaking to her in English.

'Yes,' she said, nodding her pretty head.

'With Sister Veronique until one and Sister Dominique until four?'

'Yes.'

'Lunch had been prepared when?'

'Between eleven and twelve.'

'By whom?'

'By myself and Sister Veronique.'

'And you served according to demand from the menu?'

'Yes.'

'Was there any occasion when you both left the kitchen?'

'Yes, when we were serving in the dining-room.'

'As far as you know did any of the guests leave the dining-room during the meal?'

'No, not as far as I remember.'

'So you served the lunches, washed up and put away the dishes?'

She nodded.

'Did you wash up alone?'

'No, with Sister Dominique.'

'At some point a novice was called out to serve lunch to Mr Kapp in his cell, isn't that so?'

'Yes, that's so.'

'Who took it to him?'

'I prepared it, Sister Dominique took it.'

'At approximately what time?'

'At about 2.30—maybe a little later. I'm not sure of the exact time.'

'Did any other guests call you?'

She shook her head then said, 'Yes, Dr Renoir called me once to bring some water for his wife.'

'And after the death of Mr Kapp?'

'I had to go to the cell and clean the sink where Mrs Kapp had been sick, and then I was asked to take a pot of tea to Mrs Kapp in cell number seven.'

'Did you prepare the tea yourself?'

'No, Sister Dominique prepared it and I took it.'

'And washed up the pot and cups afterwards?'

'Yes.'

'When you fetched the tray of tea things did you notice whether the cup had been used?'

The girl looked surprised at the question.

'I didn't notice. I supposed it had.'

'So some of the tea had been drunk?'

'I suppose it had.'

'You're not sure?'

'I didn't take much notice. The tea would have been cold by then anyway, so I took it away.'

'Listen carefully, Sister Marie Pierre—when you fetched the tea things, was Mrs Kapp sleeping?'

'Yes, I think she was. Yes, she was—I remember I was careful to be quiet.'

'And Miss Silverstone, was she sleeping?'

The girl hesitated, creasing her brow in reflection.

'No, of course she wasn't. She smiled at me when I walked in. She was watching Mrs Kapp.'

'She didn't appear ill or anything?'

'Ill? No, she didn't appear ill.'

'One more question—did any of the guests enter the kitchen at any time during your afternoon duty?'

The girl frowned. 'Only one, I think—the blonde woman. Madame Parmentier, I think she's called. She came for water.'

'At what time?'

'I don't know—about 3.15, I suppose. Sister Dominique was making the tea for Mrs Kapp when she came in.'

'Well,' said Inspector Joly. 'I have no more questions. What about you, Mr Donaghue?'

'Tell me,' said Donaghue, smiling at the girl, 'what made you become a nun?'

The girl blushed, averting her eyes from Donaghue's gaze.

'I don't know. I felt it was the only thing I wanted to do. I've always wanted to be a nun.'

'A vocation?' said Donaghue. 'A calling from God?'

'There can't be any other reason,' said the girl simply. She coughed quietly in embarrassment.

'That's all, Sister Marie Pierre,' said Donaghue. 'You can go now.'

'Curious that such a beautiful young woman should reject the material world,' said the inspector when the door had closed behind her, 'and the world of men,' he added regretfully. 'Still, a vocation's a vocation... So, the Silverstone girl was still alive when she fetched the tea things. Of course she could have just drunk the tea and died five minutes later. Arsenic in powder form—if that's what she took—takes longer to have effect. The question is, if the arsenic was in the tea—and it couldn't have been in anything else—how did it get there? The only guest to enter the kitchen was Madame Parmentier—and at the time the tea was being prepared. We'll have to look into that. Perhaps the other novices—what were their names?' He consulted his notes.

'Sister Veronique and Sister Dominique—perhaps they might
have something to say.'

He pressed the buzzer and the plump duty novice promptly
returned.

'Please send Novice Sister Veronique to us,' he instructed her.

Donaghue sat reflectively rubbing his fingers along his chin as
was his habit when deep in thought.

After ten minutes the plump novice knocked once more on
the office door.

'I can't find Sister Veronique,' she said. 'She's supposed to
be in the chapel for Vespers but she isn't there. It's very un-
usual.'

HALF AN HOUR LATER, after Vespers, the rule of silence among
the small community of nuns was temporarily broken. The
Mother Superior, her face etched into a frown, sent nuns and
novices hither and thither searching for the missing Sister Veronique. She had been last seen at four o'clock working in the
vineyard. The nun in whose row of vines she had been working
remembered looking up when the bell tower struck four and noticing the novice at the end of the row. After that she had kept
her eyes on her work and she hadn't noticed the novice leave.

The Mother Superior was sitting in her office in a state of
great agitation discussing the girl's disappearance with Donaghue
and Inspector Joly when the plump duty novice opened the door
without knocking and said in a shrill, stricken voice, 'We've
found her—in the wine press. She's dead. Her head's crushed.'

The Mother Superior stood up, turned white then promptly
fainted, dropping into Donaghue's arms as she fell.

IN THE OUTBUILDING that housed the wine press Donaghue and
Inspector Joly gazed sombrely at the gruesome sight of the young
novice, Sister Veronique, whose body was bent over the tub of
the press, her head crushed by the large circular wooden weight
that under normal circumstances was used to crush the grapes in
the tub. As soon as the photographs of the grisly spectacle were
taken, Sergeant Bonifay and Inspector Joly raised the heavy circular weight and the girl's body was lifted from the tub by two
ashen-faced nuns and laid on the floor of the press room. Don-

aghue peered into the wooden tub whose slats, already stained dark from the pressing of innumerable grapes, were splattered now with the reddish brown patches of the novice's blood. Something white caught his eye at the bottom of the tub. He had to bend over on the tips of his toes to reach it. Inspector Joly, who, along with Sergeant Bonifay, was straining to keep the heavy weight aloft, said gruffly, 'For goodness' sake, Donaghue, get a move on or we'll have another case of a crushed head on our hands—this thing's bloody heavy.'

Donaghue quickly retrieved the object, which turned out to be nothing more than a piece of plain white card, and the two policemen lowered the wooden weight with great relief into the tub.

Inspector Joly instructed the Mother Superior to lock the press building after their departure as nothing was to be touched until the forensic experts arrived. He would arrange for a doctor and ambulance to take the dead girl back to the abbey.

On their way back along the narrow gravel path that led from the press building to the abbey, Inspector Joly's face was grim.

'To all intents and purposes it looks like an accident,' he said. 'There appears no evidence of foul play—though how anybody could have been so stupid as to stick their head in the tub with that great wooden weight up on the shaft is beyond me. What I don't understand is why the weight was up on the shaft at all. Surely they'd leave it down in the tub when the press is not in use?'

'I put that to the Mother Superior,' said Donaghue. 'There is a simple explanation. The first crop of grapes were due to be crushed tomorrow. The weight had been lifted up on to the shaft so that the tub could be finally cleaned and sterilized. The weight normally would be secured by the thread of the screw shaft. It had, it seems, been secured too low down on the shaft. The Mother Superior believes that the thread of the shaft had not been properly restored.'

'So it could well have been an accident,' said Joly. 'But three deaths in one day—two apparently suicide, one an accident... It smells fishy to me. I think this whole situation needs careful looking into, don't you, Mr Donaghue?'

Donaghue nodded in agreement. He appeared to be deep in thought.

'It is possible,' he said, 'that the fact that the deaths occurred in the same day is pure coincidence. But if it is not a coincidence and these three people have been murdered, then there must be a reason, a motive and, as well as that, there must be a link between the deaths. It would be hardly credible that three people were murdered separately on the same day by three different murderers.'

'No,' agreed the inspector. 'That would be hardly credible.'

'Nevertheless,' said Donaghue, 'in my experience even the seemingly impossible cannot be ruled out until the facts of the matter have been ascertained.'

'Facts,' said the inspector. 'What facts are there? A man dies after taking arsenic—to all intents and purposes a suicide. He leaves a note saying "we died", implying a suicide pact. Half an hour later a young girl in the employ of his wife dies of arsenic poisoning too. From those facts anybody would be led to believe that the two had had an affair and decided to take their lives together. Then, some time later, in the same afternoon, a novice of the abbey is found dead in the wine press—accidentally, or so it seems, trapped by the press which has fallen on top of her. It might be as simple as that, pure coincidence.'

'I don't think it's as simple as that,' said Donaghue. 'And neither do you, Inspector.'

'No, I don't,' said the inspector gruffly. He put a finger to his large bulbous nose. 'As I said before, something smells bad here.'

'The first thing we must do,' said Donaghue as they approached the Mother Superior's office, 'is find out what the girl was doing at the wine press—whether working in the press was part of the afternoon's work.'

The Mother Superior looked distressfully at the two men.

'Really, really, this is most upsetting,' she said.

'Mother Superior,' said Inspector Joly kindly, 'please be so good as to tell us if working in the wine press was part of Sister Veronique's afternoon duty. In other words, was she meant to be there in the middle of the afternoon?'

The Mother Superior consulted the daily roster.

'Well, no,' she said. 'She was marked down for duty in the refectory until four. After that she was to have worked in the library until Vespers at six o'clock.'

'It seems she asked the novice, Sister Marie Pierre, to take her place in the refectory,' said the inspector. 'Sister Marie Pierre told us that herself.'

'Really?' exclaimed the Mother Superior. 'That is most irregular. I was, of course, not aware of that.'

'Can you think of any reason why she would have wanted to change places with the other novice?'

The Mother Superior shook her head worriedly. 'None at all.'

'And Sister Marie Pierre—where would she normally have worked had she not changed places with Sister Veronique?'

The Mother Superior consulted the roster again.

'She would have been working in the vineyards—you know we are very busy picking this year's grapes.'

'Would that work have involved entering the wine press?'

'Not the wine press itself, not just yet. The grapes are first taken to the processing room adjoining the press to be cleaned. We have not yet started the wine-making process.'

'So there was in fact no reason for her to be there this afternoon. Could she have wandered in from curiosity?' Donaghue asked.

'That is possible,' said the Mother Superior. 'She studied viticulture before coming here, and she is a new novice. She will not yet have acquired the self-discipline of the older novices or nuns.' She smiled. 'We learn to master such dangerous habits as curiosity.'

Donaghue studied the Mother Superior's bird-like face. A woman of great moral strength, he thought, and great single-mindedness.

'Mother Superior,' said Inspector Joly, 'the girl appears to have died accidentally. The other two people who have died appear to have taken their own lives. Nevertheless I feel that the deaths ought to be investigated.'

'Do you think they might have been murdered?' asked the Mother Superior incredulously.

'I think that that possibility should be considered, if only to be eliminated.'

'But why should anyone want to murder a novice? What possible motive could they have?'

'Aye, there's the rub,' said Donaghue softly.

The Mother Superior blushed a pale shade of pink. 'She wasn't attacked...sexually, was she?'

'That didn't appear to be the case,' said the inspector. 'The police surgeon, when he arrives, will determine the nature of the injuries. If it is the case, perhaps she was attacked by someone from outside—from the village, for instance, or by one of the guests. Is it possible that anyone could get into the abbey grounds from outside?'

'Not during a retreat,' said the Mother Superior. 'When we are not on retreat we are open to visits from the public—tourists, walkers, et cetera—but on retreat we naturally do not wish our guests to have their tranquillity disturbed by tourists so we lock the main gates. The grounds are enclosed by high walls and anyone coming in during the day would be seen by the nuns working in the fields.'

'It's possible to scale the walls,' said Donaghue, 'but I think it's highly unlikely that anyone's come in from outside.'

'You think it's someone in the abbey,' said the inspector. 'One of the nuns or the guests?'

'That's far more likely.'

'It really couldn't be a nun,' declared the Mother Superior vehemently. 'We interview our novices and nuns very carefully. They are all girls and women with true vocations. Really, Inspector, I'm sure that this novice's death is the result of a very unfortunate accident. The wine press has been badly restored. I was never in agreement with Mr Kapp that we use the old press. In my opinion it should have been destroyed long ago and a new one installed but he insisted on restoring the abbey exactly as it was before. He wanted us to make wine as they did five hundred years ago—a romantic but foolish notion, and one that has resulted in the death of a young novice.'

The Mother Superior's face flushed in anger. It was evident to Donaghue that the Mother Superior had bowed very unwillingly to the caprices of Mr Thelonius Kapp.

'You are probably absolutely correct,' said Inspector Joly graciously, 'but to set our suspicious minds at rest, we would be most grateful if you would avail us of a room where we might interview the guests and nuns—if you will give us your permission to do so, that is.'

'Well...yes...you may talk to the nuns,' she agreed somewhat reluctantly. 'But please make sure that the novices in particular keep their answers succinct. We don't want them getting back into the habit of conversation.'

'Of course,' the inspector concurred.

'You may retain the use of my office,' she said, rising to her feet. 'You'll need the telephone, I imagine—and if you need a second room you can use the library.'

'Excellent,' said the inspector, smiling charmingly at her. 'Oh, one last thing—please be so good as to furnish us with a list of the nuns and novices and of the present guests.'

The Mother Superior did so immediately, drawing the requested lists from a drawer in her desk.

'I'll leave you to your investigation,' she said as she opened the office door. She glanced at her watch. 'It's almost dinner time. I take it you'll want to start after the meal?'

The inspector nodded. He looked glumly over at Donaghue. 'Shall we go to eat?' he said. 'I'm not looking forward to the task of telling the guests that a third death has occurred. They're going to panic and want to pack their bags immediately and leave.'

SEVENTEEN

Who is the lion, who is the hind?

A TROUBLED SILENCE reigned in the refectory during dinner. The diners ate tentatively as if fearful that each mouthful might contain a deadly dose of arsenic. Only Donaghue and Inspector Joly ate the delicious daube with relish. Inspector Joly had taken Clothilde's place beside Donaghue, Clothilde having decided to dine with Sandra in her cell. The girl, during the afternoon, had become increasingly agitated and distressed.

An extra place had been set at the end of Donaghue's table for Carl Petersen who was now without table partners.

Thérèse Mendes France welcomed the new guest with a sanctimonious smile and said, inexplicably, 'Things must be very difficult for you at the moment, Mr Kapp.'

Petersen looked at her in puzzlement. 'My name is Petersen,' he said.

The colour of Miss Mendes France's face rose very slightly.

'Of course, of course—do forgive me. Whatever made me say that?'

The expression on Lady Bonnington's face conveyed exactly what she thought was behind Miss Mendes France's *faux pas*: senility, she was thinking, senility, you silly old woman.

Lady Carter Bonnington, on the other hand, appeared to accept the American's presence benignly as if he satisfied her criteria of what constituted an acceptable human being to eat with at table. Petersen ate in a distracted silence, his mind, apparently, elsewhere. Lady Carter Bonnington, stunning in a simple green sheath dress, glanced appraisingly now and again at the troubled young man.

Donaghue amused himself by trying to decide whether the colour of Lady Bonnington's eyes was real or not. He knew that eye colour could be changed quite simply by the insertion of

coloured contact lenses. As everything else about Lady Bonnington was refurbished, why not her eyes as well?

The Lady's wrinkle-free grey eyes were immaculately made
up. They were, he decided, on comparison with the grey of Carl
Petersen's eyes, perhaps her only real feature. Coloured lenses,
he had been told, were often of a false brilliance.

Lady Bonnington, aware of Donaghue's interest in her, cast
an irritated look in his direction and a disapproving one at Inspector Joly who was tucking into his daube appreciatively beside Donaghue.

She doesn't like us, Donaghue reflected. Perhaps she only
liked young men—handsome clean-cut young men like the
American of whom she clearly approved. Lady Carter Bonnington, he decided, was a snob.

Donaghue lifted a succulent morsel of beef to his lips but the
meat rested on the fork. Deep down in his IDR—his Irrelevant
Data Reserve—something stirred, a minute linking of synapses.
The image of Thelonius Kapp's face in death flashed into his
mind: the finely chiselled features, the black eyes, furious in
death, that the doctor had had to close. Furious—Thelonius Kapp
had been furious when he died, and the words he had uttered in
the church had been uttered in fury. *Come away, come away
death, fly away, fly away breath.* The origin of the words suddenly came to him, a verse from *Twelfth Night.* Silently he repeated the verse in its entirety and when he had finished he knew
what Thelonius Kapp had been trying to say as his life ebbed
away from him—a message that his violent and painful death
had prevented him from communicating. And Donaghue knew
from the unspoken message that Thelonius Kapp had not taken
his own life—that he had in fact been murdered.

Donaghue's thinking suddenly switched into reverse gear. He
had been, not on the wrong track, but travelling in the wrong
direction. He had to go back, back to those other words that had
niggled at him since Mrs Trescott's visit: *the lion and the hind.*
The question he had to find an answer to was, Who was the lion
and who was the hind?

That question would be answered, he was sure, when they
questioned Sandra Kapp.

He finished his meal in reflective silence.

As soon as the coffee cups had been cleared away, this time

by the plump bespectacled duty novice and the tall, beautiful
Sister Dominique, Inspector Joly rose and addressed the guests.

'It is my sad duty,' he said gravely, 'to inform you that a third
death has occurred in the abbey today.'

A gasp arose from among the guests.

'A tragic accident—a young novice was killed in the old wine
press. The Mother Superior asks you to avoid going near the
press building as the apparatus is evidently very dangerous.'

Adèle Bloch rose to her feet.

'Well,' she said, a note of hysteria ringing in her voice, 'I for
one, am not staying another minute in this...this mortuary. I'm
leaving immediately.'

'I am in agreement with Mrs Bloch,' said Dr Renoir, rising to
his feet. 'I think the retreat should end now and the guests leave.
I brought my wife here for three days of tranquillity and serenity
and all she has been subjected to is death—not an environment
usually recommended for pregnant women.'

'Dr Renoir is right,' said Lady Carter Bonnington. 'It really
isn't possible to enjoy a retreat with people dying all around
you.'

Carl Petersen spoke worriedly.

'Mrs Kapp should be taken away from the abbey as soon as
possible,' he said. 'And I will have to make arrangements for
the bodies of Mr Kapp and Miss Silverstone to be flown back to
the States. I agree, the retreat should be brought to an end.'

Mireille Parmentier, at the third table, lifted her blonde head
and spoke in an astonishingly beautiful throaty voice. Everybody
in the room turned to look at her fraught, beautiful face.

'I am surprised,' she said, 'that a doctor like Dr Renoir should
be intimidated by death. Death is, after all, a part of everybody's
life, particularly that of a doctor.' She smiled sweetly over at Dr
Renoir. 'I see no reason why the retreat should be ended because
one or two people are squeamish about death. Having paid handsomely for this retreat I intend to finish it.'

Nobody spoke for a moment or so—they had evidently been
impressed by the authoritative tone of Madame Parmentier's
beautiful voice. Then Lady Carter Bonnington spoke indignantly.

'Squeamish?' she said. 'I don't call it squeamish to be just a
little concerned when people are dropping dead round you like
flies.'

Maximilian Bloch lifted a hand to speak, much in the manner of a schoolboy in class. He looked around at his fellow diners.

'It's quite simple,' he said. 'Those who wish to leave may leave and those who wish to stay may stay.' He smiled brightly at the simple logic of his statement. 'I myself intend to stay—if my good wife is agreeable, of course.' He patted his wife's hand as he spoke.

A restrained cough emanated from Inspector Joly, who was still standing behind Donaghue's table.

'As a matter of fact,' the Inspector intoned apologetically, 'it is not quite as simple as that. We are obliged to conduct an investigation into the deaths that have occurred and must consequently ask all those present at the retreat to remain in the abbey until the investigation has been carried out. In my capacity as Chief Inspector of Police of the Commune of Hyères, I have to ask you not to go beyond the boundaries of the abbey's grounds until I say otherwise.'

A murmur of dissent rose from the seated guests. Lady Carter Bonnington tutted in annoyance and Dr Renoir frowned crossly but no further argument was made.

The guests rose and filed out of the refectory. Carl Petersen was the last to rise from his seat. He turned to Inspector Joly before leaving.

'Have you any idea, Inspector, how long your investigation is likely to last? You will appreciate that as Mr Kapp's secretary I have a great many matters to see to—arrangements for the funeral, legal matters, et cetera.'

'Of course, of course I appreciate that,' said Inspector Joly deferentially. 'We will do our best, I assure you, to keep the proceedings as short as possible.'

'May I ask,' Petersen said politely, 'what exactly you are investigating? Two suicides and one accident—do you have any evidence that the deaths may have been otherwise?'

'Oh no,' Inspector Joly reassured him. 'We simply have to eliminate any other possibility, that's all. It's only a matter of routine.'

'So you don't think you'll be more than a day or so?'

'I shouldn't think so,' the inspector assured him cheerfully. 'And I bloody well hope not,' he muttered under his breath.

Petersen smiled in relief, his perfectly straight teeth showing up white against the burgeoning tan of his pale face. It was the first time that Donaghue had seen him smile. Petersen was a handsome man, he noted, when he smiled.

'A serious young man,' Inspector Joly commented as he watched the tall American stride out of the refectory on his long legs. 'Takes his duties seriously—rare nowadays in the young.'

'How old would you say he was?' Donaghue asked.

'Thirty, I'd say,' said the inspector. 'Could be older—got that eternally youthful look.' He added rather glumly, 'Seems to be an American characteristic. Look at their Presidents—look like Boy Scouts, all of them. That Lady Whatsername took a shine to him, I noticed. We French...' The inspector patted his ample midriff as he spoke. '...tend to paunchiness in middle age—too much good wine and food, I suppose, but at least we die enjoying our food. You can't really *enjoy* a hamburger, can you?'

Donaghue shook his head in concurrence.

'Well,' said the inspector breezily, looking at his watch. 'It's 8.45. There's nothing much we can do this late in the day. I've booked a room at the village inn. I think I'll go back and get an early night—give the old brain cells a chance to mull this business over. I'll be back bright and early in the morning.'

'I think I'll have a word with Mrs Kapp if she's agreeable,' said Donaghue. 'And after that I have a little personal research to do. I think tomorrow we might see this sorry situation in a completely different light.'

EIGHTEEN

Donaghue investigates

DONAGHUE, ON OPENING the door to the Kapps' cell, was surprised to see Dr Renoir bending over Sandra Kapp.

Clothilde pulled Donaghue to one side and whispered, 'I called Dr Renoir for a second opinion. I examined the girl earlier. She's been in a terribly fraught state—unable to eat, and she has vomited yet again.'

'Oh dear,' said Donaghue. He frowned. 'Have you left her alone at any time since her husband's death?'

'No,' said Clothilde. 'I haven't left her side. As a matter of fact she's slept most of the afternoon.'

Dr Renoir, having finished his examination, stood up, smiled down at Sandra Kapp and said, 'It's as Dr Blanche thought. You are pregnant, Mrs Kapp—about eight weeks, I'd say.'

Sandra Kapp looked up at him, an expression of profound relief on her face.

'It didn't occur to me,' she said. 'I thought...I thought...'

'You thought perhaps you'd been poisoned,' said Dr Renoir. 'I'm afraid you're not the only one who's had the same fear. Well, in your case it's nothing untoward—a perfectly healthy sickness. Perhaps you caught it from my wife.' He tittered at his little joke and Sandra managed a weak smile.

'Well, I'd best be off to my own pregnant lady,' said the doctor. 'Try to eat, Mrs Kapp—just a little, or at least take some vitamins. You'll find the sickness will ease off after a while.'

The doctor left and Sandra sat up on the bed.

'I'd been terribly worried,' she said. 'It simply didn't occur to me that I might be pregnant.'

Donaghue noticed that Sandra Kapp's Lancashire burr was marked by a slight American inflexion.

'Mrs Kapp,' said Donaghue, 'please let me introduce myself.'

He bowed ceremoniously to the girl, who looked at him in surprise. 'My name is Ulysses Donaghue and I am a good friend of
Dr Blanche here. I am also a private investigator. A day or so
before leaving on holiday to come to this retreat I was paid a
visit in my London office by your mother, Mrs Trescott.'

'My mother!' said Sandra in astonishment.

'Yes, she came to see me to ask me to keep an eye on you
while you were in London.'

'Keep an eye on me! What on earth for?'

'She believed...she had a feeling that you were in some kind
of danger.'

'In danger? From what?'

'She wasn't sure. She thought perhaps from your husband.'

Sandra smiled. 'She never did like Theo,' she said. 'She
doesn't understand men like that. She's a darling, my mother,
but intrinsically working class in her attitudes.'

'I found her an admirable woman,' said Donaghue. 'One who
is guided strongly by her intuition.'

'Did she send you here to keep an eye on me?' Sandra asked.

'As a matter of fact it is pure coincidence that I'm here at the
same time as you. As I said, she asked me to watch you while
you were in London. I believe you were going to London after
this retreat? Mr Kapp was, I believe, in the process of making a
film.'

'Yes,' said Sandra her eyes filling with tears. 'Yes, he was.'

'Mrs Kapp,' said Donaghue, 'I don't wish to cause you any
undue distress but do you think you feel well enough to talk to
me? I want to ask you one or two questions relating to your
husband's death. Would it upset you at this stage to talk about
him?'

Sandra looked at Donaghue uncertainly.

'I...I... What do you want to ask me?' she stammered.

'You were, I believe, a very close couple?'

'Yes,' said Sandra. 'Yes, we were.'

'Did you have any idea that your husband might commit suicide?'

She hesitated. 'The thought had occurred to me,' she con-
fessed.

'And what was the reason? Why did you think he might contemplate suicide? He was, after all, in the middle of making a new film.'

Sandra twirled her fingers nervously in her lap. She looked sorrowfully from Clothilde to Donaghue.

'There's something nobody knows,' she said. 'Only I and his secretary know.' She hesitated before going on. 'Thelonius was suffering from Alzheimer's disease. It was diagnosed only a month ago. He was in the early stages of the illness but declining rapidly. I suppose all the drugs he took helped to speed it up. In the early stages the sufferer can be perfectly lucid and normal one day and completely confused the next. Over the last two weeks he was having more bad days than good. On a bad day he would remember nothing—not even my name—although I had the impression...' Sandra's voice trembled with emotion as she spoke. 'I had the impression—I could see it in his eyes—that he knew what he was looking at, he knew who I was—he just couldn't find the word that corresponded. It was as if part of his brain was malfunctioning like a computer when it prints out a jumble of letters. I don't think his thinking was impaired, just his ability to communicate his thoughts. It was terrible to see him like that, someone for whom communication was so vitally important.'

She looked earnestly, imploringly at Donaghue and Clothilde.

'For Theo words were of the utmost importance. His life's work was to seek to communicate with others through his films. He wrote all the screenplays for them himself. You can't imagine how awful it was to see him turning into a gibbering moron. And the awful thing is—I know he knew what was happening to him. That was the worst.'

She buried her head in her hands and wept.

'He couldn't bear to live like that, he couldn't bear it.'

'Mrs Kapp,' said Donaghue gently, 'did you know that he had arsenic in his possession?'

Sandra Kapp looked up suddenly, the expression on her face that of a frightened startled deer.

'I had no idea,' she said. 'No idea.'

'Did you ever partake of your husband's drugs, Mrs Kapp?' Donaghue asked.

'I...I...' She looked at her interlocutor cautiously. 'Very

rarely,' she said. 'Now and again—to please him. A joint perhaps or a line of cocaine—nothing heavier than that.'

'He kept his cocaine in a small, round, black leather box, didn't he?'

She looked at him in surprise.

'I think that's where he kept it. I can't really remember. He had so many snuff boxes. He collected them.'

'Mrs Kapp, before leaving for the Gregorian chant in the chapel this afternoon, did you partake of cocaine?'

She looked at him in astonishment. 'As a matter of fact we did. How on earth...?'

'Oh, just a guess—a little surmise on my part. Did the cocaine have the required effect? Was it pure cocaine?'

'Oh, absolutely,' said Sandra. 'Thelonius wouldn't take anything mixed. It was marvellous—it cleared my head completely. I suffer from narrow sinuses. I find cocaine clears a sinus headache.'

'It would, it would,' Donaghue concurred. 'It is a medicinal plant after all. I believe dentists used to use it to anaesthetize children's gums. Mrs Kapp,' he asked, 'do you have any idea why your hairdresser, Milly Silverstone, might have taken her life?'

A look of uncertainty once again clouded Sandra Kapp's face.

'I can't understand it,' she said. 'She had no reason—no reason.'

'Do you think she was in love with your husband and took her life in imitation of him?'

'No,' said Sandra vehemently. 'No, I'm sure she wasn't in love with him. I know that's what everyone is thinking but it isn't true. She had a boyfriend, a fiancé, back in New York. She loved life, Milly—she was full of life. I can't understand any of it.' Her face crumpled and she started to weep again.

'Has it occurred to you,' said Donaghue gently, 'that your husband intended you to die with him and that somehow Milly Silverstone died instead?'

At Donaghue's words Sandra Kapp let out a small scream. 'No,' she cried, 'no, that is not possible. He never would. He wanted me to live. He wanted me to have a child—he wouldn't want me to die.'

'But the note he left said, "we died". The thought has occurred to you, hasn't it?'

She looked at him horrified, her face pale.

Donaghue leaned forward. 'I'm going to ask you a personal
question to which, of course, you are not obliged to give me an
answer, but I would be most grateful if you would try to tell me
the absolute truth.'

Sandra nodded, regarding him warily.

'Have you recently had an affair with another man?'

Sandra looked back at him in utter perplexity.

'An affair with another man? No! Absolutely not,' she said.
'Why should I?' She gazed at Donaghue angrily. 'I loved my
husband,' she said fervently. Then she broke down, covering her
face with her hands. 'I'll never love another man as much as I
loved Theo.'

'And he wasn't, as far as you know, having an affair with
Milly Silverstone?'

The question actually made Sandra laugh through her tears.

'The idea is absurd,' she said.

'Just one or two more questions, Mrs Kapp. Did anyone enter
your cell this morning before lunch or between lunch and the
time you left for the chapel?'

'Dr Renoir came to see Theo. But apart from him no one else.'

'Did a novice fetch the doctor?'

'No, I did.'

'You left him alone?'

'Yes, but only for so long as it took to go to Dr Renoir's cell
and back.'

She stared at Donaghue. There was pain, anger and above all
confusion written large in her eyes.

'You think someone murdered him, don't you?' she said. 'I
don't understand any of it,' she said, sobbing. 'All I know is...'

'What do you know?' Donaghue asked gently.

'All I know is...I loved my husband and now I'm afraid.'

'What are you afraid of, Mrs Kapp?'

'I don't know. I feel...I feel...vulnerable without Theo. I feel
afraid. My mother's intuition is right. I feel terrified to be on my
own.'

'Don't worry, Mrs Kapp,' said Clothilde kindly. 'I'll stay with
you if you'd like me to.'

Sandra smiled at the older woman gratefully.

'I have one more question, Mrs Kapp,' said Donaghue. 'Can you give me the name of your husband's lawyer?'

'Yes, it's Hoffman and Stromberg in Manhattan—Carl has the address. I've never actually had any dealings with his lawyers.'

'Did your husband leave a will?'

'Before we married he had made a will leaving his money for a film foundation. When we married he changed it. He left everything to me and asked me to use part of it for the maintenance of this abbey and on his death, if we had no children, to create the foundation.'

'Was the condition part of the will?'

'No, he trusted me.'

'Well, thank you for allowing me to speak to you,' said Donaghue, rising to leave. 'I hope my questions have not upset you too much.'

'No,' said Sandra, her eyes now dry of tears. 'I think it did me good to talk.'

DONAGHUE WANDERED slowly back to his cell. He wasn't sure to what extent Sandra Kapp had told him the absolute truth but she had been truthful about two things—of that he was sure. She was speaking the truth when she said that she had loved her husband and she was speaking the truth when she said she was afraid.

As he opened his cell door he saw Mark Kingsford and Fiona MacKinley hurrying along the colonnade towards him. Mark thrust a sheaf of folders into his hands.

'Those documents you wanted, Mr Donaghue,' he said. 'Hope they'll be useful to you.' He was holding Fiona's hand in his. 'We're off for a spooky walk in the grounds—in the dark.' He pulled a ghoulish face. 'We want to soak up the atmosphere a bit. "Death in the abbey"—makes a good headline, don't you think?'

'I think it's all a bit scary,' said Fiona, shivering involuntarily. She pushed her shoulder up against Mark's arm. 'I'll be glad when we can leave.'

'Don't worry, Fiona,' said Mark, his voice deepening to a Hollywood baritone. 'I'll protect you.' He placed a comforting arm around her shoulder. 'No harm will come to you while Mark Kingsford is around. Personally I'm pleased that the inspector has decided to investigate these deaths. There's something decidedly fishy going on here and I want to find out what it is and be the first to get it into the headlines. Come along, Fiona,' he said cheerfully, pulling the girl along behind him, 'let's go and see if we can come across a murderer in action.'

Fiona giggled and Donaghue smiled as he entered his cell. He placed the pile of papers that Mark had given him on the table. He quickly flicked through the first folder, which was marked on the outside with the dates 1945-60. Inside were cuttings from newspapers as far back as 1950 when Kapp was beginning his career as a director. There were several pictures of Kapp as a young man. Donaghue picked up one close-up photograph and studied it thoughtfully: Kapp with hair—dark brown hair, not black as he would have expected from a man with black eyes. Did Europeans have black eyes? Perhaps Kapp had worn contact lenses—now, there was a thought. He placed the photograph back in the folder. He would study the others in detail later. First he was going to take a much-needed shower.

He rummaged in his travel bag for his towel and the Savon de Marseilles that Clothilde had given him as a present on his arrival then, closing the cell door after him, made his way up the colonnade towards the low building alongside the refectory that housed the showers.

As he was about to enter the men's section he caught sight of the white-robed figure of Brother Martin de Porres hurrying past the refectory towards the nuns' cloister. Donaghue wondered idly how a young celibate monk must feel among all those young celibate nuns and novices. A curious world we live in, he murmured to himself.

There appeared to be nobody in the showers although one cubicle door was open. He peeped inside and was profoundly shocked to see Dr Renoir sitting naked in the shower basin, his arms over his head, his white naked body curled up into the foetal position.

'Dr Renoir,' Donaghue whispered.

The doctor lifted his head. He looked up at Donaghue confusedly.

'I have to get out of this place,' he said almost imploringly.
'I think it's driving me mad.'

Donaghue lifted the doctor to his feet and wrapped his towel
around his middle.

'Why do you say that?' Donaghue asked solicitously.

'Either this abbey is a madhouse or I'm going mad myself.
Listen to this. Five minutes ago I was taking a shower—my wife
has been sick five times today and I'm reeking of the stuff. I
heard someone enter the showers and was surprised to hear my
shower door open. I turned to see that monk, the singer, standing
there at the door with his hood over his head. He looked like a
ghost and he had a knife in his hand—a scalpel, would you
believe. He held it out towards me and pointed it at
my...my...groin. He said in that falsetto voice of his, "I'm going
to butcher you the way you butchered me." Then he must have
heard you coming...' Dr Renoir hesitated. 'I was sure he was
going to lunge at me with the knife but he changed his mind and
ran off.'

'I saw him,' said Donaghue, 'heading towards the nuns' cloister.'

'It's crazy,' said Dr Renoir as he pulled on his clothes. 'As I
said, either this place is a madhouse full of homicidal maniacs
or I'm going off my head. Perhaps I imagined it. Perhaps with
all these deaths I'm becoming paranoid.'

'I saw the monk,' said Donaghue. 'You didn't imagine that.'

'But all the rest—did I imagine that he'd threatened me and
said what he'd said? He said I'd butchered him—either he's mad
or I am!'

'I can see, Dr Renoir, that you have had a troubling experience. Let me accompany you back to your cell. I think it might
be best if you lock your cell door tonight, have a good night's
sleep and wait in your cell until the inspector calls you for questioning in the morning. Then you can tell him everything that
happened.'

HAVING DEPOSITED Dr Renoir at his cell door, Donaghue hurried
back to the shower house but instead of entering the men's section he carried on past the refectory, following the direction of
the monk he had seen ten minutes earlier. Instead of entering the

nuns' cloister he turned right at the corner of the refectory and followed its long northern wall until he reached the kitchen and outhouses. In the corner of the kitchen garden stood a compost heap, barely lit by the light that came through the shutters of the kitchen window but just visible enough for Donaghue to recognize the white monk's robe that had been pushed hastily into the heap and was revealed by a flick of his brogue-clad foot. He pushed the piece of white cloth back into its hiding place and proceeded round to the south side of the refectory, passing on his way the ladies' shower entrance which was situated on the east side of the block.

Mireille Parmentier was leaving the showers as he passed. Her blonde cap of hair, darkened by moisture, clung to her head which was still wet from her shower. Smelling delightfully of an expensive eau-de-Cologne, she nodded, smiling, at Donaghue and hurried before him towards the guests' cloister. Donaghue carried on his way to the men's shower entrance and, finding the block empty, was able, at last, to take a leisurely, unhampered shower.

As he left the shower house the door to the library opposite opened and a small group of people emerged—Thérèse Mendes France, Maximilian Bloch, Carl Petersen, Olivia Carter Bonnington and finally Loic Parmentier. The last person to emerge was the monk, Brother Martin, who extinguished the light and closed the library door behind him.

'Goodnight,' he said in his soft womanish voice, 'and thank you for coming.' Then he glided quietly off towards his cell in the nuns' cloister, his white robe gleaming in the dark of the abbey walkway.

'That was quite fascinating,' Donaghue heard Lady Carter Bonnington say to Carl Petersen. Lady Carter Bonnington, Donaghue decided, had lived at some time in America. There was, as she spoke, a very slight American inflection in her otherwise aristocratic English voice. 'I had no idea that our church music came originally from the Greeks,' she went on. 'We owe those Greeks a great deal, it would seem.'

Carl Petersen muttered something in response but Donaghue didn't hear as he found himself being addressed by Thérèse Mendes France who expressed her surprise at seeing him outside as she had not seen him inside. Maximilian Bloch, followed by Loic

Parmentier, bade the others goodnight and they moved off towards their respective cells on the east gallery. Donaghue followed Miss Mendes France in the direction of the west gallery where the single cells were situated.

'I thought Brother Martin was speaking tomorrow night,' said Donaghue. 'Wasn't there a video film of the restoration of the abbey scheduled for tonight?'

'There should have been,' said Miss Mendes France, 'but the video recorder refused to function and Brother Martin stepped in and did his lecture on Gregorian chant tonight instead. Just goes to show that the human being is still more reliable than the machine—although, in my personal opinion, Gregorian chant is not nearly as interesting as the restoration of the abbey. However, once ensconced in one's seat one couldn't very well leave, could one?'

She bade Donaghue goodnight at her cell door, adding dourly that with only two hours to go to midnight, she trusted that there would be no more unexpected deaths in the abbey on this ill-fated Sunday.

Donaghue entered his cell and locked the door behind him. He opened the folder on top of the pile that he had left on his desk. As he had expected, the photograph of Thelonius Kapp as a young man had been removed.

He lit one of his small Havana cigars, picked up the sheaf of papers, settled himself comfortably on his bed, and started to leaf through them.

NINETEEN

Mark goes on a mission

AT 7.30 THE NEXT MORNING Donaghue found Inspector Joly sitting bright and breezy as he had promised in the Mother Superior's office.

'Eet...' He corrected himself, 'It's a beautiful day, Monsieur Donaghue—a fine day to find out what in God's name is going on in this abbey. I take it there have been no more mysterious deaths or heads crushed during the night?'

'Only a small case of attempted castration,' said Donaghue. 'At about ten o'clock last night.'

'You're joking, of course,' said Inspector Joly dourly.

'Not at all. Dr Renoir was attacked by the monk, Brother Martin, in the showers. Or at least he thought he was. The monk menaced him with a knife. But in fact it couldn't have been the monk as Brother Martin was giving a lecture on Gregorian chant in the library at the time. So I surmise that he was threatened by somebody dressed in a monk's habit.'

'Good God,' said Inspector Joly sombrely. 'Where is it all going to end? We've got to get to the bottom of this business before every last guest in the abbey is murdered. Do you think, Monsieur Donaghue, that it might be a case of a lunatic mass murderer?'

'No,' said Donaghue firmly. 'I don't think it's a case of that at all, but I do agree that we have to get to the bottom of it—as soon as possible, before anybody else is killed.'

'You're sure that there's a murderer, then?'

'Fairly sure.'

'Responsible for all three deaths?'

'Perhaps.'

'Any idea who it might be? One of the guests? Maybe one of the nuns?'

'I have an idea—but as yet it is only an idea. I need some proof, but I'm hoping that might come my way during the course of the day.'

'Well, Monsieur Donaghue,' said the inspector with a tone of resignation, 'you've beaten me there. I have absolutely no idea who the murderer, if there is one, could be. As far as I can see, there's no evidence whatsoever that even points to the deaths being murders—apart from this attack on Dr Renoir last night. You said he was threatened with a knife?'

'A scalpel.'

'One of his own?'

'I don't suppose so. Dr Renoir's on holiday. He's not likely to pack scalpels in his suitcase.'

'Where on earth would the attacker get a scalpel?'

'Oh, I shouldn't think that it's difficult to get hold of one— from a hospital suppliers, for instance, and I've no doubt there are one or two in the abbey infirmary.'

'It'll be easy enough to check if there are any missing,' said the inspector, noting it down.

'Yes, that'll be easy enough,' said Donaghue absently.

'Where do you think we should start, Monsieur Donaghue,' asked the inspector. 'I have to admit that in this business I am in your hands.'

'I suggest that immediately after breakfast we speak to the novices, then the guests. I think the picture will be a little clearer after that. But first, Inspector, I have to ask you a favour.'

'Ask away, *mon cher* Monsieur Donaghue.'

'Do you have such a thing as a fax machine in your office in Hyères?'

'Naturally,' said the inspector, smiling. 'We do equip ourselves with the latest in technological development in the French police force—even if our uniforms are a little out of date.'

'Better to be a little ridiculous like the English bobby than out of date like the French gendarme, eh, Inspector?'

'There's something to be said for a policeman looking just a little ridiculous,' said the inspector. 'Makes him more amenable to the man in the street, in my opinion. I believe that's how it works on your side of the water. I've suggested a change of image many a time but to no avail. Anyway, Monsieur Donaghue, what was it you wanted with our fax machine?'

'Please be so good as to ring through to the Commissariat and ask them to be ready to receive two young English people in, let us say, two hours from now, and to allow them use of the services of the fax machine.'

'If you give me the names of the two young people I'll do so immediately,' said the inspector.

'Mark Kingsford and Fiona MacKinley. They're journalists in possession of press cards. They will have four faxes to send and receive.'

'No problem,' said the inspector as he picked up the receiver. He quickly passed on the instructions then beamed at Donaghue.

'Absolutely no problem at all,' he said.

'I have one more favour to ask you,' said Donaghue.

'Fire away.'

'May they use your car to get there?'

The inspector involuntarily pulled a face.

'My car?' He hesitated. 'It's not that I would mind...but it's a new car. I only bought it six months ago.'

'The English drive very carefully and very slowly.'

'Very well,' the inspector said reluctantly. 'But I'll have to give them a note of authorization—it's got police insignia on it.'

'Well, that's that,' said Donaghue. 'I'll just pop off to see the aforementioned young people and check on Clothilde. She must be a little fed up, being cooped up for so long. It's time she had a bit of fresh air.'

Donaghue left the inspector to write his note of authorization and made his way quickly to Mark Kingsford's cell. He knocked gently on the door.

'Come in,' called Mark cheerfully, 'unless you're planning to cosh me over the head, of course.'

Donaghue pushed the door open to find Mark lying on the rug in the middle of the room doing press-ups. The young man sprang to his feet. He was wearing only a pair of jockey shorts. His neat, tanned body was lithe and supple. Donaghue, who, even as a young man, had tended to stoop, looked rather wistfully at the spectacle of upright physical perfection before him.

'Mark,' he said, 'I have a little mission I'd like you to carry out—you and your colleague, Miss MacKinley.'

'A mission?' said Mark as he dabbed beads of sweat from his face with a towel. He smiled. 'Only if it's dangerous.'

'The mission isn't dangerous,' said Donaghue, 'but it's important. If you don't do it you might find yourself in great danger.'

'You're serious, aren't you?' said Mark. His handsome face creased into a frown. 'Do you think this murderer, whoever it is, is going to have a go at me? Why? Because I'm a journalist and they think I might find things out?'

'Yes, precisely for that reason,' said Donaghue. 'I suggest that you wake Miss MacKinley so that I can explain to you both what I'd like you to do.'

'I'm already awake,' came a giggly voice from the single bed, and a dark tousled head appeared from under the duvet.

Donaghue coughed in embarrassment at the sight of Fiona's bare shoulders.

'Good morning, Miss MacKinley,' he said. 'And a fine morning it is too.' He turned to Mark, averting his eyes from Fiona who had retreated back under the bedclothes. 'As I was saying, I have a little job I'd like you to do for me. I want you to go to the Commissariat de Police in Hyères. You can take Inspector Joly's car. When you get there I want you to send four faxes, one to London, one to Paris, one to New York and one to California. Wait for the replies then bring them back as soon as you get them.'

Donaghue withdrew four folded sheets of paper from his pocket and handed them to Mark. 'I suggest that you leave immediately,' he said. 'Have breakfast on the way. Do you think you'll be able to carry out this little mission?' he asked good-humouredly.

'You can rely on me,' said Mark.

'I'll leave you to get dressed, then,' said Donaghue as he opened the door. 'Good luck!' The door closed behind him.

Mark threw the bedclothes off Fiona and pulled her out of bed.

'Come on, MacKinley,' he said, 'we've got work to do.' Then he waltzed her round the room and, pulling her close to him, looked deep into her eyes. Fiona giggled.

'MacKinley and Kingsford, *agents extraordinaires*,' he said.

Then he laughed. 'Don't you think we make an extraordinary couple?'

DONAGHUE KNOCKED on the door of Sandra Kapp's cell. Clothilde opened the door and invited him in.

Sandra, looking considerably less fraught, was sitting at the desk, sorting through her husband's papers.

'I'm sorting the private from the official,' she said. 'I want to keep the private papers. Carl can take care of the rest.'

'Mrs Kapp,' said Donaghue, 'what do you think to going out for a drive with Dr Blanche this morning? Do you think it might make you feel better?'

Sandra's face brightened. 'That's a good idea. Yes, I could do with some air—I've been cooped up in here for hours.'

'Clothilde,' said Donaghue, 'I thought perhaps you might take Mrs Kapp to Hyères in your car. She might enjoy a nice invigorating drive through the delightful country roads of the *arrière pays* and she could perhaps see an obstetrician at the hospital.'

'An excellent idea,' Clothilde agreed. She smiled, her face creasing like a concertina. 'I'm just itching to get behind a wheel—either that or a brisk walk. It's not too easy for me to remain indoors for long—you know that, Ulysses.'

Donaghue nodded. He knew his friend Clothilde very well.

'Leave as soon as you are ready,' he said. 'Have breakfast on the way.'

'Will do,' said Clothilde enthusiastically. She peered out of the cell window. 'It's a glorious day—a glorious day for a drive.'

Donaghue, contented, made his way to the refectory. It was just before eight, time for breakfast.

Only a very small number of guests were seated at two tables in the refectory. Monsieur and Madame Parmentier, in the company of Monsieur and Madame Bloch, were at their usual table. Mark Kingsford's table was empty, Dr Renoir, following Donaghue's advice of the previous evening, having stayed in his cell until called for questioning.

Carl Petersen sat at Donaghue's table alongside Thérèse Mendes France and Olivia Carter Bonnington. Inspector Joly sat in Clothilde's place next to Donaghue.

'Not many this morning,' commented Thérèse Mendes France

dourly as Donaghue took his seat. 'I suppose they're all worried that they're going to be poisoned. Such things don't worry me. The good God will call me when he's ready to and there's nothing I can do to prevent it. I'm not going to starve myself to death to avoid being poisoned.'

Lady Carter Bonnington, glancing rather disdainfully at Miss Mendes France, said, 'I don't believe in fate. I believe we create our own destiny. You don't have to accept the way you are born or the circumstances into which you are born—you can change them.'

Carl Petersen nodded in agreement. 'It's that that makes us human and not animal,' he said.

Lady Carter Bonnington beamed appreciatively at the young American.

Breakfast was served: fresh percolated coffee, croissants, light crispbread for those on diets, butter and a delicious jam made from the abbey's own figs. The novices serving this morning were two small oriental girls, Vietnamese or Chinese in origin.

'I find it quite uplifting to see so many young girls from so many nations with a vocation,' said Miss Mendes France. 'In a world that is becoming increasingly secular and materialistic it revives the spirit.'

Carl Petersen nodded as he munched a croissant.

'It was Mr Kapp's wish to create a cosmopolitan community here—particularly of young people,' he said. 'He wanted not only to encourage girls to enter the order, but to use the abbey as a centre for youth—not just on retreat but as a kind of spiritual work camp. You know the kind of thing—working holidays where young people from all over the world could meet, work together tending vines, growing vegetables, uniting at the same time in a kind of spiritual pilgrimage.'

Inspector Joly, impressed by the young man's oratory, raised his bovine head.

'It's an excellent idea,' he said. 'Rather a shame that he didn't live to see it happen.'

'And what will happen to the abbey now, I wonder?' said Miss Mendes France. 'I suppose it will become the property of his wife?' She addressed the question to Carl Petersen.

'Undoubtedly,' he said.

'And do you think she'll continue his work? She doesn't appear the spiritual type to me—not after having seen her on television,' she added dourly.

'I've really no idea,' said Carl Petersen. 'Once she gets over his death, maybe she'll want to continue where he left off. I can't really say. One would hope so.'

'She'll be a wealthy woman,' commented the inspector. 'I believe he was quite a rich man—made a fortune from his films.'

'She's quite well off herself,' said Petersen. 'She's a star in her own right, don't forget.' His tone, as he spoke, was admiring.

'So, she'll be even wealthier,' commented Lady Carter Bonnington. 'Money goes to money—that's usually how it is.'

'Perhaps she'll feel inclined to use some of it for charity,' said Thérèse Mendes France, 'or at least to maintain this abbey. That in my opinion would be a charitable act.'

'I think that the fortunes of public figures like Thelonius Kapp should go back to the public who gave it to them in the first place,' said Lady Bonnington. 'After all, film directors make their money from the public who buy the tickets to see their films. The money should go back to the government and thereby to the public.'

'What if the person has children?' said the inspector. 'Shouldn't they have the same right of heritage as any other?'

'Of course. If they have children the children should inherit—that's only natural—but if they don't, as in the case of Thelonius Kapp, I don't see why that slip of a girl who married him only eighteen months ago should get all his money. If you ask me, she probably killed him to get hold of it.'

Carl Petersen frowned at Lady Bonnington.

'That's rather a heavy accusation to make, if you don't mind my saying so,' he said. 'I've known Sandra Kapp now for two years. She's not the money-grabbing type, I can assure you of that. She loved her husband. I know that for a fact—she's no gold digger.'

Lady Bonnington pulled her beautiful face into a grimace that said, You've been taken in by her youth and beauty like him. She smiled deferentially at Petersen and added authoritatively, 'You'll learn.' Then she picked up a piece of Weightwatcher crispbread and nibbled it daintily. It was obvious that Lady Carter Bonnington was sure of her opinion and would not waver from it.

The meal was finished in silence. Then, as soon as the little novices had cleared away, Inspector Joly rose and addressed the guests.

'Mr Donaghue here and myself,' he said, 'will be spending the morning looking into the question of the deaths that occurred yesterday. We will be calling you one by one to the Mother Superior's office, which, in case you are not aware of it, is adjacent to the Chapel of La Sainte Vierge. It's a simple matter of routine questioning. Please be so good as to remain within the vicinity of the abbey buildings and let us know before you leave for your morning's activities where you might be so that we can call you at the appropriate time.'

'I shall be in the vineyards sketching,' said Maximilian Bloch.

'And I shall be with him,' said his wife.

'My wife and I planned to take a stroll round the abbey grounds,' said Loic Parmentier. 'We'll be somewhere in the vicinity of the vineyards.'

'I thought of going to see Mrs Kapp,' said Thérèse Mendes France. 'I'm sure the poor girl could do with a bit of moral support.'

'You won't be able to, I'm afraid,' said Donaghue. 'She's being taken to the hospital in Hyères for examination. She's pregnant—Dr Renoir diagnosed it yesterday and she'd like to have it confirmed. I don't suppose you were aware of that, Mr Petersen.'

Petersen looked at Donaghue in surprise. 'No, I wasn't aware—that would explain why she's been off colour recently.'

'Ah well,' said Thérèse Mendes France, casting a triumphant glance in Lady Bonnington's direction, 'he will have an heir after all so the girl will, according to your argument, be morally entitled to keep her money.'

'Absolutely,' Lady Bonnington said indifferently. 'If the child is his, of course. One never knows with these pop stars.' She rose elegantly from the table. 'I shall be in my cell reading when you are ready to call me,' she said as she turned to leave.

'As Mrs Kapp's not here I shall be in the Chapel of St Pierre la Croix,' said Thérèse Mendes France. 'There are some bronzes that I'd intended to rub.'

'And you, Mr Petersen?' asked Donaghue.

'I think I shall spend an hour in the smaller chapel. I feel in need of a bit of tranquil meditation after the disturbing events of yesterday. If I'm not there I'll be in my cell.'

The guests dispersed and Donaghue, accompanied by Inspector Joly, returned to the Mother Superior's office to start his investigation.

TWENTY

En route

MARK TOOK THE CONTROLS of Inspector Joly's car with trepidation. The car, like its owner, was large and powerful. Mark, who prided himself on his agility, in London traffic, on his 750 Yamaha motor bike, felt just a little awed by the prospect of driving a large French car on narrow French country roads where, as Fiona had already reminded him three times, French drivers tend to drive at breakneck speed in the middle of the road.

Consequently he set off very slowly, respecting the speed limits that were signposted at regular intervals but on the whole ignored by the other drivers on the road. He kept well to the right for two life-preserving reasons—one, to allow the buildup of angry drivers behind him to pass and thereby avoid crashing into the back of Inspector Joly's car and two, to avoid the central line along which the cars coming from the other direction tended to travel at life-imperilling speed. As a result Fiona, every now and again, requested him in a strangled voice to drive just a little further from the edge which occasionally, as the winding road to Hyères rose and fell among the beautiful hills of the *arrière pays,* proved to be the unprotected edge of a precipice.

'It's all right, Fiona,' Mark reassured her confidently. 'I have driven on the Continent before. I can judge distance from a left-hand wheel.'

'I'm sure you can,' Fiona said, 'but you're not used to driving a car as wide as this. Your MG is about a quarter of the width of this monster. When you hug the edge like this I find myself looking down directly into a ravine. My stomach leaps of its own accord up into my mouth—I'm chewing on it now—my head swims and I experience a powerful feeling of paralysing terror. The condition is called vertigo—*and I suffer from it!*'

'All right, Fiona,' said Mark grudgingly as he edged the car a millimetre or so towards the centre line. 'I'll move over but you wait, the next thing you know, someone coming the other way or overtaking will smash the wing mirror off—*like that!*' he yelled as something small and red flashed past him at supersonic speed followed by a black Mercedes whose huge right side wing mirror hit the left side mirror of Inspector Joly's car. Fortunately Inspector Joly's mirror was the retractable type and was only displaced by the impact and not damaged by it.

'*Maniacs!*' Mark yelled furiously. '*Homicidal maniacs!* Women as well,' he added dourly. 'I always thought women drove better than men.'

'It surprises me,' said Fiona frostily, 'that you had time to notice the sex of the drivers, I certainly didn't they were going much too fast.'

'The woman driving the Mercedes had blonde hair—rather like Salome's. It's difficult not to notice hair like that.'

Fiona glowered at Mark. 'Salome,' she said derisively. 'You're still obsessed by that Salome.' Then she added tersely, 'You do realize, don't you, Mark, that the Salome you adore doesn't actually exist, of course. The real Salome, Mrs Thelonius Kapp, is, as you have seen yourself, just an ordinary girl—like any other girl you meet every day of the week. The Salome you go all gushy about is only an artefact made up of a wig, a pair of false eyelashes, a large quantity of make-up and a skin-tight outfit. It's that you're in love with, not the person. You're not in love with Sandra Kapp, are you, now that you've seen her in the flesh?'

Mark turned his head to look at Fiona, his features crossed by an expression of unaccustomed gravity.

'You know,' he said, 'you're absolutely right. I've never looked at it like that before.'

'Anyone can dress up in a blonde wig and skimpy shorts,' Fiona went on. 'In fact half the female population of the western world are dressed like that at the moment. You'd probably go all gushy over me if I dressed Salome-style.'

Mark smiled. 'I couldn't imagine it,' he said. 'You in a blonde wig? It wouldn't be you, Fiona.'

'And it isn't Sandra Kapp either,' she said ardently. 'Salome is a figment of her and her husband's imaginations—a fiction. Tell me what you think of the real Salome, Sandra Kapp.'

Mark reflected. 'I don't know,' he said cautiously. 'I haven't had a chance to speak to her yet.'

'But from what you've seen of her—there's nothing special about her as far as I can see.'

'She's pretty.'

'No prettier than me.'

'That's true,' he said. He paused. 'I think she's clever—she looks intelligent.'

'I don't think she's any cleverer than me.'

'She can sing,' said Mark triumphantly. 'She earns an absolute fortune from her voice.'

'She can sing in tune, but so can most people—even I can—but she's no Maria Callas. She earns the money—and you know it very well—because she wiggles her backside around on stage.'

'Don't tell me,' said Mark grinning, 'that you could do the same.'

'Of course I could,' retorted Fiona indignantly. 'Any girl can wiggle her backside if she wants to.'

'Wiggle yours for me tonight,' said Mark coaxingly. He took his hand from the wheel and placed it on Fiona's knee. Fiona slapped the hand resoundingly and replaced it on the wheel.

'Keep your mind on the road, Mark Kingsford, or we'll end up in a ravine,' she said crossly.

'Well,' said Mark resignedly, 'one thing's for sure that I noticed about Sandra Kapp: she loved her husband. She was dotty about him—it just shone out of her eyes.'

'Do you know, Mark,' said Fiona softly, 'if you hadn't spent so much time watching the love shining out of Sandra Kapp's eyes you might have noticed it shining out of someone else's—for you.'

Mark turned and looked in surprise at Fiona. He smiled. 'Fiona...' he said. His hand reached out to grasp hers.

'*Mark!*' Fiona screamed. She grabbed the wheel and turned it violently. 'We're on a bend—there's a ravine on this side! Keep your eyes on the road!'

Mark dutifully kept his eyes on the road and his hands on the wheel for the next half-hour after which time they found that they had successfully negotiated the hazardous hilly section and were now on a flat, if still winding stretch of country road. Fiona, greatly relieved at having survived the hills, suggested that they stop at the first café or bistro they came across and have breakfast. She was in need, she said, of a strong black coffee and a cigarette to calm her nerves.

A sign ahead proclaimed the proximity of the Auberge des Vieux Moulins.

'An auberge, that'll do,' declared Fiona. 'Pull in.'

Mark obediently turned into the car-park of what turned out to be a rather cosy-looking country inn with rustic wooden tables shaded by frilly parasols set before its bevelled windows.

They settled themselves at one of the outside tables and Fiona ordered coffee and croissants from the pretty waitress who came to serve them and who looked rather too long and too appraisingly, for her liking, at Mark.

The waitress's appraisal, however, was lost on Mark, who was watching a low red sports car that was at that moment leaving the car-park.

'That's the lunatic who overtook us,' he said as the car disappeared with a screech of tyre on tarmac, 'and there's the other one.'

The black Mercedes that had knocked his wing mirror sat sleekly at the entrance to the auberge. Its driver had, a few moments before, emerged from the interior of the inn and was walking rapidly towards the car.

'I told you she looked like Salome,' Mark said as he gazed at the girl, who was dressed in tight-fitting cyclist shorts and matching vest, her leonine mass of blonde hair haloing her head. She was tall and slender—a very attractive girl. Mark gazed sheepeyed at her as she climbed into the Mercedes.

'You see,' said Fiona, 'you're at it again—going all moon-eyed over a blonde wig with long legs. Really, sometimes I wonder why you have anything to do with me at all.' Her tone was truculent and she twirled her dark glossy hair around her fingers as she spoke.

'She's probably mousy underneath like Sandra Kapp,' Mark said gallantly as the black Mercedes purred past them and out of the car-park. 'You're right, Fiona,' he said, taking her hand and kissing it. 'I'm just a kid at heart, mooching over pop stars.

Anyway,' he added brightly, 'let's forget Salome and her look-alikes. Let's get down to business.'

He withdrew the folder of letters that Donaghue had given him to send by fax. 'Let's see what these are all about.'

He scrutinized the four letters. The first was addressed to a Bridget Kilkenny in London, asking her to find out the date and place of birth of a Lady Olivia Carter Bonnington; the second was to the archives of the national newspaper, *Le Monde,* in Paris asking for their coverage of Thérèse Mendes France's gold medal victory in the Olympics of 1952; the third was to be sent to the curator of a film archive museum in Beverly Hills asking for a photograph and curriculum vitae of an actress called Carol Lawton; the fourth was addressed to a firm of lawyers in Manhattan, and requested a copy of Thelonius Kapp's will. The first three were signed by Inspector Joly of the Police Nationale and the fourth by Sandra Kapp herself.

'Intriguing,' said Mark. 'Now why should they be wanting the date of birth of the aristocratic Lady Bonnington? Do they think she murdered Thelonius Kapp?'

'It's not even sure that he was murdered,' said Fiona. 'To all intents and purposes he committed suicide with the Silverstone girl. Don't forget a suicide note was found and there was arsenic in his room.'

'Perhaps the police think differently.'

'Who the hell is this Carol Lawton?' said Fiona. 'An actress? I've never heard of her.'

'Obviously something to do with Kapp,' said Mark. 'And Kapp's will,' he mused. 'It's obvious that if they think he was murdered they'll be looking for a motive—and money would be the first consideration.'

'Surely his wife would inherit any money he had?'

'Not if he'd made a will leaving it to someone else.'

'But surely he'd leave it to her? She is his wife, after all.'

'You'd imagine so,' Mark agreed.

'Which means that only she would benefit from his death. Maybe they think the wonderful Salome killed him.'

'She doesn't look the type to me.'

'Well, she wouldn't to you,' said Fiona sardonically, 'but then you're taken in by appearances. Maybe she's got a split personality—maybe she's sweet and innocent when she's Sandra Kapp and a murdering virago when she's Salome.'

Mark ignored Fiona's sarcasm. 'If they think she did it,' he said seriously, 'they'd need proof. What I don't understand is why they're investigating Lady Carter Bonnington's bona fides and Thérèse Mendes France's past.'

'Everybody in the abbey is suspect, I suppose,' said Fiona. 'Even you and me.'

'And the actress, Carol Lawton,' Mark went on. 'I'm sure that Donaghue's got something up his sleeve—I'll bet my next month's salary that he's got something on somebody. I've heard of him. He's supposed never to have failed in an investigation. The thing is, if they think Kapp was murdered, then the girl, Milly, must have been murdered as well—and perhaps the novice who died in the wine press. I must admit I haven't really taken the possibility seriously up to now.'

'That could have been an accident—pure coincidence.'

'Yes, it could have been but I bet they're looking into the possibility that the three deaths are linked.'

'I don't think they've got much chance of finding a link. If there is a murderer lurking in the abbey, he...or she...is pretty clever. There's absolutely no proof as far as I know that any of the deaths were murder.'

'Donaghue might have found something, some clue.'

'But not evidence. If he'd found evidence, hard evidence, they'd have made an arrest.'

'That's true,' said Mark. He reflected as he munched his croissant. 'If there is a murderer, I wonder who it is?'

'I reckon it's Sandra Kapp,' said Fiona. 'She bumped him off to get his money.'

'And Milly? Why would she kill her hairdresser?'

'She discovered that he was having an affair with Milly and was going to leave her all his money—that's why Donaghue wants to check the will.'

'And the novice?'

'The novice might have seen her do it or she might have died quite simply by accident.'

'It would seem the obvious solution if money was the motive, but supposing money wasn't the motive. Suppose he was killed by someone who hated him. Thelonius Kapp left more than a few bodies in his wake—emotional corpses, I mean. I believe he was pretty callous as a young director.'

'So you think it could be someone from his past?' said Fiona. 'Some other director he did the dirty on, an actor or actress he had problems with, some would-be actress who refused his casting couch—someone like that?'

'That would explain this Carol Lawton. Maybe she's an actress that Kapp rejected or did the dirty on and Donaghue thinks she may be here in the guise of one of the guests.'

'It's possible,' said Fiona. 'She could be any of the women there, I suppose, apart from the older ones, Miss Mendes France and Dr Blanche—I don't suppose either of them were Hollywood starlets in their youth.'

'Starlets can become pretty ugly with age,' said Mark, 'but it doesn't necessarily have to be someone from his distant past— it could be someone from five, ten years ago.'

'That blonde woman, Mireille Parmentier—she looks bitter about something. She looks the starlet type. And the artist's wife—she could be a Hollywood starlet gone to fat. Or Lady Carter Bonnington—she's certainly glamorous enough. I don't suppose it could be the doctor's wife—she's rather young and far too plain. The problem is, without proof any story is possible.'

'Without proof,' said Mark, 'they can't arrest anybody.' He replaced the letters in the folder. 'So you're all right, Fiona, no one's going to find you out.'

Fiona leaned over to punch Mark playfully on the arm which made the pretty young waitress who had come to clear their table look at her in astonishment.

As they walked to the car the waitress gazed wistfully after Mark's departing back.

Eh bien, she thought, these English girls, they don't know at all how to seduce a man. Now, if it was me...

'ARE YOU ALL RIGHT, my dear?' Clothilde asked Sandra. 'Am I driving too fast?'

'No, no, Dr Blanche,' Sandra Kapp assured her. 'It isn't that— I'm used to fast cars. It's just that there was a car in the car-park at the inn back there that was exactly like the one Thelonius hired to come down here from Paris. A black Mercedes. It made me feel quite funny to see it.'

'It was behind us on the road for a while. I noticed it,' said Clothilde. 'Listen, my dear, I know it's difficult when you've just lost someone you love but try to think instead of the child you are carrying. I'm sure that will make you feel better.'

'It helps enormously to know that I'm pregnant,' Sandra said. She looked away at the passing countryside so that Clothilde wouldn't see the misery on her face. 'But I feel so lost without him.' Then she lost control and started to weep.

Clothilde, acutely embarrassed, said clumsily, 'Well, it's better to get it out of your system than keep it bottled up inside. Go ahead and have a good cry—don't mind me.'

She drove on in respectful silence.

After a few moments Sandra stopped crying and wiped her eyes.

'May I ask you a question?' Clothilde said tentatively.

'Of course,' said Sandra.

'Do you think your husband really killed himself?'

Sandra turned her head sharply to look at Clothilde.

'Do you think he didn't?' she asked.

'He didn't appear the suicidal type to me,' said Clothilde. 'Of course, I didn't know him as you did, but as an aged doctor I have had a great deal to do with suffering humanity and Thelonius Kapp, from the little I saw of him, seemed to be the type that fights to the bitter end and never gives in, even to illness—there are types like that.'

Sandra said nothing. She bit her lip nervously.

'I find it hard…' she began. 'I find it hard to believe that he killed himself that way.'

'What way?'

'By taking arsenic. But he must have done—they found it in our room.'

'In the container where he kept the cocaine?'

'Yes.'

'Wasn't that a bit risky, putting it there—where you might have used it?'

'I…I suppose it was,' the girl said hesitantly.

'Has it occurred to you, Mrs Kapp,' said Clothilde gently, 'that someone might have killed him?'

'Of course...of course it's occurred to me,' said Sandra frac-
tiously. 'But who would want to kill him?' She started to weep
again, her head in her hands, great wracking sobs that shook her
body. 'He must have suffered terribly. I can't bear to think that
he suffered.'

'Milly, too—don't forget that she died of arsenic poisoning.'

'I know, I know,' Sandra sobbed. 'It's just too horrible.'

'Do you have any idea of who might have wanted to kill your
husband?'

'I don't know...I don't know everything about his former life.
I suppose there might be someone he hurt in the past. I don't
know.'

'Did you notice that he recognized anybody among the guests
at the retreat?'

'Recognize?'

'Yes, did he notice anybody that he might have known before?'

'I don't think so, but even if there was somebody he knew I
doubt if he would have recognized them—he wasn't having a
good day the day he arrived. He was going through a bad patch.
He'd taken an awful lot of drugs. When he gets really bad he
hardly recognizes me. He wouldn't have recognized anybody
else.'

'So it's possible that somebody could have gone to your room
—someone he knew—and he wouldn't have recognized them?'

'You mean to plant the arsenic? It's possible, but I was with
him all the time, and in any case I had some of the cocaine that
was in the box before we went to the chapel. It didn't do me
any harm.'

'What about the meal he ate before he died? Do you think it's
possible that the arsenic was in that?'

'It's possible—but who put it in, and in any case what's the
point in thinking about that? The plates were washed up immediately afterwards.'

'If Milly didn't take the arsenic herself it must have been in
the tea she drank.'

'*If* she drank it—that's not sure—and the cups were washed
up as well.'

'The tea was meant for you,' said Clothilde. 'You are aware, aren't you, Mrs Kapp, that if Milly was murdered, she was murdered in your place?'

'I am aware of all that,' said Sandra sharply. 'I'm not stupid. I can put two and two together—but it's all conjecture. None of it can be proved.'

'If your husband and your employee were murdered, surely you are interested in discovering how and why?'

Sandra, evidently distressed, shook her head from side to side.

'I just don't know,' she said. 'I just don't know. It's all too confusing. They must have committed suicide—there can't be any other explanation.'

'I don't think you really believe that,' said Clothilde softly.

'You can think what you like,' Sandra snapped. 'I don't want to think about it at all.' She sat, her hands in her lap, looking stonily at the road ahead.

'Please forgive me,' said Clothilde. 'I didn't intend to upset you. It really was unthinking of—'

She stopped speaking abruptly and peered closely into her rear view mirror.

'Do you know,' she said, 'it's rather curious—that black Mercedes is still behind us.'

Clothilde, during their conversation, had considerably reduced her speed. The turbo-engined car was meandering along at fifty kilometres an hour. The black Mercedes behind was approaching fast, obviously intent on overtaking. The road had, about five kilometres back, entered a steeply hilly area of countryside. Signposts at regular intervals warned drivers of dangerous hairpin bends and steep zigzag descents. At the moment Clothilde noticed the Mercedes behind her she was approaching one such sharp bend, the unprotected edge of the road dropping vertically into a precipice on the right-hand side.

Clothilde, as she approached the bend, cursed. The stupid woman in the black Mercedes was going to overtake her on the bend. She wasn't signalling to do so but the speed of her approach indicated no other course. Then into Clothilde's brain crept a crazy notion: the Mercedes wasn't going to overtake and it wasn't going to slow down. The driver must be mad or out of control of the car. The Mercedes was coming straight at her and would hit her, she calculated, on the bend itself, sending her over the edge and into the ravine below.

She moved in towards the centre of the road praying that nothing was coming round the bend from the other side. Then she saw with a shock that the Mercedes had moved over too—the woman was intent on mowing her down!

She eased her foot down on the accelerator and took the bend recklessly at speed. The madwoman in the Mercedes had evidently not been prepared to take the same risk: the car did not appear in Clothilde's mirror when she looked into it some minutes later after they'd negotiated the series of bends and found themselves on a short stretch of road.

Sandra, who, in her anger, had been oblivious to the car's sudden lurch forward, suddenly noticed that they were travelling very fast indeed and looked questioningly at Clothilde.

'Are you angry because of what I said?' she asked stiffly. 'If so, I apologize.'

Clothilde laughed, keeping one eye on the mirror.

'I'm not driving like this because I'm angry—well, not with you, anyway. I'm driving like this because there's a lunatic behind us who seems to want to drive right over us.'

Sandra turned her head to look behind her. The Mercedes had just appeared on the straight stretch.

'Good God,' said Sandra, 'it's a woman who looks like me—like I am on stage. And the car is the one I saw in the car-park—like the one we hired.' She shuddered. 'It's weird. It's like looking at myself.'

'Well, whoever she is, I'm going to give her a run for her money,' said Clothilde grimly. 'There's a particularly nasty stretch of hairpin bends coming up—make sure your seat belt is secure. I think we'll lose her there.'

Clothilde knew every inch of the road from St Pierre la Croix to Hyères. She knew every bump, every life-imperilling twist, every dreadful precipitous edge. She put her foot down on the accelerator as the first of the series of bends came into sight.

Sandra, seeing the bend approach—another hairpin with a sheer drop on the passenger side—screamed and clapped her hands over her eyes.

'It's terrifying,' she howled. 'Worse than flying in Concorde.'

'And a lot more risky,' said Clothilde. 'In the South of France you put your life in peril by driving slowly. The only way to survive the hazards of the road, which consist mainly of other drivers, is to drive faster than any of them. There really is no other way. But don't worry,' she said cheerfully, 'I've driven this stretch a thousand times and in faster cars than this.'

What Clothilde had said was not, in fact, true. She had never taken these bends at this speed—but she felt obliged to reassure the girl. Sandra Kapp was pregnant, after all.

TWENTY-ONE

The novices speak

'IT'S LIKE A PUZZLE,' Donaghue said, leaning back in the Mother Superior's chair. 'There are some pieces that don't fit and some that are missing.' He scratched his head, leaving patches of his wiry hair standing on end. Inspector Joly, whose own rather thinning *chevelure* was slicked neatly to his head, looked at Donaghue askance. The Irishman looked more like one of those mad nuclear scientists than a reputed detective.

'There are three things that don't fit,' Donaghue repeated. 'The clip brooch...' He placed it on the table before them. '...the attack on Renoir and Kapp's black eyes.'

Inspector Joly looked at Donaghue, baffled. Then he looked at the brooch.

'I don't see that the brooch necessarily has anything to do with the case.'

'I think it has,' said Donaghue. 'What would a gold brooch like this be doing near one of the vegetable greenhouses?'

'Someone dropped it.'

'Why then has no one asked the Mother Superior if it has been found? It is, after all, an expensive item of jewellery.' He weighed the brooch in his hand. 'Solid gold. Whoever dropped it would surely report its loss.'

'Let the guests know that you've found it and see who claims it,' suggested Inspector Joly.

'I doubt that anyone would claim it now.'

'Why? Because whoever it is knows something about the deaths? Is that what you're thinking?'

'Perhaps.'

'A brooch like that would belong to a woman,' said the inspector. 'I doubt if a man would wear such a thing.'

'Kapp might have.'

'Perhaps it's his then.'

'If it is his, how did it get to the vegetable garden? Kapp didn't leave his cell on Sunday morning as far as I know.'

'He might have done.'

'Clothilde and I walked out towards the vineyard immediately after breakfast. If Kapp had gone before us we would have seen him.'

'So you think that whoever dropped the brooch might be the murderer?' said Inspector Joly. 'Do you think it's the same person who attacked Dr Renoir?'

Donaghue leaned further back in his chair and ran his fingers through his hair again, this time leaving the whole lot standing on end.

'I'm not sure,' he mused.

'You don't think the deaths and the attack are connected?'

'One would think they are. It's an intriguing puzzle.'

'And Kapp's black eyes—where on earth do they fit in?' The inspector's tone was very slightly sardonic. 'Perhaps you might like to tell me, Monsieur Donaghue, what exactly it is that you are concocting in that brain of yours, because I tell you, I'm baffled. I can't see any connection at all—unless it's just a lunatic out to kill everyone in the damned place.'

'Oh, no, it's not that—it's not that at all. At the moment I am a little puzzled myself, but things will become clearer when we have some proof.'

'Ah, proof.' The inspector seized on the word with relish as if it represented something concrete, a raft in a sea of troubled waters. 'Now that's what this whole business lacks—proof, evidence. We don't even have any real evidence that the deaths are the result of foul play—only your misgivings, Monsieur Donaghue.'

He looked at Donaghue, who was reclining in his seat with his hands clasped behind his head, his hair akimbo. Inspector Joly's regard was not without a trace of scepticism. If it wasn't for the fact that his friend Clothilde had spoken so highly of Donaghue's talents he would have thought that the man was a little batty. He noticed that Donaghue's linen shirt was crumpled and his trousers ill fitting. The Anglo-Saxons, really, they had no idea how to dress—they were not concerned with the body and its pleasures as the French were. They were just a little too cerebral, a little too eccentric.

'I've been hearing voices,' Donaghue said. He appeared to be talking to himself.

'Eh?' queried Inspector Joly worriedly. 'Hearing voices? Now look here, Donaghue, we can't conduct a case on hearsay from the other world, although...' He raised his eyes to heaven in a gesture of supplication. '...God knows it would help if the Almighty deigned to intervene now and again in our mundane efforts to establish an altogether non-divine justice here on earth.'

'The voices I've heard,' Donaghue explained, 'have not been from the other side. They were human voices—but voices that didn't quite fit into my puzzle.'

'Conversations you've overheard?'

'Yes. I heard a conversation yesterday morning and it's only now that I realize that one of the voices I heard *doesn't belong to any of the people here.*'

'Might I ask where the conversation took place?'

'In Carl Petersen's cell. He was talking to a woman—an American woman.'

'Can you remember the conversation?'

'Oh yes. I didn't hear much. He said, "You can't change your mind now," and she said, "I can't go through with it, I can't do it to him." He said, "You do love me, don't you?" and she said, "You know I do." He said, "There's no other way," and she said in agreement, "I suppose there's no other way."'

'Sounds like someone he was romantically involved with, who was obviously married to someone else. An American, you say?'

'She spoke with an American accent.'

'That lets out Mrs Kapp. The only American woman here was Mrs Kapp's hairdresser, the dead girl, Milly Whatsername.'

'Silverstone.'

'Perhaps they were lovers. Perhaps she was Kapp's lover as well.'

'It wasn't Milly Silverstone. Her accent was pure Bronx and I hardly see the bland and serious Carl Petersen as the lover of the rather giddy Miss Silverstone.'

'It is unlikely,' the inspector conceded. 'But then the Americans are rather bizarre in their sexual habits—as far as we French see them, that is. This case is becoming more and more obscure.'

He regarded Donaghue suspiciously. 'Are you sure, Monsieur Donaghue, that you are not just letting your imagination run away with you?'

Donaghue frowned. 'Perhaps I am,' he said. 'Perhaps I am.' Then he released his hands from behind his head, rearranged his hair into a semblance of order with his fingers and said, adopting a tone of efficiency, 'Let's get down to business then, Inspector. I'd like first of all to speak to the novices.'

He pressed the buzzer on the desk and a few seconds later the duty novice appeared. It was one of the little oriental novices who had served breakfast that morning. The novices had by now been told by the Mother Superior that, for the purposes of the enquiry, they could answer the detective's questions.

'What is your name?' Donaghue asked.

The little novice smiled back at him. 'Sister Agathe.'

'And where are you from?'

'I'm from Vietnam.'

'Do you speak English?'

'Quite well.'

He continued his questioning in English. 'The other novice who served at breakfast, is she Vietnamese as well?'

'Yes, we grew up together.'

'What is her name?'

'Sister St Jean.'

'Tell me, what duties did you and Sister St Jean carry out yesterday?'

'We worked in the greenhouses in the morning and in the vineyard in the afternoon.'

'Sister Veronique worked in the vineyard in the afternoon as well. Did you see her there?'

'No, she must have been at the other end of the field.'

'Well, that's all, Sister Agathe. Please be so good as to send Sister St Jean along.'

'That's all?' The little novice opened her dark eyes in surprise. She appeared almost disappointed that her opportunity to speak had been so precipitately curtailed. She disappeared and a few minutes later Sister St Jean arrived.

'Sister St Jean?'

'Yes.'

'How long have you been in the abbey?'

'Two months.'

'Did all the novices arrive at the same time?'

'No. Sister Veronique, God rest her soul...' The girl crossed herself as she spoke. '...was here when I and Sister Agathe arrived. Three arrived on Saturday.'

'What are their names?'

'Sister Paul, Sister Dominique and Sister Marie Pierre.'

'Well, that's all, Sister St Jean,' said Donaghue cheerfully. 'Please send me in...let me see, I've already spoken to Sister Marie Pierre...send me Sister Paul.'

Sister Paul arrived a few minutes later. Donaghue and Inspector Joly recognized her as the plump bespectacled novice who had served dinner the night before.

'Sister Paul,' said Donaghue, smiling, 'do you speak English?'

'Oh yes,' answered the girl. 'I'm American.'

'Where do you come from in America?'

Sister Paul, evidently flustered by the interrogation, stuttered, 'W...W...Wisconsin, sir. I...I...saw Thelonius Kapp on television and heard about the abbey. I...I...applied immediately and was accepted as a novice.'

Her words, emitted at speed, tripped one over the other. She was, Donaghue noted, one of those plump, self-conscious females who speak garrulously and rapidly in an attempt to hide their discomfiture.

'Are you happy here, Sister Paul?'

'I...I...I...' she stammered. 'I've never been so happy.' She smiled nervously.

In that you are speaking the truth, Donaghue thought as he dismissed her—you're probably much happier here where you don't have to use words as a means of communication.

The last novice, Sister Dominique, arrived promptly. Tall and serenely beautiful, she stood sentinel before the two men, her delicately sculpted nose in the air, her full lips set with a firm resolution that said clearly, I am breaking my vows only reluctantly and I hope for a good reason.

'You arrived on Saturday, Sister Dominique?'

'Yes.' Her elegant head inclined as she snapped out the monosyllable.

'Where are you from, Sister Dominique?'

'I'm Canadian.'

'French Canadian?'

'My origins are French, yes.'

'So you speak French fluently?'

'More or less.'

'Tell me, Sister Dominique,' said Donaghue, 'what you think of the other novices.'

A dark eyebrow arched a fraction.

'What do I think of the other novices?'

'Yes. Their characters, their dedication—whether you think they'll make it to orders.'

'Sister Veronique, God rest her soul, will not, of course, make it to orders.' A note of anger sharpened the novice's tone.

'A terrible accident,' murmured Donaghue.

'Oh yes,' said the novice, 'a terrible accident.' The tone of her voice made Donaghue scrutinize her carefully.

'You don't think it was an accident?'

'I can't believe that Sister Veronique could have been so stupid as to lift a heavy weight above her head, place her head beneath it and then wait for it to come crashing down on top of her.'

'She was not stupid then?'

'No, not at all—she was a very clever, serious novice. I've known her since we were students together. She had, like me, studied viticulture—that's why...' Her tone changed imperceptibly, became almost pleading. '...I can't believe that such a thing could have happened accidentally. She knew how those old presses functioned—she had overseen its restoration.'

'So she might have had a reason to be there in the *pressoir*—could she have been checking the press before it went into use the following day?'

'It had already been checked and was ready for the grapes. Of course, she might have gone to make sure.'

'But you don't think that what happened to her was an accident?'

'It's not for me to give an opinion. I just feel it wasn't.'

'Do you have any idea why Sister Veronique changed duty yesterday lunchtime with Sister Marie Pierre? It seems she asked to change and went to work in the fields and from there went to the *pressoir*.'

'I've no idea why—unless, as you said, she wanted to check the press.'

'And Sister Marie Pierre, what do you think of her?'

'I only met her on Saturday. It's difficult to judge after such a short space of time. She appears a little timid and a little over-awed—but that's to be expected. She didn't know anybody here, after all.'

'Have you spoken to her since she arrived?'

'Spoken to her?' The acerbic tone had returned to her voice. 'Of course not. We take a vow of silence, you know that very well.'

'And the two Vietnamese novices—what are your feelings about them?'

'They are not as timid as Sister Marie Pierre but then they are friends and have each other for company.'

'Do the new novices find it difficult to refrain from talking among themselves?'

'Of course they do. It's only normal—it takes time to acquire the discipline of silence.'

'Since you arrived have you heard any of the novices whispering together?'

'No. They have excellent self-control.'

'And Sister Paul, the American, what do you think about her?'

'From what I've seen she appears nervous and disorganized, always watching the others to see whether they're watching her—but she'll relax and get used to it in the end.'

'Do you think she's cut out for the monastic life? Do you think she'll make orders?'

'I'm not sure,' Sister Dominique answered reflectively. 'Somehow I don't really think she is.'

'NOW THERE'S A NUN if ever I saw one,' said Donaghue when the tall Sister Dominique had left. 'I must admit that I am still awed and intimidated by the power of the truly vocational nun to perturb the spirit of a culpable sinner like myself.'

'Do you think one of them might be involved?' asked Inspector Joly.

'I just wanted to hear their voices.'

'To see if one of them could have been the mysterious voice you heard?'

'Yes.'

'And did you recognize any?'

'No, none of them.'

'Not even the American?'

'The accent was not the same. The one I heard was uptown New York. I don't think Sister Paul is a great actress...' He paused, reflecting, drumming his fingers on the table. 'Nor can I imagine her saying to Carl Petersen, "You know I do," without stuttering—unless...' He paused again. 'Unless, of course she *is* a great actress.'

'Some actress that Kapp rejected, perhaps,' suggested Inspector Joly. 'And has come over to get revenge on him.'

'It's quite possible,' Donaghue agreed. 'It's quite possible.'

'Could that plump stuttering little novice possibly have been an aspiring actress?' Inspector Joly asked incredulously.

'Appearances can be deceptive,' said Donaghue. 'The appearance of a great actress can be very deceptive.'

'So you think it's a woman who killed him—some actress he had had bad dealings with. But surely he would have recognized her among the people in the abbey?'

'He was in the confused initial stages of Alzheimer's disease. He might not have recognized her and, don't forget, Inspector, appearances can be deceptive.'

The inspector scratched his head. 'I'm beginning to feel that I'm in the confused initial stages of dementia,' he said wearily. 'This case is making my head swim. Anyway, as I said, I'm in your hands. Who do you want to call next?'

'I think Dr Renoir. I suggested after his traumatic experience in the shower last night that he stay in his cell until we called him this morning, and he was so worried for his and his wife's safety that he obeyed. I think perhaps we ought to let him out now. But first I have a little call to make to Charles de Gaulle airport in Paris. While I'm doing that perhaps you wouldn't mind popping along to the Mother Superior and asking her for a list of the former names and curricula vitae of the six novices.'

TWENTY-TWO

In the abbey grounds

IN THE VINEYARD all the nuns and novices that could be spared from work in the abbey buildings had been seconded to the fields to get the ripe grapes picked and packed ready to be taken to the co-operative press in the village which, at this time of the year, had a heavy workload. They had to get the grapes picked as quickly as possible so that they could be sent in one batch. The Mother Superior had locked the door to the building that housed the old press and forbidden the nuns, novices and guests to enter it. As soon as the future of the abbey had been settled— by Mrs Kapp, she supposed—she would order a new, modern, automated press.

Loic and Mireille Parmentier wandered slowly along the perimeter of the fields, where the nuns were bent working busily. Loic's serious, intelligent face was creased into a frown.

'This is such a beautiful place,' he said, 'but don't you agree now that we should never have come?'

Mireille didn't answer. Instead tears filled her eyes and she started to weep.

'He wasn't the monster you thought he was—that's it, isn't it?' said Loic.

'I wanted to hurt him,' said Mireille, 'but when I saw his face I realized that he wasn't evil—only weak.'

'We see things differently with age,' said Loic. 'Maybe I was wrong,' he added reflectively. 'Maybe it was a good thing you came after all.'

They had turned the corner of the field and almost collided with Maximilian Bloch who was seated, sketching, on a collapsible canvas chair. His wife stood behind him, studying the progress of his sketch. Adèle, who had just returned from helping the nuns pick the grapes, was sweating profusely from her efforts.

Loic and Mireille took up positions behind the artist alongside Adèle.

'A splendid sight for an artist, this,' Loic commented. 'It's still very much the Provence of Cézanne and Van Gogh, don't you think?'

'Absolutely,' Maximilian Bloch concurred, without turning his head. 'It was Provence that inspired so many artists and in particular, of course, Van Gogh. The landscape shimmers with light and colour as Van Gogh, above all the others, was able to capture on canvas.'

'You're only sketching, I see,' said Loic. 'You'll do the paintings later, I take it.'

'Yes, sadly—that's the best I can do. I would like to paint the colours now, as I see them before me; the marvellous blue of the sky, the green of the vines, the rich ochre of the earth. But, alas, it would take me far longer than three days to do just one canvas, so I prefer to sketch. I will do my feeble best to recollect the colours later.'

Mireille picked up his folder of sketches and leafed through them.

'They're wonderful,' she said. 'I particularly like your sketches of the nuns.'

'The nuns?' exclaimed Adèle Bloch sharply. She had not, as yet, looked at Maximilian's sketches of the abbey.

Mireille held out a sketch of two novices, their heads together as if in deep conversation. One was exceedingly plain and the other extraordinarily pretty.

'One so pretty and the other quite ugly,' Mireille commented. 'A marvellous contrast. And it looks as though they're talking— an illicit conversation. How sweet. I like it.'

'I don't know whether they were speaking or not,' said Maximilian. 'It certainly looks as though they were. I wasn't interested in that. I just liked the pose.'

'You like the pretty novice, more like,' Adèle snapped. She picked up the folder and flicked rapidly through the sheets. 'Every one of them contains women,' she said crossly. 'It looks as though you've drawn every woman and every nun in the whole place.' Her voice rose to a note of hysteria which made Loic and Mireille Parmentier look at her in alarm.

'There really isn't much else to draw here,' said Maximilian calmly. 'Look around you. Apart from Monsieur Parmentier who is behind me, there are only women in my field of vision.'

'It's rather curious, isn't it,' said Adèle sarcastically, 'that the prettiest novice appears more than any other in your sketches.' She flicked the pages angrily. 'I wonder how many times the plain one appears.'

'If she appears at all it's because she appeared in my field of vision, that's all.'

'That's just an excuse,' Adèle retorted crossly. She threw the folder of sketches to the floor.

Loic and Mireille discreetly moved away from what was evidently becoming an arena of marital conflict.

'Look, Adèle,' said Maximilian, indicating the sketch he was working on. 'I draw what's in front of me. I don't really notice its component parts until I'm actually drawing them. I am objective in my art.'

'In your objectivity you can be cruel sometimes, Max,' said Adèle quietly.

'No,' said Max. 'In my objectivity I am honest. I see only what is real.'

IN THE GARDEN of the guest cloister Lady Carter Bonnington sat on one of the rather uncomfortable wooden benches and read a magazine. The magazine was one of those glossy monthly publications which contain mainly advertisements for expensive perfume and lingerie and articles on fashion and beauty aids for the chic woman about town. Lady Bonnington had chosen the magazine from the rack at the airport on the way over to France because it featured an article on cosmetic surgery which mentioned Sir Cecil Bonnington, the eminent plastic surgeon. She studied the full-page portrait of the man who had, through his extraordinary skill, not only maintained her youthful beauty but enhanced it. Dear Cecil—he was no beauty himself. His rather frog-like eyes gazed, smiling, back at her from the gloss of the page.

At that moment Carl Petersen emerged from his cell at the end of the cloister, noticed Lady Bonnington and approached her.

'May I join you?' he asked politely.

'Of course,' she said, smiling up at him, her perfect crowns white against the tan of her skin. She moved up along the bench to allow him to sit beside her. 'Are you taking a break?' she asked. 'A secretary's work is never done, I imagine—even when the boss is dead.' This she said in a joking fashion.

He smiled rather grimly back at her. 'I thought this weekend would constitute a break for me as well as for him, but it hasn't turned out like that.'

'Rather a tragic business all round,' she said. 'It doesn't seem untoward when the old take their lives—on the contrary, I find it quite acceptable. I certainly wouldn't want to live if my body was disintegrating before my eyes and my brain losing its faculties. I hope I shall be able to put myself out of my misery before I lose my wits and no one else is willing to make the decision for me in the name of the sanctity of life. But it's a tragedy when the young commit suicide. A tragedy to see such cowardice in the young.'

'You think that it takes more courage to live than to die?' Petersen asked.

'I most certainly do. Death is the easy option. It takes courage to face your problems and resolve them.'

The young man looked at Lady Bonnington in admiration. 'You think all problems are surmountable, then?'

'Absolutely. It only takes courage and determination—or guts and tenacity, as you Americans say in your films. It takes will.' She placed emphasis on the last word. 'The power of will, the greatest of all powers.'

'Where there's a will, there's a way, eh?' he said, smiling half-heartedly.

'Are you worried about your future, Mr Petersen?' she asked solicitously.

'I haven't had much time to think about it but it is a problem of course.'

'Mrs Kapp might continue to employ you.'

'I don't think I would be happy being employed by a girl ten years younger than me.'

'That's understandable,' Lady Bonnington murmured.

'And in any case she will leave the estate in the hands of his lawyer—or she'll take care of it herself. She's quite capable.'

'So you might find yourself out of work?'

Petersen nodded resignedly.

'Not a pleasant prospect?'

He shook his head.

'I've no doubt,' Lady Bonnington said encouragingly, 'that with your experience and capability, you'll find another employer of the same calibre.'

'I'm not so sure of that,' said Petersen despondently. 'Thelonius Kapp had more enemies than friends. In fact I can honestly say that he had no real friends—not in the profession, anyway. It's unlikely that anyone in Hollywood would consider taking on Kapp's secretary. It would be too much like doing Kapp a favour—and believe me, no one in Hollywood ever wanted to do Kapp any favours. No, I'm afraid that right now I'm up the creek without a paddle.'

'Look,' said Lady Bonnington kindly. She reached out a heavily ringed hand and lightly touched Petersen's arm. 'Don't worry, Carl.., You don't mind me calling you Carl, do you? Don't worry about it. Be courageous—be optimistic. Something will turn up, you can be sure of that. You are too...special...a young man.'

She gazed at him in an endearing maternal manner. 'Something will turn up.'

TWENTY-THREE

Donaghue interviews the guests

DR RENOIR, the first guest to be called for questioning, entered the Mother Superior's office in an agitated fashion and took the seat offered to him, glancing nervously at the two men behind the desk. Inspector Joly smiled reassuringly at him then said gravely, 'Mr Donaghue has informed me of the unfortunate incident that occurred last night in the showers. Do you think you could describe the person who attacked you, Dr Renoir?'

'It was the monk,' said Dr Renoir irritably. 'I told Mr Donaghue that. He saw him himself running away after he attacked me. I trust that you have arrested him—the man is a lunatic.'

'It wasn't the monk,' said Inspector Joly. 'The monk at the time was giving a lecture in the library on Gregorian chant. It was someone impersonating the monk.'

'Good God!' exclaimed Dr Renoir. 'Then who on earth was it? The person who murdered Thelonius Kapp and that girl, I suppose. Good Lord, was he going to murder me right there in the shower?'

'Was there anything about the person that you recognized—voice, carriage, something like that?' the inspector asked.

'I assumed it was the monk. He was wearing a monk's habit and his voice was high-pitched like the monk's. I had no reason to think it was anyone else.'

'Of course not. But the fact is, it was someone else. Is there anyone among the guests whom you know—someone who could have a grudge against you?'

'Someone among the guests with a grudge against me?' asked Dr Renoir incredulously. 'Impossible—they're all strangers to me. The person who attacked me was a raving lunatic—probably the one who murdered the others. I think you should find who it is and arrest him immediately.'

'That's what we're trying to do, doctor,' said Donaghue.

'But you're on the wrong track,' said Renoir passionately. 'There was nothing personal in the attack on me. I was attacked probably because I was in the shower alone, that's all.'

'Do you have any idea what your attacker meant when he said, "I'm going to butcher you the way you butchered me"?'

Dr Renoir glared at Donaghue.

'Lunatics are mad. They do and say crazy things. His words meant nothing. I've never butchered anybody.' The colour of the doctor's pale face heightened. 'I'm a doctor—a gynaecologist. I don't butcher people.'

'Sometimes,' said Donaghue, 'patients die during treatment or surgery and the family blame the doctor. The blame is, of course, unwarranted—but such things, unfortunately, occur. You must, I would imagine, have performed unsuccessful operations.'

'Naturally,' retorted Dr Renoir crossly. 'What surgeon hasn't? We're not gods—we're not infallible. But I've never had a patient or family complain. Some women are, unfortunately, sterile and no matter what you do, hormone treatment, embryo implant, et cetera, they cannot have children. Some of them think that the doctor is a god and can make them fertile—but in any case it was a man who attacked me.'

'He could have been the husband, father or brother of someone you treated,' suggested the inspector.

'I really can't accept that,' said Dr Renoir. 'Some lunatic attacks me and you try to suggest that he had some reason to? Really, such an idea is not only preposterous, it is insulting.'

'Are you sure it was a man who attacked you?' Donaghue asked.

Dr Renoir looked at him incredulously. 'Of course I'm sure.'

'Your attacker was covered by a monk's robe. You said the hood covered his head. Did you see his face?'

'Not clearly. As a matter of fact my eyes were glued to the scalpel he held in his hand.'

'Which hand, the right or the left?'

Dr Renoir frowned in reflection.

'The left, I think.'

'Can you describe the hand?'

'The hand...the hand...' said Dr Renoir hesitantly. 'He was wearing gloves—I didn't see his hand.'

'So, in fact it could as easily have been a woman as a man?'

'He sounded like a man,' said Renoir. 'He had a man's voice. It was the monk's voice.'

'The monk has a rather high-pitched voice. He has the voice of a pubescent boy that hasn't fully broken. A woman lowering her voice could conceivably produce the same effect. Don't forget, doctor, you assumed it was the monk.'

'Look here, Mr Donaghue...' Renoir, his cheeks tinged with a spot of pink, shifted irritably in his seat. 'I've told you, you're on the wrong track altogether. You're trying to imply that it might have been one of my patients—a woman whose child was born dead or deformed and who blamed me. I have, of course, brought stillborn children into the world—what gynaecologist hasn't?—but in no way have those tragic misfortunes been due to my negligence.'

'No one,' Donaghue said quietly, 'has implied such a thing.'

'And nor should they,' snapped Dr Renoir. 'And now might I suggest that you terminate this futile line of questioning and get on with the business of finding this madman before he attacks me or anyone else again?'

'Certainly, Dr Renoir,' said Donaghue. 'We just have one or two further questions to put to you. Can you please tell us where you were between breakfast and lunch yesterday morning and between 3.45 when we left Dr Blanche's cell and 4.30 yesterday afternoon.'

'That's simple. I stayed with my wife in our cell. Apart from meal times and the singing in the chapel we remained in our room. My wife, as you know, is suffering violent nausea.'

'Did you leave the cell for any reason?'

'Once, late in the morning—I can't remember the time exactly—to call a novice from the kitchen as no one responded to the buzzer.'

'And did you find a novice?'

'No, I had to clear up the mess myself.'

'When you went into the kitchen it was empty?'

'Absolutely, not a soul about.'

'Just one or two more questions, Dr Renoir. What did you think of Thelonius Kapp?'

'Kapp? I didn't really think anything. One of those Bohemian types that go beyond the pale in their behaviour—but he obvi-

ously satisfied some need of the public with his films which are,
I believe, very popular. Not the kind of man I'd like to know
personally.' Dr Renoir leaned forward conspiratorially and said
in a whisper, 'I believe he's a Jew.'

'A Jew?' queried Donaghue.

'Yes, I'm sure he is—the black eyes, you can tell.'

'I assumed he was a Catholic,' said Donaghue. 'Why should
a member of the Jewish faith buy a Catholic abbey and take part
in its retreats?'

Dr Renoir smiled a knowing smile. 'To take over, of course—
to take over the Church. A fifth columnist.'

Donaghue looked askance at Dr Renoir then resumed his questioning.

'And your wife—did she admire him?'

'Felicity—admire Kapp? No, I don't think so. She'd go to see
his films but she wouldn't be interested in a man like that—not
personally, no.'

'Well,' said Donaghue, 'that's fine, doctor. You can go. Please
send along your wife.'

'My wife?' The word exploded from the doctor's mouth.
'What on earth do you want to ask my wife? She's three months
pregnant, is violently ill and has hardly left her room since we
arrived. I will not have her subjected to the trauma of interrogation.'

'I can assure you, Dr Renoir,' said Inspector Joly calmly, 'that
we will subject her to no trauma and will take into careful consideration her delicate condition. But each person present in the
abbey at the time of the deaths must be questioned—not necessarily to ascertain their possible guilt but to see if they can, by
a chance thing seen or overheard, help in the enquiry.'

'Very well,' Dr Renoir conceded reluctantly. He frowned at
the two men before him. 'I trust that you will respect my wishes
and treat my wife with the utmost delicacy.'

DONAGHUE, when Felicity Renoir entered the office, had a dis-
tinct feeling that he was dealing, not with the delicate flower that
her husband had depicted, but rather a kind of sturdy flowering
bush—a rhododendron perhaps, or a laurier rose.

Felicity sat confidently in the chair vacated by her husband and smiled brightly at her interlocutors.

'If at any moment I turn green and run from the room you'll have to excuse me,' she said. 'I suppose my husband mentioned that I'm pregnant and am rather prone to unexpected bouts of vomiting. If he tried to persuade you that I would be adversely affected by being questioned, take no notice. André has a tendency to be a little too romantic about this our first child.' She smiled. 'I always thought that gynaecologists must be incapable of seeing sex and reproduction in anything other than a clinical manner. But I was wrong—they become, in fact, more irrational and romantic than the rest of the male population, who couldn't tell an endometrium from an implanted blastocyst.'

She looked knowledgeably at Donaghue and Inspector Joly, who squirmed under her scrutiny. It was true—neither of them had the slightest idea of what a blastocyst was, implanted or not implanted, nor an endometrium.

'You are a nurse, Madame Renoir?' Donaghue enquired.

'Yes, an obstetric nurse.'

'You met your husband at work?'

'Yes. He was taken by my efficiency—I'm a very efficient nurse—and I was taken by his little boy lost distractedness. He needed taking in hand—that was obvious to me.'

'How long have you been married?'

'One year.'

'So he was what age when you met?'

'Thirty-four.'

'Obviously after twelve months of marriage you know your husband well. Are you aware of any professional problem he might have had prior to your meeting him?'

'Professional problems? No, he has never spoken of professional problems.' She paused. 'He's a very respected doctor.'

'He has never mentioned any distressing cases—where a child died, for instance, or a mother died in childbirth, and the father and family reproached him?'

Felicity frowned. 'No,' she said. 'No. He's never mentioned such a thing.'

'But such a thing could have happened?'

'Well, yes, such things tragically happen all the time, despite all the preventive care we take. But the staff of hospitals are

rarely blamed.' She regarded Donaghue quizzically. 'You think
he was attacked by a former patient or member of a patient's
family—is that it?'

'The thought has naturally occurred to us.'

'You don't think the attack on my husband is linked to the
other deaths?'

'At this stage of our enquiry we are merely looking for con-
nections. We don't know or think anything. Tell us what you
think, Madame Renoir.'

She looked fixedly at Donaghue, her plain, intelligent face
grave. She paused for some moments before speaking, her hands
clasped together in her lap. Donaghue noticed that the fingers
were long and finely tapered and the nails short and unvarnished.

'I have no reason to believe,' she said finally, 'that anyone,
former patient or not, would have any reason to attack or threaten
my husband.'

Donaghue nodded. 'With regard to the other deaths—were you
aware that Mrs Kapp was, like yourself, pregnant?'

'My husband did tell me, yes.'

'In your opinion, Madame Renoir, do you think it possible
that Mrs Kapp might have planned to commit suicide with her
husband?'

'I'd find that hard to believe,' said Felicity firmly. 'Pregnant
women rarely commit suicide. The life force is too strong in
them. Pregnant women become like cows—they become concerned primarily with the nourishment of their and their child's
bodies. What appeared as problems before fade into insignifi-
cance in the face of the life developing inside them. I've never
known a pregnant woman, no matter how difficult her circumstances, to consider suicide—abortion, perhaps, but not suicide.'

'What do you think about the deaths that occurred yesterday?
Are you worried, as your husband is, that there is a murderer
loose in the abbey?'

Felicity smiled. 'André can get rather hysterical at times—it's
the little boy in him clutching at his mother's skirts. If you want
my true opinion, Thelonius Kapp's death was theatrical, a pub-
licity stunt of some kind that went wrong. The girl's death was
probably accidental and the novice's entirely incidental—a second unfortunate accident. No, I can't say I share André's fear

that there's a homicidal maniac at large. I don't feel that that is the case.'

'But what about the attack on your husband? How do you explain that?'

'That…well, yes, that is difficult to explain.'

'Are you not worried that the person might attack him again?'

'Of course I am,' she replied indignantly. 'That's why I'm hoping that as soon as you've finished your questioning we might be able to leave.'

'Until we have enough evidence to either cease the enquiry or make an arrest I'm afraid that the guests will have to remain,' interjected Inspector Joly.

Felicity frowned worriedly.

'It's going to be difficult for me. My husband will be very put out. You see, he is really quite frightened by this attack on him. He thinks he's going to be killed.'

'We have several police officers patrolling the grounds day and night,' said the inspector. 'I doubt very much that there will be any more attacks—you can be assured of that.'

'I do hope so,' said Felicity anxiously.

'Now, Madame Renoir, only one or two more questions,' said Donaghue. 'Where were you yesterday between breakfast and lunch and between 3.15 and 4.30? A routine question, you understand, that we have to ask everybody.'

'I was in my cell most of the time with André. I must have been there at those times. I went back to the cell immediately after Mr Kapp's death in the chapel. André, of course, was with you until about half-past three when he came back to see how I was.'

'In the morning did you or your husband leave the cell at any time?'

'I didn't. André did once or twice.'

'Did he say where he was going?'

'The first time to attend to Mr Kapp.'

'Mr Kapp? What time was this?'

'About ten. I can't remember exactly. Mrs Kapp came to the cell and called him——her husband wanted to see a doctor.'

'And did he say why he'd been called?'

'He came back five minutes later. He said Mr Kapp was asleep when he got there—that he'd taken drugs and was out of his mind on them.'

'He didn't mention it to me when I questioned him.'

'Oh, he probably forgot—what with me vomiting every five minutes. He has a tendency to panic at times.'

'And after that he left again?'

'Once, as far as I remember—to fetch a novice to clean up after me. He pressed the bell several times but she must have been occupied.'

'Just two more questions before we let you go, Madame Renoir,' said Donaghue, making a note on his pad. 'What did you think of Thelonius Kapp?'

'I think he was an extraordinary man—one of those rare men that live life to the full on both a physical and an intellectual level.'

'Was he the kind of man that appealed to you? I'm talking about the appeal of a man to a woman.'

Felicity narrowed her eyes. 'I think he did rather appeal to me despite his age. There was something of the little boy in him. It's that that appeals to me in men—the little boy in them, the appeal to the maternal instinct. It's common to many women. Yes...' she reflected, 'he was a man I could have been attracted to.'

'And your husband—what did he think of him?'

'I think he secretly admired him—was perhaps jealous of him. He didn't like his lifestyle—André doesn't like the avant-garde—but I think he admired the man. André admires those who are successful.'

'Your husband thinks that Kapp was Jewish. Are you aware of your husband's anti-Semitism?'

Felicity smiled apologetically. 'André is politically immature—I told you, in many ways he is a boy. I am, in a way, his mother. I intend to wean him off such infantile prejudices.'

Before Donaghue had a chance to say another word Felicity suddenly leapt from her seat, clapped her hand to her mouth and, grunting a muffled apology, ran from the room.

'A remarkably astute woman, that,' Donaghue commented after the door had closed behind her. 'She knows her husband well, I think—although, on the other hand, I feel that he has no idea of the kind of woman he has married.'

'So,' said Inspector Joly, rubbing his large hands together in a businesslike manner, 'what do you think? Either of them likely suspects? He went into Kapp's room yesterday at ten. He could have slipped the arsenic into the cocaine box without being seen.'

'But Sandra Kapp took cocaine from the box later and suffered no ill effects.'

'There is that,' the inspector conceded. He scratched the dome of his head. 'And he really had no motive as far as I can see— and on top of that he was attacked. I suppose we can effectively scratch him from the list of likely suspects.'

'For the moment, yes,' said Donaghue thoughtfully.

'Her too?'

'Yes,' Donaghue concurred.

'He might have been attacked because he unwittingly saw something the murderer didn't want him to see.'

'It's possible.'

'Well, we haven't got very far,' said Inspector Joly dourly. He looked at his watch. '10.15. We'd better get on. Who should we see next?'

'Carl Petersen, I think.'

As Donaghue reached for the buzzer to summon the American the telephone rang. He picked up the receiver then passed it to Inspector Joly. 'It's for you, Inspector,' he said.

The inspector listened for a few seconds then spluttered, 'Good Lord! What time was this?' A further pause then he said briskly, 'We'll get right out.'

He replaced the receiver and regarded Donaghue solemnly.

'A car has been found in a ravine on the road to Hyères. The driver, a woman, is dead. The police have reason to believe it's Sandra Kapp.'

'Sandra Kapp!' Donaghue exclaimed. 'Are you sure?'

'That's what they said.'

'Was she alone?'

'There were no other passengers.'

'She was in the driving seat?'

'Yes.'

'And the car, what was it?'

'A Mercedes, a hired one, registered in Kapp's name. Hired in Paris—the car he drove down here in.'

'But that's impossible,' said Donaghue in consternation. 'She left with Clothilde—unless for some reason she decided to take her own car. But why?'

'I need to go and identify the body,' said Inspector Joly. 'I think you should come with me. Apparently the woman is pretty smashed up. You saw more of Mrs Kapp than I did—you're better qualified to identify her.'

'Yes, I think I'll come,' said Donaghue worriedly, and he rose quickly from his seat.

AT THE POLICE MORTUARY in Hyères Donaghue and Inspector Joly looked down at the face of the dead woman whose body had been recovered from the wreckage of a black Mercedes in a ravine ten kilometres from St Pierre la Croix on the road to Hyères.

The instinct of the two men had been to turn their heads from the awful sight that met their eyes when the police surgeon lifted the sheet that covered the body—but they gazed steadfastly, albeit with difficulty. The face was shattered beyond all recognition, torn and disfigured by the shards of glass and metal that had ripped it into a bloody mangled mass of flesh. The skull was crushed horribly on one side, the brown hair that clung to it caked in dried blood. The woman—a girl, the police surgeon had deduced, of twenty-four or twenty-five—was dressed in a Salome-style outfit of tight shorts and vest. She had been wearing a blonde wig which had come off in the accident.

'Shall I replace the sheet?' the surgeon asked after a few seconds.

'Yes, you may,' said Donaghue, and Inspector Joly turned from the appalling sight with relief.

'It's Sandra Kapp, I suppose,' he said, 'but who could possibly tell?'

They left the mortuary and emerged from its cool interior into the glaring heat of the Commissariat's inner courtyard.

'What I don't understand,' said Donaghue, 'is why Clothilde didn't contact me. She left with Sandra Kapp this morning—I supposed in her car. Why would she have changed into her stage outfit? It doesn't make sense. She's in mourning, for God's sake.'

'People go funny when they lose a loved one,' said Joly.

'It just doesn't make any sense,' Donaghue reiterated, his face frowning in puzzlement.

Inspector Joly looked askance at Donaghue. When the little man frowned he looked disconcertingly like one of those monkeys you saw on the Rock of Gibraltar.

'I'll tell you what I think you should do,' he said. 'You go back to the abbey in that…that…lawnmower.' He indicated with a wave of his heavy hand the Mother Superior's ancient 2CV in which they had been obliged to drive to Hyères. 'I'll return in an hour or so after I have sorted out the paperwork here. I suppose we'll have to mark the dead woman down as Sandra Kapp, although there were no identity documents to verify it. Perhaps we ought to bring their secretary—Petersen, isn't that what he's called?—to identify her, though I doubt that he would recognize his own grandmother from that awful mess.'

'That might be necessary. He might know of some physical mark or peculiarity that could identify her. The post-mortem, of course, will reveal whether the dead woman was pregnant or not. Mrs Kapp was pregnant, or so Dr Renoir diagnosed. She was going to Hyères to have her condition confirmed.'

Donaghue fumbled in his pocket and withdrew his notebook. He quickly scribbled a message and handed it to Joly.

'I want you to do me a service,' he said. 'Phone your car and give this message to Mark Kingsford. Tell him it's urgent and of the utmost importance.'

Inspector Joly scanned the message, lifted an eyebrow and looked quizzically at Donaghue.

'It's a strange business, isn't it?' said Donaghue in answer to Joly's expression.

'Strange isn't the word,' said Inspector Joly wearily. 'I'm beginning to wonder where all this will end.'

'It will end soon,' said Donaghue grimly. He shook Inspector Joly's hand in farewell. 'I shall go back now and speak to Petersen.'

TWENTY-FOUR

Questions are answered

AS THE OLD 2CV struggled up the steep winding ascent from the U bend where the black Mercedes had spun off the road, Donaghue, at the wheel, pondered. If the dead woman was Sandra Kapp then his hypothesis about the series of deaths at the abbey was correct and there would be no more deaths. But—and this was the extraordinary thing—there was no proof whatsoever, no hard evidence, that any of the deaths were other than they appeared. This murderer, this cold-blooded killer, was astoundingly astute—had committed, it seemed, the perfect crime.

But what if the dead girl was not Sandra Kapp? The question lingered in Donaghue's mind.

Then suddenly, as the abbey came into view, two small items of irrelevant data were released from his IDR and transferred to the conscious part of his brain and he found himself with an answer to his question.

By the time Donaghue reached the abbey, lunch was under way—a quiet, sombre affair. Donaghue found himself in the company of Carl Petersen, Thérèse Mendes France and Lady Olivia Carter Bonnington. Loic and Mireille Parmentier sat as usual with Maximilian and Adèle Bloch, and Dr Renoir, conspicuous by his absence, had evidently decided to eat in his cell until his attacker was found and arrested. The subdued guests were served by the plump and nervous Sister Paul and her tall, beautiful companion, Sister Dominique.

Immediately after lunch Donaghue suggested to Petersen that he come to the Mother Superior's office at his convenience to answer a few routine questions.

Ten minutes later Petersen knocked at the office door. As he lowered his long limbs into the chair before the desk Donaghue noted that as usual the tall American was immaculately turned out—today in crisp khaki-coloured colonial-style shorts to the knee and a beige silk shirt. The whole outfit was, miraculously, without the slightest crumple. How such a state of sartorial crumplelessness was achieved defied the powers of Donaghue's imagination. His own clothes, even when new, sagged and bagged irretrievably the instant he put them on.

Donaghue put his hands together and addressed the American gravely.

'I have to inform you, Mr Petersen, that an accident was reported this morning. A car went off the road about ten kilometres from here on the road to Hyères. A body was recovered, that of a woman. The police have every reason to believe that the woman was Sandra Kapp. I have to warn you that you might at some point be asked to identify the body.'

'Good God!' exclaimed Petersen, his eyes widening. 'Mrs Kapp? But what the hell is going on? First Mr Kapp, then Milly Silverstone, now Mrs Kapp.' He looked grimly at Donaghue. 'I suppose it will be me next. Looks like the whole Kapp entourage is going to be wiped out in one fell swoop.'

'It appears to have been an accident,' said Donaghue. 'The bend was taken at speed and the car went off the road.'

'She must have been distracted. She's taken the death of her husband very badly,' said Petersen rather more calmly.

'Did you know Mrs Kapp well, Mr Petersen?' Donaghue asked.

'I can't truthfully say I knew her well,' said Petersen. 'I've known her since she and Mr Kapp met two years ago.'

'How would you describe Mrs Kapp?'

'An intelligent girl—very intelligent. Rather enigmatic to me.'

'Enigmatic?'

'Yes. In her very English way she maintained a kind of emotional reserve—never revealed her true feelings.'

'Not even towards Mr Kapp?'

'In private, yes—but never in public. I see it as an English characteristic. Her outrageous stage act does not in any way reflect her real character—in fact, she is almost the opposite.'

'A curious dichotomy,' Donaghue remarked. 'Often these singers and actors can be just as exuberant in their private lives as in their professional ones.'

'Not Mrs Kapp,' said Petersen. 'As soon as she took off her

stage outfit she reverted to what she really was—an intelligent, lower class English girl from Yorkshire or Lancashire or somewhere like that.'

'Do you think she loved her husband?' asked Donaghue. 'Many people would think that a girl married to a much older man is nothing more than a gold digger.'

'I think she loved him,' said Petersen reflectively. 'I think that was obvious to anyone who saw them together.'

'The deaths that have occurred—what do you think about them? What is your explanation, Mr Petersen?'

Petersen regarded Donaghue thoughtfully before answering.

'I feel certain that Mr Kapp committed suicide,' he said finally. 'He was very ill. He knew how ill he was. He was not the kind of man to want to live in a state of senility.'

'And Milly Silverstone?'

'I suppose she must have been in love with him.'

'Had you ever noticed signs of such feelings on her part?'

'No, I can't honestly say I had—but you never know with young girls. She may have wanted to take Sandra Kapp's place. Millions of girls all over the world do.'

'And the novice's death—that was an accident as far as you're concerned?'

'It must have been.'

'So you have no fear, like some of the guests, that there's a mass murderer in the abbey?'

Petersen smiled. 'There are people who react hysterically to death,' he said. 'Mainly women, I think.'

'Not just women,' said Donaghue. 'Dr Renoir is keeping to his cell at the moment for fear of being murdered. He does, however, have some reason for his fear. He was attacked with a scalpel in the showers last night by someone disguised as the monk, Brother Martin de Porres.'

Petersen's eyes widened in astonishment behind the lightly tinted lenses of his glasses.

'Attacked in the showers? But that's absolutely incredible—who on earth would do such a thing?'

'That's exactly the question we are asking ourselves,' said Donaghue. 'One would be led to believe that if Mr Kapp, Milly Silverstone and the novice were murdered, then the murderer must also have attacked Dr Renoir—perhaps because they believed he had some knowledge of the deaths that might incriminate them.'

Petersen smiled again. 'It's all rather too far-fetched to be credible—some lunatic among the guests who wants to kill them all...'

'But it's an idea the police have to investigate. Three deaths in one day appear too much of a coincidence to the unimaginative mind of a policeman.'

'Do you know,' said Petersen, 'such a coincidence is not at all extraordinary to me—nor would it be to anyone who knew Thelonius Kapp as I knew him. That three deaths should occur in or around the presence of Thelonius Kapp is not in the least surprising. On the contrary, there's a natural logic to it—it wouldn't be pure coincidence.'

'Can you explain what you mean, Mr Petersen?' Donaghue asked.

'You'd have to know Thelonius Kapp to understand. He was like a centripetal force—like a black hole that drew people to him inexorably whether they wanted to be drawn or not. And, like the force of a black hole, his was a negative force, a destructive force. I tell you, it doesn't surprise me at all that disturbance and death follow in the wake of Thelonius Kapp. He made enemies wherever he went, said openly what he thought about everyone in Hollywood. He used his actors and actresses as if they were mere models of human beings in Plasticine to be moulded as he wished. He was not a man who engendered peace and tranquillity. He was a man who engendered hate, and hate engenders death. I'm sure you must agree with that, Mr Donaghue.'

'Oh, I do, Mr Petersen,' said Donaghue. 'I certainly do. So you felt no great love for your employer?'

'I could have come to love him,' Petersen said softly, making Donaghue look at him in surprise, 'but like him—never. He was a man you either loved or hated—liking didn't come into it. But as his secretary I felt neither sentiment. I simply respected him.'

'Did it surprise you that he committed suicide?'

'No, I can't say it did. As I said, he was ill and conscious, on his lucid days, of his condition. No, I can't say it surprised me. As for Milly, she might have tried to seduce him and he rejected her.'

'It could, of course, be as simple as that,' said Donaghue, 'but Inspector Joly did not know Thelonius Kapp as well as you know him and feels obliged to investigate the coincidence of three deaths in one day in one place.'

'I suppose he must,' said Petersen, 'and we of course are all suspects—although what anybody apart from his wife could gain from his death, I can't imagine.'

'He left his fortune to his wife, I take it?'

'Of course. He made a new will at their marriage.'

'And the former will? Who was the estate left to in that?'

'It was left, the bulk of it, for the maintenance of this abbey and for a film foundation.'

'Did he make any provision for you in either will?'

'A small provision, of course, for the years of service I've rendered him. But he's always paid me well. I don't expect a fortune.'

'How long have you worked for him?'

'Ten years.'

'Did you resent the fact that his probably considerable estate was to go to a girl he's known barely two years?'

'Not at all,' said Petersen indignantly. 'She was his wife. It's only natural—it was her right.'

'Tell me about yourself, Mr Petersen,' said Donaghue.

'There's not much to say,' said Petersen dolefully. 'Ten years as a faithful and dependable secretary to Thelonius Kapp—that's about all.'

'Your age, Mr Petersen—would you mind telling me your age?'

'Not at all. I'm thirty-five.'

'Are you married?'

'No. My job's not suited to domestic life. I move around too much.'

'So, in a way, you are married to your job?'

'"Were" is the operative word,' said Petersen morosely, 'not "are". With both of them dead I'm effectively out of work as from now.'

'Of course,' said Donaghue. 'That's something that must have just occurred to you. But I trust Mr Kapp will have provided you with enough to keep you going until you find another employer.'

'Yes, I guess that will be the case. Still, it's a bit of a shock, as you can imagine.'

'Absolutely,' Donaghue agreed. 'But look at it positively, Mr Petersen. Now you can envisage marriage—find a more rooted position, as it were.'

Petersen eyed Donaghue diffidently.

'Why do you assume that I have some great desire for marriage?'

'A young man of your ability—good-looking, healthy—it must happen at some time. You must have women interested in you.' Donaghue winked outrageously at Petersen, making the American start.

'I...I...' he stammered.

'You must have had a girlfriend or two,' Donaghue persisted, winking grotesquely again.

'Well...I really don't see—' the American began. He was clearly embarrassed by Donaghue's questions and manner of putting them.

'Forgive me for appearing to pry,' said Donaghue, 'but knowledge of the personal lives of the guests is pertinent to our enquiry. We have to ask one or two slightly indiscreet questions. You are, of course, not obliged to answer.'

Petersen eyed Donaghue soberly.

'Do you currently have a girlfriend?'

'As a matter of fact I don't,' Petersen retorted rather sharply. Then his face reddened and he blurted out, 'I know. I know what you're getting at—but you can forget it. I'm not gay, if that's what you're thinking.'

Donaghue smiled apologetically. 'No, Mr Petersen, that's not what I was thinking at all. As a matter of fact, I'll let you into a little secret. I saw you with your young lady at Heathrow airport on Saturday.'

'What?' spluttered Petersen. 'You saw me...?'

'Yes. With a very beautiful young woman. You were taking the flight to Paris. I was in the Marseilles queue alongside. I assumed naturally that she was your wife or girlfriend...'

'Well, you were wrong,' said Petersen indignantly. 'I travelled alone to Paris. You were very much mistaken.'

Donaghue's face took on an expression of contrite apology.

'Please forgive my presumption,' he said. 'As she was standing next to you, I naturally assumed she was with you. I noticed her, as did everyone else within sight of her, because she was dressed in one of those extraordinary Salome-style outfits. I believe she spoke to you at one point. You must have noticed her.'

'I can't say I remember,' said Petersen curtly. 'Having accompanied the real Salome on many of her tours and having seen thousands of her look-alikes, I wouldn't notice one more in a busy airport—even if she spoke to me.'

'No, naturally you wouldn't,' Donaghue concurred as he dropped his eyes to his notebook. 'Yesterday morning, Mr Petersen, between breakfast and lunchtime, what did you do?'

'I stayed in my cell. I had letters to type. I'm not here on holiday, Mr Donaghue, as you probably know. I'm a working man.'

'Did you leave your cell at any point?'

'Perhaps to go to the men's room.'

'Can anyone testify to your having stayed in your room?'

'Mrs Kapp came to my room shortly after breakfast with a letter for typing. Other than that, I didn't see anyone until lunchtime.'

'And after lunch, between one and three?'

'I returned to the cell to work.'

'Did you see or speak to anyone?'

'A novice whom I called out...let me see, about 1.30. I couldn't find my lighter and I thought I must have left it in the refectory.'

'Which novice came? Can you remember?'

'The tall pretty one. I can't remember their names.'

'Sister Dominique?'

'I think that's it—the best-looking of the bunch.'

'Well, Mr Petersen,' said Donaghue, 'I think that's all. Thank you for your co-operation.'

The American rose slowly to his feet.

'May I ask you a question?' he said hesitantly.

'Of course,' said Donaghue, smiling up at him.

'You came here on holiday, didn't you? You weren't called in to investigate the case?'

'That's right. I'm actually on holiday—or supposed to be— but look what happens: I find myself slap bang in the middle of a series of quite inexplicable deaths.'

'But you're not being paid by anyone to investigate them?'

'Oh no, I just find myself doing it—can't stop myself. My job is, in fact, for me, a little like a vocation. It's not something I chose, it's something that chose me. I have no real control over it. I come across a puzzle in pieces and I have to put it back together again. But this case—it's baffling me. Do you know, Mr Petersen,' Donaghue leaned forward conspiratorially, 'I think this might be the first puzzle—I won't call it a case—that will beat me. I'm beginning to think that I might actually have been wrong to have imagined that the deaths were linked. They might well be, as you yourself said, nothing other than they appear to be, a suicide pact and an accident. The attack on Dr Renoir must have been some act of personal revenge and a complete coincidence.'

'So you think the investigation might be wound up soon and we'll be able to leave?'

'Oh yes, undoubtedly so,' said Donaghue. 'This case is either quite simple or incredibly complex—and,' he added almost despairingly, 'it might well turn out, as I said, to be my first defeat.'

'Ah well,' said Carl Petersen as he opened the door to leave, 'you can't win 'em all.'

MARK KINGSFORD, having duly sent off the faxes to their respective addresses, as Donaghue had instructed him, was driving Inspector Joly's car slowly around the delightful port of Hyères when, much to his surprise, the car phone rang. He picked it tentatively up. Inspector Joly's voice crackled through the earpiece.

'Go immediately to the central hospital,' he said. 'You'll see it signposted from the town centre. Find Dr Blanche and Mrs Kapp, who should be in consultation in the maternity section. Tell them *imperatively* not to return to the abbey before 9 p.m. this evening. When they arrive they are to go directly to Dr Blanche's cell and wait there until Donaghue calls them. Phone Donaghue at the abbey as soon as you've found them.'

'Will do,' said Mark enthusiastically and he turned the car in the direction of the town centre.

AS SOON AS the door had closed behind Carl Petersen the telephone on the Mother Superior's desk rang stridently. Donaghue grabbed it. It was Mark Kingsford, calling from Hyères to say that, because of the time lag, he would probably have to wait until the evening for the replies from America. He would have them by seven, he calculated. He had, he added, been to the hospital in Hyères as instructed by Inspector Joly but Dr Blanche and Mrs Kapp had not yet arrived. He would let him know as soon as they turned up.

Donaghue replaced the receiver with a frown. Had he made a dreadful error? He put the thought from his mind and consulted his list. Who should he interview next? Maximilian Bloch. He would talk to Maximilian Bloch next.

TWENTY-FIVE

From the artist's point of view

INSPECTOR JOLY returned from Hyères while Donaghue was waiting for Maximilian Bloch to be summoned from the fields.

'Any news of Clothilde?' he asked.

Donaghue shook his head worriedly.

'It's strange that she hasn't contacted us,' said the inspector. His large bovine face paled. 'You don't suppose this Kapp woman killed her then drove herself off the road, do you?'

'I really don't think so,' said Donaghue, then he added cheerfully, 'They'll arrive at the hospital in due course. They've probably taken a little detour.'

'So you don't think the girl in the Mercedes was Sandra Kapp?'

'No, I don't think it was. I hope it wasn't.'

'Who do you think it was, then? Some young groupie—isn't that what they call them?—who took his car for a joy ride?'

'Possibly, but unlikely in my opinion.'

'Have you got any theories about it, then?'

'Only an idea—which will have to be borne out.'

'And you're keeping your ideas to yourself for the moment?'

'Until they become more substantial than ideas,' murmured Donaghue, nodding his shaggy head.

'So what about Petersen? Any concrete ideas about him from your interview?'

Donaghue gave the inspector a brief résumé of the conversation he'd had with the American.

'Mmm,' grunted the inspector. 'He, of course, would be the best placed to kill Kapp—he virtually lived with him, knew all his habits—but, according to his statement, he stayed in his cell all morning working and didn't go near his employer. But he could have gone to Kapp's cell—say, to take the letter he had typed back—and put the arsenic into the container. Sandra Kapp wouldn't have considered it odd for him to come—not enough to mention it anyway.'

'That's possible,' Donaghue murmured.

'Of course,' the inspector went on, 'he doesn't have any clear motive, unless he desperately needed the money Kapp might leave him—although, from what he said, it's not going to amount to much. On top of that, with his employer dead, he's out of a job and worse off in the long run. No, I can't see a valid motive there. There could have been some personal conflict between them, of course. Did you get the impression that he hated his employer?'

'No, on the contrary,' said Donaghue. 'I think he felt quite strongly towards Mr Kapp.'

'So, no money motive, no hate motive. What about romance? Could he have been in love with Mrs Kapp?'

'It's possible,' said Donaghue. 'He's not a man to wear his feelings on his shirt-sleeves—but, no, I don't think there's anything between them.'

'So, no money motive, no hate motive, no love motive, and he's got no reason to be vengeful towards Kapp. As he said, he was well paid and stood to inherit something in the not too distant future. In fact, it seems to me that it would have been in his interest to keep his position for as long as possible. The longer he served his employer the more he'd be likely to get on his death.'

'Exactly,' agreed Donaghue. 'That's exactly the conclusion I came to.'

'So, who's next on the list?' asked Inspector Joly.

'Maximilian Bloch.'

'Ah, the artist,' said Joly. 'Now there's a possibility. Artists are, as we all know, temperamental, passionate people. It would be fitting for a murder in Provence to have been committed by an artist.' Joly smiled at the novelty of his thought.

At that moment came a knock on the door and Maximilian Bloch, with a folder of sketches under his arm, entered the office. Beaming broadly, he placed the folio on the table before Donaghue and the inspector then shook hands firmly with them both.

'I brought my sketches as you requested,' he said, nodding his handsome head in the direction of the folio, 'though why you should want to see them in connection with this enquiry is beyond my illogical artist's brain.'

Donaghue picked up the folio and leafed through the sketches within. There were about a dozen in all, mainly scenes of the vineyards and the toiling nuns, one or two of the abbey buildings, one of the wine press and several close-up studies of individual nuns as they worked.

Donaghue selected the sketch of the wine press and studied it for a moment or so. The sketch depicted the barrel-shaped tub with the large screw shaft rising from it.

'The circular wooden weight?' asked Donaghue. 'Where was it when you sketched the press?'

'In the barrel, of course,' said Maximilian Bloch. 'They only raise it when they put the grapes in to be pressed.'

'At what time did you do the sketch—can you remember?'

'Quite early in the afternoon. It was one of the first I did.'

'Did you return to the press later to sketch it again?'

'No. One sketch is enough. It's quite a simple object to draw.'

Donaghue selected a second sketch and held it up for the artist to look at. It was the sketch of two nuns, apparently conversing, that had attracted the attention of Mireille Parmentier earlier on, in the field. Donaghue had recognized the pretty face of Sister Marie Pierre and the rather ugly features of the novice Sister Veronique who had died in the press.

'Can you remember when you sketched these novices? You are aware, of course, that this novice...' He indicated the plainer one. '...is the novice who died tragically in the wine press?'

'Yes,' said Maximilian Bloch sorrowfully, 'I am aware of that sad fact.' He reflected. 'I sketched them yesterday...I'm not sure...let me see...was it morning or afternoon? I think it was shortly before lunch.'

'Where were they when you sketched them?'

'At the gate of the vegetable garden where they have those plastic greenhouses.'

'And were they actually conversing? They appear to be in the sketch.'

'I think they were,' said Maximilian Bloch, his black eyes smiling, 'although they shouldn't have been, of course.'

Donaghue studied the picture intently. The faces of the two novices were depicted in semi-profile, close together. Both mouths were slightly open as if one were speaking and the other listening intently. He studied the expressions of the two faces before leafing through the folder again and pulling out a third drawing—this time one of the many sketches of the vineyard where the nuns had been working for the last two days. Alongside the field ran the gravel path that led back to the wine press, the narrow path that he and Clothilde had taken early on Sunday morning.

He pulled out two or three similar studies of the same scene and compared them. Then he held the first out to Maximilian Bloch. With his forefinger he indicated two small figures, one a novice in a white habit, the other a woman in a long skirt, depicted at the end of the gravel path, apparently heading in the direction of the wine press.

'Can you remember when you sketched this person?' He indicated the woman in the skirt.

'Now, that's difficult,' said Maximilian Bloch. He cupped his face in a beautiful tanned hand. 'I've done so many of this scene. They're all studies for the painting I want to do when I get home. Now, let me see...' He peered at the small, roughly sketched figure. 'It's a woman. Now I remember—I sketched it early in the afternoon, not long after lunch. It was originally Thérèse Mendes France then, later on in the afternoon, I changed it to the person you see there.'

'Do you know who this person is? I take it it's one of the guests?'

Maximilian Bloch frowned. 'I imagine it is—it must have been. But I really wasn't looking at the identity of the person, if you understand me—I was looking at the form.'

'But you recognized Miss Mendes France earlier in the afternoon?'

'Well yes, because she had bade me good afternoon in passing and I followed her progress along the path. But this person—I happened to look up and there she was.'

'You're sure it was a woman?'

'Yes.' He smiled, revealing an array of even white teeth. 'Unless it was a nun wearing a skirt.'

'And why did you change your sketch, Mr Bloch?'

'It occurred to me that Miss Mendes France would be sure to come and look at the sketches at some point. She might not have been flattered by my representation of her. Women can be sensitive about their appearance. Miss Mendes France has a splendid physique for a woman of her age but she did appear in my sketch a little *manly.*'

'And the woman you sketched later—can you place her among the guests?'

'Strangely enough, I can't,' said Maximilian Bloch. 'As I said, I only glimpsed her as she hurried along.'

'Was she, would you say, a young woman or an older woman?'

'A young woman, I'd say.'

'And the colour of her hair?' Donaghue glanced down at the sketch.

'I couldn't say. As you can see in the sketch, she was wearing a scarf.'

'A young woman wearing a scarf,' Donaghue mused as he studied the sketch closely. The figure depicted was small, distant from the observer. It was a rough sketch, without any apparent detail, of a figure walking away from the artist, the left arm swinging out behind.

'She appears to have been walking briskly,' said Donaghue.

'Yes, she was walking quickly.'

'And you can't remember exactly when you sketched it? Can you, for instance, say whether it was before or after Mr Kapp's death in the chapel?'

Maximilian reflected carefully. 'I think it was after but I can't swear on it. When I'm painting or sketching I lose all notion of time. I enter another temporal sphere—one where time miraculously stands still.'

'May I keep these sketches for a little while, Mr Bloch? I'll return them later.'

'Of course,' said Bloch.

Donaghue regarded him intently.

'Are you a religious man, Mr Bloch?'

Maximilian Bloch smiled. 'I can't truthfully say that I am,' he said. 'I seek no explanations of life. I seek only to express it— in my own particular way.' He regarded Donaghue humorously. 'I suppose you're wondering why I came on a retreat.'

'The thought had occurred to me,' said Donaghue.

'I came primarily for my wife, Adèle. She is undergoing a

minor personal crisis. I thought the tranquillity would be good
for her, help her to see her problems in a more realistic light,
and at the same time I thought I might enjoy the opportunity of
stepping into the shoes of Manet, Cézanne and Van Gogh and
sketching the quite extraordinary landscapes of Provence.'

'You must, both of you, have been perturbed by the incidents
that have occurred.'

'Death, in whatever form it takes, is disturbing.'

'What is your opinion as to the nature of the deaths?'

'I would imagine that they need investigating—as you are doing now.'

'Do you think that the three people who died were murdered?'

'I have no opinion on the matter. I'm not a detective—as I
said, it's not my nature to seek answers. I am an observer of
life.'

'Are you not afraid that, if the deaths were, in fact, the result
of foul play, you might be a potential victim?'

Maximilian Bloch laughed—a loud, hearty, infectious laugh.
'I can't imagine that anyone in the world would want to murder
me. If some maniac was out to get us, surely he would have
found a way of killing us all at the same time and not have left
us the time to identify him? If, on the other hand, Kapp and the
two young women were killed for a reason, then that reason has
nothing to do with me. I'm in no danger.'

'Had you ever met Thelonius Kapp before coming to the abbey?'

'As a matter of fact, yes,' said Bloch. 'He once attended the
opening of one of my exhibitions in Paris. He bought one of my
paintings.'

'Would you say he was a cultured man?'

'Oh yes, a highly cultured man. I spoke to him briefly about
the painting he had bought. He was interested in it as a work of
art, not simply as an investment as so many of the big buyers
are. I am always happy to sell a painting to a person who appreciates it for its true value. We spoke also of his work. I believe
he was an artist himself—a man essentially concerned with the
art of creation. He was, I think, profoundly saddened by the
spiritual dearth in modern man.'

'Did Mr Kapp show any signs of recognizing you when you
arrived at the abbey?'

'No, none whatsoever.'

'Did that not surprise you?'

'Not in the least. He met me once. He must have met thousands of people in the course of one year. I doubt that he would remember the face of every artist he bought a painting from. I believe he had quite a collection in New York.'

'Had your wife met Kapp before coming here?'

'Yes, on the same occasion as me.'

'And he didn't recognize her either?'

'I think not—in any case, my wife has changed considerably in appearance since that time.'

'In what way, may I ask?' said Donaghue.

'Over the last two or three years she has put on a lot of weight. Fifteen years ago when we met Kapp she was very slim—quite another woman.'

'And this weight gain—is that the cause of her present crisis?'

'The cause or the symptom, I'm not sure,' said Bloch, a little mournfully. 'I'm no psychologist. It's all rather silly, her concern about her weight, because it doesn't change my feelings for her. It's that she doesn't understand. She's concerned about what others think of her, men like Kapp for instance. She didn't want to come when I told her that Kapp was going to be here. She'd read in some magazine or other that Kapp had once said that ugly women were only fit to clean up after men and that older women should be mercifully put away at menopause.'

Donaghue's eyebrows raised themselves a millimetre. 'Kapp said that?'

'I doubt that he did,' said Maximilian Bloch. 'You know what journalists are like—if they don't actually lie they can quote people in such a way that what is printed appears the exact opposite of what was actually meant. From what I've seen of Kapp I would say that he, like myself, was the kind of man who appreciates women primarily for their character and not for the purely transitory beauty of their bodies.'

'Describe to me your wife's character, Mr Bloch,' said Donaghue.

'My wife?' said Bloch in surprise. 'My wife is a very special woman, a supremely intelligent woman, an art historian. She is fundamentally a kind, sensitive woman who is burdened with a little too much empathy for those who suffer, whether they be starving children or lonely old people or beggars in the street. When we married she was a beautiful, intelligent young woman with everything life can offer but even then she suffered profoundly at the distress of others. She suffered along with them. Now, at this personal crisis in her own life, she feels she has become one of them. She sometimes says that I lack empathy for her suffering—which is true. But she knows me well. Where she feels empathy I see absurdity. I provide her with the humour she lacks and she provides me with the compassion I lack. We complement each other.'

'And Mr Kapp's wife, Sandra Kapp—do you think he married her for her character rather than her youth and beauty?'

'Absolutely,' said Maximilian. 'Her beauty is banal—mere prettiness. He was getting old, getting weaker. He was attracted to her, I am sure, for her strength. Sandra Kapp is a very strong woman.'

'You think she is stronger than her husband?'

'Oh yes, much stronger. Kapp was, despite his media panache, an essentially weak, frightened man. That is why he created all this...' He indicated with a flourish of his hand the surrounding abbey. '...this abbey, this spiritual monument. He was terrified of death.'

'Tell me, Mr Bloch,' said Donaghue, 'if you had to describe the Kapp couple as a lion and a hind which designation, in your opinion, would fit whom?'

'That's simple,' said Maximilian Bloch, smiling broadly. 'She is the lion, he the hind—undoubtedly.'

Donaghue, apparently satisfied with Maximilian Bloch's answer, picked up the folder of sketches and handed them to the artist. 'Thank you for your co-operation, Mr Bloch,' he said. 'You may go. Please be so good as to send your wife to us.'

Maximilian Bloch bowed ceremoniously and, with a last brilliant smile, left the room.

'So, Inspector,' said Donaghue to Joly, 'what do you think? Still like the idea of an artist murderer?'

'You didn't ask him where he spent the morning and afternoon.'

'I didn't need to. I saw him myself in the fields in the morning. I shall ask his wife about the afternoon. I'm sure she knew where he was at all times.'

'This case makes my head ache,' Joly grumbled. He pressed the buzzer and a novice appeared immediately.

'A pot of strong coffee for Mr Donaghue and myself,' he said, 'and an aspirin,' he added.

The girl, the dumpy Sister Paul, retreated and Inspector Joly continued his lament. 'It's like a maze where every pathway ends in a brick wall—that's how I see it. All the people you've spoken to up to now could have killed Kapp—apart perhaps from Madame Renoir. All the others could have gone into his cell during the few minutes that Mrs Kapp left to fetch Dr Renoir. Anyone could have put the arsenic into the box.'

'But you forget—Mrs Kapp took cocaine from the box later on in the day.'

'Perhaps she was mistaken, or perhaps he'd taken all the arsenic and she was left with the cocaine at the bottom of the box.'

'Yes, that is possible,' Donaghue agreed and Inspector Joly's face brightened into a satisfied smile.

'At last, something that's possible!' he exclaimed. 'So any of them could have done it and none of them had a motive. No alibis and no motives—bloody marvellous.'

'It's true that up to now none of the guests have any fast alibis for the hours prior to the deaths, but what use are alibis when we are not sure when and how the arsenic was administered?'

'It was put into the cocaine box while Sandra Kapp was out of the cell—that's obvious. Or Carl Petersen could have put it in any time—his presence in the cell would not have been considered untoward. And then again, Sandra Kapp herself could have administered it at any time. She's the most likely candidate if you want my opinion. Motive—she stood to inherit his fortune—and opportunity—she could have put arsenic into his cocaine box at any time. It could have been a mercy killing. She knew he was incurably ill.'

'And Milly Silverstone—why should she kill her?'

'Jealousy. Perhaps Milly Silverstone was in love with her husband and had tried to seduce him. Nothing easier than popping the arsenic into her tea then pretending to sleep. But if Sandra Kapp is innocent any of the guests could have slipped into Dr Blanche's cell while you were all busy with Kapp's death and put the arsenic into the teapot. They could have gone in on the pretence of seeing how Mrs Kapp was.'

'That is all possible,' Donaghue conceded and Inspector Joly beamed again.

'When it comes down to it, the only person with a motive is Sandra Kapp—but you don't think it's her, do you?' He looked sideways at Donaghue.

'I'm not sure of anything yet,' said Donaghue evasively.

'Well, if it isn't her I'm blowed if I think this murderer had a motive at all.'

'The old homicidal maniac theory,' said Donaghue, 'but I really don't think so.'

He looked up as the door opened and Adèle Bloch tentatively entered the room. She placed her large bulk in the proffered chair and looked hesitantly from one man to the other. Then she fumbled nervously in her handbag and drew out a paper handkerchief with which she proceeded to wipe the beads of sweat that glistened on her forehead. Her plump arms wobbled as she lifted her hand and the sleeve of her loose top fell back to reveal the pale flesh beneath.

'It is hot, isn't it, Mrs Bloch?' said Donaghue as he glanced at his watch. '2.30—the hottest part of the day. As far as the sun is concerned it's now 12.30—at its height. Shall I turn the fan up?'

Adèle Bloch smiled weakly in gratitude as Inspector Joly switched the fan on the desk to its highest setting.

'The heat in the South of France in September is almost intolerable,' she said.

'You were not very keen to come here then, Mrs Bloch?'

'No, I wasn't keen at all. My husband persuaded me to come. I should have resisted.'

'But you're not in the habit of resisting your husband's advice?'

Adèle Bloch looked sharply at Donaghue. 'His advice is usually sound,' she said curtly.

'Your husband is an admirable man,' said Donaghue. 'Successful and renowned as a painter, I believe.'

'He is quite well known, yes.'

'As well known, would you say, as Thelonius Kapp?'

'Maximilian is an artist, not a film director. They move in different worlds.'

'I believe you met Thelonius Kapp about fifteen years ago at one of your husband's exhibitions. Do you remember the occasion?'

'Yes—yes I do,' said Adèle. She regarded Donaghue suspiciously.

'Can you tell me what you remember of the occasion—your impression at that time of Thelonius Kapp?'

'I was quite young at the time, twenty-three or twenty-four. He must have been fifty, I suppose...' She smiled and her plump face suddenly brightened, becoming almost beautiful. 'I was, of course, immensely attracted to him as young women are at that age to older, powerful men.'

'You saw him as a powerful man then?'

'Oh yes. Not in a physical sense—he wasn't a big man—but he possessed a certain charisma, the charisma of power, I suppose. When I saw him at the exhibition he was dressed entirely in black, black leather trousers and jacket. His black eyes were deep and penetrating—a little, I imagine, as Picasso's might have been. As a rather naïve young graduate I was immensely impressed by him, as was every woman in the room, I might add. He, of course, flirted with every attractive woman there.'

'Including you?'

'Of course. He flirted with me outrageously right in front of Max.'

'Was your husband jealous?'

'Max, jealous?' Adèle laughed almost gaily. 'Max isn't capable of feeling jealous. To feel jealous you have to feel threatened and nothing in the world could threaten Max's absolute sense of the absurd.'

'He sees all life as absurd, your husband?'

'Everything. Life, God, death—everything. He laughs at everything. It's a wonderful philosophy. Max is a very happy man.'

'And you, Mrs Bloch, do you subscribe to his philosophy?'

'No. I sometimes wish I could, but I have a different nature. I can't help but react to suffering when I see it and there is so much suffering in this sad world. Max is very good for me.'

'He sounds like the perfect husband,' said Donaghue. 'A man who isn't jealous when another man flirts with his wife. Is he jealous if you flirt with another man?'

Adèle's colour rose. 'I'm not...' She shifted her bulk in the chair. 'I wasn't the flirtatious type. I never have been.'

'But men flirt with you?'

'They did…' She blushed a bright pink, evidently finding the conversation embarrassing. 'I've put on rather a lot of weight recently. Men don't flirt with fat women.'

'Tell me, Mrs Bloch,' said Donaghue as he steered the conversation away from the rather perilous territory of Adèle Bloch's weight problem, 'do you have any children?'

'No, I don't.'

'From choice?'

'Yes. I am a career woman. Children would have interfered with my work.'

'And your husband—did he ever express a desire for children?'

'He accepted my decision.'

'Have you ever been pregnant?'

Adèle Bloch looked at him in surprise. 'You mean, have I ever had a miscarriage or an abortion?'

'Yes.'

'Yes, I've had an abortion.'

'Are you aware that Mrs Sandra Kapp is pregnant?'

'No, I wasn't aware of that. I noticed that she looked ill.'

'Do you think that Mr Kapp committed suicide or was murdered? Please give me your honest opinion.'

'I think he was murdered,' said Adèle firmly. 'I think he was the kind of man who inevitably dies by violence.'

'Why do you say that, Mrs Bloch?'

'I have no concrete reason—just a feeling. He was a man who wanted power over others. Those men always incur hatred and enmity—it's inevitable.'

'I take it that you didn't like Mr Kapp.'

'Like him?' Adèle laughed. 'No, I didn't like him. I detested him, but not enough to kill him, if that's what you're thinking. I have no reason to want him dead—but you're right, I didn't like him at all. I suppose that admission will put me high up on your list of likely suspects, but nevertheless I admit it because it's the truth.'

'Yesterday morning, Mrs Bloch, what did you do between breakfast and lunch?'

'I stayed in my cell. I wasn't feeling too good. Max took off to the vineyards to sketch and I stayed in the cell. I was feeling a little...fragile.'

'Because of Kapp?'

She looked sharply at Donaghue. 'Yes,' she said, narrowing her eyes. 'You're very astute, Mr Donaghue.'

'And did you leave your cell at all?'

'Just before lunch, to go to the toilet, that's all.'

'And after lunch, between one and three?'

'I went to pick grapes in the vineyard. I was feeling better. I felt the work would do me good.'

'And after the death of Mr Kapp?'

'I really can't remember. I stayed for a while in the cell then I think I wandered out to join Max in the vineyard.'

'What time would that have been?'

'About four, I think.'

'Did you meet any of the other guests on your journey out to the fields?'

'I saw Miss Mendes France going into the Chapel of St Pierre as I left my room, and Lady Olivia Carter Bonnington going into the library.'

'How were they dressed, Miss Mendes France and Lady Carter Bonnington?'

'How were they dressed? Goodness me—I don't know if I can remember...'

'Were they wearing trousers or skirts, or dresses perhaps?'

'I think they were both wearing skirts—longish, cotton, summer skirts...'

'Similar to the skirt you're wearing now?'

Adèle looked down at her skirt, which was of blue silk and draped down over her knees to mid-calf. 'Similar in style but the colour, I really have no idea. I didn't notice.'

'Was either woman wearing a scarf—a headscarf, I mean?'

'A scarf—let me see. Miss Mendes France was wearing a light summer scarf around her neck. I'm not sure about Lady Bonnington. I just caught a glimpse of her as she went into the library.'

'And did you see any of the other guests on your way to the fields?'

'No. There were only the nuns working in the vines.'

Donaghue delved into his pocket and pulled out the gold clip

brooch that he had found the morning before. He held it out for
Adèle Bloch to see.

'Is this yours, by any chance?' he asked.

'No,' she said, shaking her head. 'No, it's not mine.'

'Do you know whose it is?'

'I haven't the faintest idea.'

'One more question—would you mind very much telling me
how old you are?'

'Not at all,' said Adèle. 'I've already told you indirectly—I'm
thirty-eight.'

'Thank you, Mrs Bloch,' said Donaghue. 'You may go now...'

Adèle left the room with a faint rustle of her silk skirt.

Inspector Joly stretched and sighed. As he did so, the plump
Sister Paul entered bearing a tray of coffee and biscuits which
she deposited on the table before scuttling rapidly out of the
room.

'What do you think, then?' Joly enquired of Donaghue as he
munched happily on a Breton shortbread. 'A motive there. She
admitted she hated Kapp and she's evidently an unstable
woman—a very unhappy woman, I'd say.'

'She's emotionally fragile, that's obvious,' murmured Donaghue as he regarded his list of guests' names. 'Shall we call Lady
Olivia Carter Bonnington—a woman, I think we'll see, who is
not in the least fragile and who possesses all the confidence and
stability that Adèle Bloch lacks.'

TWENTY-SIX

Lady Olivia Carter Bonnington

OLIVIA CARTER BONNINGTON arrived promptly and seated herself gracefully before Donaghue and Joly. The latter offered her a cup of coffee which she politely declined. The tall Lady Bonnington shifted in her seat to make herself comfortable with the result that her tight white skirt rode up her thighs a couple of centimetres. Donaghue and Joly found themselves gazing rather too openly at the Lady's legs which were crossed elegantly and tanned to a dark perfection in contrast to the white of the skirt. The legs were long and flawless without a trace of cellulite or varicose veins—they were as perfect as the rest of Lady Carter Bonnington, whose face was so discreetly made up that she appeared to be wearing no make-up at all and whose dark hair, tied back into a chignon, was as sleek and well groomed as the coat of a pedigree dog. Above the white skirt she wore a silk T-shirt that revealed the contours of her large, evenly tanned breasts.

She sat, confident of the effect of her beauty, waiting for the two men to start questioning her.

'Thank you, Lady Olivia, for coming so promptly,' said Donaghue deferentially.

'I came immediately,' she said as she smiled graciously from one man to the other, 'because I would like to get this business over with as quickly as possible so that I can leave what has turned out to be a very unpleasant place altogether.'

'I think all the other guests feel the same, Lady Bonnington,' said Donaghue. 'So we're conducting the interviews as rapidly as possible. Now, first of all, please tell me why you came on this retreat?'

'For tranquillity. I lead a very busy and stressful life. As it turns out there has been precious little tranquillity on this particular retreat—rather the opposite!'

'When you booked the retreat, were you aware that Thelonius Kapp would be here?'

'Not at all. I had no idea that the abbey was owned by a celebrity. I doubt that I would have come had I known he owned it.'

'Had you ever met Thelonius Kapp before coming here?'

'Met him? No, I've never met him.' She looked at Donaghue in puzzlement. 'Where would I meet such a man?'

'Your words carried a judgement on him. I deduced from that that you might have met him before coming to the abbey.'

'You deduced wrongly, Mr Donaghue. We don't mix socially with film people. My husband is a highly respected surgeon. He has actresses and actors as his patients, of course, but there are social milieux that do not mingle.' Her tone as she spoke implied strongly that a person of Donaghue's lower breeding could not possibly be aware of such nuances of social interaction.

'You may not have met him, Lady Bonnington,' said Donaghue, 'but nevertheless it seems that you have made a judgement on him. Can you tell me what that judgement is?'

'I find such men crass, physically mediocre, very definitely megalomaniac and, to put it bluntly, rather nasty pieces of work. It's written for all the world to see in their faces. I've read quite a lot about him—his history is not without moral blemish.'

'What do you feel about his death?'

'Feel? I feel nothing. I didn't know the man.'

'What do you think then? Do you think he committed suicide or do you think he might have been murdered?'

Lady Bonnington looked wearily at Donaghue. 'If you want my true opinion,' she said, 'which I imagine you do, I don't actually care how he died. It's nothing to me whether he was murdered, committed suicide or succumbed to a perfectly warranted death from poisoning as a result of all the drugs he took. Early death from drug abuse seems to be an occupational hazard of those in the media world.'

'Are you worried, Lady Bonnington, that there might be a murderer in the abbey?'

'Of course I am,' said Lady Bonnington. 'That's why I want to get this questioning business over with and get out of here.'

'Tell me what you did yesterday morning.'

'I stayed in my cell and read.'

'And after lunch?'

'I returned to my cell to continue reading.'

'Might I ask what you were reading?'

'The Psalms. I find them beautiful and uplifting. I'm currently reading The Song of Songs—the most beautiful love song ever written.'

'And after the death of Mr Kapp—between 3.30 and 6—what did you do?'

'I went for a walk in the grounds. To witness a death is disturbing. I needed the warmth and heat of some sun on my skin.'

'Did you walk as far as the vineyards?'

'Only to the first field.'

'Did you drop this by any chance?' He held out the clip brooch.

Lady Bonnington peered at the brooch then shook her head. 'No. I have a brooch similar to that, but that's a scarf clip. I didn't bring one with me—one doesn't wear scarves in summer.'

'The bible you were reading from after lunch—did you borrow it from the abbey library?'

'No, it's my own. I brought it with me.'

'On your walk in the grounds, did you see or meet any of the other guests?'

'I saw Maximilian Bloch in the fields.'

'Was his wife with him?'

'His wife? I'm not sure. Yes, perhaps she was with him.'

'And you met no one else?'

'No.'

'Did you see any of the guests in the fields, perhaps working with the nuns or just walking?'

'I saw two people walking towards the press building along the gravel path. One was a nun—or rather a novice dressed in white—the other must have been a guest as she wasn't wearing a habit.'

'You're sure it was a woman?'

'Yes, fairly sure although I was some distance away at the other end of the field.'

'Would you say it was a young woman or an older woman?'

'Oh, a young woman—definitely a young woman—a girl from the way she walked.'

'Do you know who it was?'

'No, I can't say who it was. She was wearing a headscarf.'

'And how was she dressed?'

'In a skirt or dress—normal length or perhaps on the long side.'

Donaghue consulted his notebook then looked up pointedly at Lady Bonnington.

'I am obliged to ask you one or two personal questions. You are, of course, not obliged to answer them.'

Lady Bonnington frowned then inclined her head in reluctant acquiescence.

'Do you have any children?' Donaghue asked.

'I have two children—two daughters.'

'Would you be so good as to tell me your age?'

'Absolutely not!' snapped Lady Bonnington. 'My age has nothing whatsoever to do with this enquiry.' She stood up and glared at Donaghue then turned and smiled charmingly at Inspector Joly who had not addressed one word to her throughout the interview. Joly, on reflex, leapt to his feet.

'I take it that's all?' she said.

'That'll do, Lady Bonnington,' said Donaghue, who remained seated as Inspector Joly saw Lady Bonnington to the door.

'A disarmingly beautiful woman that,' sighed Inspector Joly, 'and hardly likely to be our murderer. Married to a renowned surgeon—well-known social figure, I imagine, in England, where titles count a lot more than here. She's hardly likely to bump off some Bohemian film director just for the fun of it.'

'How old would you say she is, Inspector?' Donaghue asked.

'Hard to tell. She looks thirty, although you know she's older. There's something about an older woman that all the plastic surgery in the world can't hide—blessed if I can put my finger on it, though.'

'Give a guess—forty-five, fifty?'

'Fifty, I'd say. Maybe a bit more, maybe a bit less.'

'I'd say the same,' Donaghue murmured. 'Around fifty—a very stable woman.'

'Confident too,' added Joly admiringly. 'Sure of herself. I suppose it comes with the breeding.'

'Ah, breeding,' said Donaghue, smiling. 'That peculiarly English notion. And do you know what is its true mark, Inspector Joly?'

The inspector shook his head.

'Discretion,' said Donaghue. 'The well-bred Englishman is always honest but will never reveal his true feelings.'

'Which makes life all the harder for a policeman,' said Inspector Joly glumly. He consulted his notes. 'Who's next? Mireille Parmentier. Let's see what the enigmatic Madame Parmentier has to say.'

TWENTY-SEVEN

The Parmentiers speak

AS MIREILLE PARMENTIER took her seat before Donaghue and Inspector Joly, both men thought the same thing—a beautiful woman, but a sad and bitter one.

She nodded silently to them, brushing a strand of platinum blonde hair back off her forehead.

'Madame Parmentier, your husband is a chemist, is he not?' Donaghue asked.

'Yes, he has his own pharmacy.'

'And you, Madame Parmentier, do you work?'

'Yes, I run an analysis laboratory.'

'You're a chemist too?'

'Yes.'

'How long have you and your husband been married?'

'Four years.'

'Might I ask your age?'

'I'm forty.'

'Had you been married before you met your husband?'

'No.'

'What was your maiden name?'

'Sassoon.'

'Do you have any children?'

'No.'

'Was it your choice not to have children?'

'Yes. I chose a career instead of motherhood.'

'Have you ever been pregnant?'

'Mr Donaghue,' said Mireille, a little impatiently, 'I fail to see what my fecundity has to do with your enquiry.'

'To an enquiry of this nature everything is relative,' said Donaghue quietly. 'Although I must add that you are not in any way obliged to answer my questions. I'm not a policeman. I can only assure you that if I ask a question it is relevant.'

She regarded him intently for a second or two before answering. 'I was pregnant once—a kind of pregnancy. An ectopic pregnancy.'

'The embryo developed in the Fallopian tube?'

'Yes.'

'And you had to undergo surgery?'

'Yes. Such pregnancies can be fatal.'

'What was the name of the surgeon?'

'It was ten years ago,' said Mireille tartly. 'I can't remember. I was taken to the nearest hospital for emergency surgery. It was the on-call doctor who operated, not my own gynaecologist.'

'Where did this take place?'

'Lyons. Really, Mr Donaghue, I must insist that you bring this line of questioning to an end. My medical history is my business and nobody else's.'

Donaghue smiled apologetically.

'Yesterday morning, before lunch—tell me how you spent your time?'

'I went for a walk in the abbey gardens. Loic was tired—he'd worked late the previous night—so he decided to sleep in the cell. On my return, at about ten, he was still asleep so I sat in the cloister garden and read for an hour.'

'Did you borrow a book from the abbey library?'

'Yes.'

'On what subject?'

'The history of the abbey.'

'Was there anyone else in the library when you went in?'

'No, nobody.'

'Did you see any of the guests during your walk and during the time you sat in the cloister?'

'Of course.'

'Can you remember who?'

'Goodness me—I really wasn't taking too much notice.' A frown crossed her fraught, beautiful features as she reflected. 'I saw the young English couple, the journalists. I think they were arguing. I saw you and Dr Blanche stop and talk to them.'

'Really?' said Donaghue. 'You must have followed the same itinerary as us.'

'I followed the path around the vineyard. Oh, I saw the artist, Maximilian Bloch. He was setting up his easel at the other end of the field. I wandered around the vegetable garden. I wanted to check that the vegetables were indeed organically grown.'

'And are they?'

'Oh yes.' Her face brightened for an instant into an unaccustomed smile. 'But you can tell from the taste if you're not a chemist.'

'So they use no insecticides or artificial fertilizers?'

'No, they're very competent. They put plants together strategically so that the pest attracted to one is repelled by the other.'

'There are rats, I noticed. What would they use for them?'

'The perfect organic solution is a cat.'

'But there are no cats in the abbey. I suppose a cat would tempt the novices to speak to it.'

'Then they'd have to use rat poison. There's no other way—they'd be overrun.'

'Arsenic-based poison?'

'Undoubtedly.'

'What form does commercial rat poison come in—powder or liquid?'

'Both. Powder is more practical—easier to deal with if spilled.'

'What colour is the powder?'

'White—similar to a kitchen scouring powder.'

'Or cocaine?'

She looked at Donaghue in surprise. 'I suppose it does resemble cocaine.'

'Did you see anybody in the vegetable garden?'

'Only the novices working in the greenhouses.'

'Did you hear any of them speak?'

'No. There was only one novice in each tunnel. They were working in silence.'

'Did you by any chance drop this when you were in the garden?' He held out to her the gold clip brooch.

'No,' said Mireille. 'It's not mine.'

'And you saw no one else?'

'As a matter of fact, now I come to think of it, I did catch a glimpse of Miss Mendes France.'

'Miss Mendes France? What time would that have been?'

'I don't know, perhaps 9.30. I can't be sure.'

'Where was she?'

'She must have been doing the same as me, checking that the vegetables were organically grown. She was on the path at the other end of the tunnels. I caught a glimpse of her going into one of the greenhouses.'

'Are you sure it was her?'

'Almost—I recognized the white skirt she'd worn at breakfast.'

'And later, when you were sitting in the cloister, did you see any of the guests entering or leaving their cells?'

'There wasn't a great deal of coming or going. I saw Miss Mendes France again, this time coming out of the chapel at about 11.15 and Dr Renoir rushed along the gallery at one point. I suppose his wife had been sick again. The duty novice passed a couple of times. I didn't take any notice of where she was going.'

'Did you see anyone entering or leaving Kapp's cell?'

'Dr Renoir. He almost bumped into me as I entered the colonnade.'

'What time would that have been?'

'Just after ten, I think—after I'd come out of the library.'

'Did you see anybody else going into the cell while you sat in the garden?'

'No, but that doesn't mean nobody did. I was sitting with my back to the colonnade.'

'Tell me, Madame Parmentier,' said Donaghue, leaning conspiratorially towards Mireille, 'what do you think about the Kapps?'

'The Kapps? They're not my kind of people,' said Mireille hesitantly. 'Too Bohemian, too extreme in their habits and thinking.'

'Nevertheless, you came to Mr Kapp's abbey.'

'I don't confuse the person with his work. I like Kapp's films. I don't deny that he was a creative genius. I just don't like his type. I think he was a cruel man—not perhaps to those he loved but to everybody else in the world.'

'You don't like cruel people?'

'No.'

'Are there any other kinds of people you dislike?'

Mireille smiled. 'Like all women who use the intelligence they possess in absolute equality with men, I dislike certain types of men—those who are foolish, bigoted, macho and incompetent.'

'I've no doubt that intelligent men think the same about women,' commented Donaghue with a smile.

'Of course,' countered Mireille. 'I would be less than intelligent to say otherwise.'

'Tell me what you did immediately after lunch.'

'I accompanied my husband on a tour of the abbey buildings.'

'And after Mr Kapp's death?'

'We returned to our cell.'

'Did you have occasion to go to the kitchen?'

'To the kitchen? Ah yes, as a matter of fact I did pop into the kitchen to fill my carafe with water.'

'You didn't call the duty novice?'

'With all the coming and going after Mr Kapp's death I thought the novice would have enough on her hands.'

'Was anybody in the kitchen when you entered?'

'Only the novice preparing tea.'

'And in the afternoon?'

'We stayed in our cell. We were disturbed by what had happened.'

'On Sunday evening your husband attended the lecture in the library. You didn't accompany him. What did you do instead?'

'I think you know what I did. You saw me coming out of the shower. I have no interest in Gregorian chant. I enjoy listening to it but not talking about it. I took a shower instead.'

Donaghue sat back comfortably in his chair. He smiled at Mireille. 'Well, that will be all, Madame Parmentier. Please send your husband along.'

LOIC PARMENTIER smiled deferentially at Donaghue as he took his seat.

'Monsieur Parmentier, you're a chemist, are you not?'

'Yes, that is my profession.'

'Mr Kapp and Miss Silverstone died from arsenic poisoning. In your professional opinion, is arsenic commonly used as a means of suicide?'

'It's not the most pleasant way of killing oneself—not one I'd choose anyway. There are easier ways.'

'Had you ever met Thelonius Kapp before coming to the abbey?'

'Never.'

'From what you've seen of him, would you say it was in keeping with his character to kill himself with arsenic?'

'Not with the arsenal of drugs I believe he had available. He had no real need to add arsenic unless, for some perverse reason, he wanted to die in pain.'

'Do you think it more likely that he was murdered?'

'I have absolutely no idea. I know nothing about his private or business affairs. I simply find it scarcely credible that a man of such an obvious hedonistic bent should choose to kill himself with arsenic unless, as I said, he took some perverse pleasure in pain.'

'Are you a religious man, Monsieur Parmentier?'

'Not at all.'

'Why did you come on a retreat?'

'My wife wanted to come. She thought the tranquillity would do her good.'

'But you were not very keen?'

Parmentier smiled again. 'I prefer to play golf at the weekend. I have to admit that I find retreats rather boring, although this one hasn't turned out quite as uneventful as I expected.'

'What did you do yesterday after breakfast?'

'I stayed in my cell. I slept, as a matter of fact. I was tired after a late night.'

'And after lunch?'

'My wife and I did a tour of the abbey buildings—the churches, the library and the nun's cloister.'

'Did you see any of the other guests on your tour?'

'Strangely enough, no. I suppose they were keeping to their cells—keeping out of the midday heat—but the interior of the abbey is wonderfully cool even at that time of the day.'

'Was there anybody in the library when you visited it?'

'Only the duty novice arranging the books.'

'Can you remember which novice it was?'

'I can't say. I didn't see her face. She was reaching up to the top shelves with her back to us. She was tall though, tall and slim.'

'And after Mr Kapp's death what did you do?'

'We returned to our cell. We found the experience disturbing.'

'Naturally, Monsieur Parmentier,' said Donaghue, nodding his untidy head. 'That's all then. Thank you for your co-operation.'

Parmentier, apparently surprised by the abrupt termination of the interview, rose and left the room.

Donaghue leapt up from his seat, making Inspector Joly jump. 'Come along, Inspector,' he said. 'We're going to pay a little visit to the library.'

Joly, mystified, followed Donaghue's short figure as he hurried past the Chapel of La Sainte Vierge towards the library, whose vaulted interior offered a cool respite from the heat outside.

Once inside, Donaghue cast his eyes around at the shelves that lined the ancient stone walls. He made his way rapidly towards the section marked 'History of the Abbey', and scanned the titles of the leather-bound books. He drew a finger along the tops of one or two of the books and turned to Joly holding up the soiled digit, a triumphant expression on his smiling face.

Joly looked at the little Irishman as if the latter were mad.

'Dust!' exclaimed Donaghue happily. 'But on this one...' He drew out a slim volume. '...there is no dust.' He opened the volume at the title page—*Wine Presses of Provence*. A small cardboard pocket was glued to the facing page. Then he drew from his jacket the piece of white card that he had found in the wine press and placed it into the pocket.

'I think this belongs here,' he declared. The card did indeed fit the small pocket as if it had been made for it.

Carrying the book with him he crossed to the single desk that stood between two vaulted pillars. He picked up a small box that contained a dozen or so cards similar to the one he had placed in the book then leafed rapidly through the book until he found the page he was looking for. Joly peered curiously over Donaghue's shoulder. On the page was a photograph of an old wine press. The caption beneath read, *The wine press of the Abbey of St Pierre la Croix, believed to date from 1461, said to be the oldest of its type in Provence.* A picture on the following page showed a similar press but in much newer condition. The caption read, *Model of St Pierre press as it will be when restored.* Accompanying sketches depicted the various parts—weights, screw shaft, handles of the press—and how they fitted together.

'Well, well, well,' said Donaghue. 'Somebody wanted to see

how the press worked.' He indicated the outer edge of the pages. 'Look, Inspector, no dust. This book has been borrowed very recently.'

'We could check for fingerprints.'

'You'll only find the fingerprints of the novice who put it back on the shelf—and mine, of course.'

'So whoever killed the novice borrowed the book to check on the workings of the press.'

'Almost certainly.'

'Who do we know went into the library?' asked Joly. 'Lady Bonnington and Mireille and Loic Parmentier. But then anyone could have gone into the library at some time or another. They're the only three that admitted it. We've only got the words of the others for what they were doing most of the time.'

Joly realized quite suddenly that he was talking to himself. Donaghue was studying the picture of the old wine press. Then he closed the book abruptly and placed it back in its slot on the shelf. Then, apparently satisfied with his work, he proceeded to leave the library.

Rubbing his hands together in the manner of a small boy who had successfully solved a problem in maths, Donaghue said cheerfully to Inspector Joly, 'Well, there's only one person left to interview, unless you think we should include the Mother Superior.'

'She's as likely a suspect as any of the others, if you ask me,' said Joly glumly. 'I can't make head nor tail of any of it.'

'Don't worry, Inspector,' said Donaghue as they made their way back to the office. 'Very soon...' He looked at his watch, which read 4.15. '...in about three hours from now, things will become a great deal clearer.'

THÉRÈSE MENDES France arrived a few minutes after being summoned from the Chapel of St Pierre where she had been busy rubbing the recumbent brass figures of the founders of the abbey, whose effigies lay on top of their tombs in the side chapel of the church.

She was wearing baggy cotton dungarees over a T-shirt and was rather pink in the cheeks from the exertion of the work.

'Thank heaven they knew how to build in the thirteenth cen-

tury,' she said breathlessly. 'It's tolerably cool inside the church.'
She sat inelegantly on the chair.

'Well,' she said looking sternly from one to the other, 'can
we get this over as quickly as possible—I'd like to get back to
my rubbing.' She raised a muscular arm and wiped her brow
with a hand covered in charcoal. Both men were struck by the
almost masculine aura of strength that emanated from the former
judo champion.

'Miss Mendes France, can you remember what you were wearing yesterday?'

Miss Mendes France looked at Donaghue as if he were de-
ranged. 'What I was wearing? What kind of question is that?'

'It's slipped my memory. I believe you were wearing a skirt—
a white cotton skirt, perhaps?'

'I believe I was—and a blue blouse. What possible relevance
has my clothing to anything?'

'Did you wear that outfit when you visited the vegetable garden after breakfast?'

'After lunch, you mean. I didn't change, as far as I can remember. I must have been wearing the same clothes. I'm not a
great one for skirts but on Sundays I make an effort to dress up
a little.'

'You say after lunch—are you saying that you didn't go in
the morning?'

'No, I went to Mass after breakfast. You have a bad memory,
Mr Donaghue—don't you remember, I invited you and Dr
Blanche to accompany me.'

'And you didn't go to the garden after Mass?'

Miss Mendes France tutted irritably. 'I've already said I went
after lunch.'

'What did you do after Mass in the morning?'

'I remained in the chapel to meditate for half an hour or so
then I went to the library.'

'To look at a book on wine presses? *Wine Presses of Provence*
by a certain M. Verrier, perhaps?'

'How on earth did you know that?' exclaimed Miss Mendes
France in astonishment.

'Simple deduction,' said Donaghue modestly.

'I suppose you know what I did for the rest of the day as
well—but I'll tell you, as you may well have got it wrong. After

lunch I took a walk out to the wine press then came back to witness Mr Kapp's death in the chapel. After that spectacle I visited the Chapel of St Pierre to check what brasses I could rub. I returned to the Chapel of La Sainte Vierge for meditation at five before Vespers at six.'

'You visited the wine press at what time?'

'About two, I think.'

'Did you take the book to the wine press with you?'

'No. Why on earth should I have done that? I simply wanted to see the press as it had been, in order to assess the quality of the restoration.'

'Was the circular wooden weight up on the screw shaft or below in the barrel?'

'Inside the barrel, of course. It's only put up on the shaft when the barrel is full of grapes to be pressed. I should have thought that was fairly obvious. It's highly dangerous to leave the weight up on the shaft—the thread stops half-way down and at that point the weight would simply fall.'

'As it did on the young novice's head,' said Donaghue.

'Yes,' said Miss Mendes France. 'I simply can't imagine what she was doing with her head in the barrel and the weight up on the shaft—she obviously had no idea how these old presses work.'

'I think she had a very good idea,' said Donaghue. 'It seems she was a highly experienced viticulturist.'

'Well, she must have had a brainstorm or else she wanted to commit suicide in a manner fitting her trade.'

'In your opinion, would she have been able to lift the weight from the barrel to the shaft?'

'Not by herself. Not even I could do that and I'm pretty strong for a woman.'

'It would take two?'

'Yes, of course. Can you see yourself lifting that weight?'

'Me, no,' laughed Donaghue. 'The only weights I am capable of lifting, Miss Mendes France, are emotional burdens from other people's shoulders. So, in your opinion, it's unlikely that she committed suicide by lifting the weight and letting it fall on her head?'

'Yes—and in any case a novice wouldn't commit suicide. It is a mortal sin, you know—one of the worst.'

'Do you think it possible that she was killed accidentally?'

'Very unlikely, if she knew what she was doing.'

'So what is your explanation?'

'Somebody killed her.'

'What about Kapp and Milly Silverstone—what do you think about their deaths?'

'Probably murdered too—he was an evil man. She was probably just a victim of his evil.'

'If you thought him evil why did you come to his retreat?'

'I came to the Abbey of St Pierre la Croix, *not* to the Abbey of Thelonius Kapp. I was interested also to see whether he was a true repentant. His action of buying and restoring the abbey indicated a spiritual change. I thought that it might be the action of a man who has repented his former evil ways and was treading a new path of spiritual light.'

'And was that the case, in your opinion?'

'Not at all. The evidence is there for all to see. He came armed with the tools of his evil. He had enough drugs in his cell to intoxicate an army. No, you could tell by looking at him that he hadn't changed. He was a man concerned primarily with the pleasures of the flesh, not the soul.'

'Do you have any opinion as to who might have killed him?'

'His wife probably, to get his money. Don't people usually murder for money?'

'And the girl, Milly?'

'She probably murdered her too. Maybe she saw her putting the arsenic into his food—doesn't one murder usually lead to another?'

'And the novice—why would she have murdered the novice?'

'Perhaps she too saw something. As I said, one murder leads to another. Evil begets evil.'

'How old are you, Miss Mendes France?'

'I'm sixty-three.'

'Have you ever visited the United States?'

'Yes, once, a long time ago. I was nineteen or twenty. I was junior champion of judo for France at that time.'

'Did you, during your visit, have occasion to meet Thelonius Kapp?'

'As a matter of fact I did. He contacted my trainer and asked if I would take part in one of his films. He was very young at the time, only two or three years older than me.'

'And did you take part?'

'No, I didn't...' Miss Mendes France faltered. For a moment her poise broke and a curious expression crossed her features. 'I...I wanted to. I was young at the time—attracted by the false glamour of Hollywood—but my trainer was against the idea. He contacted my parents and they, of course, refused. I suppose they worried that I would be lured from the glorious career that lay ahead of me in judo to the corruption of the film world. They were right, of course.' Miss Mendes France had regained her poise. She straightened her back and sat stiffly in her chair.

'Did you ever return to the States again after that?'

'No, never. It is not a culture that attracts me—too materialistic. Even believers in America are sham and superficial. Do you know, they actually sell God in TV commercials? It's disgusting.'

'One last little question, Miss Mendes France. Have you ever had any gynaecological problems?'

'What!' spluttered Miss Mendes France. 'What kind of question is that?'

'You are not obliged to answer but I would be grateful if you would deign to.'

Miss Mendes France hesitated. For the first time in the interview she appeared embarrassed.

'As a matter of fact, I had a hysterectomy five years ago.' She glared at Donaghue. 'But I suppose you knew that already.'

'Was Dr Renoir the surgeon?'

'Need I answer?' said Miss Mendes France sardonically. 'You know he was—I suppose you deduced that as well.'

'In fact, Miss Mendes France,' Donaghue confided to her, 'I know nothing of your health problems. I would have deduced from your fine physique that you'd never had a problem of health in your life. I was simply guessing. Well, that's all, you may go. Thank you for your time.'

Miss Mendes France, somewhat abashed, frowned at the two men as she left the room.

Donaghue pushed his chair back, stretched and placed his feet up against the Mother Superior's desk. Then he let out a long sibilant sigh.

Inspector Joly stretched too, placing his hands behind his head. 'Well, that's that,' he said. 'Now I'm completely befuddled. She could have killed the novice—more or less described how it should be done. She has no love for Kapp, that's obvious. There's probably more to her story about this film affair than meets the eye—could be a revenge motive there. You never know, she might have been a beauty at nineteen.'

'An interesting woman,' Donaghue commented. 'A powerful woman—the kind of woman Kapp would have been attracted to. I can imagine that she was a very striking nineteen-year-old.' He mused, 'So she met him when he was about twenty-four.'

'And she, of course, would hate his wife. It's only natural. She probably fell in love with him—her parents refused to allow the relationship and she's carried the bitterness over it with her all her life. Perhaps she killed Kapp simply to incriminate his wife—you never know.'

'There are many hypothetical explanations,' said Donaghue. 'But there is only one real one.'

Inspector Joly looked pointedly at Donaghue. 'You've been asking the guests their opinion as to how Kapp died. Now I'm asking you, Donaghue. Do you think that he committed suicide or was murdered? Answer me honestly and not evasively.'

'I think he was murdered.'

'Ah,' said Joly triumphantly. 'Something concrete at last. And who do you think murdered him?'

'I have an idea, but as yet it's only an idea.'

'So you're not telling?'

'Soon, Inspector,' said Donaghue, glancing at his watch. 'Very soon. It's 4.45. Shall we take a break for tea?'

'Ah,' sighed the inspector. 'I forgot—the English and their tea. At five o'clock everything, even murder investigations, stops for tea.'

TWENTY-EIGHT

Inspector Joly sums up

'WHILE YOU WERE DOING all the talking,' said Inspector Joly, 'I was making notes. Would you like to hear my summary?'

'With pleasure,' said Donaghue with satisfaction. He was feeling replete after a pot of English tea served with *petits fours* and biscuits.

'OK. We'll start with the deaths.'

'3.10: Kapp dies in chapel—arsenic poisoning. Arsenic found in his cocaine box, put there either by himself or by person or persons unknown.

'3.30: Milly Silverstone, beautician to Mrs Kapp, dies in Dr Blanche's cell of arsenic poisoning. Arsenic possibly introduced into tea brought to cell for Mrs Kapp. How arsenic got into tea is unknown.

'Between 4 and 5: Novice (Sister Veronique) dies in wine press—apparently an accident.

'Assuming that the deaths are the result of foul play, we can rule out the possibility of them being perpetrated by someone from outside the abbey. The gates were locked at the beginning of the retreat and no strangers were seen in or around the grounds. The perpetrators must therefore be among either the guests or the community of nuns. As the community of nuns depends for its existence on Mr Kapp it is highly unlikely that one of its members killed him, so our investigation concerns principally the guests at the present retreat.

'First of all, Sandra Kapp, wife of dead man—in my book the most likely suspect. Had at all times the means of killing her husband—never left his side except for five minutes to fetch Dr Renoir. Had a strong motive—stands to inherit a considerable fortune. Could also conceivably have killed him for love—euthanasia.

'Petersen: says he stayed in his cell working during the morning and after lunch. As he was Mr Kapp's secretary, a visit to his employer's cell would not have been considered untoward—although Sandra Kapp does not mention any such visit. No apparent motive—on the contrary, he stands to lose his job on his employer's death.

'Dr Renoir: the only one, as far as we know, who went into Kapp's cell. No known motive apart from irrational prejudice against Jews (believes Kapp is a Jew). He himself was attacked—possibly by murderer.

'Felicity Renoir: didn't leave cell except to go to refectory and chapel—no known motive.

'Maximilian Bloch: seen by several guests in fields where he spent most of day. Could, of course, have left at some time unseen. Saw Sister Veronique approach wine press in company with another woman. Previous contact with Kapp—possible motive of jealousy.

'Adèle Bloch: like other guests she could have entered Kapp's cell when Sandra Kapp left to fetch doctor. Met Kapp previously—possibly in love with him and jealous of Mrs Kapp. Personal observation—an unhappy woman.

'Lady Carter Bonnington: said she remained in cell but seen going into library—might be simple omission. Saw Sister Veronique approaching wine press in company of another woman. Her description confirms that of Maximilian Bloch. No connection with Kapp. No known motive.

'Loic Parmentier: Slept in cell all morning. Toured abbey buildings with wife after lunch. They could have entered kitchen and slipped arsenic into tea. He is a chemist so would have access to poisons. No connection with Kapp—never met him before. No known motive.

'Mireille Parmentier: like husband would have access to poisons. Spent morning in garden—one hour in cloister. Could have entered Kapp's cell when Sandra Kapp left. Husband and wife could be working as a team—but no known motive. Personal observation—a troubled woman.

'Thérèse Mendes France: seen in garden in morning though denies it. Met Kapp in States when nineteen—possibly vengeful or jealous of his wife. Visited the press after lunch. Took book on same from library. Personal observation—a bitter woman.

'Mark Kingsford and Fiona MacKinley: English journalists here to interview Kapp. Not yet interviewed by us. Young, ingenuous but could conceivably have perpetrated whole thing as a journalistic scoop.

'Clothilde Blanche: retired surgeon. Well known to myself and you, Mr Donaghue. Unlikely to have brought about the deaths unless she had a brainstorm. In fact it's as likely that Clothilde Blanche committed a triple murder as it is for an Englishman to reveal his true feelings about anything.' Inspector Joly looked accusingly at Donaghue as he finished his summary.

'If you are implying that I reveal nothing of what I feel about this matter to you, Inspector,' said Donaghue, 'I have to remind you that I am an Irishman not an Englishman.'

'So there you have it—and if you want my opinion, which I am at all times ready to give,' Joly interjected dourly, 'I place my bets on Sandra Kapp with Thérèse Mendes France a close second and Adèle Bloch a possible outsider.'

'You think it's a woman, then, Inspector?' Donaghue asked.

'It smacks of a woman's crime to me—and a woman was seen approaching the wine press shortly before the novice died.'

'It's curious that you should think it's a woman,' said Donaghue, 'because Kapp thought the same thing.'

'Kapp thought the same thing? What on earth do you mean by that?'

'It's evident from what he said before he died.'

'He said something about death,' said the inspector. '"Come away death"—he didn't mention a woman.'

'He didn't have time to finish what he wanted to say but I know what he was thinking, what prompted him to say those particular words.'

'Well?' said the inspector. 'Are you going to tell me?'

'Ah, Inspector, if you had paid more attention to your Shakespeare at school you would know.'

'You're keeping things from me again,' the inspector grumbled petulantly.

'All will be revealed,' Donaghue assured him, smiling, 'in due course—when I have a little more in the way of concrete proof of my ideas. Ah!' he exclaimed. 'Perhaps that's the evidence now.'

Steps could be heard hurrying along the walkway outside, then the door to the office was flung open and Mark Kingsford and Fiona MacKinley entered breathlessly.

'Did you get my message, Mr Donaghue?' Mark asked worriedly. 'I phoned from the hospital as soon as Dr Blanche and Mrs Kapp arrived.'

'I did indeed receive it—we were having tea at the time,' said Donaghue, smiling reassuringly at the young journalist. 'Where are they now?'

'They're at Dr Blanche's house in the village.'

'Did you make it clear that they must not return to the abbey before nine?'

'I did exactly as you asked,' said Mark.

Donaghue sighed with relief and satisfaction.

Mark placed a manilla envelope on the desk before him.

'Your answers, Mr Donaghue,' he said. He rummaged in his pocket and produced a bunch of keys. 'Your keys, Inspector,' he said, smiling. 'It's great driving a French police car. No one stops you when you go through a red light.'

'You went through a red light!' exclaimed Inspector Joly. 'In my car!'

'They put them so high you just don't see them,' explained Mark. 'I don't understand why they can't put them where you can see them as they do in England.'

Before the indignant Joly could reply a loud grunt of appreciation came from Donaghue who was scanning the documents Mark had brought him.

'Well, well, well,' he muttered. 'Well, well, well.' He passed the documents over to Inspector Joly, who scrutinized them closely. One was a copy of the birth certificate of Lady Carter Bonnington, the second a newspaper article depicting a young Thérèse Mendes France triumphantly holding up her first Olympic gold medal, the third a copy of Kapp's last will and testament, and the fourth a black and white photograph of a fair-haired young woman. The woman was dressed and coiffured in the style of the early fifties. Then he looked up and regarded Donaghue solemnly.

'You are an extraordinary man, Mr Donaghue,' was all he could say.

Donaghue inclined his shaggy head modestly then turned to the young couple.

'Thank you, Mark and Fiona, for your very great help. Now, may I ask you to carry out one last mission for me?'

Mark looked at Donaghue warily.

'As long as it doesn't involve driving Fiona along any more mountain roads. The stress is more life-imperilling than the roads themselves.'

Fiona scowled at Mark and Donaghue shook his head.

'This mission involves only a ten-metre walk. Go to the Mother Superior—you'll find her in the Chapel of La Sainte Vierge—and tell her to cancel the video show booked for this evening. Tell her I shall be inviting the guests into the library after dinner to tell them a story.'

Mark took Fiona's hand and led her from the room, saying, 'Stay close, Fiona—I'll need you to guide me through the door lintels.'

Donaghue leaned back in his chair, loosened his tie and placed his feet up against the desk.

'Ah,' he sighed. 'It's been a long day.' He pressed the buzzer to summon a novice. 'I think a little aperitif before dinner wouldn't go amiss. Perhaps some of the abbey's orange wine— what do you think, Joly?'

TWENTY-NINE

Donaghue tells a story

AFTER AN EXCELLENT dinner of avocado salad followed by Poulet Provençal the guests assembled in the library. Donaghue and Inspector Joly sat at the library desk in the company of the Mother Superior while the guests took their seats in a semi-circle before them. As soon as everyone was seated Donaghue rose and ambled around to the front of the desk, then, leaning casually against it, he addressed the gathering.

'I have invited you here to talk to you about the deaths that, tragically, occurred in the abbey yesterday,' he began. 'At ten past three Thelonius Kapp, benefactor of the abbey, took his life. Half an hour later Milly Silverstone, beautician to Mr Kapp's wife, followed suit and took her life too. Two hours later a novice, Sister Veronique, was found, her head crushed, in the abbey's wine press—apparently a tragic accident.'

Donaghue gazed gravely around at his audience.

'I am obliged to inform you that another death occurred today, not in the abbey this time but on the road to Hyères several kilometres from here—a road accident, in which the driver of a black Mercedes was killed. The police believe the victim to be Sandra Kapp.'

Several of the guests gasped at this news and Adèle Bloch let out a stifled scream.

'Two deaths by suicide and two accidents,' Donaghue went on. 'An extraordinary coincidence that so many deaths should occur in an abbey such as this during its inaugural retreat—almost incredible, but nevertheless a coincidence. Or is it a coincidence? It may, of course, have been pure chance that two suicides and two accidental deaths should occur in the course of one weekend but, to the stolid and logical brains of a French policeman, such coincidence is too improbable so the possibility of foul play had to be investigated. It's for that reason and one or two personal reasons that I agreed to conduct the investigation with Inspector Joly here. During the course of today we have interviewed each of you in turn and reflected deeply on the question and have invited you here to inform you of the conclusions we have come to.

'I will begin our answer,' he said, 'with another question. The question I asked myself after witnessing the death of Thelonius Kapp was this: why should a successful film director, at the summit of his career, in the middle of negotiating a new film contract and on the first day of the inaugural retreat of his newly restored abbey, take his own life by the painful method of arsenic poisoning? There is one answer as to why he might have committed suicide, although it doesn't explain the method chosen: the fact, revealed to me by his wife, that he was suffering from Alzheimer's disease, a form of incurable senile dementia. Such knowledge would, I am sure, have distressed a man like Kapp— although, at a certain point in the illness, the sick person loses conscious knowledge of his state. It seems that Thelonius Kapp was rapidly reaching that point, if he had not already reached it. But it is in the nature of the illness that before total senility sets in the sufferer can have days when he is quite lucid, his normal self. It was confirmed by his wife that yesterday, after lunch, he enjoyed one of those lucid intervals. Perhaps he became profoundly aware of his condition and decided to take his life. Having indulged in a large variety of drugs for many years he might have doubted their efficacy on a system inured to poisons so assured his death by adding arsenic to his normal cocktail of drugs. His suicide is further substantiated by a note found by his secretary which states that he "died as he had lived, high in the saddle of life"—a quotation from his most popular film—but, as the English journalist Mr Mark Kingsford pointed out to me later, Mr Kapp had misquoted his own film. Kapp wrote on his note "*we* died as *we* had lived"—not "*I* died" as the character in the film had said.

'Why does Kapp write "we" and not "I"? The reason becomes apparent half an hour later when Milly Silverstone dies in a similar fashion to Mr Kapp of arsenic poisoning. It would seem that there had been something between them and they'd decided to die together. Three hours later a young novice is found dead in the abbey wine press—apparently a tragic accident.

'As I said before, I had one or two personal reasons for suspecting that the deaths might not have been as they seemed. Shortly before I left London to come to Provence, a charming lady came to see me expressing concern about the safety of her daughter and asking me to keep a professional eye on the same daughter when she came to London the following week. The lady, a Mrs Trescott, was Sandra Kapp's mother. She believed that her daughter was in danger from her husband Thelonius Kapp, whom Mrs Trescott had not exactly taken to as a son-in-law.'

Donaghue paused and regarded the guests who gazed blandly back at him in the manner of children listening to their teacher. One or two coughed and shifted in their seats. Donaghue cleared his throat and continued.

'When I saw Sandra Kapp on my arrival I was concerned. She appeared distracted and fraught—a worried young woman. Her husband, far from appearing dangerous, seemed to me to be a very sick man barely in control of his own most simple actions.

'We set about our enquiry, which consisted mainly of interviewing the guests present in the abbey, at the time of the deaths. We interviewed Sandra Kapp first. After speaking to her I was left with the impression of a very distraught, confused and fearful woman. I understood her distress—her husband had just died— but I didn't understand her confusion nor her fear. The question that niggled at me for some time was, why was Sandra Kapp confused and of what was she frightened? It seemed to me that she understood and yet at the same time didn't understand that her husband had committed suicide. She understood that he might have taken his life in one of his lucid moments, knowing that he could not tolerate the idea of becoming senile, and yet she didn't understand why he had died the way he had.

'After interviewing the other guests I came to the conclusion, as did Inspector Joly, that Sandra Kapp was the most likely person to have killed her husband. She had the means to introduce the arsenic that killed him into the cocaine box in which it was found, and she had the motive—a double motive. It was my belief that she had killed him primarily for love and only incidentally for the vast fortune that she would inherit. Although it

was obvious that she loved her husband I had reason to believe
that she was secretly involved with another man.'

Donaghue paused and his gaze rested on Carl Petersen. 'I believed she was in love with her husband's secretary, Carl Petersen.'

Petersen gasped then shook his head vehemently from side to
side.

'No, Mr Donaghue, that's not true. It's an outrageous libel.'

'It's all right, Mr Petersen,' said Donaghue placatingly. 'I said
it was what I *believed*. I do not believe it now.'

Petersen relaxed visibly and subsided into his chair. He
avoided looking at the other guests, whose eyes were devouring
him avidly. He kept his own eyes fixed on Donaghue, who had
resumed his narrative.

'It seemed, as I said, a straightforward case of the wife mercifully killing her suffering partner. But if that was the case, why
had Milly Silverstone died? Perhaps Sandra Kapp killed her because the girl knew what she had done—or perhaps she had
discovered that something had transpired between Milly and her
husband. But all that is hypothetical. There is no proof, no evidence to support it. And then the novice died in the wine press
while Sandra Kapp was in the care of Dr Blanche. There is no
possibility that Sandra Kapp could have murdered the novice and
yet I felt somehow that this third death was in some way linked
with the other two.

'I began to see the events that had occurred in the abbey as a
kind of jigsaw puzzle. There were pieces that didn't quite fit like
Sandra Kapp's fear and confusion and pieces that didn't fit at all
like Thelonius Kapp's black eyes, a clip brooch that I found in
the vegetable garden and two conversations that I overheard quite
by chance on Sunday morning. The first was a conversation between two novices in a vegetable greenhouse. I only heard
hushed whispers—I didn't actually catch the gist of what the
novices were saying, but from the intonation I knew that they
were speaking English with a British rather than an American
accent. I discovered later that the tall and slender novice that I
saw working in the greenhouse was a Sister Marie Pierre from
London. By this time her talkative partner had disappeared, but
I was sure that she also was English, not American nor Canadian—the music of the language is quite different. I was baffled

later to discover that, of the six novices in the abbey, only Sister
Marie Pierre was of English origin. Of the other five one was
American, one Canadian, one French and two Vietnamese. Who
then had Sister Marie Pierre been speaking to?

'The second conversation I found equally baffling. I overheard
Mr Petersen speaking to a woman—a young woman—in his cell.
He spoke of love. This was at eleven o'clock, before Mr Kapp
died. I assumed naturally that it was Sandra Kapp he was speaking to, or Milly Silverstone, although of the two I judged that
Mr Petersen was more likely to be in love with his employer's
wife than with her beautician. But again something niggled at
me. The woman I heard had an American accent. Sandra Kapp,
after several years in the States, has a slight American inflexion
to her voice, Milly Silverstone had a marked Bronx accent, but
the voice I heard had been neither Sandra Kapp's nor Milly Silverstone's. After interviewing the novices and guests it finally
came to me that the voice I had heard in Carl Petersen's cell *did
not belong to anybody in the abbey*. But that was extraordinary.
I questioned Mr Petersen about his personal life and he denied
having a current lover or girlfriend. I began to think that perhaps
I had imagined the whole thing.'

Petersen stood up, his face red with anger.

'Really, Donaghue—this is going too far. My private affairs
are nothing to do with you, let alone the rest of the company.
Please be so good as to drop this totally irrelevant subject.'

'I am sorry, Mr Petersen, but private affairs, not just yours,
are very relevant to our enquiry. You will simply have to bear
with me, as will the others.'

Petersen sat down reluctantly, glaring crossly at Donaghue.

'As I said,' the investigator went on, 'it's possible that I imagined the second conversation—but then, in addition to the other
pieces that didn't fit, I discovered another. I am—as I am con-
strained to inform you at this point—a great admirer of Shakespeare.'

Donaghue's Dublin brogue inexplicably became more marked
as he spoke of the revered bard.

'It came to me shortly after his death that Kapp's last words—
the words he had called out in the chapel, *"Come away, come
away death, fly away, fly away breath"*—were taken from
Twelfth Night, a verse I had quoted once as a student of literature

at Trinity College. But Kapp had not completed the verse. I must modestly admit that I have devoured every word of Shakespeare's works and have a great facility, no credit to myself I might add, of recalling them. The words that Kapp had intended to say before death interrupted him were:

'Come away, come away death,
And in sad cypress let me be laid,
Fly away, fly away breath,
I am slain by a fair cruel maid.

'Kapp wanted to let us know that he had been slain, and slain by a fair cruel maid. What fair cruel maid was he thinking of? Did he mean his wife, Sandra Kapp? But my impression of the Kapps was that they were a loving couple—that she loved him and he loved her. Would he refer to her as cruel? Wouldn't he have known that if she had killed him it would have been for love?

'What other fair cruel maids were there in the abbey who could have had reason to kill Kapp? Having interviewed the guests we discovered that two women, Adèle Bloch and Thérèse Mendes France, had previously met Kapp—both of them at a much younger age, and at a time when Kapp's notoriety as a *tombeur de femmes* was at its height.'

The heads of the guests turned curiously towards the two women mentioned.

'Either of these women could have entered Kapp's cell—as could any of the guests, I must add—when Sandra Kapp left in the morning to fetch Dr Renoir, and placed arsenic in the cocaine box.'

Adèle Bloch's face blushed a bright red and Thérèse Mendes France set her lips into a tight line.

'Be careful, Mr Donaghue,' she said in a low voice.

'Both women may have harboured feelings of jealousy or revenge towards either Kapp or his wife. In addition Miss Mendes France was seen in the vegetable garden in the morning—which she denies—and showed a manifest interest in the wine press.'

Miss Mendes France stood up and shook a fist at Donaghue.

'This is monstrous,' she cried. 'Are you implying that I killed three people?' She glared round at the other guests. 'What he is saying is absolutely preposterous!'

'Please sit down, Miss Mendes France,' said Donaghue sternly. 'I am simply cataloguing my train of thought.

'It occurred to me that if the crimes had been committed by a woman known to Kapp, as was evident from his words, then it was somebody who had, at some time, had dealings with him—probably of an intimate nature.'

'My dealings with Kapp were never intimate,' Adèle Bloch protested.

'Nor mine,' said Miss Mendes France tersely.

'Nevertheless,' said Donaghue, 'he had recognized somebody with whom he had had some intimate connection—perhaps much earlier in his life.

'I conducted a little personal research. I discovered among some documents lent to me by the journalist, Mark Kingsford, a photograph of Kapp at twenty-five. Looking at it, I discovered something extraordinary—*the young Kapp bore a remarkable resemblance to one of the guests present in the abbey.* When I left my cell to take a shower on Sunday evening the picture disappeared—as I had expected that it would. Among the same documents I also found an article about a young Hollywood actress called Carol Lawton. In 1956, at the age of seventeen, she filed a paternity suit against Kapp who, at that time, was thirty years of age. The young actress lost the petition and had to pay the court costs. By the time the case was over she was too far gone in her pregnancy to have an abortion. She was obliged to have her baby adopted. She had claimed that Kapp had promised her a role in one of his films if she slept with him but, discovering that she was pregnant, he had dropped her like a hot potato, denying his involvement. Such an experience could leave a girl of that age very bitter indeed. After interviewing the guests I came to the conclusion that there were three very bitter women among them—Adèle Bloch, Miss Mendes France and Mireille Parmentier. Adèle Bloch and Mireille Parmentier were too young to be the actress Carol Lawton, and Miss Mendes France at sixty-three was a little old. Now, it's a curious law of nature that a human being can be made, by artefact or surgery, to look younger than their years but it is, I believe, impossible to make an individual appear—let us say—ten years older than they really are. There are signs of youth—texture of skin, distribution of bodily fat and above all posture—that are impossible to conceal, unlike the signs of age which are much more easily camouflaged. I am convinced that Miss Mendes France is, as she says she is, sixty-three years old.'

Miss Mendes France glared at Donaghue, her expression not, however, without relief.

'I had, I must admit, harboured the suspicion that Miss Mendes France was not who she said she was but an impostor who had knowledge of the real Miss Mendes France's early connection with Thelonius Kapp—'

'Impostor!' shouted Miss Mendes France, rising once again to her feet. 'You dare—'

Donaghue silenced her with a sudden disarming smile and a firm hand on her shoulder which pushed her back into her seat.

'But an archive photo of her Olympic gold medal award...' He held up the faxed newspaper cutting. '...confirmed that Miss Mendes France is indeed who she says she is and that the fine physique that gained her the gold medal for her country has scarcely changed over the years.'

Miss Mendes France's face crumpled into an expression of acute embarrassment and pleasure as the assembled guests applauded Donaghue's statement with an enthusiastic clapping of their hands.

Donaghue went on, 'I was forced to the conclusion that none of those three bitter women could have been the former actress, Carol Lawton. This conclusion was confirmed when I received a faxed copy of a photograph of the actress. I was disappointed to discover that she bore no resemblance to any woman in the abbey. Of course, she would now be a woman in her fifties and would have changed with age, but usually one can see something of the young person in the old—the shape of the face, the colour of the eyes, the expression of the features that rarely changes with age. There was no woman among the guests who resembled this girl in the picture in any way. But—and this was quite extraordinary—the photograph resembled somebody I had seen. *It resembled the picture of the young Kapp that had disappeared from my room.* The two faces were remarkably similar, apart, of course, from the colour of the eyes. Kapp's eyes were black and Carol Lawton's were grey. And it was then that I realized that my brain was actually playing tricks with me—*it was not Kapp that she resembled but the guest whom I had found quite remarkably similar to Kapp as a young man.* Carol Lawton resembled one of the guests, but not a woman. She resembled one of the male guests—the same finely sculpted bone structure, the same grey eyes, the same pale skin. She resembled Carl Petersen, Thelonius Kapp's secretary.' Donaghue turned to face the American.

Carl Petersen frowned at Donaghue but he said nothing.

'The pieces of the puzzle began to fit together. If the young actress Carol Lawton bore a remarkable similarity to Carl Petersen, was it not possible that he was her son—the son who had been taken from her when she was seventeen? She had, as a matter of interest, returned to England, her native country, as soon as the baby had been taken from her. If Carol Lawton was telling the truth, then Kapp was Carl Petersen's father, and indeed the photograph of Kapp as a young man bore a striking resemblance to Carl Petersen—the resemblance with one of the guests that I had noted before the photograph was taken from my cell.

'There is, superficially, little resemblance between Carl Petersen and Thelonius Kapp as we know him now. One would not take them for father and son. First of all Carl Petersen is tall and fair, Thelonius Kapp small and dark. Carl Petersen has grey eyes, Kapp black eyes and, as every schoolboy knows who paid attention in his biology class, dark eye colour always dominates genetically over light—which means that Carl Petersen cannot be the son of Thelonius Kapp, unless...' Donaghue paused dramatically. '...unless Carl Petersen does in fact have black eyes—beneath his pale grey contact lenses.'

'Contact lenses?' scoffed Petersen. 'Everybody can see that I'm wearing glasses.'

'Coloured contact lenses need not be prescription lenses. They are very often sold for purely cosmetic purposes.' Donaghue turned his attention from the American back to the other guests. 'Then I remembered something, a small detail. When Miss Mendes France first met Kapp and his group she called Petersen "Kapp"—a curious slip of the tongue, I'd thought at the time, as everyone knew that Kapp was in his sixties, but Miss Mendes

France *had recognized in Petersen the young Kapp that she had met forty years before.*

'And if you look closely you'll see that there is a similarity in the bone structure, something fine and sculpted, between the two men, but who would expect a small man like Kapp to produce a tall son like Petersen? Now, there is another interesting law of nature, one that I learned recently from my friend, Dr Blanche, that a boy will always be taller than his mother—apparently it is an invariable law of heredity. My mother, as you can deduce, was very petite.' Donaghue smiled at his little pleasantry but none of the guests reacted—not one of them smiled.

He went on, 'It was easy enough to discover Carol Lawton's vital statistics—the nomenclature of a budding actress in Hollywood at that time. Five feet ten inches, thirty-six, twenty-two, thirty-four—a very beautiful, *tall* young woman, fair-haired, grey-eyed, elegant with a perfect figure. One can easily see from the description that Carl Petersen could be her son. But is he Kapp's son? And if so, does he know that he is? It is quite possible that he didn't know and that this is the first time he has heard such a hypothesis. On the other hand, perhaps he did know and if so how did he come to know? He had been anonymously adopted and never informed of his true origins as is the law in the State of California. He could only have known if his real mother found him and informed him.'

Donaghue paused and paced theatrically around the semicircle of listeners, his hands behind his back. He stopped in front of Carl Petersen.

'That,' he said, 'is what I believe happened. Am I right, Mr Petersen?'

Petersen looked stonily up at him.

'You have a fertile imagination, Mr Donaghue. I am, as far as I know, the natural child of my parents and am not adopted. I certainly would never claim to be Mr Kapp's son.'

'Not during his lifetime,' said Donaghue quietly. 'He would have denied his paternity as he did at your birth—but after his death it would be in your interest to claim to be his natural son. As his son you would feel morally, if not legally, entitled to his inheritance—is that not so? Would you not agree that a natural son, whether born in or out of wedlock, is morally entitled to the legacy of his father?'

'On strictly moral grounds, yes, of course.'

'I think your mother felt that much more strongly than you. I think Carol Lawton felt denied, not only her child, but her career and her child's rightful heritage. She must have become, over the years, a very bitter woman indeed, bent on avenging the terrible wrong done her by Thelonius Kapp. Let me tell you what I think, Mr Petersen. When I have finished you can say whether I am right or wrong.

'I think she spent several years as a young woman trying to trace you. She failed. The authorities refused in cases of adoption to reveal any information until the child is eighteen. When you reached that age or perhaps a little later she finally found you. She persuaded you to seek a career in Hollywood. This you did and, with her encouragement, finally gained the post of Kapp's secretary. Carol Lawton, then, would have been a woman in her early forties—probably still very beautiful and easily recognizable as the former budding starlet. She was living in London, divorced or widowed—perhaps not as wealthy and celebrated as she would like to have been. At some point she became the mistress of a renowned British plastic surgeon who used his exceptional skill to transform her, not only into a woman ten years younger than her age, but into *an entirely different woman altogether.*

'Her figure she streamlined, her heart-shaped face she remodelled, her nose she bobbed. She couldn't do much about her height, of course. Artefact can only add to height; nothing other than old age can contract bones. Her fair hair she darkened. She wanted to make herself utterly unrecognizable to Thelonius Kapp—and she succeeded. When she arrived at the abbey Kapp—even if he had been lucid—would not have recognized her. Nobody...' Donaghue paused and withdrew from a folder on the desk the photograph of the young, fair-haired Carol Lawton. 'Nobody, no matter how much they stretched their imagination, would have recognized Lady Carter Bonnington as this young woman.'

All eyes turned to Lady Bonnington, who sat rigidly in her seat staring stonily at Donaghue.

'A fair cruel maid, Kapp described his killer. Lady Bonnington is neither fair nor a maid—she may or may not be cruel. Was Kapp referring to another young woman or to Carol Lawton? He had, surely, not recognized the young actress in Lady Bonnington.'

'No, he had not,' Lady Bonnington called out shrilly, 'because it isn't the case. Your imagination is running away with you, Mr Donaghue. But do carry on with your story. I find it quite fascinating.' She smiled around at the other guests, confident of the idiocy of Donaghue's implied accusations.

'I will continue, Lady Bonnington, with my little tale of greed and vengeance—for that's what it is in the end.

'Carol Lawton saw her chance of taking revenge on Thelonius Kapp when she learned from her son that Kapp was dying of Alzheimer's disease. She knew that his wife was heartbroken by the knowledge and suggested to her son that he persuade Sandra Kapp to put her husband out of his misery. Sandra Kapp agreed. She knew that her husband would not want to live as a senile vegetable. So Carl Petersen and Sandra Kapp planned his death. She would feed him a mortal dose of his favourite drugs so that he would die happily in the euphoria of drug-induced ecstasy. The death would appear, naturally, as suicide with a note to substantiate it. They planned that his death would take place during the first retreat of his abbey and Kapp duly died; but—and this was why Sandra Kapp betrayed confusion and fear after her husband's death—the death was not as she had planned. She had not planned that her husband die of arsenic poisoning and the note that she had written had not read, "we died",—it had read "I died as I lived—high in the saddle of life," the exact quotation from his film. Then Milly Silverstone died of arsenic poisoning half an hour later. Mrs Kapp became truly frightened. She realized that the poison in the tea had been meant for her. The "we" in the suicide note was meant to refer to Kapp and his wife. Carl Petersen removed the note when the body of Kapp was brought to the cell and produced it fifteen minutes later, by which time he believed Sandra Kapp to be dead. But he had not been aware of Sandra Kapp's condition. He could not have foreseen that she would be unable to drink the tea provided for her and that Milly would drink it instead. What confused Sandra Kapp was why Carl Petersen would want to kill her too. What benefit could her death possibly be to him? He stood to lose his job, which could in no way be compensated by the small legacy Kapp had left him in his will. But what Sandra Kapp didn't know was that Petersen had, on one of Thelonius Kapp's confused days, persuaded him to sign another will, leaving his entire estate to his secretary.'

'Absolute nonsense!' snapped Petersen. 'You're making this up as you go along.'

'Please, Mr Petersen,' Donaghue said patiently. 'Allow me to finish my story.

'The problem for the investigators was to discover how Petersen and his mother had actually carried out the murders. A large quantity of arsenic was found in Kapp's cocaine box but it was not that arsenic that killed him. Kapp and his wife partook of cocaine from the same box before leaving for the chapel to hear Brother Martin sing and Sandra Kapp suffered no ill effects. I myself was the last to leave Kapp's cell after the body had been brought there. I noticed at that time a small quantity of cocaine at the bottom of the box. *The arsenic was therefore placed in the box after I and the police surgeon left the cell.* The only people to enter the cell after I left were Thérèse Mendes France, to pray for the soul of the dead man, and the duty novice to clean the sink where Sandra Kapp had been sick.

'It is almost certain that the arsenic that killed Kapp was in the food he ate before he left for the chapel and that the arsenic found in the box was placed there as a decoy. The question is, how did the arsenic get into the food? According to the evidence of Sister Dominique, the novice on duty in the morning, none of the guests entered the kitchen during the morning and only one after lunch—Mireille Parmentier to fill her water carafe. The novices on duty at lunchtime yesterday were Sister Dominique, a Canadian, and Sister Marie Pierre, the only English novice— the novice I had overheard in illicit conversation in the greenhouse in the morning. She, in fact, had not been scheduled to work in the kitchen after eleven o'clock—she should have been in the fields. The novice scheduled for kitchen duty was Sister Veronique, who tragically died in the wine press. According to Sister Marie Pierre, Sister Veronique had asked to change duty with her.

'And then, curiously, I discovered that this second illicit conversation—Sister Marie Pierre was evidently not a very disciplined novice—was witnessed by Mr Maximilian Bloch, who sketched the two novices whispering together.'

Donaghue returned to the desk and selected the picture from among the pile of Bloch's sketches. He held it up for the gathering to see. 'I think you will agree with me that the person talking is this one...' He indicated the pretty Sister Marie Pierre. '...and that the other one, Sister Veronique, is listening. I think that is fairly obvious to anyone. The conclusion I came to was that Sister Marie Pierre was lying when she said that Sister Veronique had asked to change duty; that in fact it was she who asked to change and sent Sister Veronique to work in the fields in her place. I was then brought back to my former question— who had Sister Marie Pierre been speaking to that morning in the greenhouse, the mysterious novice with a British accent? I had caught a glimpse of a white robe and Mireille Parmentier, a little later, thought that she saw Miss Mondes France, recognizing her white skirt. But perhaps she had been mistaken—perhaps she had seen someone else wearing a white skirt. Perhaps I too had been mistaken—perhaps I had seen a woman in a long white skirt and not a novice in a white habit as I had thought. Perhaps the person she had seen and that I had overheard was Carl Petersen's mother—the only other woman in the abbey with a British accent. This idea brought me back to the other mysterious conversation that I had overheard—that between Carl Petersen and a young woman with an American accent, someone he had professed love to.'

Donaghue suddenly smiled broadly, gazing around at his audience.

'Now, I will let you into a little secret. Despite his denial when I questioned him, I had suspected that Carl Petersen did, in fact, have a lover. I had seen him at Heathrow airport prior to coming to the abbey in the company of a young girl who bore a surprising resemblance to Sandra Kapp. I had, in fact, momentarily thought that she was Sandra Kapp. Girls dressed in Salome-style outfits, so fashionable at the moment, are disarmingly alike—and the girl with Petersen had those somewhat too regular features, rather like Sandra Kapp herself, that can become unrecognizable when concealed beneath extravagant make-up and hair-dos. Sister Marie Pierre, among the novices, had that same perfect prettiness. It occurred to me during our first lunch when she was serving us, in a moment, I must confess, of middle-aged fantasy, that if you dressed Sister Marie Pierre in a Salome-style outfit and put her in the company of the real Salome and, for example, the girl I saw with Petersen at the airport—all girls of the same height and bland prettiness—*you would not be able to tell them apart.*

'And there were other similarities. The girl at the airport had coughed asthmatically. Sister Marie Pierre exhibited a persistent nervousness and coughed nervously when I questioned her. I assumed of course that it was the nervousness of the new novice. She had only arrived the day before. It is my belief that the girl I saw Petersen with at Heathrow airport and the novice Sister Marie Pierre are one and the same person.'

The Mother Superior looked aghast at Donaghue.

'Perhaps I should call Sister Marie Pierre,' she suggested worriedly. 'She is in her cell—in seclusion for talking. I found her talking to one of the guests this morning.'

'Might I ask you which guest she was speaking to?'

'I believe it was the English Lady.' The Mother Superior looked anxiously in the direction of Lady Carter Bonnington. 'Yes, I'm sure it was.'

Lady Carter Bonnington gazed darkly at the Mother Superior then glared at the other guests who were watching her avidly.

'I think you'll find that Sister Marie Pierre's cell is empty,' said Donaghue to the Mother Superior. 'I think you'll discover that instead of going to her cell as you instructed her she left the abbey, took Kapp's car—the keys having been given to her by Carl Petersen—and followed Sandra Kapp and Dr Blanche on the road to Hyères with the intention of driving them off the road.'

A buzz of excited murmuring rose from the guests and Inspector Joly quietened them with a wave of his large hand.

'I came to the conclusion,' Donaghue continued, 'that the person I had heard in Petersen's cell was Sister Marie Pierre and that she was not English as she had pretended to be but a quite excellent American actress who had taken the same plane from Heathrow to Paris as Petersen and in fact had sat in the next seat to his. Her name was Angelica Sherman. She came from San Francisco. She would have become Petersen's protégée, a new Sandra Kapp, when Petersen took over Kapp's role. But she was not experienced enough, as an American driver, for French roads. She instigated the deaths of Kapp and Milly Silverstone by serving them arsenic and that of her fellow novice by changing duty with her—and she did it all for love. Love of Carl Petersen.' He regarded Petersen gravely and accusingly.

'Your fair cruel maid,' said Petersen sardonically. His face had regained the colour it had lost during Donaghue's narrative. He looked confidently at his accuser. 'A delightful tale, Mr Donaghue,' he said. 'Perhaps it's true, perhaps it isn't. Who knows? There is no proof either way. As far as I can see the murders were committed by a novice who was obviously not in her right mind.'

'And your preposterous idea that I am Mr Petersen's mother is nothing but ludicrous,' said Lady Carter Bonnington. 'I can't imagine from what depths of your sordid little imagination you dredged that idea up.'

'Mr Petersen,' said Donaghue, 'you are wrong on one count. The novice did not commit all the murders. She placed the arsenic in Kapp's food and she administered it to Milly Silverstone in the pot of tea and she placed the decoy arsenic in Kapp's cocaine box—but she did not kill Sister Veronique. Ironically, she had a personal reason to kill her fellow novice, although she had no personal interest in the other deaths. Sister Veronique had seen her handling the rat poison in the kitchen—had possibly seen her putting it into the food. But Sister Veronique was killed by someone else, somebody who couldn't risk another death by poisoning. The death of Sister Veronique had to appear an accident and indeed there is nothing to prove that it wasn't. Sister Marie Pierre asked Sister Veronique to change shift with her on the instruction of Carl Petersen's mother. Sister Marie Pierre took her place in the kitchen and Sister Veronique went off to work in the fields. There she was invited by one of the guests to show them the wine press. The person who accompanied her into the press was seen by two of the other guests—by Maximilian Bloch and by Lady Carter Bonnington. Maximilian Bloch depicted her in one of his sketches as a youngish woman wearing a long white skirt and a headscarf. Lady Carter Bonnington also saw a young woman accompanied by a novice walking towards the press. Maximilian Bloch saw what he thought was a young woman. The figure was some distance from him—a tall slender figure, a young shape. Mr Bloch, as an artist, was looking at the shape not the identity of the person. Lady Carter Bonnington lied.'

'I did not,' Lady Carter Bonnington declared angrily. 'You are the only liar in this room!'

'I put it to you, Lady Bonnington, that you lied. You saw no one walking towards the wine press because it was you who were walking there. You accompanied Sister Veronique, who you knew was the acknowledged expert on viticulture. You asked her to show you the mechanism of the wine press. You showed her the book you had borrowed which contained a picture of the press as it had been before restoration. You invited her to help you lift the circular wooden weight—then, on the pretext that you had dropped the library card from the book, induced her to look down into the barrel. You then released the screw shaft handle and the weight fell on the poor girl's head. Unfortunately you did actually drop the card which I picked up when the girl's body was lifted.'

'A fanciful tale,' sneered Lady Bonnington. 'You can't construct the evidence of a case on an artist's sketch.'

Donaghue, without replying, held up the sketch for the guests to see.

'Mr Bloch's sketch depicts a woman wearing a headscarf. As you can see, with one hand she is holding the scarf which is in fact a neck scarf and rather small to place over the head. She is holding the scarf which is too small to tie because she has lost her scarf clip—she dropped it that morning when she visited the greenhouse to instruct Sister Marie Pierre on the poisoning of the Kapps.'

Donaghue paused and retrieved something from the desk behind him.

'I believe this is yours, Lady Bonnington,' he said as he held out the gold clip brooch towards her.

Lady Bonnington smiled disdainfully. 'I told you before that it is not mine.'

Donaghue turned the brooch over. 'It has your initials on it—C. M.'

'My initials are O. C. B. not C. M. Everyone in this room knows that.'

'I beg to disagree, Lady Bonnington. Your true initials are C. M. You were born Carol Maudesley. When you went to Hollywood you changed your name to Lawton—Maudesley is hardly a name glamorous enough for a Hollywood starlet—but you reverted to your real name on your return to England.'

'My name is Olivia Carter Bonnington,' Lady Bonnington protested vehemently. She stood up as if to leave the room. 'I won't stand for this nonsense any longer!'

'Please sit down, Lady Bonnington,' said Donaghue quietly. 'The inspector has not yet authorized anybody to leave the room. I have it on the authority of Somerset House that Lady Carter Bonnington was born on 20th January 1927. I don't think that even the exceptional skill of Cecil Bonnington could make a sixty-four-year-old woman look as young as you do. You have the body of a thirty-five-year-old but the hands of, shall we say, a woman of fifty-two, fifty-three—about the age Carol Lawton would be now. I put it to you, Lady Bonnington, that you are not the wife of Sir Cecil Bonnington—you are his mistress. You do not have two daughters as you said in your interview. The real Lady Bonnington does have two daughters, as you well know, but you, Miss Maudesley, have one child—a son—who is sitting here with us in this room. His name is Carl Petersen.'

Donaghue turned his head towards the American, who sat stiffly in his chair. He looked pale and uncomfortable, but was evidently making an effort to maintain his sang-froid.

'This charming story is exceedingly entertaining,' he said boredly. 'But you haven't one shred of evidence for any of it—it's all conjecture on your part.'

'You're wrong, Mr Petersen,' said Donaghue. 'I have evidence of the true Lady Bonnington's age and I'm quite sure that a search of this bogus lady's belongings will reveal other items of jewellery with the initials C. M.'

Lady Bonnington looked around at the company, a weary expression on her face as if to say, When is this ugly little man going to stop spouting his fanciful ideas?

'You are complacent,' said Donaghue patiently, 'because you feel sure, even now, that you have succeeded in what you considered, not just a perfect crime, but a perfectly *justifiable* crime. You were a little put out when Sandra Kapp did not die as you had planned with her husband. Your plans began to go wrong when neither husband nor wife ate the lunch laced with arsenic by your accomplice Sister Marie Pierre. Kapp didn't eat because he was unaware even that there was food before him and Mrs

Kapp because she was pregnant and unable to eat at all. It was for the same reason that she failed to drink the poisoned tea. As soon as Milly Silverstone died I felt strongly that I had to protect Sandra Kapp—so I put her in the care of Dr Blanche. I took a calculated risk and sent them this morning to Hyères.' He regarded the two. 'Your complacency is misplaced. You believe that Sandra Kapp is dead and that you are inviolable—but I am pleased to be able to inform you that she is alive and well. It was not Sandra Kapp who died this morning but your accomplice, Angelica Sherman, who was in no way qualified to take on a driver of the calibre of Dr Clothilde Blanche.'

Carl Petersen let out an involuntary cry. The guests turned their heads to look at him. He gazed, stricken, at Donaghue, who turned and nodded to Mark Kingsford. The journalist rose and left the room. A few seconds later he returned in the company of Sandra Kapp and Dr Blanche. The two women took up position behind Inspector Joly.

Lady Bonnington gasped and clutched at the side of her chair. Petersen's already ashen face blanched.

'Mrs Kapp will testify that she planned her husband's "suicide" with your help, Mr Petersen. The jury will, I am sure, come to their own conclusions about my "fanciful tale" when it is presented to them by the prosecuting counsel.'

Inspector Joly rose to his feet.

'Carl Petersen and Lady Carter Bonnington, I am placing you under arrest. Be so good as to remain in your seats. The other guests may leave.'

Before anybody had time to move Dr Renoir rose to his feet and cried out angrily, 'This is all very well—but what about me? Not one word has been said of the attack made on me. Am I to assume that this "lady" here and her son attacked me? If so I'd like to know why.'

Lady Bonnington looked disdainfully at the doctor.

'Attack him?' she sneered. 'Why on earth should I want to attack him?'

'Dr Renoir,' Donaghue said, 'I offer you my profound apologies but I have to admit defeat on the identity of your attacker. I can find no possible reason why either Mr Petersen or Lady Bonnington should have attacked you. But I am confident that you can rest assured that you are in no further danger.'

'Rest assured!' blurted Dr Renoir. 'Rest assured! I shall rest assured when I am five hundred kilometres from this place.' He pulled his wife, Felicity, to her feet. 'I'm leaving this madhouse right now,' he exclaimed crossly as he led his wife from the room.

The remaining guests, glancing sidelong at Petersen and Lady Bonnington as they filed out of the room, gathered in a cluster in the walkway outside.

'I take it,' said Loic Parmentier, 'that the retreat is effectively over.'

'Not for me it isn't,' said Thérèse Mendes France. 'I for one am going to do my three days. There are some souls to be prayed for.'

'I should very much like to stay on and finish my sketches,' said Maximilian Bloch. 'If my wife is agreeable, of course.' He smiled at Adèle and squeezed her hand. Adèle smiled hesitantly back.

'If you wish to stay, Max—we'll stay,' she said meekly.

'And you, Mireille?' Loic said to his wife. 'Would you like to stay?'

'Yes,' said Mireille absently. 'Yes, I'd like to stay.'

A sudden bright flash of light made the guests turn their heads. Fiona MacKinley was taking unauthorized pictures of Petersen, Lady Bonnington and Sandra Kapp. Inspector Joly managed to avert his face before she snapped him. Mark Kingsford grabbed her by the elbow and dragged her from the room. Before the startled eyes of the small knot of guests he pulled Fiona into his arms and danced her around the ancient pillars of the walkway.

'The story of the decade!' he sang out. 'We've got the story of the decade!'

THIRTY

Donaghue reveals a secret

ONE HOUR LATER, after Petersen and Lady Bonnington had been taken into custody, Clothilde, Donaghue and Inspector Joly sat in the company of the Mother Superior in her office. The Mother Superior looked contrite.

'I can't believe that I was taken in by that girl. I've never been wrong yet in my judgement of a novice. She fooled me completely.'

'Her accent fooled me at first,' said Donaghue. 'Americans usually find the British accent very difficult to imitate. She would have made a great actress. Petersen knew that. He would have set up his own company with the money he hoped to inherit from Kapp and would, no doubt, have made her a star. He wanted to imitate Kapp—step into his shoes. I suppose he felt that, as his natural son, he had that right.'

'What about the will?' asked Clothilde. 'Surely it's a legal document? Won't it mean that Sandra and her child are effectively disinherited?'

'Not if Kapp's doctor will swear that it was signed while Kapp was not in control of his faculties—which I have no doubt he will.'

'Tell me,' said Inspector Joly, 'do you know who attacked Dr Renoir?'

Donaghue's monkey-like face adopted an expression of innocence. 'I have absolutely no idea,' he said blankly. 'Do you?'

TWO DAYS LATER, as Clothilde drove Donaghue at lightning speed from the abbey back to her house in the village of St Pierre, she repeated Inspector Joly's question.

'You do know who attacked him, don't you?' she added accusingly.

Donaghue smiled rather wryly. 'If I tell you, will you promise not to tell Joly?'

'Guide's honour,' said Clothilde.

'It was Mireille Parmentier,' said Donaghue. 'She gave herself away on two counts. First, she was the only left-handed person amongst the guests and Renoir said that his attacker held the scalpel in his left hand; secondly, when I asked her about her activities on Sunday evening, she said that she wasn't interested in Gregorian chant. But she couldn't have known beforehand that the schedule had been changed. She thought that there was a film show of the abbey's history. She would not have been so stupid as to dress up as the monk when all the guests could have witnessed to his presence in the library.'

'Why did she do it—do you know?'

'Her husband explained to me. She was rendered sterile after an ectopic pregnancy. Dr Renoir was the young intern who operated on her. I imagine he bungled it. Her maiden name was Sassoon. She's Jewish. I can well imagine that the rather anti-Semitic Dr Renoir didn't take as much care with her as he would have done with his other patients. She wanted to exorcize her bitterness towards him—she wanted to frighten him. I think she succeeded.'

A WEEK LATER, tanned and noticeably wider around the midriff, Donaghue released the blind of his bedroom window and gazed out over the familiar vista of Hampstead Heath. A fine drizzle clouded the landscape into grey mist. Donaghue sighed. He had spent the last week of his holiday reclining on Clothilde's favourite nudist beach near Hyères so that no demarcation line would mar the splendid uniformity of his tan when he wore shorts and T-shirt for his first brisk walk to work across the Heath. But the English summer rarely called for shorts and this one had proved no exception. He shivered. It was, he realized, too cold for shorts and he would have to wear his track suit and deprive the population of Hampstead of the sight of his demarcation-free *bronzage*.

Mrs Percival, serving him a breakfast of tea and wholewheat toast, regarded his midriff with what amounted to an expression of contempt.

'You've been stuffing yourself with all those French cheeses—
I can tell—and washing it down with litres of wine,' she scolded
him. 'Animal fat and alcohol and all that lying around in the
sun—it'll be the death of you, Mr Donaghue. It's no wonder
you're getting fat!'

She pronounced the last word with such derision that Donaghue became painfully aware of the flesh of his mid-section as
it pressed against the elastic of his track suit pants.

'You're quite right, Mrs P.,' he sighed. 'It doesn't *do* you any
good to eat the things you like or indulge in activities that give
you pleasure—it just makes you *feel* good.'

He gulped his tea and picked up his umbrella.

'Still,' he called out as he opened the front door to be sprayed
lightly in the face by the fine summer drizzle, 'I don't suppose
we were put on this earth to feel good, eh, Mrs Percival?'

At his office on the other side of the Heath he changed into
his grey working suit and settled himself at his desk. He heard
his secretary, Bridget, singing as she usually did in her pure
soprano as she hung up her coat and brolly. Then his office door
opened slowly and her bright auburn head peeped cautiously
around it.

'Are you there, Mr Donaghue?' she said. She remained, mys-
teriously, where she was with only her head visible in the doorway.

'Why don't you come in, Bridget?' queried Donaghue.

'Because...' She hesitated. 'Because...of what I'm wearing.'

Donaghue gazed at Bridget in perplexity.

'What on earth are you wearing that you have to hide yourself
like a snail in its shell? I'm all agog.'

The door opened slowly and Bridget appeared. She stood still,
rigidly, as if on display.

Donaghue gaped, his mouth hanging slackly open in shock.

Instead of her usual tailored suit Bridget was wearing a mini-
skirt and some sort of transparent chiffon top. Her mass of red
curls billowed out around her head and cascaded over her shoulders. With her three-inch heels she looked like some unearthly
Celtic goddess dressed up as a go-go dancer.

'I thought you might not mind, just for once,' she said cheerfully. 'It's the Salome look...it's all the fashion at the moment.'

She twirled on her heels, affording Donaghue an inspection of her long shapely legs.

'It's...it's...' Donaghue stammered.

'Oh, before I forget,' Bridget interjected before he could find a suitable adjective. 'Mrs Trescott phoned to cancel her appointment—but she sent you a letter. It's on the desk.'

Donaghue picked up the envelope and opened it. Inside was a cheque for one thousand pounds and a card which read simply, 'With my heartfelt thanks, Angela Trescott.'

'Well?' said Bridget.

'Well what?' asked Donaghue.

'My outfit—do you approve or not?'

Donaghue regarded Bridget mournfully. He couldn't say what he really wanted to say—that her outfit was magnificent, that she was magnificent, that she was the most delightful, the most beautiful creature he had ever set eyes on, that—were she not engaged to her tall architect fiancé—he would ask her to marry him, and that only their daughters might be small—their sons would almost certainly be taller than her. He couldn't say any of that so he said nothing at all.

'You don't approve, do you?' she said reproachfully. 'You think I look ridiculous, don't you?'

'It's not that, Bridget,' he said. 'It's just that your outfit reminds me of a tragedy—a double tragedy. The death of a hind and the wasted life of a fair and cruel maid.'

Bridget looked at Donaghue, mystified.

'Make me a nice cup of milky coffee, Bridget,' said Donaghue, 'and bring one for yourself. Then you can sit down here at my desk. I have a fanciful tale to tell you.'

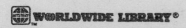

FAMILY PRACTICE

Charlene WEIR

First Time In Paperback

A Susan Wren Mystery

"Susan Wren...is a winner."
— *Mostly Murder*

The Barringtons are a wealthy family—prominent and respected in their small town. All but the youngest are doctors. Then the eldest, Dorothy, is shot to death—gunned down—in her office. But there is a surviving witness to this heinous crime: eleven-year-old Jen Bryant has also been shot, but not mortally wounded.

As the young girl struggles for each breath in hospital, police chief Susan Wren begins an investigation that opens up a Pandora's box of dark, tormented secrets in the prominent Barrington family. As two more lives are claimed, the former big-city cop must follow a grisly trail to a truth as tragic as the crimes.

"A slam-bang finish." — *Kirkus Reviews*

Available in May 1997 at your favorite retail stores.

 **WORLDWIDE LIBRARY** ®

FAMILY

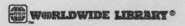

A Bleeding of Innocents

A Castlemere Mystery

DESPERATE MEASURES...

The Castlemere police force loses one of its own to a
hit-and-run. Adding stress to an already understaffed
force, a young nurse is brutally murdered in her car with
her husband as the only witness. Is there a shotgun killer
walking the streets, or is her distraught husband guilty of
more than he'll admit?

But after another horrible shooting murder, it's clear
there's a serial killer on the loose.

Jo Bannister

"Bannister keeps the suspense tight as a drum."
—*Publishers Weekly*

Available in June 1997 at your favorite retail stores.

NOT FOR SALE IN CANADA.

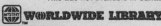 **WORLDWIDE LIBRARY®**

WBLEED-R